ZOMBIE PARK

ZOMBIE PARK

SIMON MARLOWE

Matador
9 Priory Business Park,
Wistow Road, Kibworth Beauchamp,
Leicestershire. LE8 0RX
Tel: 0116 279 2299
Email: books@troubador.co.uk
Web: www.troubador.co.uk/matador
Twitter: @matadorbooks

ISBN 978 1788037 457

British Library Cataloguing in Publication Data.
A catalogue record for this book is available from the British Library.

Printed and bound by CPI Group (UK) Ltd, Croydon, CR0 4YY
Typeset in 11pt Aldine401 BT by Troubador Publishing Ltd, Leicester, UK

Matador is an imprint of Troubador Publishing Ltd

For the patients.
Whoever they may be.

Turning and turning in the widening gyre
The falcon cannot hear the falconer;
Things fall apart; the centre cannot hold;
Mere anarchy is loosed upon the world.

W. B. Yeats, *The Second Coming*

PROLOGUE

… to recite the poem:

I shake and reel in morbid pain
And shiver down the spine again
As mad dogs bark, reveal the dark
Of brick and mortar, Zombie Park.

The Clock Tower is striking out
The towers of my fear and doubt,
Above the path to mourn the loss
Of bitter patient graves of moss.

I pass the wards of urine wipes
And ulcers in their creaking pipes,
The shattered boards of jagged floor
And trolley beds stacked near the door.

Sustained in life like old estates
On sulphur soup and mashed fishcakes,
Their shit congealed and hanging out
Through laxatives of Brown and Stout.

I hide behind a stone grave head
To watch the march of crawling dead,
Who sleep within a rotting past
And heave and sigh, 'Revenge at last!'

The spiders spread a thin white web
Then earth begins to flow and ebb,
Awakening and brought to boil,
Steam and heat secreting soil.

The crashing mush of blood and brain
As skulls are split and drip and drain,
No mercy shown to flesh and bone
When screams and cries of death atone.

This place has met its reckoning
For sins I witnessed happening,
This justice is a waiting game
Which now will speak its hidden shame.

CHAPTER 1

SUICIDE IS DANGEROUS

'You fucking wanker!'

'I want to die! I want to die!'

'No, you aren't going to fucking die! Hold his arms! Hold his wrists!'

Franks was slippery, as Roland tried to grab his flailing arms. He managed to press him down again, just for a few seconds, before slithering across his bloodied torso.

'Hold him!' barked Douglas.

Alright, thought Roland, but there was not much else he could do against a man twice his size.

In the rigid metal panel running along the side of the ambulance, Roland looked at his reflection: a smear of his face, a thin, angular, freckled thing, shaped like a rectangular box. He hated his hair, his thick, ginger bouffant hair, and his thick brown-rimmed glasses. He looked down, looked away, and crawled back on to Franks.

'Please, I won't do anything,' said Franks, his owl-like eyes bulging due to the shock and exertion of his attempted suicide.

1

'Don't let go of him,' instructed Douglas, taking out a packet of cigarettes, anxious to feel the comfort of tobacco in his fingers.

He leant back on the double doors, swaying nonchalantly as the ambulance continued to swerve. There was a wily handsomeness in the deputy nursing manager, a swarthy, pitted face, full of creases along his brow. He was also blessed with a mischievous grin, and a glint in his blue eyes which he used to its full advantage.

'I think I've got blood on me,' said Roland, pressing down harder, holding Franks' arms by his side, preventing him from snatching at his drip-feed.

Douglas snorted, fingering his unlit cigarette and nodding in the direction of Franks.

'How did it happen?'

'It's my fault,' interrupted Franks.

'You... keep quiet!' instructed Douglas. 'You need to learn how to behave.'

Franks nodded submissively. Roland let go and sat on the other side of the weaving, wailing vehicle. He put his arms down by his sides and flattened his hands on the foam bench to keep his balance. Douglas continued to fondle his cigarette, looking at Roland for an explanation.

'We didn't have enough staff to keep an eye on him,' said Roland, wondering whether he should say this in front of Franks.

'Oh, I'm sorry, I'm so sorry,' interjected Franks, unable to maintain his silence. 'What a terrible thing I've done!'

Douglas ignored him and continued to look Roland directly in the eye.

'You were on Lilywhite Ward, so who was meant to be watching him?'

'It was me,' said Roland, regretful and anxious to add some detailed mitigation.

'Oh, don't blame Roland, it's not his fault,' said Franks, offering a consoling glance.

'Keep quiet,' said Douglas. 'You're the patient and not responsible for your actions.'

'Where did you find him?' asked Roland.

'It wasn't me,' said Douglas. 'You have Mr Fitzpatrick to thank for that.'

Fuck, even worse, thought Roland.

'Oh, yes,' continued Douglas, 'our friend here was well away when Mr Fitzpatrick got to him.'

Roland narrowed his eyes trying to fathom how one event had led to another. Douglas turned to Franks as he continued his mini investigation.

'Where did you get the glass from?'

'I broke a window,' said Franks sheepishly.

'Was that from the potting sheds?'

Franks was silent, reluctant to give away any more information.

'You did a good job on yourself then… didn't you?'

'How's your patient?' shouted the paramedic from behind the driver's seat.

'He'll live,' said Douglas.

The ambulance continued to scream, rocking the cargo backwards and forwards. Franks began to play with his drip again and Douglas barked at him to leave it alone. This only encouraged Franks to make another sudden pull on the drip, prompting Roland to lurch across and keep his arms restrained. Franks continued to moan and groan: he wanted to be left alone, so he could finish it all without anyone bothering about him. It was a meaningless mantra: Franks had failed, and Roland doubted he had seriously wanted to do it anyway. But what Roland really needed to know, what he desperately needed to know: was he in trouble and was his career going to be fucked?

'How did you get involved?' he asked, looking at Douglas, continuing to press his body down on Franks.

'You couldn't miss it,' he replied. 'He was right in the middle of the grounds. He punched me before he let go of the glass.'

Douglas paused, his adrenaline dropped and his mind regained a sense of proportion.

'You're from the September '84 intake, aren't you?'

'Yes,' said Roland, 'this is my first placement.'

Douglas allowed himself a little self-knowing grin.

'This must all be a bit of shock for you, then?'

'It is,' said Roland, also sensing he had a chance to state his case, 'but I shouldn't have been put in this position.'

'It's simple, Roland, you should never leave a patient if they are on special obs.'

'I know,' said Roland, looking at Franks with a simmering sense of injustice.

Franks then closed his eyes.

'We're pulling in!' shouted the paramedic.

Roland eased himself off the vast bulk of Franks and turned to look straight into Douglas' eyes. He had little to lose and this was his one opportunity to make his case.

'I know we were understaffed,' said Roland, moving up close to Douglas. 'I am not going to keep quiet if anything comes of this.'

The ambulance came to a sudden stop. Douglas avoided a response as he pushed his hands down on the levers of the double doors and swung them open. He turned back to instruct Roland as Franks began to stir.

'You can stay with him,' he said, 'until we know what the damage is. I'll talk to Mr Fitzpatrick. Don't worry, we've all messed up one time or another. Anything else we can take up with the sister on the ward.'

'Right,' said Roland, with a barely disguised sigh of relief.

'But just remember, Roland, I am part of the management team.'

'Yeah, I know,' said Roland, who jumped down on to the forecourt of the A&E department.

'Oh, I am sorry,' said Franks again, as the paramedics clambered in to extract the trolley.

'Let's just say,' said Douglas, close to Roland's ear, 'you've got lucky on this one.'

★

After A&E had assigned Franks to a surgical ward Roland was left to babysit until the operation in the afternoon. Douglas was keen to get back to Wellington Park and left Roland with his standard wink of reassurance (an indication, Roland assumed, that everything would be alright). He certainly did not trust Douglas, Fitzpatrick or any other manager, especially as he was the perfect scapegoat given the circumstances, but Roland rationalised that any investigation would cause more trouble for them than it would for him. Okay, he knew he had fucked up, made a mistake with Franks, but that was a mistake anyone could make, especially after only a few weeks on a ward full of nutcases. In fact, things were pretty much in his favour as long as he didn't panic.

Roland stared out at the grey blanket of cloud which hung in the window, slumped in a high-backed armchair at the side of Franks' bed. They had been allocated one of two isolation wards, the other occupied by a hapless individual covered in red blotches and a victim, so they said, of AIDS. They were on the fourth floor so Roland thought about standing up and seeing if there was a good view across the town, but decided it was not worth the risk of waking the mad retired professor. Fuck knows why he had done it, thought Roland, especially as he had trusted him not to do it. But it was a bad judgement call, the same old mistake he had made so many times before: trusting people. *Why do they do it? Why do people lie; why do people say things when they have no intention of ever sticking to them?*

Franks opened his eyes. He turned his head like a wise old owl and stared intently at Roland. He lifted his arm and used his fingers to fondle the thin bandage covering the wound over his throat.

'I wouldn't touch it,' said Roland, trying to sound authoritative.

Franks obeyed, moving his hands down by his sides, feeling the cotton sheets; a comforting but suspicious material.

'You're on a ward now,' said Roland, raising his voice. 'You're going to have an operation to stitch up your throat.'

'I'm so sorry,' said Franks, his voice weak from the trauma.

'You don't have to be sorry,' said Roland, looking out through the window again.

'But I am, for getting you into trouble.'

'You haven't got me into trouble.'

'But I should have come back with you,' said Franks. 'It was my fault. I know you did your best.'

This was the last thing Roland needed: Franks conscious of the events.

'Look,' said Roland, leaning forward and prepared to be explicit, 'why didn't you come back to the ward when I asked you then?'

Franks lowered his voice.

'I knew when you left me I was going to do it... I told you I was going to do it.'

'I didn't believe you,' said Roland, also keeping his voice low. 'I didn't think you'd do it. I came back for you, but by the time I came back you were gone.'

Franks shrugged his shoulders. Clearly, it was not his fault.

'Okay,' said Roland, 'you're right. I made a mistake, but it doesn't matter... I won't get into trouble for it.'

'Oh, that's good,' said Franks, folding his arms across his chest. 'You don't deserve it. I know you trusted me and I betrayed your trust. I'm sorry.'

Roland leant back in his chair.

'Are you going to stay with me?' asked Franks.

'Yeah…'

'Good,' he said, looking sideways and then back at Roland. 'Do you know, there are people after me?'

'I don't think so, not in here,' said Roland, keen to reorientate Franks. 'You do know you're in a general hospital… you're not in Wellington Park. You cut your throat this morning. We came in an ambulance. You're just waiting for surgery.'

Franks looked bemused. He then pursed his lips to indicate he needed to remain silent. He shook his head from side to side, then held his breath, ready to burst.

'Shush!' said Franks, bringing his finger to his lips. 'They've been after me for ages.'

'You've never said anything before… about people being after you?'

Franks tightened his lips again in order to maintain his silence. This was good, thought Roland, in one way: Franks being more overtly symptomatic could mitigate Roland's cock-up if he could reveal Franks was harbouring a latent psychosis. However, just before surgery he needed Franks composed and compliant.

'You're going to have an operation soon,' said Roland, his voice acquiring a higher pitch, 'to fix your throat… where the bandage is…'

'No, no, no, no, no,' said Franks, 'you don't understand. I did a terrible thing. You know, I marched them all the way to Moscow and then they died because of me, in the snow, in the wasteland!'

Ah… just what you would expect from a professor of history.

'Yes, that was Napoleon,' said Roland, 'but you're

not Napoleon. He failed, didn't he, Napoleon – he didn't prepare his army for the winter.'

'I am the army!' shouted Franks.

Roland looked behind him towards the nurses' station. A female nurse stared and Roland smiled to offer some reassurance. He was doing his job, this time…

'You do know why you're here, don't you?' said Roland. 'You know they are going to have to operate, to stitch up your throat?'

Franks' eyes flickered.

'Will you come with me to the theatre?'

'I'll stay until they take you in, but I can't come with you. Anyway, you'll be asleep during the operation.'

'Oh dear,' said Franks, who had obviously found another point of distress, 'you must stay with me… this is a terrible thing I've done.'

'What have you done that's so terrible?'

Franks looked around again, making sure prying eyes and ears were not going to get his story, or not without high-quality equipment, that is.

'I was a member of the Communist Party,' he whispered.

Roland wanted to laugh, but knew he needed to remain serious.

'That's not a crime… yet… as far as I know,' he said.

'Trotsky,' said Franks, in hushed tones, 'they got him in the end.'

'True… but you're not Trotsky,' said Roland.

Franks had to rethink: Lenin… Trotsky… Stalin?

'You mustn't tell anyone,' said Franks. 'You had to keep quiet about that sort of thing… back then.'

'Don't worry,' said Roland, oblivious to the historical threat Franks was referring to, 'I won't tell anyone.'

'Oh, please, please, don't say a thing.'

'My lips are sealed.'

Franks paused, thinking again about Trotsky and Stalin.

'I had a pickaxe in my head,' he said, his face stern and determined.

'I think all you did was cut your throat.'

Franks moved his finger like a knife across his bandage.

'They got him in the end... in Mexico,' continued Franks, 'Stalin's agents. You can't disagree with them, or that's it.'

Clearly, thought Roland, Franks was deluded, but it was interesting because he had never met a real Communist.

'So, why did you become a Communist?'

'Oh, you had to back then, terrible things were going on. They were going to destroy the world. We had to stop them.'

'Well, they're always trying to destroy the world,' said Roland, 'but I'm not a Communist. I don't believe you have to be a Communist to change things.'

Franks slammed his hand down on the mattress.

'They're after us, you know! In the end they'll get you. They've got files on me... they've got files on you. You can't stand up to them... spies all over the place. They've got the technology, you know. There's nothing we can say to each other that they don't already know.'

'Who is after you?'

'The Russians,' said Franks dismissively. 'They are all Russian spies. You're a fool if you don't know that!'

'I don't think the Russians are listening to us. I can assure you there are no bugs in here.'

Franks paused, trying to separate fact from fiction.

'We need to make sure,' said Franks, 'that the army is a revolutionary force which cannot be diluted by bourgeois insurgents, or worst of all, agents provocateurs!'

'We're only waiting for your operation,' said Roland, realising it was probably a mistake to indulge "the professor".

Franks looked confused. He was calculating, trying to hold on to something.

'You won't let them do anything to me, will you?'

'You need to go for surgery, that's all.'

Franks hesitated and touched his thin crêpe bandage. This seemed to bring about a moment of self-awareness.

'You've been very good to me,' he said. 'I've got you into all this trouble and all you want to do is help. I'm very grateful, you know. You'll make a good nurse.'

'It's just my job,' said Roland, cautious of Franks' ingratiating praise.

'But you've got a lot of training to do before you're qualified?'

'Yes, you're right,' said Roland, wondering if Franks had turned into his tutor. 'I am just a first-year student.'

'I'm sure you'll make it… just don't make any more mistakes.'

Roland blushed.

'Are you looking after Mr Franks?' asked a voice from behind Roland's shoulder.

Roland turned to see a baby face leaning around the side of the door frame, a stethoscope hanging from the obligatory white doctor's coat.

'Can I have a word?' he said, in a manner which immediately grated on Roland. 'You can leave him for a minute, can't you?'

'You'll be alright,' said Roland to Franks. 'I'll just be in the corridor.'

Roland followed the white coat and viewed Franks through the frosted glass panel.

'We'll be doing the operation shortly,' said the white coat, 'but we were just wondering what is wrong with him, psychologically?'

'Well,' said Roland, 'I think I've discovered he has paranoid and grandiose delusions.'

The white coat looked at Roland as if he was being far too presumptuous. He then checked the name tag on Roland's uniform, before glancing in another direction.

'Would you consider him to be a danger to himself or to others?' asked the white coat officiously.

'Well, he did try to commit suicide,' said Roland acerbically.

The white coat was unimpressed.

'On a measure of one to ten,' said the white coat, 'can you give me an evaluation of his propensity for self-harming?'

'He'll be alright, as long as you don't mention ice picks.'

The white coat was offended, and stared sternly into Roland's face.

'What's your name?'

'Roland.'

The white coat squeezed his eyes in an attempt to focus on his name badge again.

'Roland Cauldron,' said Roland.

The white coat nodded and then walked off through a set of double doors which swung back obediently.

'Fucking wanker,' said Roland under his breath.

Franks looked worried as Roland returned and sat down.

'It won't be long,' he said, still smarting from being spoken to by some snotty-nosed twat.

'Okay,' said Franks. 'Is it too late for dinner?'

CHAPTER 2

A STARR IS BORN

Starr bent his nose so it was close to the blood drying on the lawn of Wellington Park Psychiatric Hospital. The thick glob had congealed and contained little bits of leaf and twig. If he'd had a stick he would have poked it, but there was no implement to hand. He turned his head towards the breeze-block visitor centre and wondered if the blood belonged to any of the patients positioned scenically on the benches. No, he was sure, instinctively, it was none of them.

'And what are you up to?' boomed the authoritarian Irish accent of Fitzpatrick.

Starr froze, reluctant to look at the eyes, the piercing, demanding eyes which always required a response.

'Six... one-five... one-five... one-two,' mumbled Starr, concentrating on the thick bloodstain as a source of comfort.

'Get up, man!' commanded Fitzpatrick. 'I'm asking you, what are you doing?'

Starr stood up, looked down at his feet, then faced his inquisitor.

'Shouldn't you be with Ms Colgate?' asked Fitzpatrick, looking at his watch.

Starr blinked uncontrollably at the yellow domed head glinting in the autumnal sun. He remained static, uncertain, mesmerised by the green hue of Fitzpatrick's jacket.

'It's ten past nine,' said Fitzpatrick, always alert to time, procedure and activity. 'You have five minutes...'

Starr acknowledged the instruction, his buttocks wobbling off, saliva lined along his lips and his face flushed like a red varnish. After a few paces he decided to accelerate at top speed, supersonic speed, his legs marching like a distressed road walker's, heading towards the sandstone columns which buttressed the entrance to the main reception. He kept his head down as he got closer; *Do not look up*, he said to himself, *do not look up at the Clock Tower*. The four clock faces stood in the centre of a wheel of wards and had once emanated time across the manicured landscape. It had been the controller, the indicator of the daily routines – although time had now caught up with the faces and no money would ever be found for its repair.

Starr ambled into reception, glancing over at the unmanned visitors' desk, and considered his next move. He opted for a north-easterly direction along the white-painted corridors. As he strutted, he watched the thick tubes of ductwork above his head move at a similar pace to his own.

'Watch out!' shouted an aggrieved trodden-on patient. 'Who do you think you are? You don't run this place!'

Starr was in no mood to tolerate more tiresome, repetitive admonishment and moved quickly away. He knocked on the door of the staff canteen, glanced at Slaney's big chief's office door, then pushed with a great effort through the plastic panels which covered the fire exit. To his left was Ms Colgate's ark, a flat-roofed prefab of rotting windowsills. Next door was the humming boiler house, then the mortuary and the dilapidated triangular potting sheds. Lastly, he acknowledged a dark, carnivorous opening, an archway of shrubs, hedges and trees. Starr knew it well, beyond and within, as the patients' graveyard.

Not today, Starr said to himself, none of this was for today.

Instead, he took to the circular tarmac road, used by delivery vehicles to drive around the hospital. As he travelled once more, bobbing along, he watched the sunlight reflect off the high rectangular windows of the red brick tentacle wards. He soon reached a new point of consideration, his next option: should he head into the woods behind the nurses' hostel, or carry on into the sweet shop in the visitor centre? The woods were best for galloping and there was no need to gallop just yet. So he powered onwards, ignoring the isolated Lilywhite Ward near the entrance to the old gates, and slipped through the heavy white panelled glass doors and into the malaise of the visitor centre purchasing area.

The debris of institutionalisation sat abandoned on the brown benches against the walls. With their small allowances they had purchased chocolate, crisps, fizzy drinks and rolling tobacco to get them through their tedious day. Starr walked purposefully across the beige tiled floor to the shop counter. He feasted his eyes on the small shelves of desirable commodities, but the sweet lady had already decided she was not going to waste her time on him.

'No,' she said prescriptively, 'you know I can't serve you... I've been told you're meant to be on a diet. There are no crisps or chocolate for you here!'

Starr continued to look at the prizes before him. He pointed with his fat-fingered hand.

'Chocolate...'

The sweet lady fussed around her trays, her grey voluntarism displayed in her brown uniform and name badge.

'No, I told you, look at you, you're a roly-poly man and there's no way I'm serving you. Now, off with you!'

Undaunted, he stood in front of the pleasure palace, his salivating mouth beginning to dribble, his doe eyes appealing for sympathy. Another patient moved forward and the sweet lady held her bosom as she reached up to retrieve a chocolate bar. Starr needed food, needed feeding, needed fuel. Stubborn persistence sometimes delivered the result; unblinking motionlessness, all absence of thought might yet get her to yield.

He waited, bowing his head.

'Are you still here?' she said, pushing her hands down on the counter. 'You're wasting your time with me, young man.'

Persistence, thought Starr, *do not look into her eyes, but wait, ever so patiently*. And he waited, waited as the slow stroll of patients came and went, waited against all the odds, with all the gods possibly against him.

Eventually, Starr decided reluctantly to withdraw, spinning around to look through the seascape windows. *There should be something*, he thought, *something else to search for, to find in the earth, in the firm body of life.* He had after all found some red stuff, some essence of life. There must be more life out there, more things to do with stuff up there, floating above his head, and stuff down there, near his feet, in the earth.

He walked down the steps of the visitor centre and stood in between two tall hedges. He was almost back to where he had started from, near the spot where he had been looking out across the well-groomed lawns.

And again, behind him, he heard a voice, but a different voice, a slow, rich tone from low down on the register, rising up to a high-pitched syllable on the end.

The hedge was talking.

'Ad… am! Ad… am!'

Starr peered into the dense foliage.

'Ad… am! Ad… am!'

He giggled.

Then he noticed, embedded in the centre, a grey-bearded man perched like a rigid frog. Starr approached, stimulating the release of the trapped voice from its suspended position. The voice of Adam regained some composure, ignored Starr's greetings and headed off along one side of the hedge. Starr was tempted to follow, but he was heading towards the reception, possibly too near the environment of compulsory activities he was seeking to avoid.

Starr resumed his gaze across the carpet of lawns. He recognised Agnes holding her bag of things tightly against her conjoined breasts, her worldly possessions stuffed into a plastic supermarket bag. She was resilient, but unapproachable. Starr would avoid her, but he could see to the right of him a good prospect, known as the most persistent traveller beyond the grounds of Wellington Park. This was a tall, gangly man whose athletic build meant he could drive forward all day, in all weathers, in a constant fugue-like state. Not a word had ever passed his lips, no one ever knew where he went, but he was always back in time for tea, always back in time for bed, before resuming his remorseless treading of the paths, fields and roadways.

Starr kept his eye on the great big walking boots and decided to follow.

However, it was not long before the enthusiasm which had carried him forward dissipated. He did not care about the distant traveller as he tired mentally and physically. He stopped at the old cricket pitch, screened from the Clock Tower by a line of trees, sitting beneath the twigs of a hanging branch on a green, mouldy bench, looking out over the rarely used wicket. He knew, although he did not know why he knew, but he had to find something, something to do – perhaps something that was looking for him, or something that could help?

He restarted his motor, propelled by the hypomanic energy fuelling his routine, and wobbled across the cricket field towards the small pavilion. As he peered in he avoided pressing his face against the glass, peeled off some of the stale white paint from the window frame and scanned the home and away changing rooms. The wooden floors were covered in cricket gloves, pads, bats and stumps, all left to decay because the ship had suddenly been abandoned and the game abruptly stopped. Starr walked behind the rotting pavilion through a small wooded area and kicked the flaking leaves on the moist, frosted floor. Then he found a forgotten building, a lost ward. He had lived there once, years ago, or only a few years ago, until he had moved into the big spider's web. He peered into the space through a cracked window. Time was changing in there as well; the wheels were turning, going another way, going anticlockwise, backwards, sending everything into oblivion.

He had another thought, an old thought, the same thought. The boots... he remembered the marching boots, marching onwards to victory! He must find him, find where he was going and find the eternal path.

Starr got back on to the tarmac and followed the route towards the very last outpost, the very last thing on the remote boundary of Wellington Park. He walked over a rusty cow gate, along a straightened concrete path and into dangerous territory. He was near the one place where very few would ever go: Chaolla House. He stopped, listening to the sweeping seeds of grasses, and looked suspiciously at the low roof of the solitary building. No, he said to himself, there was something not quite right with the world out there.

With his head bowed he slowly trundled back from the perimeter, following cracks in the tarmac, spotting objects on the ground. And then he saw it: the thing, shiny in the pitted soil, the meteor which had fallen last night as he had explored the star-filled sky. No more than the size of a small stone; he bent down and retrieved the compressed mineral which had smashed through the atmosphere.

What a find! In the earth, the precious earth, the precious star releasing into his palm the amino acids, the structures of life, the osmosis of life, the life-giving chances of life confetti and the restoration of things.

He spun around in ecstasy, released a horse-like laugh and set off at a canter. He galloped back across the cricket field, on to the circular tarmac path, rushing like a runaway train, exhilarated with the discovery held tightly in his grubby, fat hand. As he looked up he saw a tall, Amazonian figure coming towards him. Unable to contain his excitement, he walked straight up to Sophie Smith.

'Star!' said Starr.

'Hello,' said Sophie, smiling tactfully.

'Look!'

Sophie looked at the granite-type stone.

'A star!' he said triumphantly.

Sophie leaned forward to examine it more closely.

'Are you sure it's a star, Alan, and not a stone you found?'

'Yes,' said Starr, giggling.

'And where did you find it?'

'There,' he said, pointing with his arm to the exact angle and position.

'And why is it a star?'

'Because it's singing.'

'It's singing… you can hear it singing?'

'Yes.'

'Is it singing now?'

Starr furrowed his brow, unsure as to how he should respond.

'Was it singing… was it singing?' he said, out loud and to himself.

'Perhaps you're just singing to yourself?'

'No,' replied Starr adamantly.

'I sing to myself sometimes, when I am happy,' explained Sophie.

Starr withdrew. She was wrong.

He bowed his head and remained wobbling on the spot. He was undaunted. He knew there was far more he could do with the power he had been granted.

He galloped at great speed, accelerating his legs, punching his pistons on the ground and almost falling over with happiness. He was in no doubt: he had a cure. It had come from the sky, come from the gods, the special material: a star for Alan Starr.

CHAPTER 3

THE POTHEAD PIXIES

Roland kicked the bottom of the heavy swing-back doors to the front entrance of the nurses' hostel and stepped into a wide corridor on the ground floor. He looked over at the noticeboard full of irrelevant warnings, advice and guidance, checked the downstairs TV room, the large common room and the communal kitchen, before leaping up the concrete stairs to the staff accommodation. There were approximately eighty rooms housing staff and students in hollow, soulless residencies of dank, faded yellow. Roland walked along a U-shaped corridor, pushed through a fire safety door and listened to it thunder back on its tight retention. He ignored his own little box room and tapped lightly on Jas' door. There was only one thing on Roland's mind: he needed to get stoned with the Pothead Pixies, Terry and Jas.

On Roland's first day of training he had immediately found an affinity with Jas, and admired enviously his undoubted handsomeness and sexual conquests. Jas unashamedly boasted about his hedonism and obliterating any sensitivities to sexism, language and discretion. He had been happy for a number of years living and working in the hospital as a domestic: cleaning toilets and floors, serving dinners and washing up on the wards. He played up to the stereotype of the cheeky South London Indian, whilst failing as a male model because he was too short and continuing to harbour ambitions as a clubbing DJ. But he had reached a point where he had to get serious, if only to keep his parents quiet with their constant talk of arranged marriage, and avoid such a commitment by taking the plunge and enrolling on the student nurse training programme.

Roland was always more cautious and circumspect with Terry (also part of their September '84 intake), who blended the anxious and the sardonic with unfaltering accuracy. There was also a rather uncanny likeness in appearance: although Terry had curly brown bouffant hair, they possessed the same pale pink skin which needed constant attention and Jas' advice on male grooming. But for Roland, Terry failed on one crucial level; a lack of commitment or passion which was the prerequisite of a "proper friend".

Stepping into Jas' room was like entering a five-star deluxe version of the nurses' hostel. Some years ago he had bagged the best room, furnishing it with four of the largest speakers known to the home audio aficionado, complemented by top-of-the-range decks, a TV wired to the temperamental quadraphonic sound system, a sofa bed, an extendable clothes rack (full of the latest fashion) and a variety of illegal martial arts weaponry.

Inside the den of iniquity Roland immediately

revealed the trauma of his day with the suicidal Franks. This was greeted with the inevitable: "We've heard" and "You just need to try this".

Roland was invited to examine a variety of paraphernalia and settled on an initial test run called the "soft option": a butane gas burner-heated "hot knife". As Roland waited, crouched with his legs wide open, Jas reached forward and placed a heated knife on Roland's bulging bollocks. Roland remained passive, failing to notice the unprovoked assault. Only at the point of the smoking fabric did he leap backwards in pain.

'What the fuck?!'

Both Jas and Terry convulsed, rolling on the floor in a state of stoned euphoria.

'Why the fuck,' asked Roland, inspecting his crotch, 'did you do that?'

'Because it's there…' said Jas, only slightly surprised by his own impulsiveness.

'Yeah, those are really tight jeans,' said Terry.

'Fuck!' said Roland, continuing to inspect his nether region. 'What does it take to get a fucking smoke out of you guys? Jesus!'

A few more minutes of self-indulgent laughter prevailed before Jas was suitably composed to begin proceedings.

'Are you going to do it then?' asked Roland of a tearful Jas. 'And leave my bollocks alone this time, please.'

'Yeah, yeah, yeah… just let me get my head together first.'

Finally, Roland was invited to dip his head and use the improvised bottle funnel to suck the burning smoke into his lungs. This ensured a greater quantity of the amber nectar's, rapid diffusion within his bloodstream and optimum navigation towards his brain. Then Roland collapsed for all the right reasons.

'That's him fucked,' said Jas.

Terry nodded sagely.

Jas suggested they proceed with a few more rounds before they consider the more advanced experimentation. All three took turns in providing or administering the succulent hashish. Once they were all sated they began to discuss the "ultimate experience", but their unbridled joy at devising an intricate solution to consumption was disturbed by a violent thud on the door. This sent them into an immediate state of stoned paranoia.

In such situations it had been agreed by all that a general principle should be applied:

1) If you are stoned, ask yourself this question: do you have the composure to answer the door and maintain a conversation with someone who is not in the same condition but who can be persuaded, at least for the duration of the social interaction, that you are coherent and in full capacity of mind and body?

2) If you realise option one is unrealistic, will a muffled conversation behind the door avoid unnecessary suspicion?

'Who the fuck's that?' whispered Terry, preparing to throw some of the evidence in the ashtray out of the window.

'It's the police, open up!' shouted the voice behind the door.

'Is it fuck,' said Jas, who then raised his voice. 'If you don't tell me who the fuck you are I'll crush your nuts and eat your penis!'

'Come on,' they said, trying to maintain the voice of pseudo law enforcement, 'open up!'

Jas was having none of it.

'I'll fuck your daughter and your mother and sell them off as sex slaves if you don't tell me who the fuck you are!'

Terry looked at Roland, and Roland looked at Jas.

'I think I know who it is,' said Jas.

'You've got one more chance,' said the voice, beginning to lose the will to maintain the pretence.

'Are you going to let him in?' asked Terry, who also seemed to know who the stupid dick was.

Jas, in a swift coordinated movement, swung a jailer's chain of keys into his hand (all illegitimate and inherited from his time in the hospital as a domestic). He found his own room key, demonstrating the accumulated experience of locking and unlocking doors, to reveal the smirking Dr Jonas, who did not hesitate to invite himself in.

'You fucking bastard!' they all said in unison.

Dr Jonas laughed hysterically, taking off his John Lennon glasses, rubbing his eyes and observing the collective scene of indulgence and degradation.

'I thought I'd see what the Pothead Pixies were up to,' he said, seeking to seat himself on the sofa bed, causing Roland to shuffle along to make room.

He wore corduroy trousers and a check jacket, also

known as the informal uniform of the junior doctor. He had effortlessly fulfilled his predetermined trajectory of a career chosen for him, but he felt trapped in a straitjacket constructed by his doctoring parents. The pixies discreetly acknowledged he was from a different class, which permitted associate membership of the puffing gang.

'So, what are you guys up to then?' he asked, sniffing the fumes. 'You can smell it all down the corridor.'

'You motherfucking faggot,' continued Jas, in his usual politically incorrect manner, 'have we got a surprise for you!'

Dr Jonas examined the butane gas burner and was underwhelmed.

'Fear not,' said Terry.

'We've got hot knives and amyl,' said Jas, rather like a proud chef.

'Cool...' said Dr Jonas, enthused by the propensity for student deviancy.

'But it's more than that,' offered Roland, his head still humming after the consumption from the initial experimental processes.

'We've got a mega head rush,' explained Jas, eager to promote the process. 'You get the hash, the amyl rush and the fucked up scene from *Apocalypse Now*, all rolled into one.'

Dr Jonas yelped with joy.

'Oh my God! That sounds crazy! I like it. What do I need to do?'

Jas offered up Roland as "demonstrator".

'The trick,' said Jas, eager to explain, 'is to get it so

the head rush coincides with the helicopters flying into the village. I've got the speakers rigged so the music's coming at you from all sides.'

Dr Jonas looked at Roland's eyes.

'I take it you've already done this?'

'No,' said Terry, 'he's just stoned.'

'He also burnt my bollocks,' said Roland, as he opened his legs to reveal a distinct fraying over his testicular area.

'That's barbaric!'

'I know,' said Jas, sniggering, whilst preparing the knives, 'I just saw his bollocks staring at me.'

'And so you burnt them?'

'He's got big balls,' said Terry.

'Mega gonads,' said Jas, as he turned on the butane gas and slid the ends of the knives over the flame.

Dr Jonas offered his sympathy.

'And he's your friend… how do you put up with it?'

'I don't… normally,' said Roland.

'That's what you say,' said Terry. 'I think he needs to go to A&E.'

Dr Jonas paused, gauging his acceptance within the group before launching into a pre-prepared statement.

'So,' he said, directly facing Roland, 'I hear you took a ride in an ambulance today.'

'He'll only try and freak you out,' said Jas, acutely aware of Dr Jonas' propensity for one-upmanship.

'He's going to eat you for breakfast,' added Dr Jonas.

'He means Fitzpatrick,' said Jas, who dropped the needle on to the deck before lifting it back on to its armrest.

'The man runs this place,' said Dr Jonas, 'and he

won't stand for anyone trying to challenge him.'

'What are you fucking talking about?' said Roland, anxious for a little clarity. 'I'm not doing anything to challenge Fitzpatrick. I haven't said anything to Fitzpatrick.'

'The word is, you are going to make a formal complaint,' said Dr Jonas, who was momentarily distracted by the reddening knives.

Roland held up his arms in protest.

'I don't believe this place!' he said. 'I've had one conversation with Douglas and it's gone all round the fucking hospital. All I said was, I'm not going to be done for it, or if they want to, I'm not going to sit back and take it. You know what it's like on the wards. What was I supposed to do when there's only me and Sister Bernice?'

'Look, who cares about the shit that goes on?' said Jas. 'Nothing will happen to you... trust me, I've been here long enough to know they won't do anything. They just cover things up.'

'I wouldn't bet on that,' said Terry.

'Have you heard what happened to McEmery?' asked Dr Jonas, leaning back to pursue his prey.

'No,' said Roland, who knew he was now going to hear all about McEmery.

'Fitzpatrick waited,' said Dr Jonas, narrowing his eyes, 'and then they got him, right at the end.'

'Yeah,' said Jas, as he searched through the video player for the appropriate scene, 'he was a great guy, always standing up for things.'

Roland looked to the ceiling. 'What the fuck... ?'

'The story goes,' said Dr Jonas, happy to provide Roland

with further details, 'that he finished his training, passed all his exams and was walking back from the social club and then decided to take a short cut through the hospital. Fitzpatrick was in the corridor, spotted him and gave him a formal warning there and then for being drunk on the premises. The next day, Fitzpatrick went to the school and they forced him to resign and withdraw his registration.'

'Hang on,' said Roland, 'why would he be walking through the hospital if he was walking back from the social club? He doesn't need to walk through the hospital.'

'I know,' said Dr Jonas. 'People said he was really looking for Fitzpatrick so he could tell him what he thought of him... that's why he got the boot.'

'Even at the end?' asked Terry, who had become mildly interested in the tale, in case Roland's behaviour had potential ramifications.

'Trust me,' said Dr Jonas, 'if they don't like you they can do anything they want... anything...'

'Like what?' asked Roland.

'Yeah, like what?' asked Terry.

Dr Jonas laughed.

'They decide how they get you,' he said, trying to turn his head 360 degrees.

'How?' asked Roland.

Dr Jonas smiled.

'Alright,' said Roland, prepared to give Dr Jonas the benefit of the doubt, 'how do they get you?'

'No, I won't say anything. You guys can find out for yourselves because you won't believe me.'

'I believe you,' said Terry, happy to facilitate the targeting of Roland.

Dr Jonas paused, calculating how he should play to the rest of his audience.

'Go on then,' said Jas reluctantly.

'Well, they won't actually tell you about it,' he said.

'What a surprise…' said Jas.

Dr Jonas raised his finger; he had not said his piece.

'Let me ask you a question,' said Dr Jonas. 'Do you believe that everybody here, I mean the patients, that every patient here is really mad?'

'No,' said Roland.

'That's a fact,' said Jas.

'Right, so therefore, there is room, let's just say, for other people who may not be mad… some faking it, some needing it, some labelled by it.'

'There are all sorts of people here,' said Roland.

'Exactly – casualties.'

'And your point… ?' asked Roland.

'We can all become casualties,' said Dr Jonas, his eyeballs bulging.

'We know that,' said Roland. 'We all know there are people here who are not really mad and there's nowhere else for them to go. We all know it's a safe haven for the socially dysfunctional.'

'And…' said Dr Jonas, indicating Roland had got close to his premise.

'And what?'

'Well, I'll leave it for you guys to work it out for yourselves.'

'I know what he's saying,' said Jas, grasping the rather opaque meaning.

'What is he saying?' asked Terry, who was losing interest.

'He is saying,' said Jas, 'that we can all become patients. You don't have to be *mad* mad, just a bit deviant. Then they can diagnose you, section you and lock you up... especially if they don't like you.'

'Who's they?' asked Roland.

'Fitzpatrick, Slaney and that other fucker who runs Chaolla House, Dr Caldwell.'

'Rubbish!' exclaimed Roland.

'No, it's true!' said Jas. 'If they want to, they could have you sectioned, make you so fucking paranoid you'd easily end up being put away. And you know what... you'd all end up like all the other sad fuckers here with no one giving a fuck about you.'

'But they would have to prove that you'd gone mad,' said Roland.

'They can do that easily enough,' said Dr Jonas. 'Anything you do here can be interpreted as a sign of mental illness.'

'How does that work then?'

'Simple,' said Dr Jonas. 'Just look at you guys here... I could have you all sectioned for criminal behaviour and drug dependency.'

'Smoking dope doesn't mean you're mad!'

'Of course it doesn't,' said Dr Jonas, 'and the consequences are far less serious – negligible outside of the institution. But you are all working in a mental hospital, looking after the mentally ill. You're all under the microscope and your behaviour will be interpreted differently. However, as I said, they only use it if they want to keep you quiet.'

Terry looked accusingly at Roland.

'What?'

'Nothing,' said Terry.

'We'll ask Gobi next time we're in school,' said Jas.

'As I said,' said Dr Jonas, 'nobody will admit to it.'

'Then he's making it up,' said Roland, no longer prepared to be taken in. 'Freaking us out.'

'That's up to you guys,' said Dr Jonas, 'but don't say I didn't warn you.'

'I've not heard anything about it,' said Roland. 'Anyway, the point is, I'm not making a formal complaint unless I have to.'

'Don't worry,' said Terry, 'you've got almost three years before they kick you out.'

'Thanks,' said Roland.

'Right,' said Jas, keen to focus people's attention, 'shut the fuck up while I concentrate.'

But the seed had been planted in Roland's mind. That was typical of Dr Jonas, thought Roland; it was just his way of being superior, all-knowing. No way… no way were people locked up because they complained to Fitzpatrick or whoever. That was crazy. Fuck it! Bollocks… complete and utter paranoid bollocks!

Jas had renewed his tasks and cut a thin blob of hash, ordering Roland to prepare for take-off. Roland held the bottomless glass bottle. Dr Jonas was instructed to hold the amyl so it could be administered up Roland's nose. On screen, the rising helicopters hit the skies and began their advance.

'You've got to wait for the bit where the helicopters start smashing the village,' said Jas, as general advice to the waiting pixies.

The music and imagery rampaged towards a crescendo. As the first rockets flew and the machine gunfire began strafing the peasants, Jas removed a knife from the butane gas flame and dropped the hash on to the red-hot blade. Roland relaxed his lung movement so he could infuse his bloodstream. Jas took the other knife and placed the two ends together. The smoke began to rise.

'Go, go, go!'

Roland let the hashish collect inside the bottle. The first ammunition exploded on screen as the attack worked its way to its Wagnerian climax.

'Here we go!'

Dr Jonas unscrewed the bottle of amyl and thrust it under Roland's nose. Roland consumed as much as he could and then pulled away, choking.

'Hold it in! Hold it in!'

The head rush was emphatic, the drug concoction fusing through Roland's body. Bellows of ingested smoke flew out of his mouth as the amyl kicked in and his heartbeat began to race, shot through like an electrical current. He keeled over on to the sofa bed and uttered a few constricted words of pain and pleasure. Jas, Terry and Dr Jonas looked on like demented Frankensteins, laughing uncontrollably as Roland groaned in a contorted muddle.

'I'll have some of what he's having,' requested Dr Jonas.

They set about administering the narcotic combination with the efficiency of a coherent surgical team. It was now just a question of how much each could take before they sank back into a stoned and satisfied stupor.

Once their mission was completed Dr Jonas began to speculate on their ability to move off the sofa bed. All three pixies confirmed that Dr Jonas' observation was correct and their arms and legs were completely useless. This induced a degree of exaggerated laughter as they all tried to stand up. They all agreed that they should all be admitted as soon as possible under section. With their hearts beating, their heads swathed in mild hallucinogenic, Dr Jonas was suddenly able to free himself from his muscular rigidity and shake his arms and legs like a beetle turned on its back. Full of drug-induced energy, they continued to shake their limbs in the air. Then a sound, an alien, intrusive *bleep-bleep*, cut through the air.

'Oh fuck!' said Dr Jonas, fumbling to find the source of the noise.

The pixies looked at each other, convinced the authorities had discovered their degeneracy.

Bleep-bleep, bleep-bleep…

'What the fuck's that?' asked Jas, shaken by the intrusion.

'Oh fuck!' said Dr Jonas again, bending his head down to look at his belt and pull the offending noise closer for examination. He read the message on his pager. 'Is there a phone somewhere?'

'A phone… what do you need a phone for?' asked Roland, even more perplexed than Jas.

'I need to phone in.'

'Phone in for what?'

'I'm on call,' said Dr Jonas.

'You're kidding!' they all exclaimed.

'You can't go out there,' said Jas.

'Why not?'

'You're stoned!' said Jas, stating the obvious and managing to control his limbs so he could stand up.

'You've got to phone in sick,' said Roland, uncharacteristically concerned for Dr Jonas' welfare.

Dr Jonas headed towards the door.

'I'm not opening it,' said Jas, attempting to impose a physical barrier.

Dr Jonas smiled reassuringly. Their concern was appreciated but everything was under control.

'There's no way you can go on to the wards. They're bound to find out… they'll look into your eyes!'

'Why… what's wrong with my eyes?'

'You know what we mean,' said Roland, looking into Dr Jonas' glazed, murky eyes.

Dr Jonas turned to Jas.

'Let me find out what it is first. You guys are so paranoid!'

There was little they could do to stop Dr Jonas. Jas unlocked the door and pointed to the phone further down the corridor.

'Can you believe that?' said Terry. 'That man's got some balls.'

'He shouldn't be doing it,' said Roland. 'How can he get so stoned when he's on call? That's mad!'

As they waited for Dr Jonas to return, they speculated on the likelihood of him going back on to the wards. If he was discovered incapable of any clinical function, would he reveal how he had got into such a state, and by implication, their own role in it?

There was a faint knock on the door and Dr Jonas stepped back into the room.

'Right, guys,' he said, 'I've got to go.'

'You can't do that,' pleaded Roland.

'I've got to... there's an admission and they need an assessment.'

'But how can you do that stoned out of your mind?'

'Easy,' said Dr Jonas confidently. 'It's the challenge.'

'The challenge?'

'To see if you can keep it together. It's what makes life interesting... to see if they can tell.'

'Who, the patients?'

'Maybe.'

'That's crazy!'

'Well,' said Dr Jonas, 'it's something you should try one day. Everything else is boring until you've tried it. They're mad, you might be mad, but who can tell?'

Dr Jonas thanked them for the entertainment and headed back out to attend to the admission on Lilywhite Ward.

'Fuck!' said Roland. 'No way could I do that.'

'He's a crazy fucker,' said Terry.

'Anyway,' said Jas, turning to face Roland, 'when are you going to fuck Sophie?'

CHAPTER 4

VIRGIN ON DECEIT

Roland returned to his room, crashed on to his bed, looked up at the shadeless light, shut his eyes and drifted through a comforting stoned haze. He meandered through the sense that he was present but also absent, his consciousness suspended in time, a trapped moment which always proved there was more than one way to look at the world.

So much for abstinence and a new start. He was back to his pothead ways. Yet again, he had gravitated to the puff heads, drawn like a powerful magnet to the stoned stupor. But this time he was not out there in the mad world, he was doing it on the inside, inside a mad, fucked up place. In hindsight, choosing to live and work in a mental hospital was a crazy thing to do, the sort of crazy thing he tended to do: impulsive and instinctive. Although, there was some sense to it, a kind of logic. He probably would not be here if it was not for his mad, fucked up friends. He had just been so stupid, so naïve about them. It was embarrassing even to think about it, difficult to explain to anyone. And in some way, he really had no reason to feel aggrieved, betrayed by them... but he did.

It was the lie, the deceit, the great big fat fucking joke they must have been having at his expense for all those years. It was the gay thing, the great big fucking lies behind it, the secret life being played out in front of him whilst he was blind and blinkered to it all.

Well, what could he say? Was he right? Was he wrong? Should he have been more understanding? Had he failed to understand what it means to be gay? Fuck! Maybe he should try and understand it. That is what everyone else said: understand how difficult it is to "come out". But there was more to it. Oh yes... a lot more! It was not just about "coming out", it was about "coming out" and also saying to him: he was gay, how he needed to accept it, how it was so obvious.

Obvious! Obvious to whom?

No, it was not that he was gay. But fuck, yeah, that was what really blew his mind. How dare they – how dare they presume, just because he hung out with them (and yeah, okay, he had never had a proper girlfriend), it meant he was gay? There they were, expecting to be understood, expecting to be accepted (even though it had been going on for years behind his back), and all they could think about was whether he was gay, and how they probably thought now that they were "out" it was just a matter of time before he "converted".

What a load of self-indulgent, self-satisfying, self-serving, narrow-minded bullshit!

Fuck it! Fuck it!

Can someone not have a girlfriend and not be gay? Am I

allowed to be who I am: a sensitive soul, so sensitive, scared and anxious? The prospect, the actual thought, the process of meeting a girl (having sex), is almost impossible, unobtainable. And of course you cannot say that. In fact, the more you protest, the more you are in denial.

But it was not – not ever – about his sexuality.

What it came down to, what he had to come to terms with, what he had to accept, admit to, so he could grow up and move on, was his need to cross the Rubicon, because the fucking horrible, humiliating, vile and disgusting truth was… he was still a fucking virgin!

So, he had to learn one big thing, he had to, and he could not put it off any more, but he just had to overcome his shyness and anxiety. And as bizarre as it might seem, Wellington Park, the madhouse, the crazy, fucked up hospital, was the perfect place to do it. Because, as Jas kept saying, the place was full of opportunities, he just needed to grab them. And it all came down to one thing, so Jas had told him: confidence, confidence, confidence…

The thing was, if it came to politics, if it came to arguing about something, if it came to literature, books, films… well, no one would think that he was a jabbering, introverted wreck. But when it came to women, oh my God, what a hopeless fucking basket case! If only he could convert the same level of self-confidence he had with those things into the sex thing, the girl thing, the being-with-women thing.

And there was Sophie. There was a chance with Sophie, who, as far as he could tell, or so Jas said, was definitely interested. Which was weird: why would a stunningly beautiful woman like Sophie Smith have any interest in a skinny, ginger-haired virgin? Not that she knew he was a virgin. Not that anyone knew, unless Jas had some instinct for that type of thing. And maybe, maybe Jas did know. But with the ratios so high here (i.e. male to female), the chances and opportunities, so Jas said, massively increased.

Roland pushed himself up on his bed and looked into the mirror above the small washbasin. Man, he looked really out of it. How the fuck could Dr Jonas pull himself together to go on to the ward? On the other hand, Roland used to do something similar when he was living in London, doing that stupid fucking warehouse job. He laughed as he remembered the routine of a great big fucking bong going down in one, running like fuck for the bus, getting to work and then loading the lorry for the p.m. deliveries. Then, by the end of the shift, his head had usually cleared and he had the rest of the day free to work on the music with the band.

But everything went wrong because of his so-called friends, because of all their secrets, because of their fucking agenda. It was not the band for them... all they cared about was their sexuality. They were happy they had "come out", they were happy they had "become", but they had no insight into the damage their secret life had on him! They had suffered – sure, he accepted that – but not one miserable, considered grain of thought for what it meant for him. His only option was to accept their suffering, their plight and their difficulties. *Well, fuck me! Must I just jump for joy because they find themselves? They may have found themselves but I am still a fucking virgin!*

Well, he knew he had to carve out his own course in life, independent of their fucked up shit. Roland's needs had always been subsumed under the needs of their peer group. Now, after putting it off for so long, he had taken responsibility for his lack of action, his lack of being. And bizarrely, he found the answer based on the following criteria: get away from London (i.e. get away from the band and the so-called friends because otherwise he would never be able to be himself), get a job that paid enough money to put a roof over his head, and get a proper career where he could study and they would not mind a minor criminal indiscretion.

And somehow it had become a reality. His first genuine achievement. For a brief moment he believed he would leave all the dope-smoking behind. It was hardly his fault; once he was ensconced in the nurses' hostel he discovered a rampant misuse of drugs, various shades of deviancy and inappropriate employment. He was just one of many recruited to keep the sick, redundant institution going. He was here now, for better or worse... and into one mad, fucked up journey.

And as he lay back down on the cold bedspread he wondered how it was all going to end: whether he would survive, how he would come out of it – dead, alive or completely fucked up?

CHAPTER 5

THERE IS NOTHING REALLY WRONG WITH ME

Once Annie Buchanan had been assessed and admitted by Dr Jonas, she sat in a high-backed armchair in a corner of the day room on Lilywhite Ward. She knew everything about the place: the thirty beds upstairs in the dormitory, the isolation post-natal bed downstairs, the ward office at the other end and the meds room next to it. She had been in and out of the ward two or three times a month, carrying bags of instruments, fully aware that there was little respect among the staff for her therapeutic interventions. Now she was part of it…

The large white-framed rectangular windows rose up in front of her like an unforgiving parade of altars, passing judgement, telling her she was mad. She looked away and stared back at the flickering TV, watching but not watching, her thoughts racing at a thousand miles an hour. It was difficult to fathom, to get a handle on it, to get to grips with it, but this morning (thinking it through, because she had to now; she had no choice but to think it through), this morning, she was not mad, but within a few minutes, maybe hours, she had gone completely steaming mad. And all she could remember was sitting in a meeting discussing her budget – cutting back on things; cutting back on what she wanted – and then... nothing... just her head exploding, a firework going off, an eruption of pure anger and frustration, brimming over and boiling over, pouring down a rain of vitriol on the intransigent bastards.

What did they say... what did that doctor say? She was a bit manic. A bit manic! She was fuming. She was angry. She had every right to feel angry. Everything she had worked for, cut down and thrown on the scrap heap. They did not care if all her hard work was smashed into another meaningless saving, another meaningless restructuring. As long as they kept within budget, calculating, rationing, putting things here, putting things there, putting things on hold, moving things back or moving things forward. Where was the sense in that? Where was the justice in that?

Calm down, Annie said to herself, *I must calm down. There I go again, going off on one. But I can't stop thinking. How do I stop thinking? I must stop thinking. I must sort out what has happened here. This is mad. No doubt about it. This is madness. Something has definitely gone wrong. The old wires have got crossed. The old fuse box has blown a gasket. The spark plugs ignited. The motor is running. The car cannot stop. The lights are green. The ship is sailing. The plane is taking off. Here we go... whoosh!*

Annie let out a loud laugh. She could not contain herself. Because it was so mad, ridiculous, that here she was on the ward where she worked, having crossed over the great big river of insanity, right across the bridge, not waving but drowning, laughing and laughing and laughing…

This is me, she said to herself. *Yes, I am here, I am looking at something, looking at a patient who is looking at me. A strange companion who I do not recognise.*

She tried to focus. Right, yes, the low coffee table with a few coffee mugs and a tinfoil ashtray… yes, that was here. She touched it to make sure, to make it tangible.

Well, at least she did not smoke… it would make things easier if she had to stay a little bit longer. *But why should I*, thought Annie, *what have I done wrong? This is a terrible mistake. I must have miscalculated. I must have missed something along the way. Somewhere, somehow, the message got confused.*

Yes, it's all about the message. That is where I fell down. That is how they got me. They caught me, just as I was about to trounce them, just as I was about to show them how they were wrong. They caught me unawares. What a smarmy, devious lot, always plotting and planning their way. You cannot trust them. Not for a minute. They will steal your mother, grandmother, take them away and lock them up. Just like me… locked up, banged up, put in here just because I said no.

Annie burst into tears. Her tears began to flow down her cheeks and she clasped her hands to her face. But the tears kept coming, dripping, draining and flowing down her long, thin hands.

She must keep quiet. They must not see them. The tears must stop. *I must stop crying. Think, think, think! Am I really mad? I must be. I am here. This is reality. It is not a dream. I have to accept it. I have to come to terms with it. I need time to work out what went wrong and how to get out of here. I need time to get things straight. I need time to make them realise there is nothing wrong with me. I need time to be composed. I need time to be normal.*

I must not shout. I must not get angry. I must not be emotional. I must appear in control of my feelings. My feelings do not rule me. I am cool, calm and collected. I can see clearly how things have been misinterpreted. Yes, I have been under a lot of stress, but that is normal in this line of work. Stress, yes, but nothing out of the ordinary. I can cope with that. Apart from once, at the meeting, where things, I admit, got a little out of control. But that is not me. That is not me, normally. I mean, anyone would have been upset if they had their whole programme cut. Cut! Just like that! But I can see. Yes, I can see how they want me to be.

She looked at the floor. It was a rich red carpet. She followed the texture and noticed how it was glowing, a thick, red, ambient glow. Then the floor seemed to be moving, gently moving, like the sea.

Perhaps there is something wrong? But then she thought: *All I know is, there is nothing really wrong with me.*

CHAPTER 6

ON THE OTHER SIDE OF THE FENCE

Roland sat on the inside ledge of the bay window in the Lilywhite Ward day room, watching the various depressives, schizophrenics, obsessive compulsives and borderline personality disorders stare aimlessly into a vacuous space. There was nothing Roland could do, left to his own devices whilst waiting for something to happen. And Roland knew, just like the patients knew, that the only person who really mattered in all of this madness was the consultant, also known as the all-seeing, all-powerful, Great Beneficence.

For the patient, their future was in his or her hands, with judgements made in the democratic illusion of the patient case conference: risks assessed against the conditions of their section, calibrations of their dosage and the granting of privileges to soothe their passage through the doped-up therapeutic regime. But the truth was, it was in nobody's interests (staff or patient), whatever the knowledge of the patient's condition, to contradict the Higher Being. To go against the consultant's expertise would be detrimental to the patient's interests, potentially leading to a tightening of the chemical straitjacket, or fewer privileges within the narrow tunnel of circumscribed freedoms.

In this pitiless vacuum, a dark void in which everyone waited, the antipsychotic injection took on a profound and symbolic ritual. It was the quantitative measure by which the skill of the nurse was informally celebrated or denigrated. Roland had at least managed to pass this hurdle, imposed on the most docile patient on the ward. He had hovered over the emaciated bottom, needle poised like a dart, hesitated as he tried to recall the practice of stabbing an orange, before plunging in, flinching as the patient squealed. He had managed to get something right, he thought, before yesterday's disaster with Franks.

With Roland so absorbed in his own thoughts, he had failed to notice Annie Buchanan standing in front of him.

'Hi, I'm Annie,' she said, meekly, wondering why she had not caught his attention.

'Oh, hi,' said Roland, startled.

Annie smiled between the streaks of her purple braided hair, cocooned in a peacock shawl draped over her sloping shoulders.

'I saw Mr Fitzpatrick here this morning,' she said. 'Is there anything wrong?'

'No, not really,' said Roland, unsure if he was talking to a patient or a member of staff.

'I heard there was an incident yesterday,' she said, her pale, narrow face looking inquisitively up at him.

'Something like that,' said Roland. 'There was a bit of trouble off the ward.'

'Oh,' said Annie excitedly, 'I heard someone tried to... you know...'

'Yes...' said Roland, acknowledging Annie's code.

'That must have been awful... is he alright?'

'He'll live. Mad as a hatter though... if you know what I mean...'

Roland blushed. Why did he say that?

'Sorry,' he said, 'I didn't mean to...'

'Don't worry, I'm not offended. I was admitted myself last night.'

'Oh, really?'

Fuck... he'd got that wrong. *Quick, think, patient...*

'Well, you don't look mad,' said Roland, trying to sound apologetic.

That was just as bad, he thought, but she seemed remarkably tolerant of his ineptitude.

'I saw Dr Jonas last night,' Annie said. 'He thought it might be manic depression. But the thing is, and don't say anything because I do know things go on here, but he looked stoned to me.'

'Well,' said Roland, blushing even more, thinking quickly how to diffuse his part with the drug-infused Dr Jonas, 'they're probably all on something.'

Annie laughed.

'Oh, I know all about doctors and what they get up to. Are you a student?'

Roland pointed to his name badge.

'Yes, first year...'

'You know,' said Annie, stepping in closer in order to sound purposeful, 'I've worked on this ward.'

Roland's pupils widened.

'What, you're a nurse?'

'No, I'm the music therapist for the district. I've worked with some of the patients here.'

'Fuck!' said Roland. 'Now that's crazy! In fact, that's more than just crazy. How did that happen?'

'You won't believe it,' she said, seizing her opportunity to explain. 'It's like a nightmare. I was in this meeting yesterday and Morten Slaney was there – he usually attends. Anyway, all I can remember… they were going on and on about the budgets and then they said they were going to cut my budget. I was really angry and then things just started getting really out of hand. They weren't listening to what I was saying… they just didn't care… all the work I had put in… all the things I had wanted to do… they were just saying they didn't want me to do it any more…'

Annie paused.

'And then I think I just went for it. It was like my head was exploding. I just couldn't control myself.'

Roland suddenly realised, the penny dropped, the pure and utter madness of it all: was the warning from Dr Jonas real, personified by this staff member-cum-patient? And was Dr Jonas carrying out orders from Slaney?

'Why would they do that?' asked Roland, expressing his immediate thoughts.

'What do you mean?'

'I mean, what did they say to you about why you're here?'

'Oh, I don't know, I can't remember. That sister…'

'Sister Bernice?'

'Yes, she said they had a report from Morten Slaney saying I had a manic episode. Apparently, I had got on the table and was shouting and screaming that I was going to kill Slaney and they were all going to die…'

Annie looked to the ceiling, hoping for redemption.

'What's wrong with that?' said Roland, laughing, desperate to make light of her predicament.

'Not if you end up here as a consequence,' she said, with a deep, exasperated sigh.

'So,' said Roland, pausing, thinking how best to help, 'you can't remember anything once you lost it in the meeting?'

'Not really, I felt a bit funny when I got here. I don't know, perhaps there is something wrong with me? But they've put me on a six-month section.'

'What?!' exclaimed Roland, his conspiratorial thoughts quickening. 'Six months?!'

Annie nodded.

'You're joking?'

Annie shook her head.

'Six months for having a go at those wankers? You know what,' said Roland animatedly, 'you should've killed them… then they'd have good reason to give you six months.'

Annie shrugged her shoulders.

'Six months?' said Roland again, slightly exasperated. 'How can you be on six months?'

'I don't know,' said Annie, sighing again, demonstrating her sense of powerlessness and shivering with the aftershock of her trauma.

Was she really a proper patient? wondered Roland. Could they seriously whack a section on her like that?

'How are you feeling?' he asked. 'Do you feel manic? Are you depressed?'

'No,' said Annie. 'Well, I'm depressed about being here. I hate it. The thing is, I don't know if I am ill. I just hope they'll take me off section by next week or I'm afraid I'll never get out of here.'

'But this was only a budget meeting, right?' said Roland, trying to get a sense of proportion.

'Well, it wasn't *just* a budget meeting. I've spent three years building up a music therapy programme.'

'But you shouldn't be here!' interrupted Roland. 'On this ward! Not if this is where you work. That can't be right.'

'Oh, I don't mind,' she said, twirling a braid running down the side of her face. 'I mean, I would rather be here than anywhere else. I know what the other hospitals are like.'

'You mean there are worse places than this?'

'Unfortunately.'

'But you must know the patients here… are you sure you want to be on this ward?'

'I've got no choice… I've worked in every hospital in the district. Also, I thought it might help if I continued to do some work here.'

'Even while you're a patient?'

'I know, sounds silly really.'

That was odd, thought Roland, things were not quite adding up. No way would he want to be on the ward. If he was in Annie's situation, he would be demanding a transfer. Let's say, even if Dr Jonas was making it up last night, even if this was all just a coincidence, there was no way you would want to stay here, with patients knowing you were a member of staff.

'You don't think I've done anything wrong, do you?' asked Annie.

'Wrong… what do you mean, wrong? You've stood up for yourself. So what if you lost it? It doesn't mean all of a sudden you've become a manic depressive. Christ!'

'Oh, it's so nice to hear someone say that. You know, I've been thinking it's my fault.'

'Listen, you haven't done anything wrong. Trust me, maybe they just like to freak people out, to keep them quiet, if you know what I mean?'

Annie looked perplexed.

'Eh… listen,' said Roland, realising he had probably said too much, 'things are never black and white, are they?'

'Can you help me?' she asked suddenly.

Help? How could he help? He had to be careful, especially after what had just happened yesterday with Franks.

'Look, I'm only a student,' he said. 'I'm not supposed to know anything. They're not going to listen to me, and I'm not sure what I could say.'

Annie looked down. She needed someone to help her.

'The thing is,' said Roland, trying his best to compensate, 'they might be making you ill rather than you being ill, if you know what I mean?'

Annie looked quizzically at Roland. Fuck, should he have said that? Out of the corner of his eye he could see Sister Bernice, hovering, trying to catch his attention.

'Sorry, but I think I'm needed for once.'

'You will come and talk to me again?'

'Of course, that's my job. Heh, hang in there... just remember, it's not you that's mad, just everyone else.'

Annie nodded because she understood the meaning, the principle. *Yes*, she thought, *it's not me but everyone else.*

Roland walked over to Sister Bernice. She was prudently slim at the waist, a perfectly ironed uniform fitting tightly to her body. Her brown hazelnut eyes peered out from beneath her classic bob. She always looked out of place, thought Roland, especially with the patients.

'What was Annie Buchanan saying to you?' she asked, parting her well-groomed hair.

'Oh, she's just upset, that's all,' said Roland. 'She doesn't really understand why she's here.'

'She's not the only one!' said Sister Bernice, smoothing down her uniform around her hips. 'Do you want to do the meds with me later?'

'Yeah,' said Roland, surprised he was allowed to do anything after yesterday.

Sister Bernice parted her hair again. She had something more serious to say.

'Mr Fitzpatrick came over this morning. Don't worry – he obviously wasn't happy, but I don't think anything will come of it.'

'Right,' said Roland.

Just as he had thought, Douglas had obviously

communicated the message. There was no way they would want to look into that cock-up.

'Okay, we'll try and do the meds before handover,' said Sister Bernice, who immediately headed back into the ward office.

CHAPTER 7

DEATH AND METAPHYSICS

The rest of the morning moved as slowly as ever for Roland. The conversation with Annie Buchanan still permeated his thoughts, but at the same time he was desperate to avoid her. He just did not know what to think; whether there was anything credible in what she said. Could Dr Jonas be part of such an insane thing, when he was supposed to be on their side, the just side, the humane side? Why would Dr Jonas be party to a wicked conspiracy to section someone who happened to disagree with a budget cut? But once Roland had completed the drugs round with Sister Bernice, there was a sense of being part of a process, a benign process. It was surely absurd to view the therapeutic world of Wellington Park as pernicious and spiteful. Logic dictated that at best it was struggling with a lack of resources and at worst it was just a victim of the changes sweeping throughout society.

With his momentary sense of belonging, Roland sat down with the rest of the staff in the ward office. The early and late shifts sat like squashed tomatoes around a grand old oak desk, piled with residues of equipment for minor medical procedures. Someone, anointed for the day (Roland had no idea who), routinely dribbled through the metal folder of care plans for patients on the ward: so-and-so was down again today, so-and-so did not eat their breakfast, so-and-so probably hid their tablets. As each dry cliché was trotted out, so Roland laughed at the patients when he was meant to and sighed at the patients when everyone else sighed.

'Mr Cornwall… depression… came in yesterday. Wife says he's not been eating for two months. He's on high-energy drinks… lacks a sense of humour.'

Everyone laughed.

'Probably dead…'

Everyone laughed again.

The door to the ward office flung open and an excited nurse apologised for the intrusion.

'You know Mr Cornwall?' she said. 'I think he's dead…'

*

Roland offered to stay late so he could gain experience with the procedures for the dead. He had been assigned the support of Staff Nurse Maria. She had not been there long, having arrived with the most recent wave of Northern Irish recruitment. Like every wave of immigration that propped up the ailing hospital, she was just doing time before moving on to somewhere better. Roland knew she was going out with Dr Jonas and it was an open relationship. Dr Jonas rarely mentioned her, except to say she was a "mad fucker" just like himself. She was well known for her manic, eye-bulging energy, which attracted Roland but also made him wary.

They were in the upstairs dormitory, with all the patients given a strict instruction not to enter. It was a sparse, depersonalised environment, even for those patients who had been there for months. An artificial panel, made of hardboard and frosted glass, separated the sexes. Relationships occasionally developed but were formally frowned upon, or prohibited by removing one of the potential couple.

The curtain was pulled around Mr Cornwall's bed to retain some privacy. Roland, wrapped in a pink plastic apron and a warm soapy cloth draining in his hand, read the protocol and was ready to perform the duties. Maria stood on the opposite side as they both stared at the naked body.

There it was, flesh and bone, death, life extinguished, a cold fait accompli. *It all comes down to this*, thought Roland: nothing, nothing but the emptiness, the finality of it all... all the struggle, all the strife, it all was just a case of becoming a slab of meat, a memory for others and a tragedy for the few who still loved you. He looked over at Maria and wondered what she was thinking. Was it the same for her, just another body, just another procedure? Death, here, with Mr Cornwall... the reality, the undeniable truth.

Well, he had better get on with things, but the flesh... he was not keen on touching the dead grey flesh. And should they observe something before they start? What could they say? It was just a plain old man who needed to be washed and wrapped in a crêpe white shroud with some ridiculous labels tied on his appendages. He just hoped Maria would tell him where.

Roland leant forward, pulled Mr Cornwall's arm towards him, and a deep sigh hushed from the dead man's mouth.

'Fuck!' said Roland, jumping backwards and dropping the arm. 'Did you hear that?'

'Don't worry,' said Maria, laughing, 'it's just the gas in his lungs.'

'Fuck me,' said Roland, 'I thought he was alive.'

'They do that sometimes,' she said. 'Gas gets trapped.'

'Fuck, that really freaked me out! Can you imagine if he was still alive?'

Mr Cornwall stared into space.

'It's the eyes,' said Maria, 'I can't stand them. I always think they're looking at me.'

'Yeah, it's weird, isn't it?' said Roland, still reflecting. 'And it all comes down to this – you know... we just end up like a piece of meat.'

'Oh, I'm sure Mr Cornwall has a soul as he speaks to his Maker.'

'You think so?' said Roland sceptically.

'Here, give me that,' said Maria, pointing at the soapy cloth in Roland's hand. 'I'll start if you like.'

Roland was grateful for the temporary intervention.

'You know,' he said, as Maria efficiently began to clean, 'you'd think death would be something profound, meaningful... but it isn't.'

'Aye, you get that in this job. He'd probably had enough, you know. People get tired of living and just want it over and done with.'

Roland watched as Maria applied her practised hands to Mr Cornwall's body.

'Did you hear what happened in the handover?'

'Aye, I did… anyway, let's make him look good for the relatives.'

'And have you heard about the new patient, Annie Buchanan?'

Maria paused, before looking up at Roland.

'The crazies can always get you… it doesn't matter who you are.'

'But should she be on the ward… don't you think that's wrong if she works here?'

Maria shrugged as she rinsed the soapy cloth in the plastic bowl.

'You shouldn't worry yourself too much, Roland. You know, you can't be putting yourself forward as an advocate for patients, if that's what you're thinking of doing.'

'I'm not,' said Roland, his voice rising and betraying his thoughts. 'It's just that we saw Dr Jonas last night—'

'Oh, him!' exclaimed Maria. 'I don't believe a word he says and neither should you or any of your friends.'

'I know that,' said Roland. 'It's just, you know, a coincidence…'

'What is?' asked Maria, as she moved the cloth over Mr Cornwall's legs.

Roland did not know how to put it; about the coincidences, the possibilities…

'Well…' he said, before he paused again.

Maria got down to Mr Cornwall's feet and ran the cloth in between his toes.

'Aye?'

'Well, you know, Slaney and Fitzpatrick.'

Maria stopped.

'You need to be careful, Roland,' she said, 'especially after what happened with that patient of yours yesterday. Those two, Fitzpatrick and that Slaney... well, they strike me as being a bit nasty... if they wanted to be.'

'Exactly!' said Roland, seizing his moment to reveal his fears. 'You know Annie Buchanan was in a meeting with Slaney when she lost it. I've heard they can go as far as...'

Roland stopped. Even he thought what he was about to say sounded ridiculous, unbelievable.

'... lock you up,' he said, almost whispering.

For a moment Roland thought Maria was going to confirm everything Dr Jonas had said: how he had been right all along and there was an evil conspiracy to deal with troublemakers. Instead, she laughed; laughed so loud she had to clasp her soapy hand to her mouth, and then spat across the legs of Mr Cornwall.

'Fuck me, I think I'm eating dead flesh!'

That was that then, thought Roland, he did sound like a paranoid android.

'Sorry,' he said, assuming he was culpable for Maria's lack of concentration.

'Here,' said Maria, handing back the cloth, 'you're meant to be doing this, not me.'

'Sorry,' said Roland again, as he took the cloth and wondered where he should start.

'Just do his face,' said Maria, 'and we'll put these stupid fucking tags on him.'

Roland looked at Mr Cornwall. There was still some humanity about him, he thought, the features and everything... but it was death, there was no denying it.

As Roland moved the cloth gingerly around the face, they could both hear the grating of Mr Cornwall's stubble.

'You know,' said Maria, 'I think we'd better shave him.'

From behind the curtain she pulled out a Philips shaver and handed it to Roland. He turned on the motor and applied the triple blades.

'So, Roland,' said Maria, raising her voice so she could be heard above the shaving, 'tell me why are you here then... why are you doing this?'

Should he tell her the truth, the real truth?

'I want to find out,' he said, pausing, 'what makes people tick... why people do things.'

'Go on,' said Maria, 'finish his face.'

Roland did as he was instructed, manoeuvring the blades over the chin and cheekbones.

'We had a tutor, when I was training,' said Maria, 'and he had a word for some of us.'

Roland reached around the sides of Mr Cornwall's sideburns.

'Metaphysicians, he used to call us. People who question, I think that's what he meant. There was a group of us and we always wanted to know what lay behind the illnesses, how it might all connect up, in some way, to everything else that was going on. We were looking for the true meaning of things, I think... but we were crazy fuckers though.'

Roland stood back to check his work.

'Perhaps that's what you and your friends are up to,' said Maria, 'and good luck to you. But just remember, it can be a dangerous journey if you don't know what you're getting yourself into.'

Roland admired the smooth chin of the dead Mr Cornwall. He liked the term metaphysician, even if he was not sure what it meant in practice.

'Did you all finish your training?' he asked.

'Oh yes, did we fuck! We were all desperate to get out of the North, that's for sure. But whatever is going on with yous Pothead Pixies, don't take too many risks or they will get you. This place is fucked up, Roland, just remember that... you're right to think that if that's what you think.'

'Well, everything here is a bit crazy, and not just because people are supposed to be mentally ill.'

'Trust me, don't get into thinking there's nothing wrong with the patients here. You can help them, and they all need the help of good people like yourself. You know, the best way to survive in this place is to find someone you can trust, someone to love. If you don't have a girlfriend and you've got your eye on someone then I would make a move. That really helps, smooths out all the rough edges. Experiences like this change you though, Roland. They challenge you, force you to take on things you've never done before. You can do it as long as you don't do the wrong thing.'

Perhaps Maria was right, he thought, he had to stop being afraid – afraid of living, afraid of sex because he had never done it before – and help people, help people who needed it most. He had to trust people again, embrace the journey, travel on this crazy trip until he found out… found out what the truths were. *Yes*, he said to himself, in a satisfied manner, *I could also be a metaphysician*, because he could never stop questioning. And perhaps that was part of it, as Maria said: to see what was behind things, try and connect things up, look for truths and expose the lies and all the illusions. But could he do it all on his own? And didn't he want to change, to get away from his past, perhaps even make a career out of this? He was caught a bit: between not losing the essence of his Self, his true nature, whilst perhaps compromising in order to fit in for once and benefit from what was on offer.

CHAPTER 8

A QUESTIONING SOUL

'What do you think the truth is?' asked Roland, as he passed the joint back to Jas.

'About Annie Buchanan, you mean?'

'Yeah… and what Dr Jonas said.'

Jas sniggered.

'Don't get taken in by him. You can't trust him. In fact, you can't trust anyone around here… there's only yourself.'

'I know that,' said Roland, 'but don't you think it's a bit weird? First he tells us management can get to you if you disagree with them, then he does the admission on her and she's sectioned as if she's a raving psychotic… and I don't think there's much wrong with her.'

'Look,' said Jas, 'even if there is something in it, there's nothing you can do. All we need to do is get through our training.'

'But will we get through, you know, if they don't like us?'

'Well, I've never had any problems.'

'Rubbish! You told me Fitzpatrick can't stand you… you said he was a racist.'

'He is,' said Jas, certain of the prejudices he knew exuded from the old-fashioned military mindset, 'but that doesn't mean they are going to do anything to me. They need people like us. Why do you think the likes of you and me are here? It's because this place is on its knees. They're desperate for people to work here and the school needs students. Don't get taken in by all the bullshit Gobi gives out about needing something different. He knows the only way to keep the school going is to take on anyone who has applied for training.'

It was a painful truth, thought Roland, a truth which helped puncture some of the illusion that he was worthy of a genuine chance of doing better.

'Well,' said Roland, 'that doesn't mean we have to be like them. You know, patients here are treated like shit and students here are treated like shit.'

'Tell me about it; I've seen it going on for years, but don't think I'm going to throw this chance away by getting up the noses of Slaney or Fitzpatrick.'

'I'm not saying that,' said Roland, 'but just because they think we're supposed to be fodder for this place doesn't mean we have to behave like it. I was just going to get through, like you, but I don't know any more... it's not me... I wouldn't be true to myself.'

Jas drew on the joint, maintaining the diffusion for as long as he could, then watched his stream of smoke barrel wistfully out of the open window. Roland also followed the smoke roll out towards the woods.

'It's all out there, not just in here,' said Jas, musing on the destination of the succulent smoke. 'You ought to go have a look sometime... go for a walk through the woods. There's even some old abbey or church where the patients go to hang themselves on some old tree.'

'Nice,' said Roland.

'That's what this place is about: they only come here if they're really mad. And you can't stop them, you know, suicides, not if they want to do it. Listen, what happened with Franks wasn't your fault. They put you in a situation where there was not much you could do about it.'

'Exactly,' said Roland. 'I shouldn't have been put in that situation. Christ, we're only just out of school after two months' training and I'm left with a ward full of acute patients with only me and Sister Bernice!'

'Get used to it because it isn't going to get any better.'

'So we're always going to be at risk, whenever we are on placement?'

'More than likely,' said Jas, who thought he had the experience to negotiate his way through it all, 'and there's nothing we can do about it.'

Roland paused, as he realised, once again, he was in a situation which most people would walk out on.

'Are you going to resign?' asked Jas anxiously.

'No... no way... I'm not running... I've got nothing to run back to.'

'I bet you feel like you've jumped from the frying pan into the fire – you know... after your mates did the dirty on you.'

'Something like that,' said Roland stoically.

Jas flicked some burnt ash on to the brown tiled floor of his room.

'Why do you think everyone gets so wasted in this

place? It's the only way to survive. If I didn't smoke, I'd go mad. Honestly, the best thing we can do is keep our heads down and just get through it.'

Roland grimaced. If he had no choice, if he was stuck here, he was not sure he could just pretend there was nothing wrong.

'You know, I was talking to Maria, Dr Jonas' girlfriend. She told me when she did her training there was a group of them who questioned what was going on. She said they called themselves metaphysicians. It means looking for truths... the true meaning of things.'

Jas looked thoughtful.

'I would fuck her,' he said, handing back the remains of the joint he had devoured.

'I was thinking of something a bit more profound, something we could do to keep ourselves going.'

'Yeah, as long as it means I get to fuck Dr Jonas' girlfriend.'

'It doesn't mean that, it just means we think about things. I mean, we do anyway, but we should make a point of it, questioning and not accepting everything.'

'Listen, as long as we can get wasted I'm with you.'

'Right,' said Roland, who thought that was as good as he would get from Jas. But he knew he was probably alone in his thinking. There was very little hope of getting a group of like-minded students together.

'I was also thinking,' said Roland, 'perhaps Dr Jonas was right in a way. Where are the borders between what is normal?'

'The borders are false,' said Jas, 'you and I know that. It doesn't take a doctor to work that one out. But on the other hand, people here are ill. Some of the staff here are even more fucking crazy. But it's true, the patients don't get treated right.'

'So, it's wrong, isn't it?'

'Lots of things are and we can't do much about it. If you get to talk to someone like Fitzpatrick, he's not all bad. He can tell you how it once was here... a lot better than it is now.'

'What, even back then?'

'Well, there was still crazy shit going on, but when they knock this place down – which they will, that's what Slaney's all about – then these poor fuckers will really suffer.'

'Why's that?'

'Because no one gives a fuck about them! The threat for these nutters is out there. At least in here there is something for them to hang on to... however crap it all is.'

Roland wasn't sure now... perhaps all he could do was rely on his instincts and just question everything.

'You should speak to Sophie Smith,' said Jas, 'she's a lot like you. As I've told you before, you need to get your leg over or your balls will explode!'

CHAPTER 9

COOL, CALM AND COLLECTED

The social club was situated just outside the hospital grounds, about a hundred yards from the open gate and the bus stop. It was built during the Second World War to house a Spitfire or Hurricane, hence its substantial single-span roof. The building had been condemned on numerous occasions, but somehow, every year, a Fire, Health and Safety Certificate was approved, with a long list of recommendations, deferred to a defunct social committee to action. With a chequered licensing history and a tendency for the bar managers to go missing at the end of the financial year, most people suspected there was divine intervention whenever the threat of closure failed to materialise.

Roland sat on the corner of a badly sprung seat, away from the bar where all the usual drinkers congregated. He was bathed in a bright, stale light, the fibrous current running over his head and all the way down to the toilets at the bottom of the hall. He pretended not to look at anyone as they walked in, mediating his consumption of beer with a cigarette, checking the time and hoping Sophie would not stand him up.

It was not long before she was ten minutes late. *Be positive*, thought Roland; at least he had knocked on Sophie's door and asked her out, and that was an achievement in itself and should be recognised as such. Alright, he could make a complete tit of himself if he was nervous and anxious... and then he imagined Sophie wandering off to speak to someone else or making excuses about wanting to watch something on TV.

He looked up again as the door to the social club swung open. This time it was Sophie, dressed in her usual bright red dungarees, her jet black perm glistening in the artificial light. Roland was infatuated, smitten with Sophie's open-hearted smile. He was always amazed at how beautiful she looked, how her eyes perfectly matched her dark brown skin, and how beneath her utilitarian clothes he could trace the outline of a body which was sleek and desirable. Why nobody had snapped her up, grabbed her at the first opportunity, was a mystery, but there she was, prepared to go for a drink with a bespectacled ginger virgin.

'Hi,' she said, standing in front of the small circular table, 'sorry I'm late.'

'Don't worry,' said Roland, fixing confidently on her eyes. 'Do you want a drink?'

'Don't be silly,' she said, as she motioned for Roland to sit back down.

'Sophie!' shouted a voice across the hall.

It was Cranfield, who had just walked in behind

her. He was tall and skinny, enormous glasses covering his face and greasy blonde hair trailing down his neck. Roland had nothing to do with him, and Cranfield kept to his own little gang of pixies in the nurses' hostel.

'Didn't you hear me?' he said, as he positioned himself next to her. 'I was right behind you all the way down here.'

Sophie feigned surprise.

'Do you want a drink?' he asked, aware he was probably unwanted.

'No,' said Sophie, who said it so that Cranfield knew he was not welcome, 'I can get my own, thank you.'

Cranfield focused on Roland.

'She's a feminist, you know,' said Cranfield.

'Shut up, you!' said Sophie, as she playfully cuffed Cranfield.

This was not what Roland needed.

'Remember,' said Cranfield, speaking directly to Sophie, 'be safe.'

Sophie rolled her eyes.

Satisfied he had caused as much offence as possible, he kissed her on the cheek and slipped into the bar.

'Sorry about that,' said Sophie.

'Man, what a dick!'

'I don't know why I ever went out with him,' she said apologetically.

'We all make mistakes,' said Roland, offering Sophie a cigarette.

'Tailored… you don't mind?'

'Of course not,' he said, as he watched Sophie light up. 'You'd better get yourself a drink.'

'Oh yes. Don't worry about Cranfield... he's just jealous,' she added, as she turned and walked up to the bar.

That sounds promising, thought Roland, *and stage one complete*. He was at ease and relaxed. He just needed to maintain the trick, avoid thinking about having sex with Sophie... because if he started thinking about sex then he would crack, turn into a gibbering wreck and destroy his self-confident persona.

He looked towards the bar and checked to see if Cranfield had pursued her. Fortunately, he appeared to keep his distance whilst she got her drink.

Sophie walked self-consciously back through the bar and placed her pint of cider on the table as she sat next to Roland.

'I went to see Jas before I came over,' she said. 'He told me everything he knew about you.'

'Oh,' said Roland sheepishly.

Sophie looked into his eyes and laughed.

'I'm not stoned,' he said.

'It doesn't bother me,' she said, taking pleasure in teasing him.

'Do you smoke, then?' he asked.

'Yes, but not as much as you guys.'

'You mean Jas and Terry?'

'All of you,' she said, laughing. 'The Pothead Pixies!'

Roland blushed.

'Don't worry, it's always gone on as far as I know.'

'I was going to give it up before I came here,' said Roland, in mitigation. 'I thought there was no way I could smoke once I lived on-site.'

'There's a lot worse goes on,' said Sophie reassuringly, 'but you're fairly safe here if you're worried about getting caught. They're desperate for staff, students, anything… as long as it walks and talks.'

Yet again, thought Roland, more confirmation that his new career was based solely on the ability to fill in an application form for the Wellington Park School of Nursing.

'You're not the usual type of intake, are you?'

'No,' said Roland, 'we've heard we're different. Gobi told us none of us would have normally got in. We know now that the school is struggling to recruit and had to take a chance with us.'

Sophie smiled.

'Where did you live before?' she asked, fumbling in the depths of her various side pockets.

'London,' he said assertively.

'What made you do something like this, then?'

'Oh, lots of things,' he said, as he watched Sophie place a crumpled wrap of tobacco and torn Lizra packet on the table. 'I needed to do something. I needed to get out of London.'

'Don't you like London?'

'Oh no, it's a great place but you need money… it can be really depressing otherwise. Plus, it depends on what you're doing I suppose.'

Sophie packed her cigarette paper with a thin strip of tobacco. Roland watched the semi-proficient process.

'What were you doing?' she asked, with a mischievous grin.

'Oh, nothing really. I was working in a warehouse…'

Sophie drew deeply on her cigarette as she tried to get it started.

'You might have rolled it too tightly,' advised Roland.

'I know,' she said, 'I always do that.'

Roland paused, wondering if he should reveal his sense of bitterness, deceit and betrayal as his main motivation.

'I think I'll have to roll it again,' she said, as her roll-up failed.

Roland waited.

'Are you going to tell me then?' she said, as she set about rolling another.

'About what?'

'Why you really decided to come here?'

'Oh...' he said, looking across the empty hall, pretending to see if anyone was in earshot. 'Something happened with my friends... well, unexpected. It was a shock, I suppose, part of the reason for doing this, to try and understand why people do what they do... the human condition, if you like.'

Sophie looked quizzically at Roland.

'What did they do?'

'They betrayed me,' he said emphatically.

'That doesn't sound nice. People can be really awful sometimes. What did they do that was so bad?'

Roland hesitated. He was not sure how it would come out now, but he could not hold back.

'Well, we all hung out together in the same boring town, and one by one, made our way up to London. We were all into music and the idea was to get a band going. I shared a flat with a guy called Kevin, and Seb and John shared a bedsit. I didn't think anything about it, and then one night they took me to this bar, a gay bar, and then Seb and John just came out with it: that they were gay, and together... boyfriend and boyfriend.'

'What's wrong with that?' asked Sophie, as she completed her rejuvenated roll-up.

'Nothing, if you mean being gay, but I felt betrayed because they'd kept it a secret.'

Sophie sipped her cider.

'But is that their fault? I'm sure it wasn't easy for them. It's probably why they had to keep it a secret.'

'I know,' said Roland. 'I suppose it was because I was best friends with one of them. I was really close to John. He never said anything to me about it, but it had been going on for years. You know what it's like with best friends, you tell them everything. I was angry because they were leading this secret life behind my back.'

'I think I understand,' said Sophie. 'Don't you ever want to get revenge?'

'Revenge? Well, yeah... but there's not much I can do to them. They are what they are, self-absorbed and self-obsessed. I hate them for it, but I don't know what revenge is... what it looks like.'

Sophie appeared ready to expand, and then retreated. It was odd, thought Roland, that Sophie had picked up on the notion of revenge.

'So, what happened to the band?' asked Sophie, moving Roland away from further exploring the consequences of his personal trauma.

'That was it, finished... that's why I had to get away. I had to go my own way.'

'Well, nothing exciting like that has ever happened to me,' said Sophie. 'I came here because I just wanted to get away from my parents.'

'Don't we all?' said Roland. 'So, how long have you been here?'

'A couple of years.'

'So, you're in your second year?'

'Just finishing… starting my third year in January.'

'And what did your parents think?'

'What, about doing this – working and training here? They were okay about it. My brother's a nurse anyway. He got me into it. I wouldn't have thought about it otherwise.'

'Right. My parents didn't want me doing it. However, I have nothing to do with them. It's my life. All they've ever wanted me to do is to get a job in an office.'

'That's boring.'

'I know,' said Roland. 'Anyway, there's a lot of stuff with my parents.'

'You've got a lot of stuff, haven't you?' said Sophie, teasing him again.

Roland frowned. Sophie was sorry. She didn't mean to annoy him, and rubbed his arm. Roland relaxed. Sophie had offered something physical – a sign; an indication.

'You are different,' she said, smiling. 'You must be on your first placement by now, then. Are you on the dementia wards?'

'No.'

'Just you wait,' she said, enthusiastically drinking a large amount of cider and fumbling for her cigarette in the ashtray. 'What goes on there is criminal.'

'I've heard it's bad.'

'That's what this place is made up of... full of dementia. There isn't much else, some acute stuff and the alcohol unit over at Chaolla House.'

'Yeah, well, they don't tell you that when you come for an interview,' he said, flicking open his cigarette box.

'Who interviewed you?' asked Sophie, offering her own tobacco if he ran out.

'Gobi.'

'What do you think of him?'

'He's alright, but he's not going to do anything for us. He says you should tell him what goes on, but I bet if it came to it he'd come down on the side of management.'

'Why don't you stand for the student council?'

Roland shrugged his shoulders.

'There are elections coming up soon.'

'I don't know,' said Roland doubtfully. 'For me, it's all part of the system. You just end up legitimising what goes on.'

'So, what's your alternative?'

'Metaphysics,' said Roland, unpersuasively. 'Philosophy... questioning things.'

'Is that an excuse for doing nothing?'

'No,' said Roland, realising he was going to struggle to sound convincing, 'but you asked me what I thought the solution was.'

'You're just like my brother, and he doesn't do anything about it either.'

'Hang on!' said Roland.

Sophie straightened her back, pretending to ready herself for Roland's response.

'Look,' he said, 'I'm not sure if that's what I want to get into. I came here to get away from things, start a career and everything. I don't want to get into trouble again.'

'Why, what trouble have you been in before?'

'None, as such,' he said falteringly.

'Why are you so vague about everything?'

'I don't really know you… do I?'

Sophie laughed.

'I'm sorry,' she said. 'I do like you anyway.'

And she smiled.

Okay, thought Roland, he just needed to remain cool, calm and collected.

CHAPTER 10

CROSSING THE RUBICON

Roland and Sophie stayed until it was throwing-out time. As they walked back to the nurses' hostel, they kept their distance from drunken groups of students, in an attempt to ignore the friendly abuse aimed at them. But goaded, Sophie responded with a few cutting reminders of widely known indiscretions, before passing quietly by the illuminating lights emanating from the day room on Lilywhite Ward. Roland was still on his placement and told Sophie he would be back there in the morning.

'I don't suppose you want a coffee if you are on an early?'

'No, no,' said Roland, 'a coffee and a joint sounds good to me.'

They continued to walk and talk until they were inside the nurses' hostel and needed to make a decision on whose room they were going to use. Sophie preferred her own as she had all the creature comforts of an established residency. As she searched for her keys outside the door, there was the usual late-night commotion as everybody settled down for more drinking, smoking and organising sleeping arrangements. A few stereos started up and loud exaggerated laughter rattled through half-open doors. Roland looked down the corridor to his own room. His hope was that he would not be going back there tonight.

Sophie's room had been arranged to suit its narrow, rectangular space, with her bed and wardrobe down one side and a small made-up kitchen crammed near the window. With the poor choice of music from other residents thudding through her door, Sophie searched for some music and settled on the Cocteau Twins, her favourite band at the moment. Roland sat on the floor and commenced rolling. He read the titles of a collection of books which stretched along the shelf above her bed. He was impressed; there was some good reading there, the types of books he had read: a mixture of politics, philosophy, psychology and existential fiction along with a few nursing and medical textbooks.

'So,' said Roland, keen to pick up on the themes which had preoccupied them in the social club, 'I am a feminist as well, you know.'

Sophie was sitting by the open window, waiting for the kettle to boil, which was balanced precariously on the edge of a dark wooden cabinet.

'You can't be a feminist,' she said. 'Although it's nice you think like that.'

'Well, yeah, I know what you mean. I mean, I know I am not a woman. But I understand why women need to fight for their rights. You know... how women have been treated like shit by men throughout the ages. But I don't go as far as you on other things, like animal rights and environmentalism. I am not really into all of that. It's humans first for me.'

'But all the other things should matter... they are all part of the same thing.'

'Not if there is a choice,' said Roland, continuing to work diligently on the joint. 'I'm not really convinced by some of the stuff... especially on animal rights. I mean, I'm not trying to be offensive, but I'm not one of those who believes dolphins are more intelligent than humans... if you know what I mean.'

'That's possible,' said Sophie, who was now going to make the case. 'You are just arrogant about our species, a species which is destroying the world. There's no point in drawing a dividing line between species. We should be guardians if we are superior, instead of devouring everything we see.'

Roland moved his head from side to side, pursing his lips.

'And... you should also know I am a vegan,' continued Sophie. 'Which is why I don't have any milk for your coffee. And also, most of those books are my brother's and I haven't read them... if you were wondering.'

Roland paused. Were they agreeing or disagreeing?

'You know,' he said, nodding in the direction of the bookshelf, 'you should really try and read some of the existentialism.'

'What's that, then?' asked Sophie, challenging Roland to prove he knew what he was talking about.

'Well, it's a philosophy,' he said, adjusting his crossed legs and lifting the joint to seal the paper. 'You come to the realisation that everything is absurd. It's a psychological state of mind where you are alienated from the world... where you realise everything is just ridiculous... where you realise it has all been a load of lies: everything you have been told, everything you are meant to believe in... family, school, society... it's all bullshit... all an illusion.'

'Is that how you feel about your family?' asked Sophie, moving off the windowsill to make the coffee.

'What?' said Roland, shuffling to make room.

Sophie opened the cabinet door and pulled out a jar of "instant" and a bag of sugar.

'Don't you like your family?'

'No,' said Roland dogmatically, 'I hate them.'

'Oh,' said Sophie, as she spooned in the coffee granules. 'Do you like it strong?'

Roland shrugged his shoulders.

'I don't drink coffee normally,' he said, twisting the end of his perfectly formed conical joint.

Roland waited for Sophie to make the coffee. She cooled down the hot liquid by pouring in a little bit of cold water and left Roland's mug above his head. She then sat opposite Roland, seated on her bed.

'I know what you mean about families,' said Sophie. 'I was desperate to get away myself. But I do miss them, my mum and dad.'

'I don't,' said Roland, burning the twisted end of the joint so the tobacco ember was just showing.

'Why, did they treat you badly?'

'I think so,' said Roland, puffing on the lit joint.

'You don't have to talk about it if you don't want to.'

'No, it's alright, I'm better off having nothing to do with them. I mean, they didn't do anything really terrible. I wasn't, you know, abused as such, although I did get a few beatings now and then. They were just oppressive psychologically, trying to run my life, trying to tell me what to do. There was no love...'

'Oh, that's so sad.'

'Well, yeah, once you discover all the "loving family" thing is just an illusion, then it does make life easier. But then things are not easy... to get there... to get to that point. You know, it can make you suicidal.'

'I know... I've felt suicidal...'

'Yeah, it's easy to feel like that, especially when you realise how fucked up the world is! Plus, I couldn't believe how people fell for all that Thatcher bullshit. She's just one nasty piece of work.'

Roland handed the joint to Sophie.

'She got away with a war,' she said, as she inhaled.

'Exactly, and people still voted for her! Her and Reagan have the finger on the button... those two nutters could destroy the world!'

Sophie nodded and then praised Roland's joint-rolling technique.

'You'll need to show me how to roll,' she said. 'I smoke roll-ups and they never work.'

'No problem,' said Roland, as Sophie handed back the joint.

They were very alike, Roland decided; they both had the same ideas, really, the same experiences, the same basic philosophy on life.

'So,' said Sophie, 'is that why you are a... meta-something?'

'What, because of the fucked up world we live in?'

'It is a mess…'

'The thing is,' said Roland, warming to his subject, 'I'm probably a bit of an anarchist as well. Anarchism's always portrayed as being about chaos and terrorism, but it's not about that at all.'

'Well, isn't it?'

'No!' said Roland, preparing himself for a longer explanation. 'It is about revolution, it is about changing things, but not every anarchist is some nutter trying to blow people up… not that any anarchist would do that these days. It's about the individual being in a state of permanent revolution, whatever system is in place.'

'That must be difficult to keep up. If we've had the revolution, do you just carry on being revolutionary?'

'Yes – whatever system you have, there will always be faults with it. An anarchist should always be against the system, because the system ossifies into a new status quo, a new state of oppression.'

'But if we have created a better society, people will want to be part of it. They wouldn't want to make more sacrifices to change something that might not need changing.'

'It will always need changing,' said Roland uncompromisingly.

Sophie paused.

'Well, how about doing something about it now… here? The thing is, I've never had anyone to work with to try and change things, but all the students have grievances.'

Roland hesitated. He knew, after all his bold talk, Sophie would think him a fraud if he didn't back it up.

'Well, we are just used to fill gaps on the wards,' acknowledged Roland. 'Patients and staff are put at risk. I've been there myself!'

'Everyone knows about what happened with you and that patient.'

'Do they?' laughed Roland.

Sophie nodded.

'Fitzpatrick will never forgive you.'

'Fuck! It wasn't my fault!'

'Don't worry,' said Sophie, 'he doesn't get everyone he hates.'

'He hates me? He doesn't know me!'

Sophie shrugged.

'He does now.'

'Well, that doesn't leave me much choice then, does it? But I don't want to end up playing along with management with no real changes… playing the game of dissent.'

'It won't be a game,' said Sophie earnestly.

'No, what I mean is, the way in which the system lets you believe you have the freedom to change things, but in reality, you end up changing nothing. It is the game of siphoning off everything into reports, committees, investigations, and recommendations which never get implemented. It is the illusion of dissent, dissent up to a point, up to the point where the status quo still remains.'

'I think that's a bit abstract for what I have in mind. I could easily carry on and not bother. I just think we can do something about it together. There are things we could achieve, concessions… if we started getting involved and using the mechanisms available.'

'What mechanisms?'

'The student council,' Sophie explained. 'There's no one on it at the moment and elections are coming up. If we both stand, we could easily get on.'

'Okay,' said Roland, noticing he had hogged the joint, 'but there is one thing, which I know is going to sound a bit weird, but we're in a strange situation... a strange place. Have you heard about Annie Buchanan? She went up against Slaney and look what's happened to her. No one thinks there is anything really wrong and yet she is under section.'

'Well, yes, the place does make you question your sanity. But there is a difference between staff and patients. If you try to blur the boundary, you'll be going down the wrong road and definitely end up in trouble.'

'Of course,' he said. 'I don't really know her, but I hate that divide.'

'Look, we're not anti-psychiatrists, or what was that other thing you said... metaphysicians. We're just student nurses. You're new to everything. But there is a reason why people are here: they are ill, they need our help. By not accepting that, you can end up condemning them to even more neglect.'

'I know people are ill, but patients are not being treated as people, as human beings. They are just dumped and forgotten. Perhaps if the boundaries were blurred a bit they would be treated better.'

'Why would they? For some of them this place is a lot better than where they came from,' said Sophie, as she fixed eye contact with Roland. 'Look, will you stand with me for election to the student council, or are you just all talk?'

'Aha! A challenge!'

'And… ?'

'Yes, I will do it… of course I will. Anything to get back at those heartless bastards.'

'Good,' said Sophie, pleased she had achieved what she had set out to do.

And Roland, for once, was committed to doing something. But then, he would have agreed to anything, as long he got the chance to sleep with Sophie.

And, as their animated conversation turned into silence, it became obvious to Roland that there was a chance something could happen. This was probably it, he thought: the time when they might kiss.

'I was wondering,' he said, feeling the adrenaline coursing through his body, 'if Cranfield… you know… is something you've finished with?'

'Oh, him… that was months ago… six months ago. In fact, I haven't had sex since then. I think I'm going frigid!'

That's a message, thought Roland, *clearly a great big message*. But he must not tell her he was a virgin. If he said anything, then he'd blow it. The trick was not to think like a virgin… do not think like a virgin and you will not be.

He could feel the anxiety, the thing he hated most. But should he ask to kiss her? Should he just try and kiss her? What were the rules?

'Can I ask you a question?'

'Yes,' said Sophie, aware of what the question might be.

Roland could barely speak, his mouth was so dry.

'Do you want to sleep with me?'

Sophie's face went red. She looked down, embarrassed, but she was thinking about it.

Roland did not expect that... but he did not know what to expect. Perhaps defeat? *Yes, she is probably going to say no.*

'Okay,' she said. 'I just need to go to the toilet.'

Did she say yes?

'Sorry about this,' she said, as she opened the door and walked down the long corridor to the communal toilets.

Roland was in shock. Now what? They had not even kissed and yet they were going to have sex.

He sat there in a moment of undiluted satisfaction, but what should he do when she returned? Should he take off his clothes? No, no, that was stupid. Just wait. Relax. She had agreed to it.

He stood up and looked at the books on the shelf again. Was there something he should read? *Don't be stupid. Calm down. I need to remain calm.*

He walked over to the window and looked out. He traced the residency lights as far as the wire fence which bordered on to the woods.

This was it, he thought, no more separateness. He had conquered his worst fears. Alright, he had not kissed her yet, but he had got over that awful hurdle: no rejection, no ifs, no buts...

Then Sophie opened the door.

He waited.

She walked over and kissed him.

★

Roland did not really sleep, it was a half-sleep, a dozing tiredness, combined with a high level of awareness of what he had done. He had finally, at last, crossed the Rubicon. No more fucking virgin, no more fucking living in a quiet hell. No more having to make up stories. No more hiding. No, he had grown up. Tonight, or what was left of the night, was the greatest moment of his life. To be cured of the foul stigma of virginity!

So, not only had he been cured of his virginity, but he had done it with someone who was desirable. In fact, there would be people all over the hospital who would be thinking, *How the fuck did he do that?* This woman was meant to be out of his league. You are not supposed to have sex with the likes of Sophie Smith. But oh yes, he had triumphed! He had joined the adult world with a great big fuck-off triumph! This was what it felt like to be a fully-fledged, paid-up member of the human race. This was what it felt like to be a normal person. Alright, he had only done it once, but once was enough, once was enough to mean he now knew what it was like to kiss, to feel a breast, to penetrate. At last, he now knew. He could, if he wanted, go back to his so-called friends and parade his new girlfriend… well, not parade, but show off. *There you go, you lying, deceitful fucking wankers, you who committed the ultimate sin of leading secret lives, hiding everything, hiding and laughing at me, thinking you knew everything about me. Well, I have become!*

Sophie stirred, curling back into herself, pushing out her legs, trying to find more room. Roland pushed his body back against the cold wall. He didn't care… he was not looking for comfort. He knew that tonight, Sophie meant everything to him. It was not just about having sex for the first time. It was not just to get the first notch on his belt. Roland knew, from within his heart, from the first time they kissed. It was crazy, as he thought about it, as he played around with the word, but it made sense to say it, in his head… he was sure, certain, he was in love.

Of course, he did not know what Sophie might think. Perhaps she might wake up and tell him to fuck off? No, that was rubbish, ridiculous. Even if she did, he would not listen. That would be madness. No, he knew something had happened. They had a deep, deep connection. There was nothing superficial here. It was truth, the type of truth he had been seeking, the type of honesty he had been seeking, the experience which reveals a new understanding, an unbreakable cord. He had crossed into a new state of being and he had found… love.

CHAPTER 11

WHITE HEAT

Starr was watching the star-speckled sky through the eighth windowpane to his right. He viewed it patiently, waiting, watching, listening to the communication that travelled through the cosmos, his pupils moving like a juddering stenograph. He let out a short, horse-like laugh, before burying his head beneath the duvet cover. He remained submerged for a while, before emerging and muttering a few thematic words.

'Fat, fatso, fat man… fat, fatso, fat man!'

But his declaration was suddenly interrupted, as the curtains to his dormitory bed were abruptly pulled apart.

'Don't say it!' said the male nurse, in a pre-emptive instruction, his brown skin amusing Starr once again. 'I've already heard enough. You know you're not supposed to be in bed. Come on… out, out, out!'

There was no point in resisting. Starr slid from under the duvet, rolling, crumpled on to the floor.

'Right, now don't lie there like a sack of potatoes, get yourself up.'

In a reluctant daze, Starr hauled himself up on to the

bed and pushed his head into the mattress. This pulled his trousers down so low that his half-naked buttocks reared up.

'Thank you… that is not a sight I like to see so late in the day, or at any other time of the day.'

Starr swivelled his head round to look at the upside-down nurse.

'Look at you… what a state. Now, go to the bathroom, wash your face and come to the dinner table.'

The nurse left, continuing his search along the dormitory for any more recalcitrants hiding away in the forbidden beds.

Starr lumbered like a moody adolescent into the cold chamber washroom. He looked around at the white tiled surfaces, contemplating the action he should perform. There was a row of white basins in front of him. He stood over the one he always used. In amongst a beaker of toothbrushes he identified his personalised tooth cleaner, his name written in thick black ink capitals on a thin white plaster: *A. STARR*. He sighed, rubbed his fat, hairy chest, protruded his thick red lips and considered his reflection.

'Wash, please!' shouted the nurse, who had kept an eye on him whilst still checking the beds.

Starr looked down at the taps.

'Use the water!'

He struggled to turn the tap on, and felt the effort drain his reserves. It was pointless, meaningless. He decided to wait for some intervention.

The nurse returned, having failed to hear the flow of water.

'Let's have a look. You haven't washed your face, have you? I can tell... there's no water there.'

The nurse turned the tap on and used a flannel to rub soapy water into the bleary-eyed Starr.

'I know you can dry your face, so there's a towel... and do it properly, please.'

Starr felt the coarse fibres rub against his skin.

'Now, off you go and put a jumper on. It will get cold later on... seeing as you're a creature of the night.'

As instructed, Starr waddled to the back of the dormitory and into the linen cupboard of coagulating ironed detergent. He sifted through the shelves of pine battens filled with charity-funded clothing and the uniform of the long-stay patient. He moved a few pairs of expandable cotton boxer underpants, flicked through some trousers, pulled out vests and shirts, before uncovering a pile of plain knitted jumpers.

It was tedious. His penis was far more interesting.

Starr undid his trousers so they hung around his thighs. He felt the partially engorged appendage.

'Leave that alone,' said the controlling voice of the nurse, who had returned to check on Starr's progress. 'It's the jumper you need... yes, that one there will do. Put it on, please... thank you.'

Starr obeyed. There would be no peace until he had complied with the relentless barked commands.

He walked through the centre of the dormitory, acknowledging the perfectly arranged duvet covers on the beds, and emerged blinking into the day room. The twenty or so patients on Daffodil Ward sat around square Formica tables, sipping soup from green plastic bowls.

Starr sat down at his usual table, opposite the spindly frame of Andrews, who flicked his tongue out like a snake sniffing the air, his fingers fidgeting involuntarily (a legacy of his many years on a potent brew of antipsychotic drugs). Opposite Andrews sat McCarthy, rigid and silent during the day, loud and expressive at night when vocalising excerpts from popular opera.

The domestic moved from table to table, uniformed in a pink plastic apron, supplementing soup with cardboard chicken burgers, stewed tomatoes and cold, lumpy mashed potato. She approached Starr's table.

'Custard?' he asked, with baleful eyes.

'No!' she said, with a ladle of soggy stewed tomatoes balanced in her hand. 'No custard. You've already missed your soup. It's dinner first. You get custard after you've had your dinner. This is dinner.'

Starr kept quiet. She ladled out two stewed tomatoes, which steamed uninvitingly on the plastic plate. McCarthy continued to gobble what was in front of him. Andrews had his food cut up into small morsels, enabling him to use quick, darting actions with his fork, estimating the best moment to grab what he could.

By one of the high white-framed windows, Mr George (whose first name was also George) danced to an internal tune, his dreadlocks swinging from ear to ear. He would only sit down if he could be provided with a bowl of sunshine.

'George, are you not going to have anything?' asked the nurse, as he left to fetch the drugs trolley.

Mr George was in no mood to be persuaded, and was going to dance all evening.

The patients' supper continued in silence, the societal rejects diligently swallowing their basic nutritional diet – all, that is, except for the soft-shoe-shuffling Mr George and the frustrated Starr.

Once the nurse had returned with the drugs trolley, Starr leapt from his chair to be first in line to receive his medication.

'Have you eaten your dinner?'

'No, he hasn't touched a thing,' responded the domestic, who was collecting plates for an early finish.

'Well, you can take this then,' said the nurse, handing Starr a miniature plastic cup.

Starr emptied the white coated tablet into his hand and swallowed.

'You'll need some water.'

But Starr, who was skilled at swallowing, rushed off down the day room and pushed open the door with the full force of his arms and hands. He wanted out: out of the ward, out of the constant denial of his needs.

He tumbled down the concrete stairs and into the circular route of the main hospital, making his way along the curved ceiling corridors, listening again to the drone of pipes and ductwork above his head. But as he suspected, around the corner was the commanding, interrogative voice of Fitzpatrick. He backtracked, completing a full circumference of the corridor, just to ensure he could drift undetected through the reception and out on to the open lawns. Without any further impediments to his progress, he sped across the grassy surface, floated by the visitor centre and the nurses' hostel, travelled across grassier lawn, jumped over the wire fence and then deep, deep into the frosting woods.

This was Starr's place, the place of secrets and the unknown. It was always best when the sun was down, when the branches and autumnal leaves of trees dimmed the light. And so, with the freshness of the chill evening touching his face, his chest beating with the desperate need for freedom, he set off on his mission to correspond with the communication he had received through the eighth windowpane to the right.

He galloped along the dank, trodden tracks, chirping, burbling and singing aloud:

> *'The grand ol' Duke of York*
> *He had ten thousand men*
> *He marched them up to the top of the hill*
> *And he marched them down again!'*

Laughing like a baying horse, on and on he went, stretching further away from the boundary of Wellington Park, further and deeper into the clumps of wood, before pausing in the opening of a grassy meadow.

Another verse came to him, which he released through his singing voice:

> *'They seek him here, they seek him there,*
> *They seek him in his underwear,*
> *Up and down and all around,*
> *Oh, where will I go underground?'*

Starr continued on his trek and reached the top of a rising track, and looked down on the fibrous fingers of Wellington Park. He avoided the gaze of the tall brick Clock Tower and reflected.

'Tick-tock, tick-tock,
There's fire in the Cauldron pot,
Tick-tock, tick-tock,
The rocket now is taking off.'

He puffed out his cheeks and his exhausted face turned red. He sat down and felt the tickle of seeded grass on the lower part of his back. Up above, a quarter of the moon began to relay. Thin wisps of white clouds moved effortlessly across the communicating rock. It was time to laugh again. He nodded knowingly, assimilating the vast threads of information.

Starr bade farewell, thanking the stars, the planets and the moon for keeping him sane. He propelled his chunky legs headlong down the hill and back into the padded woods. His message drew him further in, into the clumps of ferns, nettles and prickly bushes. Peeling back the threads of foliage, he came to his point of destination.

'Smithy Palace,' said Starr, giggling. 'Smithy Palace.'

There was not much left of the ancient structure, battered and bruised by the Reformation, the relentless march of nature reclaiming land. Starr moved around its edges, the broken walls of flint stone worn down to the foundations. The only structure left was a tall, high window with its arch perfectly framed in the veins of reflecting moonlight. As he stumbled further around its perimeter, he decided to move in through the stumps of a door, striding purposefully towards an old oak tree in the centre of the old abbey.

He sunk to his knees, clasped his hands in prayer and felt the tears run down his cheeks. Starr whimpered, a childlike noise; short, pitying bursts. Above him, the patient twisted, a half-corkscrew, the rope hanging on to the burden of its weight.

Starr pulled from his pocket the magic star, the unearthly piece of mineral, and laid it in front of him. He giggled and bent his torso forward so his head rested on the ground. Saliva dribbled from his mouth and he sucked it up for taste and texture. Mucus rolled again through his nasal passages and dripped on to a decaying leaf. He rocked backwards and forwards for a while, eventually letting the dead man speak.

'The pain is gone – the long, long days of pain. I am now at rest. I have seen out the light. I am happy to be dead. Why waste time living when you can make the one decision worth making, the one thing you have power over? You know what it is like in there… that place. You know they make no difference, how they prolong the agony, eke it out, a drip-drip-drip of mind-numbing non-existence. I have made it out, out of their vicelike grip and into the arms of freedom. Did they ever listen? Did they ever let me make a choice? No. They compressed and pushed me into the floor. But I have beaten them.

'I was not meant to be a part of the living. I was not meant to be part of the days and weeks, months and years which make up the pain of life. I have put back into place the destiny of things. I am of the soil again, part of the atoms and the universe of everything. I now swim with all the stars and planets, rocks and moons. Time now is on my side... time now to think. But what should I think? What can I think in this universe of time? Can I go back? Can I revisit the uselessness of my time? Can I go down the pipes, down through the drains, the puke and the sewage... down through the brains and the blood and the fluid, where the evidence is up there, up above me, in the mystery of truth... where the evidence is the evidence of illusion? Can I lift my eyes and mouth from the sewage and spit out the vomit, wrap myself in the blanket of shame?

'The clock is ticking. The hands are moving as I spread my vermin across the waves. Oh, the evidence, you say? Because it is irrefutable, irretrievable, incontrovertible, undeniable, as clearly as black is black and white is white. Do you not see the evidence before you? There is truth! Eat it. Swallow it. Puke on it. Suck it up like a grovelling, pig-swilling pile of shite. But the fire, the fire that burns you, I can feel the heat, the white heat, the white trauma... with all the flesh hanging, with all flesh burning as I sink deeper into the mass, into the waves and the sea and the salt. Oh, I can see, with screaming eyes and pain, it is like no other pain, that strips the surface of all things... dripping, sinking... down, down, down into the ship, the ship of no returns, when boys and men no longer scream in the melting cups of sinking, stinking blood. I can feel the fire, the hot breath, touching, peeling and stripping... third degrees, so many degrees of convulsive agony. Can you feel it? It is my true love, my true love, my one reliable clock: tick-tock, tick-tock.

'Truth and evidence – don't waste your time on that. Who does? No one does. No one says anything about truth. They say it's truth, all dressed up... looking lovely, looking ever so right. No, understand, please, listen very carefully, whisper it ever so silently, the evidence of things, the truth of things, a tricky, slippery sort of thing. Don't trouble yourself with all these little trifling things. Dream, dream, just for tonight. Sleep and rest your head on the pillow. Are those waves you hear now? Is that the dream you can hear now, where they, the dead, must seek revenge, bitter and justified? When the dead must speak and demand retribution? When penance must be paid? When the perpetrators must be dragged from the comfort of their beds and hung for the crimes of the few and the many? At some point, they must rise and claim their right to be counted among the living, to demand acceptance in the category of humanity. Soon, the sword will be unleashed, slashing and burning. Soon, the victims will run in the streets and dance. Soon, the hour will come when the history of things can make only one conclusion: justice will come to those who know injustice and justice will come to those who have behaved unjustly.

'But let's not fester. No, now, rejoice, rejoice, rejoice in the glow of success, in the triumph. For I have done my service, service to the queen of things, service to the false and lying bosom, the asylum of things waving in the winds, the vile and cancerous growth, the malignant tumour of pride... bellowing trumpets, calling all to their shallow deaths.'

Starr laughed, lifting his head and placing the star possessed of powers on the foot of the dead weight. He shook his head from left to right and up and down. He had heard, as best he could, the testament, the voice of truth, the exact truthfulness of all that could possibly be known. It, the swinging, dangling patient, whose black shadow swung so gently in the cool wool of the night, had spewed forth the elements of satisfaction, regret, anger and bitterness. As a vessel, Starr had received, understood, what no one else can hear, what no one else cares to hear, the absorbing sponge, the transmitter, the conduit of pain.

There were voices... other people's voices.

He grabbed the star and began to crawl away from the encroaching sound, with his hands hurting as his palms grazed the rough undergrowth of the foundation stones. He manoeuvred his large bulk until he felt safe to stand, ready to move, away from Smithy Palace. *Clip-clop, clip-clop*, he jogged along, the movements of his limbs the imitation of a horse, moving rapidly again, all the way back, all the way back to the place where he was safest.

Brushing aside the bits of fern, nettle and bramble, he soon emerged at the boundary of Wellington Park, scrambled over the wire fence and sauntered casually across the lawns. As he strolled, he was back in verse again:

> *'Like vegetables in cooking pots*
> *Round and round like spinning tops,*
> *Boiling up a funny brew*
> *Of peas and cabbage, mash and stew.'*

Starr laughed again, his hyena laughter travelling across the wide open space. He spotted the last dregs of the wanderers, the patients who stepped outside of the wards and spent their days weaving in and out of the cracks, crannies and hideaways, filtering back to their dormitories, back to the comfort of a safe bed. As he passed reception he caught sight of the imposing figure of Fitzpatrick, hovering under the shadow of the entrance, deep in conversation with a bright florescent jacket. Starr immediately turned back on himself and found another route to his destination, a more circuitous journey, but one that was still necessary and vital to his mission. He curved around the brick edges of the wards, poking his face into the windows, the bright lights of the night shift burning out into the end of the day.

There was another verse ready to come to the surface, to echo out into the broad, opaque crevices of the brick and mortar that he rubbed with the side of his body. But sadness creased his face, a bleak, woeful sigh; a heartfelt, anguished groan for custard, for something, for anything. Compressed into his stub-like face, pity and despair etched his brow and ran along the furrows that crumpled his forehead. A burden had slowed him down, made him stop and consider the ramifications, the consequences of his actions, the questioning of his motives. It only lasted a moment before his old state of consciousness picked him up again. Sliding skilfully against the walls, he plunged his hand into his pocket and felt the star, the unearthly message of magic, of powers which had communicated so many things. So much to do and to be acted upon, so much to gather, accumulate and synthesise, so much to put into practice.

At last, he had found where he wanted to be, behind the spider-like threads of Wellington Park and in amongst the neglected buildings at the back of the hospital. The old boiler house cranked and hummed as he wobbled around the dilapidated potting sheds with the shards of glass hanging from the peeling window frames. In the distance, in the pale, moonlit night, he could see the sign of the ark above the Portakabin. But none of this was of interest to him. Ahead, hidden in between the thick bushes of undergrowth, entwined in the open-jawed entrance, he moved stealthily towards the old patients' graveyard. He passed under the thin, unstable wooden arch warped by the thick vines of wisteria, following his instincts into the dark. He could feel underneath his feet the difference, the change in textures, walking slowly through the bedding of thick, wet moss. As the blocks of bent gravestones became more tangible, he knelt again, just as he had done before, laying the star on the soft green carpet. The canopy above his head whispered against each branch as the gentle breeze of the closing night rustled through.

Starr felt satisfaction, his lips burnt by the cold, with the last juices of energy thumping through his veins. And he raised his star so the dead could speak in unison:

'Revenge at last! Revenge at last! Revenge at last!'

Starr nodded.

Yes, he had heard, heard so much about their pain.

'Revenge at last! Revenge at last!'

CHAPTER 12

A SIMPLE TOOL

Gobi, head of Wellington Park School of Nursing, started his career in the late 1950s when he had been part of an overseas recruitment drive from one of the islands off the east coast of Africa. He had retained a heavy accent, slowly articulating, and prefacing or ending every sentence with a distinctive "you know". Short and introspective, he was likened to a toad by most students, which meant there was always one willing to make toad-like noises to alleviate the boredom. In response, his bald brown head would glisten under the stress, accompanied by sweat trickling down his thick black-rimmed glasses.

Tuition was supplied in short, weekly spurts, compressed into a few downstairs classrooms which historically had been part of the lounge and reception of the converted old gatekeeper's cottage. White plastic concertinaed partitions divided the spaces, with both floors covered in a nondescript beige carpet, whilst every available space on the walls was saturated in didactic posters of dos and don'ts for the aspiring psychiatric nurse.

In theory, students were taught in the school to do things properly, but as they attended their ward-based placements they soon became disillusioned by the gap between theory and practice. Gobi always listened, showed concern, even dissatisfaction, but he had no intention of changing anything. Plus, it was rare if any student had the energy or commitment to challenge the status quo between the school and the hospital. As far as Gobi was concerned, he had to maintain the balance between encouraging students to learn whilst providing free labour for the wards. If he failed to maintain the quota, Slaney and Fitzpatrick had considerable influence over the ability of the school to continue.

However, when Gobi was informed of the results of the revitalised student council, it was not the election of Sophie Smith as treasurer and secretary which warranted concern, but the unknown quantity of the newly elected president: Roland Cauldron. Once he had looked into it, his incredulity amplified, as apparently Roland had stood unopposed, achieving presidential status due to receiving the prerequisite two nominations, one from Jas Jaswinder and the other from Terry Alcock. With two elected and functioning officers, Gobi would have to reconvene the student council. Whilst he was all in favour of students having a voice there was a risk he would have less control over matters, especially in regards to the bitter experience of student placements. This was always a delicate and thorny issue which, with some justification, was top of the list of student grievances.

There was one other factor which intrigued Gobi.

He did not usually go out of his way to involve himself in students' personal relationships, but the liaison between Roland Cauldron and Sophie Smith had certainly surprised his teaching staff. What was the attraction of Cauldron, they said, who was clearly out of his league, when she had the pick of anyone she wanted? It merely confirmed for Gobi that this particular young man had a quality (if he could call it that) which had to be treated with suspicion.

After the '84 intake had completed their first placements, Gobi decided to treat them to a lesson on "historical development of therapeutic interventions at Wellington Park". It would also be an opportunity to gauge the temperature after their first experiences on the wards.

'You know,' said Gobi, as he placed his bulging black leather briefcase against the leg of the desk, 'if there's anything you're not happy about, you must tell me first. You know, I like to know what students are feeling. We can only do something about it if you tell me what's wrong. Not that I'm promising, you know, I can solve everything for you, but if you're not happy about something, we all need to know.'

The '84 intake of Roland, Jas, Terry, Claire and Judy all hesitated. They had, one way or another, been through a baptism of fire.

'And, you know,' said Gobi, 'I must congratulate Mr Cauldron on being elected president of the student council. You can say things here, or to Mr Cauldron, who could say things on your behalf, you know, when we meet as the student council.'

There was a restrained silence in the small, partitioned classroom. A few gazed at the blackboard.

'You know, you can talk to your tutors as well,' said Gobi.

They looked along the line at each other, their elbows leaning forward on their note-taking desks.

'Are you all happy then?' asked Gobi, as a final opportunity.

'Well,' said Roland, predictably breaking the silence, 'I don't think we are…'

Gobi nodded, whilst Roland checked to make sure he was not making a rash or non-consultative statement.

'We're not happy with a lot of things,' said Roland, who felt he had the green light to say his piece. 'We're not happy with the fact that we are used on the wards to fill the gaps in staff shortages. We're not happy that we and the patients are put at risk.'

'Are you put at risk?' asked Gobi, pretending this was something new.

'I can give you an example, if you like,' said Roland eagerly. 'Judy here had to manage a ward all on her own, for a whole shift. She contacted Mr Fitzpatrick and he said there were no qualified nurses available… she would just have to manage on her own because all of the patients could look after themselves. I mean, we are only three months into our training… do you think that is fair or acceptable?'

'Oh, I didn't know that,' said Gobi. 'You know, you should always tell me about these things.'

'We are telling you!' said Roland, focused on airing the collective disquiet. 'I mean, there are things on the wards we find difficult to fathom. We're meant to be training to become nurses, to bring new ideas, to do things in a better way, but everything is so backward here. The only therapy is chemical… the only thing that seems to matter is an injection.'

'Oh, I think that's a bit harsh,' said Gobi, scanning the rest of the students to see if Roland had the full support of his colleagues.

'But it's true!' said Roland, slightly exasperated.

'We're not criticising you,' said Claire, stretching her bony fingers forwards and then parting her fringe to reveal her ski-slope nose, 'but it is difficult to know what we should be doing on the wards… everyone is so busy. I don't think they have much time to do anything else but the basics.'

Gobi nodded, thanking Claire for her more measured contribution.

'Well,' said Jas, 'I agree with Roland. All we do is drug them up to keep them quiet.'

'The liquid cosh,' said Roland. 'It's a system without thought, just going through the motions, a benign form of barbarity.'

'Oh, I don't think it's like that,' said Judy, immediately dissolving the united front Roland thought he had agreed beforehand. 'I'm sure things are a lot better now than they were in the past.'

'You know, I think that's a very useful point, Judy,' said Gobi, who was pleased Roland was not monopolising the feedback. 'You know, if you look at the history of mental illness, we have made a big step forward in the treatment of some illnesses.'

'I don't doubt that,' said Roland, glancing at Judy, 'although they still use ECT here… and that is barbaric! The point is, it's about how the drugs are used as a means of control, so this place can function at the lowest common denominator… on the cheap!'

'Ribbit,' said Terry surreptitiously.

'There was another thing,' said Claire. 'We've heard the hospital is going to close. What would that mean for our training?'

'Oh, yes, you know,' said Gobi, keen to move things on, 'there are always rumours.'

'Yeah,' said Jas, 'I heard they are going to shut the place down, move everyone out into the community or something naff like that.'

'What community?' said Roland rhetorically.

'We'll have to see about that,' said Gobi. 'You know, there's no need to worry at the moment.'

'Does that mean the school will close?' asked Claire.

'No, no, no, no, no, no… you know, we'll see how things go.'

Everyone looked blankly at each other. No, they did not really know. Gobi again looked along the line of the '84 intake. He did not want to get bogged down in things which were bound to be rather speculative.

'Let me get the projector,' he said, swiftly exiting the classroom.

They all sat back in their chairs, all dissatisfied for varying reasons.

'I hope it's a dirty movie,' said Jas, attempting to alleviate the mood.

'Why, will you be in it?' asked Claire sarcastically.

'No, I don't do that any more.'

'That doesn't mean you won't be in it,' said Terry.

'Why?' asked Jas, looking at Claire. 'Do you want to see me shagging?'

'No thank you, I've just had my breakfast.'

'She might have a point,' said Terry.

'I thought the point was,' said Roland, whose frustration was etched across his face, 'we all stood together on this. We were all meant to say we were unhappy.'

'I thought we did,' said Jas.

'Really?' said Roland, unable to disguise his annoyance with Judy. 'Well, it's not going to end here. We can't let them get away with it and pretend nothing has happened. We all know how bad this place is, and with me and Sophie reconvening the student council, we're going to make things happen. That means we are going to need everybody's support. Not say one thing and then do another.'

'Of course,' said Jas, who felt he had played his part.

'Right!' said Roland, assuming that signalled agreement once more.

Gobi reappeared with a large projector hanging from his shoulder, placed it on the stand at the back of the classroom and hesitantly returned to the blackboard.

'You know,' said Gobi, as he attempted to unfurl the screen from its curled cavity, 'have you ever wondered why Wellington Park is where it is, its location?'

'You need to pull it at an angle,' said Jas helpfully.

'Oh, yes, I see, it always does that, you know,' said Gobi, as he waited for the screen to behave.

'I think that's alright now, sir,' said Jas, who had a habit of adopting deference at inexplicable moments.

'Oh yes, let's see,' said Gobi, who walked back to the projector whilst anxiously eyeing the screen. 'So, you know, the whole of London is surrounded by old asylums like this one, with a lot of institutionalised patients. You know, a long time ago the relatives would pretend to take them out for a nice day in the country – you know, the old horse and cart and a nice picnic – and then leave them here.'

'But not any more?' said Claire hopefully.

'They still do,' said Terry. 'It's called the 174.'

'That's right,' said Jas, eager to offer his own evidence, 'I've read loads of patients' notes. Agnes – you all know Agnes – well, she's had everything going: zapped, drugged, the lot. She's been here since she was sixteen and she must be over sixty by now. Well, it said in her notes she was put in here because she was pregnant and it was going to be a bastard. There was nothing wrong with her. She had the baby and had to give it up. That's bound to send you crazy!'

'That's terrible,' said Claire, looking at Jas, because he might have a heart.

'You're telling me,' he said. 'I've got more stories like that if anyone is interested.'

'You'd also get a lot of the staff living near here,' continued Gobi. 'The old houses down the road used to be staff houses. So, you know, we're a bit old and faded, but things have changed.'

'Have things changed?' asked Roland cynically.

'Why did they build the hospitals outside London?' asked Judy, again coming to Gobi's aid.

'Oh, yes,' said Gobi, moving back to the projector. 'These old asylums, you know, were not built in the country for the fresh air. It was a good place to put them, you know, out of the way.'

'You mean lock them up and throw away the key,' said Roland.

'Also,' said Gobi, continuing along his tangent, 'there's lots of history around here, if you like that kind of thing. There's an old abbey which is built on a Roman burial ground for some reason, you know – Neolithic as well, you know. There's not much there, but some patients like it… you know.'

'Suicide…' whispered Jas.

'Oh yes, you know, it's not good for that.'

'Vilnous…' said Jas to Roland. 'Burnt to fuck from the Falklands.'

The projector lights suddenly came on.

'Oh, that's good,' said Gobi. 'You never know if these things are working properly.'

'What's the film about, sir?' asked Jas.

Gobi replied by flicking a switch.

'Oh, good, a picture,' he said, promptly turning the switch off again. 'So, you know, I like to show this to students. It's an old film. Wellington Park was internationally famous in the 1950s. You know, they would all come to see what we had done here. We were the first hospital to take down the gate and the walls. Patients can come and go as they please.'

'Apart from the locked wards,' said Jas.

'Oh, yes, you know, you won't work on those wards until your final year.'

'That's where they put the real nutters,' said Jas, feigning disbelief at the disapproving looks from everyone.

'So, you know,' continued Gobi, 'some of you might not like this film, but you need to look at it as history, how they did things.'

Gobi flicked the switch of the projector, but the reel remained stationary and a bright light shone on the screen.

'I can fix it,' said Jas, leaping out of his seat.

Gobi stepped back as Jas wound the reel with his pen.

'What is the film about?' asked Claire.

'Oh yes, you know, has anyone heard of Dr Prize-Bomka?'

No, no one had heard of Dr Prize-Bomka.

'Oh, so, you know, he was a consultant here, and, you know, he came up with an experimental surgical procedure for the prefrontal leucotomy.'

'That's taking your brains out,' said Jas, as he continued to act as temporary technician.

'Well, you know, it's only a short film, which we keep here in the archive, but if you view it in context, you will see he was only trying to improve things.'

'Do we still do that?' asked Judy nervously.

'No, no, no, no, no, we don't do that any more,' said Gobi. 'But some people still want it, you know, privately, but we don't do it here… no, no…'

'There you go, sir,' said Jas, turning the switch and projecting a still image on to the screen.

'Oh yes, that's very good,' said Gobi, who then turned the projector off again.

'I wouldn't turn it off,' said Jas. 'It might not work again.'

'Oh, well, we shall see,' said Gobi. 'So, you know, see this film, it's only ten minutes long. He describes what he has invented, and, you know, you see what it does.'

'Should we draw the curtains?' asked Jas, painfully helpful yet again.

'Oh, yes, thank you.'

Gobi waited for the ever-diligent Jas to close the curtains, then, with a flick of the switch, he started the film.

Against a rich blue background, the white-coated Dr Prize-Bomka introduced his revolutionary approach to the prefrontal leucotomy. He had invented a simple tool, which could be inserted into the brain in order to take a precise slice out of the patient's troubling thought processes, preferable to the pioneering but rather imprecise hammer and chisel. Dr Prize-Bomka's innovation was to adapt his own wristwatch so the spring could be expanded and retracted once it had penetrated the small hole in the side of the patient's head. There was already a strong body of evidence for the positive effects of this procedure and he would happily perform it in his own kitchen. This prefrontal leucotomy would be able to demonstrate a significant change in the patient's behaviour, in those who suffered from obsessive compulsive disorders, acute paranoid schizophrenia and bipolar depression. After a short operation and allowing for a period of recovery, these improvements were more clearly identifiable in OCD cases, where the compulsive behavioural traits were markedly reduced or disappeared altogether.

Dr Prize-Bomka introduced Thomas, a Wellington Park patient, who had classic OCD symptoms: obsessive cleaning of the hands with an added psychosexual deviancy, or compulsive dimension.

'He means masturbation,' said Jas.

Thomas, dressed in a dark brown suit, shirt and tie, his hair curled up at the front, smiled inanely. He thanked the doctor for all the help he had been given. No, he had no fear in regards to the operation and just wanted to get better.

The mechanism with which Dr Prize-Bomka would extract the offending organic dysfunction had its intrinsic parts revealed. As promised, it was no more than a simple adaption of a retractable ballpoint pen and the arch of a watch spring as the cutting tool. With local anaesthetic, iodine and a green sheet, the shaved side of Thomas' head had a hole drilled in it to remove a small part of the skull, no more than the size of a shilling. Having secured access, Dr Prize-Bomka inserted the tool, measured the length by a system of grading, rather like a ship's Plimsoll line, twisted, cut and removed.

Dr Prize-Bomka was able to confirm the operation was a success, as was the case in over 30 per cent of similar cases, with some degree of reduction in symptoms with another third. He then presented a consultation with Thomas, who agreed with the doctor that he felt relaxed and less concerned about things.

Clearly, in conclusion, said Dr Prize-Bomka, there was a place for surgery in psychiatry and the benefits it could bring to those afflicted.

FINIS.

'Okay, so, you know,' said Gobi, turning off the projector, 'that means the end.'

'Ribbit…'

'That's just like in the film *One Flew Over the Cuckoo's Nest*, with Jack Nicholson,' said Jas. 'They took out his brains to shut him up because he wouldn't play by the system.'

'Oh, you know, that's very good,' said Gobi, moving to the front of the classroom, 'but I don't think Thomas, the patient in the film, is like that. We can see when we look back at things how things were not very good. But at the time, this was considered to be very progressive. Now we know better and can rely on the patient's medication.'

'Is it cure or is it control?' said Roland. 'Don't we just shut people up with antipsychotic drugs to keep the peace, to keep things rolling along so management can manage the system?'

'You know,' said Gobi, 'you must remember these drugs were a big advance on what used to be done here. We don't want to go back to the bad old days.'

'So, when did it become the good old days?'

'I feel sorry for that poor man,' said Judy. 'I don't think he looked any better. He looked just the same.'

'Well, you know, not everything went right for him. You know, if you go and look in the patients' graveyard, you will see a grave for that young man and a few others there.'

'They died?!' exclaimed Judy.

'Oh, yes, you know, a little history, you know. We would all like things to be done better. But, you know, today there are lots of people who come here, get better and go.'

'Yeah, but not everyone in here is ill,' said Roland conspiratorially.

All of a sudden, the projector sprang to life and Gobi was startled by an intense beam of light.

'Oh…'

'Freaky…'

'Shall I turn it off, sir?'

'Oh, you know, blinded by the light…'

Jas jumped out of his seat, flicked a few switches on the projector and then pulled out the plug.

'Sir, what do you think was wrong with Jack Nicholson then?'

'Can someone, you know, open the curtains?' asked Gobi, pulling on the projector screen, which refused to budge. 'That's a good question.'

'He was a rebel, an individual, a nonconformist,' stated Roland, proudly aligning himself.

'Ah…' said Gobi, as the projector screen flew rapidly back into its cavity, 'you know, these are social types, you know.'

'What does that mean?' asked Roland suspiciously.

'There are people, you know, who find refuge in groups outside our normal society,' said Gobi, facing the class. 'You know, they will be disguising their illnesses, you know, hiding in alternative lifestyles.'

'You can't say that!' said Roland in protest.

'Of course Mr Gobi can,' said Judy, annoyed at Roland again. 'He is our tutor. You don't know everything!'

'We're students and we are supposed to question,' said Roland, who was not going to be put off. 'You can't say that people who just want to live a different way are mad!'

119

'That's not what he said,' said Claire.

'He suggested it.'

'That's a bit iffy I think, sir,' said Jas.

Gobi remained unmoved.

'You know,' he said, 'someone who is manic might dye their hair purple, you know, live in transient groups, take drugs that make their underlying illness worse, you know. We have patients like that.'

'That's us,' said Terry proudly.

'Are you seriously saying,' said Roland, raising his voice, 'that people who choose to live a different lifestyle from all the consumer capitalist bullshit we have to put up with could actually be harbouring mental illness?'

'No, no, no, you know,' said Gobi, smiling to himself, 'we measure moods and behaviours to know what is normal, you know, and what is abnormal.'

'Yeah, I know that,' said Roland, 'but where do you draw the line so that people who just think differently are not labelled mad?'

'Oh, you know, you have to wait and see, over time, you know.'

'Well, that's me fucked,' said Jas, laughing.

'Don't be paranoid,' said Roland.

'Ribbit...'

Gobi scanned the classroom. He was not going to tolerate the baiting.

Everyone kept their faces blank.

'Well, you know, I think it's time for coffee,' he said, with sweat trickling down his thick black-rimmed glasses.

'Ribbit.'

CHAPTER 13

THE AMAZING DR CALDWELL

From its birth in the 1960s, Chaolla House was built separately from the main body of the hospital, reflecting the differences between Dr Caldwell's clients and the institutionalised long-stay and dementia-infested patients of Wellington Park. Dr Caldwell was the more distant member of the powerful ruling triumvirate, along with Slaney and Fitzpatrick, who essentially ran the hospital through their positions on the senior management team and board of governors.

Roland, as he walked to Chaolla House in the frosty morning, was acutely aware he was stepping into the territory of Dr Caldwell's citadel. He had tried to mitigate the cold by wearing a high-neck jumper, but he could still feel the chill winter morning pierce through the gaps in his uniformed blazer, sending a bleary-eyed shiver through his body. He longed for the comfort of lying next to Sophie in bed after another long night of shagging.

In the first few weeks he had kept count, but they had done it so many times now he was beginning to lose count. If Sophie was on a different shift pattern, Jas and Terry were always available to offer alternative entertainment. Roland's day-to-day existence consisted of working, a little study, shagging and getting stoned. But usually, all he had on his mind was shagging and talking with Sophie about how fucked up and crap everything was in Wellington Park. They would end up discussing how they were going to use their positions on the student council to tackle the inequities of a decrepit and failing system. With Roland having the voice of the first-year intakes, Sophie the second and third, they had decided on a solution, something Gobi and the rest of them would be unable to ignore: a petition, to kick-start the issue of misusing students on the wards.

In theory, Roland was lucky to have a chance to spend a day with the "amazing Dr Caldwell", internationally renowned for alcoholic rehabilitation. His clinic had a very exclusive client list of judges, lawyers, politicians, journalists, doctors, managers, celebrities and businessmen, or, so Roland liked to call them, "all the privileged wankers who couldn't cope". Dr Caldwell would treat them all, as long as they adhered to the strict regime of Alcoholics Incognito or AI. Straying from the path would lead to expulsion, damnation and probably the end of their lucrative career, including family and associated benefits.

But for any student in Wellington Park with serious aspirations to be more than just a "shit and piss nurse", they needed to get a foothold in the therapeutic nirvana of Chaolla House. They had one opportunity, one day to impress and put down a marker. In truth, a few hours in Chaolla House had little or no impact. If you wanted to get yourself noticed there were certain prerequisites, not least a higher education, combined with social and cultural compatibility with the staff. They were the elite, the only practitioners of genuine psychiatric intervention in the morass of discredited institutional care. They had escaped the horrors of the dementia-ridden "back wards", the long-stay wards full of misfits and mavericks, or the socially dysfunctional throughput from acute patients on Lilywhite Ward. No need for elite staffing to waste their high-level skills on the intractable complexity of patients, dulled into submission through the chemical straitjacket of compliance or the legacy of eccentric pseudoscientific experiments. They had the privilege of being schooled in the more advanced techniques of psychotherapeutic approaches, soft and gentle practices compared to the institutional.

Roland took a short cut through a small wooded area, passing the isolated closed ward, where ivy spread its tentacles over the red brick walls. He peered through the downstairs windows: the old day room was mainly empty, just cracked tiles and a few trolley beds pushed up against the main door. This was where Gobi had said Dr Prize-Bomka had specialised. *Poor bastards*, thought Roland, as he continued on through the wooded patch, crunching the frost-frozen oak leaves, then sprinting across the cricket pitch, conscious he was probably going to be late (again).

He turned his head to look up at the Clock Tower. Fuck it! If there was one thing Gobi had said, it was "Don't be late for Dr Caldwell's placement".

Once Chaolla House was in sight he decided to relax. He could just see the top edges of the flat-roofed complex hidden in the tall, overgrown grasses. The whole cut-off area was a bit like an obscure government research facility, a vague building punctuated by narrow, regular, rectangular windows.

Roland approached along a jagged concrete path before taking a right-angled approach to face the glass-doored reception. Gobi had said if he failed to turn up on time they would not let him in; they were that strict. Roland pressed the buzzer to the intercom system. The seconds passed, which then stretched into what he thought were minutes. This was getting serious. He pressed the buzzer again. *Shit, shit, shit! Come on!*

Just when he thought it was all over and he would have to account for his lack of discipline in front of Gobi, a voice came through the intercom.

'Can I help?'

Roland bent down, near the speaker. 'My name is Roland Cauldron, I'm here for my one-day placement.'

He heard the click of the intercom and waited. After a painfully short amount of time, a tall and tanned Chaolla House member of staff, dressed in blue slacks and blue striped shirt, looked through the window of the door.

Roland looked back, innocently smiling at the handsome figure.

'You know you're late,' he said, his voice muffled by the glass door.

'Am I?'

'You have to be on time.'

'Oh, I thought I was,' said Roland, convinced he had

timed it accurately by the Clock Tower. 'I'm sure I'm on time… that's weird…'

'We don't normally let you in if you're late.'

'I didn't know,' pleaded Roland. 'Honestly, I thought I was on time.'

The handsome face looked Roland up and down again.

'Okay, but don't say anything.'

The door was unbolted, top and bottom.

'Thanks,' said Roland, as he stepped into a stale, vacuous space. 'It is cold out there.'

The handsome face gave Roland a look of incredulity.

Roland followed, dutifully walking behind through a mini maze of corridors, then into a wood-panelled day room. It was a mixture of sunken leather sofas, leather-backed armchairs and a coffee table full of magazines.

'Take a seat,' the nurse said, pointing to a sofa.

'I will in a minute,' said Roland, who moved into the centre of the room.

'That's up to you, but I'm afraid there's not much for you to do.'

'Why is that?'

'Depends on what day it is. Any sessions today are closed.'

'What do you mean?' asked Roland, who was genuinely hoping to experience something far more progressive for once.

'You can't go into any of the therapeutic sessions this morning. Plus, you would need to be at the right level. It probably wouldn't make much sense to you.'

'Why? I thought that was the point: we got a chance to see some proper therapy.'

'Chaolla House is not like the wards,' the nurse said. 'And another thing: you can't just go up to the clients and start talking to them. You must stay out of the clients' rooms. Here, it's different: clients have a right to privacy and should not be disrupted or disturbed.'

'So, what's the point in me being here?' asked Roland, his blood beginning to boil.

'Well, Dr Caldwell is more than generous in allowing these opportunities to students. Keep out of the way of the clients and wait until this afternoon. Dr Caldwell will be holding his clinic and he has allowed students to be present. However, you must not speak, you must not do anything to upset the clients or Dr Caldwell.'

Roland stared back, angry and frustrated.

'You can make yourself a coffee... the kitchen's through there,' the nurse said, pointing through the door.

'Is that it?' asked Roland, thinking that he would face hours of waiting.

'Did you bring a book to study?'

'No.'

'Didn't they explain any of this to you?'

'No.'

'Look,' he said, mildly sympathetic, 'just sit here till about eleven... slip out for a few hours and take a long lunch... just make sure you're back here by 1.30 p.m. for the clinic.'

Roland sat down on the sofa, acquiescing.

'What if a client comes in? Do I speak to them or pretend I'm not here?'

'They won't come in,' the nurse said, turning towards the door. 'Listen, I'll make you a coffee.'

Great, thought Roland, *an existential moment; I don't actually exist.*

He looked around the day room, focusing on the strange handwritten chalked affirmations on a narrow blackboard fresco running along the walls. These were positive reinforcements, a religious declaration, reminding clients that strict abstinence was the only way of life open to them. In one corner a flipchart rested on an easel. In neat, joined-up handwriting, someone had gone to great lengths to record the rules and regulations; Chaolla House instructions on behaviour, lifestyle and method.

Rules, rules, rules. Roland hated it. All he could think about was the stuck-up prick of a fucking nurse. *What a load of bullshit! My level... whose fucking level? So, what level is he then? So far up my fucking arse level that I cannot see I am a fucking arsehole. Well, fuck you!* Roland had seen it all before. Fucking class... that was what it was all about: some stuck-up fucking wanker with his fucking class and his fucking privilege. *Oh, he's so very special... so fucking special he doesn't have to give a shit about the fucking peasants!*

His Lordship returned.

'I forgot to ask if you take sugar?'

'Well, I usually have it black,' said Roland, as he received the coffee with milk.

This triggered a look of recognition.

'Sorry, are you Sophie Smith's new boyfriend?'

'Yes,' said Roland, with some pride.

'I knew... *know*... Sophie, that's all... when she started out. How's she doing?'

'Okay,' said Roland, wondering if they were once an item.

'She must be finishing soon?'

'Yeah, one more year…'

'Right, yeah, I remember… that was an odd one, because they started her year in January so she finishes in January. She's a good nurse… lots of potential. Well, listen, tell her Felix said hi.'

'Felix?'

'Yeah, I'm sure she remembers me. Listen… just read a few magazines and I'll see you back here after lunch.'

'Right,' said Roland, as Felix disappeared.

Oh well… Felix says hi… I'll be sure to say Felix says hi.

★

When Roland returned from lunch, Felix escorted him into Dr Caldwell's clinic, a consultation room sheathed by oak wood panelling, centred by an enormous desk of intricate inlay. Roland expected to be introduced to the "great man", but was immediately directed to a large green leather chair by the side of the desk. Felix held a finger to his lips to indicate he was not to say anything because the most important man in the room needed to concentrate.

Roland pushed himself back into the chair, which caused his feet to be just above the floor, increasing his sense of insignificance.

'I'll be back in a minute,' said Felix.

Dr Caldwell continued to write, a bold silver stylus scratching out the words into a client's notes. He was a giant, thought Roland, six feet plus, probably, with grey tufts of hair wrapped around his head.

Felix returned and stood in front of Dr Caldwell's desk.

'We're ready when you are, Dr Caldwell,' said Felix, pointing up at the clock behind him to emphasise the time.

Dr Caldwell merely nodded, readjusted his seat and continued writing. Roland sat forward in his chair, expecting to be introduced, but Felix turned and walked out of the room again.

Roland's hands were cold and so he pushed them under his thighs. Should he say something, he thought? *Hi, I'm Roland Cauldron, existentialist, anarchist, metaphysician. No, apparently not. I am supposed to keep quiet. What am I? An ant, an insignificant insect, a blob on the wall? What does it take to have some degree of courtesy and acknowledge my presence? Or is this just the way things are done around here? What "they" are like… the superior beings, the great gods of psychotherapy? Oh*, said Roland sarcastically to himself, *we are so intelligent, so skilled and knowledgeable, we cannot waste time, not a minute, not a second, not a fraction of a second, on anyone or thing that is not pertinent. Therefore, we must ensure our superiority is communicated at all times, so that those who are not at the required level are kept at a distance.*

Felix returned with a large bundle of files and placed them on the corner of the desk. Dr Caldwell turned to acknowledge Roland. He smiled. It was an inscrutable, self-confident, implacable smile. There was power, perhaps benign power, thought Roland, but controlled, designated power, the power to alter lives, for better or for worse.

'Okay, Felix,' said Dr Caldwell, 'let's get the show on the road.'

'They are all outpatients,' said Felix to Roland. 'Please do not interrupt and just observe.'

Roland had his instructions.

One by one, Dr Caldwell's clients knocked obediently on the door before entering. One by one, they sat across from the enormous desk whilst Dr Caldwell pondered his inscrutable medical notes.

It soon became apparent they were on a journey of redemption, but only some could move on, whilst others could not. There were those still trapped in the strict disciplines which they struggled to adhere to, whilst others were granted more liberty, more freedom, rejuvenating lifeblood for their reconstructed soul.

However, Roland soon caught on to what the clients were adept at doing. It seemed that if they were grateful recipients of the most advanced therapy available under the consultancy of the amazing Dr Caldwell (appeal to Dr Caldwell's ego), their wishes would be granted: laser off a tattoo, increase access to their loved ones, letters of mitigation to employers or delays on mortgage and interest repayments. But for the client who showed resistance, or a lack of deference, Dr Caldwell seemed reluctant to move their lives forward. Dr Caldwell was indeed a god, a cut above, the man who had the doctor gene in him. This was just destiny for him: all in a day's work, all in day's diagnosis and benevolence.

But was there really any point in resenting the good works of Dr Caldwell?

As the procession of ingratiating, nauseous self-flagellation progressed Roland stretched out his legs, slumped into the chair and struggled to stay awake. After all the hype of the messianic Dr Caldwell and his Chaolla House, Roland decided there was not much to it. Of course, he could only guess at what really went on, but was that his fault if he was denied access to anything remotely interesting? He had just been tolerated for a day. And, thought Roland, the whole thing stank when he compared it to the rest of Wellington Park.

Clearly, Dr Caldwell had hived off his own little city-state, unsullied and untouched by all the dirty peasants that made up the rest of the hospital's population, dragooned and manoeuvred by the omnipresent Slaney and Fitzpatrick. Roland was just being trained to look after all the detritus, all the fucked up rubbish washed up on to the wards. He was cheap labour for the "forgotten". Come to Chaolla House and you get the full-on treatment, the top-notch service, the exclusive hotel-like facilities and nice posh nurses for nice posh people.

Or, perhaps, thought Roland, *I am just bitter and twisted because I will never, ever, be part of it.*

★

At a break in proceedings Roland followed Felix to relieve himself.

'So, what do you think?' asked Felix, who unzipped with a self-confident smile, as they both stood facing the urinal.

'Interesting,' said Roland, emptying his bladder.

'Well, these are only outpatients,' Felix said, fixing his eyes on the mortar in the wall.

'So, how do you get to work on Chaolla House?' asked Roland, pissing in the trough.

'Not as a student,' said Felix.

'That's not true,' said Roland assertively.

'What do you mean?'

'I know some of you started here as students,' said Roland mischievously.

Felix sighed.

'A few of us,' he said, in acknowledgement.

'So, that means you *can* work here as a student,' said Roland, all too pleased at catching Felix out.

'Very rarely,' said Felix, who was not going to be unsettled. 'You would have to be a special case, an outstanding student for Dr Caldwell to consider you.'

'Oh,' said Roland, smiling, 'and what does it take to be outstanding?'

'If you mean me,' said Felix, 'I had a degree in psychology before I started my training.'

'Right,' said Roland, thinking Felix was only boasting. 'Do you think that's fair, that only a privileged few have the opportunity to prove themselves?'

Roland watched his stream come to an end, zipped himself up and walked over to the washbasins. He turned his neck to check if Felix had finished.

'At the end of the day,' said Felix, moving away from the thick stench of toilet cleaner, 'you need to be at a certain level.'

'Oh, the level again,' said Roland sarcastically.

'You know,' said Felix, 'you seem more than capable to me. You could do it if you wanted to.'

'What, go to university? You must be joking!'

'It's hard work, that's all,' said Felix, 'but if you want it, that's what you need to do.'

'I can't see it,' said Roland, disgruntled. 'Plus, I can't see myself ever being accepted in a place like this.'

'Well,' said Felix, reassured he had turned the onus back on to Roland, 'you'll never know unless you try.'

Easy for him to say, thought Roland, *the guy hasn't got a fucking clue.*

They both moved towards the exit and walked almost shoulder to shoulder through the doorway.

'Where's your tie?' Felix asked.

'Here,' said Roland, pulling it from underneath his jumper.

'Make sure he sees it when you go back in.'

'Okay,' said Roland, rather bemused.

He then pulled the tie up to his collar, felt it constrict before loosening it again. *Fuck it*, he said to himself, *it is only a tie.*

CHAPTER 14

THE PRIZE-BOMKA CUP

TERRY: Well, here we are today to witness the much-anticipated clash between two giants of the mental health profession, competing for the highly prestigious Prize-Bomka Cup. We have to our right Wellington Park, in a mixture of white and grey, and to our left, Cladham, in dynamic red and black. I'd also like to welcome my fellow commentator, Jas Jaswinder, who although he has never played the game, I am sure will still be able to provide some vital insights. So, Jas, how do you think the match will go?

JAS: Thanks, Terry. Well, with both sides warming up this gives us an excellent opportunity to look at the physical condition of the players. I think I can safely say, without fear of contradiction, both teams will do well to last the full ninety minutes.

TERRY: Thanks, Jas. So, who do you think will be the key players for both sides today? Shall we start with Cladham?

JAS: Thanks, Terry. Well, I think Cladham are out for revenge after experiencing defeats in the last couple of years. There is a rumour of a ringer for Cladham, based on his reputation as a deadly striker who used to play in the Portuguese 2nd Division. In fact, I think we can see him near the goal, limbering up, looking fit and athletic. I must say, he does look impressive, especially with *No. 9* on his shirt.

TERRY: Yes, there has been this rumour, and I think we can tell from the way he strikes the ball he could pose a threat to Wellington's back four.

JAS: Yes, I think that's right, Terry. I would have to say, unless Wellington's Chopper Chaney is on his game, Wellington will have to rely on the mud to restrict the score.

TERRY: Well, thanks, Jas, that's a great insight. And is there anyone else who you think deserves special mention before the game starts?

JAS: Well, of course, Terry, there is the surprise inclusion of Roland Cauldron, whose qualities as a player remain unknown.

TERRY: Yes, I can see young Cauldron over there on the other side of the pitch. Shouldn't he be limbering up? However, as you say, little is known about Cauldron's footballing abilities, especially as he was pulled in at the last minute.

JAS: Yes, that's right, Terry. The story is, Wellington were struggling to ensure they had eleven players on the pitch until young Cauldron offered his services. You would have to say though, Terry, there are some concerns here. Not only does he lack the necessary kit and footwear, but he does look a bit isolated…

TERRY: It's not only that, Jas, you can tell he's struggling to cope with the fresh air. Now, that must be a shock to his lungs!

(Laughter.)

TERRY: But let's give the boy a chance.

(Laughter.)

Roland stood on the only green patch of grass he could find because he knew he would struggle to stay on his feet without football boots. On the other side of the pitch Wellington Park and Cladham staff were laughing, rooted to the touchline and shouting occasional abuse at friends and colleagues. Roland calculated he could avoid the worst of this (especially from Jas and Terry) by sticking exclusively to one side of the pitch... at least for the first half.

Wellington Park's captain, Chopper Chaney, trotted over, his big leather boots squelching in the mud. He was a well-known bruiser, a reputation he had earned on the wards and off the pitch.

'Thanks for stepping in,' he said, his baby-faced cheeks burning red from the cold.

'No problem,' said Roland, responding by jogging up and down, his white collared shirt billowing in the wind.

Chopper Chaney looked down at Roland's feet.

'Are you sure you can play in those shoes?'

'Yeah,' said Roland, 'I'll just have to stick to the grass.'

Chopper Chaney paused, still pondering the wisdom of his decision.

'Okay...' he said, deciding he'd rather have eleven players. 'Play on the wing, but make sure you get plenty of crosses in.'

Roland nodded, as Chopper Chaney headed back towards the centre circle.

TERRY: Well, Jas, I think it's time for kick off, as Chopper Chaney greets Cladham's captain to begin this much-anticipated Prize-Bomka Cup Final.

JAS: Yes, Terry, it's great being here today, although there's only so long my bollocks can stand this cold.

TERRY: Yes, Jas, you might be right there, but let's hope the game can keep us warm inside. So, Jas, do you have a prediction for the result today?

JAS: Well, Terry, these games are always difficult to predict, but I would expect utter humiliation for Wellington Park.

(Laughter.)

Chopper Chaney kicked off and booted the ball as hard as he could towards the Cladham goal. Everyone on the touchline cheered as it sailed high over the crossbar.

TERRY: If I'm not mistaken, that's three points for a conversion.

JAS: Yes, Terry, but this is football, so I think that's called a goal kick.

TERRY: Quite right, Jas. I think we can see where Chopper Chaney might have gone wrong.

Just as Roland had feared, with Chopper Chaney there was only one player for Wellington Park who was going to touch the ball today. It was why Roland gave up playing football: there was always some dickhead who was crap at it, shouted his mouth off and played in central defence.

'Come on, lads... get stuck in!' screamed Chopper Chaney, as he ran back to his defensive line.

As soon as the ball was booted forward, Cladham's No. 9 trapped the sphere, turned effortlessly, jumped the first tackle and sped on down the wing. Roland tracked him on the other side of the pitch, but by the time he had got to his own penalty area the ball sped through the goalposts, bypassing their goalkeeper, on and on, all the way to the hedge at the bottom of the playing field.

'Shit! Did you see that?'

Roland shrugged. He was now more concerned about his own fitness. He felt his chest tighten. He would have to pace himself if he was going to survive the full ninety minutes. The Cladham players congratulated their star player and everyone along the touchline clapped in appreciation, but the Wellington Park players stood around looking resigned to their fate as they waited for the ball to be retrieved.

TERRY: Well, Jas, after a goal like that I think we can safely say the rumours about Cladham's No. 9 must be true.

JAS: Yes, I think Wellington Park have an uphill struggle. In fact, I wouldn't like to be in their shoes.

TERRY: Well, there's only one player who is wearing shoes and I wouldn't want to be in those shoes either.

(Laughter.)

The demoralised faces of the Wellington Park players galvanised Chopper Chaney. He was having none of it!

'Come on, lads! Let's get into the game!'

He then purposefully whispered in the ears of a few players. It was clear where Cladham's threat came from, and it needed to be sorted.

Chopper Chaney stood back in defence and Wellington Park kicked off with a little more finesse to their play. A couple of passes and Roland was running down the wing. He was in a good position to receive the ball and held his hand up as both teams piled into an intense midfield. The ball pinged around, tackles flew, before a desperate kick saw the ball trickle towards Cladham's goalkeeper. The cajoling Chopper Chaney offered direction.

'That's it, lads, force them back!' he shouted, gesturing with his arms as if guiding in an aeroplane. 'Hold the line here.'

The Cladham goalkeeper booted the ball forward and a few players let it bounce before attempting to trap it in the sludge. Cladham's No. 9 stood away from the mêlée until it dropped kindly at his feet. With another skilful turn, he sped towards Wellington Park's goal and directly at Chopper Chaney. This was Chopper Chaney's chance to take him out. He lunged with a flying boot, spun ungracefully, stuck out his hand to grab his shirt and ended up on his backside. The ball accelerated towards Wellington Park's goal, flew by the hapless goalkeeper and drifted onwards to nestle again on the edge of the playing field.

TERRY: Well, Jas, I think we can safely say Chopper Chaney will have his work cut out this afternoon.

JAS: Yes, Cladham's No. 9 certainly is a flyer, or is that a ringer? Certainly a notch above the rest and capable of scoring at a rate of one goal per minute.

TERRY: Well, with forty-five minutes each half I'd estimate Cladham – or their No. 9 – could score ninety.

JAS: You could be right there, Terry, but it does take a long time to get the ball back.

(Laughter.)

Chopper Chaney showed no sign of submission. The football gods would turn in his favour through sheer will and determination. As they waited for the ball to be retrieved, he looked over at Roland and clapped his hands.

'Come on, lads, let's get into the game!'

Roland despaired; the man was riddled with footballing clichés.

As the game progressed, Roland ran up and down the pitch a few times and was acutely aware he was unfit for playing. If Chopper Chaney expected him to do anything they needed to pass the ball to him before he got exhausted.

TERRY: So, Jas, have you any advice on how to contain Cladham's super deluxe No. 9?

JAS: Thanks, Terry. Yes, I'm glad you've asked me that... I would suggest a good kicking.

TERRY: I think you're right, but they have to catch him first.

JAS: Yes, Terry, that won't be easy.

TERRY: But what about Wellington Park's Roland Cauldron? We've yet to see him play any part in the game.

JAS: Well, Terry, you're right there.

TERRY: However, he has been effective at running decisively on the wing. In fact, I am particularly impressed he hasn't asked for resuscitation. There's a resilience there I never thought the young Cauldron possessed. But I'd agree with you, Jas, we do want to see him with the ball.

JAS: Oh, yes, Terry, I think we'd all like to see him with the ball.

(Laughter.)

Roland jumped up and down on the halfway line, ready for another kick off. As he looked at the bedraggled Wellington Park team Chopper Chaney pointed at him, tactically directing Roland towards the centre of Cladham's goal. Roland nodded, acknowledging the responsibility, and prepared to move into the mud when required.

The whistle blew and all the players converged towards the centre, but the fierce competition led to a Cladham counter-attack. This time the ball was kept out and Chopper Chaney screamed at their goalkeeper.

'Kick it!'

The ball flew over the top of Cladham's last defender and stuck in the muddy glue. This was Roland's chance.

He ran forward, with a head start on the Cladham's defender. Roland could make a name for himself if he could just get to it in time. His feet began to slip as his shoes slid in the sludge, but he was still on target to get to the ball first. He focused, striving for the elusive sphere, but it felt like running up an escalator. There were screams from the crowd as Roland decided the best option was to kick it straight at the goal rather than move the ball forward. He drew his leg back, sure he could strike it into the top corner. The screams got louder. *Sweet*, thought Roland, *I've got this one*.

Crunch!

'Fuck!'

Roland flew through the air, his legs removed from underneath him and his body crashing into a muddy puddle. The crowd laughed and groaned at the same time. Roland spat out the mud. The ball was booted back out by the goalkeeper as the Cladham defender turned and looked at him.

'For fuck's sake!' pleaded Roland, still on the ground.

'What?' said the innocent-looking fouler.

'You could've broken my leg.'

'Play to the whistle,' he said nonchalantly.

'What whistle? There's no referee!'

'Heh, Kes, come on!' shouted a teammate.

TERRY: Well, we've had a chance now to compare two new players today, with Cauldron perhaps failing to live up to the crowd's expectations.

JAS: Oh, I don't know that, Terry… that's a bit harsh. After all, he only had an open goal and it's difficult playing in these conditions in your Sunday best.

TERRY: That's right, Jas, but I am sure his mum would be proud of him.

Roland trotted along, the pain in his left leg forcing him to limp off the pitch. He pulled up his trouser leg and inspected his knee. There was a large gash where the stud had successfully impeded Roland's potential glory. There was also blood, blood mixed in with mud.

TERRY: Oh dear, this could be bad news for Wellington Park. Although, I suppose it depends on your perspective. I must say, it doesn't look like anyone is particularly concerned by Cauldron's absence from the pitch.

Roland looked over at Terry and Jas, laughing like crazed, stoned, Pothead Pixies. He then looked along the line at all the other staff laughing. Fuck it! He had made a right prick of himself. Well, some fucking cheating bastard had made him look a right prick! But then he noticed someone else, someone who he had not seen for ages, who he had essentially forgotten. It was Annie Buchanan, a pale, shadowy figure, standing slightly separate and peering over from the touchline. Fuck, what was she doing here? He supposed it was alright... it was bound to be alright, as everyone knew about her predicament. He did not want to look too long, and he did not want her to see he was looking. But it was too late. She stared intently and smiled in recognition. What else could he do but smile back?

He felt the gash in his knee seeping blood and stretched it backwards and forwards, testing the flexibility. *That was dirty*, thought Roland, *he should have had a penalty*.

There was a brief cheer as another goal went Cladham's way. Wellington Park lined up for another kick off. Roland did his best to trot back into the action. Chopper Chaney asked if he was okay and Roland nodded.

By now, there was a definite air of despondency among the Wellington Park players. They knew they were going to get slaughtered. Chopper Chaney's optimism had all but evaporated. Roland could hardly move, but he wanted to play on, he wanted to prove he was not there to make up the numbers.

However, goal after goal went Cladham's way and Roland became even more peripheral to the game. A thin drizzle of rain began to soak into the players and a chill wind was stinging their skin. Roland's thoughts drifted back to all those vile days of playing through inhospitable conditions, satisfying the sadism of PE teachers.

TERRY: Well, Jas, at half-time with the score at sixteen-nil, it would be a miracle if Wellington Park gets back into the game.

'Fuck it,' said Jas, disengaging from the mock commentary, 'it's pissing down with rain and my nuts are frozen.'

'You're right,' said Terry.

'Bucket-bong?'

'Sounds good to me!'

Both teams left the pitch to suck on half-cut oranges provided on a sodden plastic tray. Roland stood around in a huddle with the Wellington Park players. It was not their year. A gallows humour gripped them all as they began to joke about the possible scoreline. This was anathema to Chopper Chaney, who insisted they strive to score at least one goal. But everyone complained there was little they could do against the ex-Portuguese semi-professional. Also, Roland chipped in, he should've definitely had a penalty when he was in on goal.

'You should've stayed on your feet,' replied Chopper Chaney, identifying the scapegoat.

'How could I? He hacked me down!' said Roland, hoping his teammates would back him up.

There was a shivering silence.

'Let's have a look at your leg,' said Chopper Chaney.

Roland rolled up his trouser leg and a few players winced.

'Nasty.'

'You need to get that cleaned up.'

'Early bath for you, mate.'

It meant failure for Roland, but he was happy to opt out if they didn't want him to play. *Fine*, he thought, *suits me – the same old crap… one big-head telling everyone else what to do.*

The rain intensified as he hobbled along, feeling the stinging pain of his open wound. And fortunately, Annie Buchanan had gone.

★

Roland sat in Sophie's room, his bloodied leg resting on the bed. He needed to forget about the match and catch up on some studying for once. He had his first assessment on the wards soon, probably on the worst ward possible: the "death ward", as everyone called it.

He picked up the drugs book and opened it at the section for psychotropics. He hated it, memorising commercial names, relating them to generic names, learning dosages, underlining side effects. It was a totally fucking mindless chore. He managed ten minutes and then decided he needed a coffee.

The kettle roared into action. Above the steaming noise he heard a knock on the door.

'Who is it?' he asked cautiously.

The only response was another, louder, distinctive knock.

'Okay, hang on,' he said, as he hobbled over and opened it.

Shit! Annie Buchanan smiled from underneath her dyed purple hair. Fuck, thought Roland, she looked just like a patient.

'Hi…' she said, blushing, as she looked behind Roland to peer in. 'So, this is where you live. I asked someone in the corridor and they said you'd be in sixty-six, and then you weren't in so I saw someone else and they said you'd be here.'

'Annie,' said Roland, 'you know you can't come here.'

'Why?'

'This is the nurses' hostel,' he said, looking up and down the corridor. 'You know patients are not allowed in.'

'But I was bored, there's nothing for me to do on the ward. You said I could come and talk to you any time.'

'Yeah, but that was ages ago and not like this,' he said. 'I can't be seen having patients round… you know that I'd get into serious trouble.'

'Oh,' said Annie, 'I didn't mean to be any trouble.'

'You're not,' he said, trying to sound sympathetic, 'but it's just the way things are… you know that.'

'I'll go then,' she said, her eyes full of disappointment.

'Heh…' said Roland, thinking how best he could

146

appease her. 'It's just that I've got to be careful. I mean, I know what's happened to you is bad, but I have to be cautious, now that I am trying to change things through the student council.'

'But nobody's telling you you're mad,' she said resentfully.

'Who says you're mad?'

'Everyone.'

She was right: everyone now said she was mad and she had a proper diagnosis: manic depression.

'Look, Annie,' said Roland, 'I don't think you're mad. I'm not sure what's gone on. You seem normal to me, but I can't change things for you. I wish I could, but I've got no influence over your case.'

'But if you're fighting to change things here, why can't you help me?'

'Your situation is different... yours is clinical. I'm just fighting to improve things on the wards for students.'

Annie stepped back a few paces into the middle of the corridor and stared grimly at Roland.

'Why am I still here?' she asked.

'Well, you're under section, aren't you? Whether that's right or wrong I don't know. But trust me, I don't think there's anything seriously wrong with you. Perhaps it's just a matter of time. I mean, you must be improving if they let you go out today.'

Annie quietly shook her head.

It was not working, Roland thought – he was failing... failing to help.

'You do believe me, don't you?' he said unconvincingly.

147

'They're going to renew my section,' said Annie. 'I know they will, and then I will really go mad. They will leave me with no choice. They're not going to help me... they're just going to make me feel worse.'

Roland was powerless.

'I wish I could do something... I'm sorry,' he said, desperate for Annie to leave in case she was seen by another resident.

'I'll go then,' she said, her body curving in on itself.

Roland would have liked to have said no, he was wrong, he would challenge everything... but this was just a step too far.

'Yes, I'm sorry, but I think it's best,' he said, beginning to close the door.

A few tears trickled slowly into the semicircle of her eye sockets. He wanted to say sorry again, but she turned and walked briskly down the corridor.

Fuck, that was terrible, but what could he do? He was way out of his depth. Maybe there was an injustice, but it would complicate things too much if he got involved in something like that. Hopefully, no one would say anything about her coming into the nurses' hostel. He'd just have to keep quiet about it and say nothing to Sophie.

CHAPTER 15

NAZIS CAN'T DANCE

Jas stood in front of Roland and Sophie in full Nazi regalia, the brown-shirted kind with a long black tie, puffed-out baggy trousers and knee-length black leather boots. The only thing missing was a swastika.

'What do you think?' said Jas, twirling around like a debutante in the middle of his room.

'That's disgusting,' said Sophie.

Jas laughed at the success of his desired effect.

'It's pretty outrageous,' said Roland, offended and impressed.

'You're not really going to wear that?' asked Sophie despairingly.

'Why not?' replied Jas, genuinely perplexed.

'Do you want me to tell you why you should not dress up as a Nazi to the student and staff nurses' Christmas and New Year's party?'

Jas laughed again, looking in the mirror, proud as a peacock.

'Do you think people won't get it, then?' he asked, bending his knees as he checked out his profile.

'What is there to get?' asked Sophie.

Jas looked thoughtfully at his reflection. He got it, if nobody else did.

'Perhaps he is a Nazi,' said Roland.

'Don't encourage him,' she said. 'Anyway, I'm not going with him dressed like that.'

Jas twirled around on his black heeled boots, jigged a little riff and froze his body in classic "jazz hands".

'It's the police,' said Terry as he entered.

Jas clicked his heels and stood to attention.

'Oh, fuck!' he said, as he sat next to Sophie on the bed. 'Please tell me you're not going dressed like that?'

'He is,' said Roland.

'Okay, cool,' said Terry, who knew there was no point in trying to persuade Jas of the inappropriateness. 'Can you do the voice – you know… with the accent?'

'It's not about the voice,' said Jas.

'What is it about, then?' asked Terry. 'Or is that a stupid question?'

'He wants to be the centre of attention,' said Sophie, resigned to what lay ahead.

'Oh, you'll definitely be that,' said Terry.

'Don't worry,' said Jas, 'I'm going to wear a coat.'

'That's alright then,' said Terry sardonically.

'You know,' said Roland, in a concession to Sophie's disapproval, 'we should be trying to keep a low profile.'

'You mean you should,' said Terry pointedly.

'Why should I have to keep a low profile?'

'You mean you don't know?'

'No, I don't!'

'We all should,' asserted Sophie.

'Well, I don't think I'll be associating with any of you lot, then,' said Terry. 'Is anyone going to skin up before we go?'

'I will,' said Jas.

'Make it strong,' said Terry. 'I'll also have some of the other.'

'What's that?' asked Jas, unable to disguise his guilt.

'The diazepam,' stated Terry.

Jas laughed, far too wasted to mount any denial.

'Where did you get that from?' asked Sophie.

'Off the ward,' said Terry, telling on the younger sibling.

'And how do you know?' asked Sophie, in full investigative flow.

'Because it's missing,' advised Terry.

'Are you crazy?' she said.

Jas raised his heavy head.

'You know,' he said, 'it really does space you out.'

★

They all strolled falteringly towards the social club, meandering along the tarmac path which led out of the hospital grounds, in a state of mind which suggested the last – very last – joint was super-strength.

'What did you put in it?' asked Terry, in an attempt to seek reassurance.

'Don't blame me,' said Jas, wrapped up inside his coat, beginning to feel slightly equivocal about his fancy dress. 'You told me to load it, so I did.'

'Well, I think we should all separate once we're in there,' said Terry. 'That way, we won't look like four stoned pixies.'

'Whatever you do,' said Sophie to Jas, 'don't take that coat off.'

'He'll blend in,' said Terry. 'Most of them are fascists anyway.'

'You know,' said Jas, 'that diazepam makes you feel really weird. I think I'm here, but I'm not sure if I am.'

'Spoken like a true metaphysician,' said Terry.

'What's that?' asked Roland, concentrating on how he was going to cope at the party.

'Hand signals,' said Terry, on a separate, but what he thought was a related train of thought.

'What?'

'We should use hand signals to communicate.'

'You mean like semaphore?'

'Yeah,' said Terry, warming to the subject and turning to Jas. 'Can you spell out "not waving but drowning"?'

Jas stared ahead into the pale neon light.

'I think he's gone catatonic,' said Roland.

'No surprise there,' said Terry.

'You're going to have to look after him,' said Sophie to Terry.

'Why me?' protested Terry. 'What have I done?'

'You encouraged him.'

'What, to take drugs? I don't think so… he needed no encouragement from me.'

Roland, Sophie and Terry retreated slightly behind Jas and resorted to an infantile giggle. It was, after all, too late.

★

The main hall of the social club pumped out a high-tempo Christmas song. Sophie and Terry plunged for the dance floor, drawn to the shiny globe hung from a rafter, sparkling excitedly in the randomly decorated hall. Jas sought the refuge of a soft foam chair, burying his head in his coat. Roland watched briefly as Sophie and Terry gyrated in semi-coordinated symmetry, then took the risk that he could bluff his way through any challenge to his state of mind and headed for the bar.

As drinking voices flowed and ebbed in a socialised wave, Roland cocooned himself in the warm glow of being stoned. He had no intention of speaking to anyone unless they spoke to him. A procession of people bought drinks whilst Roland tried to project an air of self-containment and aloofness. More and more people crammed into the bar to get served, which caused Roland to be pushed further along towards one end and eventually into the orbit of Douglas. Roland knew he only ventured into the habitat of the lower echelons because the social club was his hunting ground and meeting place for scheduled assignations. Roland also suspected that socialising helped him maintain respect among the nursing staff and to keep a foothold in both camps.

Roland sensed Douglas glance occasionally in his direction. He felt the seconds tick slowly by and self-consciously checked to see if Douglas wanted to say anything. Then, as they were almost leaning against each other, Douglas stared intently into Roland's eyes.

He knows, thought Roland, *he knows I am off my fucking head*.

'Glad you've finished the ward?' asked Douglas, looking deeply into Roland's glazed eyes.

Roland nodded. He wanted to speak, but he could not... not yet.

'Have you seen our Mr Franks at all?' asked Douglas, before turning his back to finish his pint and ask for another.

Speak, speak, said Roland to himself, *I must speak*. And then the words came...

'No,' said Roland, released from his constricting noose.

'He was a warning,' said Douglas, as he waited for his drink. 'Now one of 'em's gone and done it!'

'The real suicide, you mean?'

Douglas nodded, as he lifted his pint and pocketed a packet of cheese and onion.

'They've done the investigation, haven't they?' said Roland, as the cacophony of music and voices forced him to lean into Douglas' ear.

Douglas remained expressionless and fiddled in his pockets.

They continued to stand side by side, looking out across the congested bar. Douglas smiled and acknowledged a few people who looked his way.

'Well,' said Roland, pausing to make sure he had his sentence constructed, 'at least they might do something about it this time.'

Douglas remained distant, listening.

'I mean,' said Roland, struggling, 'as you say, they had a warning.'

Douglas offered a pained expression and a jaded laugh.

'How's your campaign going?'

'What campaign?' replied Roland, who intended to keep quiet about the petition.

'To change the way things are done around here, you and your girlfriend.'

'What do you mean?'

'I don't know... you tell me.'

'I haven't got anything to tell,' said Roland warily.

'What's the point of you being on the student council then? You got elected, didn't you? You've got a way in there, to put across your views, to try and shake things up.'

'Well, we will,' said Roland, feeling slightly indignant, 'when we meet with Gobi.'

Douglas burst into cynical laughter.

'You'll be waiting a long time, then.'

'Why? Gobi's got to hold the student council...'

Douglas looked away, demonstrating his scepticism.

'I am not going to tell you what to do,' he said, facing Roland again. 'You're intelligent enough to work that one out for yourself... but you'll need to decide.'

Decide, wondered Roland, what did he need to decide?

'And,' continued Douglas, 'whatever you may think of what goes on here, it's not all bad. Believe me, there are worse places than this. It's getting nasty out there in the real world. For a lot of people in here – and I don't mean just the patients – it's a safe place to be.'

'I know that, but we will do things,' said Roland, wondering if he was being encouraged or discouraged.

'You're the kind of person who will always end up doing something,' said Douglas. 'That's in your nature… you can't help yourself. But when you do, just remember, not everybody is rotten, even the ones who you think are the most obvious targets.'

Douglas remained inscrutable for a few moments, before offering a conciliatory arm around Roland's shoulder. He then pulled him closer and hugged him tightly, in an incongruous brotherly hug.

'You've really rattled their cage,' he said, pulling Roland even closer into his chest. 'Someone had to do it. Good on you!'

Had he? How the fuck had he done that?

Douglas let go and leaned back on the bar and took a large gulp of his pint.

'Just remember,' he said, 'they're capable of anything in this place.'

Roland paused, suspicious of Douglas' candour.

'Why… what do you think will happen?'

'Look, have you heard about McEmery?'

Everybody knew about McEmery. Not bloody McEmery again!

'Yes,' said Roland fatalistically.

'He was just like you, a real bolshie character,' said Douglas, smiling. 'He used to get right up Fitzpatrick's nose.'

'I know,' said Roland, eager to cut short a repetition of McEmery's downfall.

'Just remember, there're ways they can get you… and you lot are taking far too many risks.'

Ah, so that is the point of this conversation, thought Roland.

'I can't tell you how to live your life, but people notice things. They know everything that goes on in that nurses' hostel and you lot are always top of the agenda.'

Fuck! That must mean only one thing: the Pothead Pixies.

Two hands moved up over Douglas' neck, and lips appeared and pecked him on the cheek. The kissing lips looked at Roland, identifying him as an imposition which had lasted long enough. The lips became a body, sliding in between the tight fit the two had established at the bar. She apologised profusely, hoped Roland did not think her rude and then politely turned her back on him.

Fine, he was only too happy to escape.

He desperately wanted to grab hold of Sophie, Terry or Jas, and warn them, warn them all. *Top-top information, from a top-top source: they are coming for us, one way or another, they are coming for us… they are going to bring us down, flush us out, expel us, ruin our careers, drive us out because we do not conform. Oh yes, it is coming, the full force of reaction… the intolerant beast has awakened and we are going to be beaten down, beaten into the ground, just because we like a smoke!*

Roland squeezed through the drunken, celebrating bodies and into the hall. In the darkness, a circular, rotating body bopped and weaved, hands moving up into the spinning, turning colours beamed from the DJ's console. Sophie beckoned him to take the dance floor, but he only wanted to reveal what Douglas had told him, sit everyone down and get the pixies to realise how they needed to stop and calm things down… immediately!

But as he waited, he began to cast doubt over his thinking. Perhaps he was just being paranoid? Perhaps Douglas was only playing a joke, because he knew, because he could see, because he could tell that Roland was stoned? So, perhaps Douglas was just playing with him?

Yes, that could be it… that could be another way to look at it. Things were not doomed. Things might not be so bad. Who could tell? How could he tell, based on one bit of information, from a dubious source, a mischievous, patronising source? Anyway, why was Douglas trying to tell him how to change things? After all, Douglas didn't give a flying fuck about anyone or anything! All he cared about was going around shagging nurses.

Suddenly, Sophie pulled Roland into the dancing throng. This was awkward. He just really, really hated dancing. He looked around and found the perfect excuse by pointing at the abandoned figure of Jas.

'I'll check him out!' shouted Roland into Sophie's ear.

'Don't let him take off his coat!'

'What?'

'His coat!' she shouted, pointing at her own body.

'What?'

'Don't let him dance!'

'Oh yeah, don't worry, he's out of it!'

'And don't wake him!'

'No, no, I won't.'

Roland slipped passed a few flailing arms, pleased he had absolved himself of any gyration. He sat down next to Jas, the low, comfy chairs still cradling the sleeping space cadet.

Jas stirred, coming round from a deep, deep sleep.

'I've been told not to let you dance and expose yourself,' said Roland.

'Fuck! You're kidding. Whoa... I tell yer... I have been to some strange places.'

'You've been out of it,' said Roland.

'Fucking hell! That's my song! *Dancing Queen!*'

Jas looked across the dance floor. Perhaps it was not too late.

In one movement he propelled himself forward, wobbled unsteadily as he achieved the few steps required to arrange himself in the middle of the dancing throng. A great cheer went up as Jas contorted his arms and legs, spun himself round and twirled his arms in a giant windmill.

Roland followed to the edge of the circle as clapping started for the resurgent Jas. He could only laugh, as the display built on ever-increasing heights of innovation and originality. Then Roland looked for Sophie and her eyes communicated a desperate unease.

'He's alive then!' shouted Terry into Roland's ear.

Roland shrugged his shoulders.

'Oh fuck, here we go!'

Jas swung his hips and skilfully undid his buttons to his coat. A few cries of 'Take it off... take it off... take it off' encouraged Jas to initiate a form of striptease. The song was still playing but Jas had reached his moment. Spreading his arms wide open and posing cabaret style, he ripped open his coat to reveal his fancy dress.

'Oh well, at least we've learnt something tonight,' said Terry.

'What's that?' asked Roland regretfully.

'Nazis can't dance.'

CHAPTER 16

RING-A-RING O' ROSE WARD

The "death ward", formally known as Rose Ward, accommodated the dying who had gravitated from the "back wards" to their final days in a mixture of morphine and minimal fluid. The ward also had beds for an eclectic mix of patients with long-term mental and physical conditions, while a few side rooms were allocated for Fitzpatrick's favourite therapeutic intervention: electroconvulsive therapy or ECT. Roland had been warned by Gobi to watch himself there, because 'Maybe, you know, you might find things not strictly by the book… and people are talking about you as causing trouble.' Whilst there was an attraction to being the resident dissenter, thought Roland, it was also grossly exaggerated.

However, Roland and Sophie were mobilising, getting signatures for their petition to be presented at the reconstituted student council. But Roland's preference for just talking and getting stoned with the Pothead Pixies was creating an unwelcome tension in his relationship with Sophie. Yes, he was all about trying to change things; it was not that he did not want to do something (of course he did!), he just didn't believe in all the committee-type formal crap! Roland kept repeating his own favourite mantra: things had to change, suddenly, rapidly, everyone together. It was alright for Sophie because she did not have the reputation Roland did – not that he was paranoid, but it felt like he was being targeted when so far he had done nothing wrong… apart from the "Franks thing".

All this was swimming around in Roland's head as he rang the bell to Rose Ward. He listened to the telltale cries of anguished souls penetrating through the door, the moaning, groaning, high-pitched wails of patients. The noise was temporarily stopped by the punctuated order of a nurse shouting, 'Shut up!'

Here we go again, thought Roland.

A female nursing assistant opened the door and looked him up and down.

'I'm the new student.'

'Oh yes, we knew you were coming,' she said, before turning to head back down the corridor.

Roland obediently followed.

'We're just doing the washes…'

'Right,' said Roland, wondering if he would have to get started straight away.

She pulled out a bundle of keys on a thick, heavy chain and slotted a key into the lock of the ward office.

'You can wait in here,' she said, as she pushed open the door before returning to the audible mayhem.

Roland looked around and hated everything about it: the nauseating smell, the frayed A4 box files on the shelves, the metallic care plan folder, the plastic specimen bottles, used and unused sanitary gloves, stacks of randomly selected medical packs and a leather-bound transistor radio. He could still hear the distressed patients reasserting their anguished sighs, probably being pushed through some meaningless routine in order to sustain life without purpose. Did anyone ever stop to question the absurdity of it all, thought Roland, did no one ever stop to ask themselves: *What exactly am I doing – am I actually making things better or am I making things worse? What is the point of prolonging and contributing to more agony and despair?* And the worst thing (the worst thing of all): he was part of it, he was part of the whole ridiculous institution which, day after day, blind, without thinking, went through the mechanics of keeping everyone just alive, just barely conscious, ticking over like some lethargic slug. Nothing was ever cured. Nothing ever changed. The plodding, inane absurdity of it all, the status quo, went marching on.

Roland shut his eyes. He needed to escape. He needed to run.

'Make yourself a coffee,' said Douglas, as he poked his head round the door. 'I'll be with you in a minute.'

So Roland looked, but there was nothing to make coffee with and he was reluctant to start wandering around the ward looking for the kitchen. Instead, he counted: one minute gone, two minutes gone, three minutes gone. He was feeling sick at the thought that it was all going to start up again: the drudgery of hauling human flesh, wiping bums, in one end and out the other... and pausing, just for a moment, before starting

162

the whole process all over again. *The patients are just like tin cans on a conveyor belt*, thought Roland, *but due to oversupply we leave them to rot in the back of a warehouse.*

Douglas returned with a mug of coffee and sat down on a well-worn office chair.

'Right,' he said, turning to face Roland, 'why were you late this morning?'

'I'm not late!' said Roland, surprised by Douglas' aggressive formality, whilst confident that for once he was on time.

'The shift starts at seven and you arrived at nine,' said Douglas, maintaining a disciplinary tone.

'That's because I was told to come at nine,' said Roland indignantly.

'Who told you that?'

'I don't know,' said Roland. 'I phoned the ward over the weekend and they said come at nine.'

Douglas paused.

'Okay, I'll accept your word on that,' he said unapologetically.

Fuck me, thought Roland, *it has already bloody started!*

Douglas picked up his coffee and took a long sip.

'I'm going to warn you now,' he said, as he put his mug back down, 'this is a heavy ward to work on. You may find things here not by the book, but it's up to you as to how you want to play it… but my advice is not to stir things up.'

Roland's mind was racing. Was this fair, legitimate? Could Douglas get away with talking to him like that?

'I know you like to catch people out,' said Douglas, anticipating Roland's response. 'I suggest you watch, listen and learn, instead of trying to look for all the negatives. People are not all bad, you know.'

Roland was speechless. He knew he should say something, fight back and tell Douglas where he could stick his little bit of advice. But what was the point? The message was clear.

'Think about what I've said before you go running off to the school and start complaining,' said Douglas. 'You're on my ward now and you play by my rules. Okay, that's the end of the lesson. Have you got any assessments to do on the ward?'

'Yes, drugs,' said Roland, resenting his own compliance.

'That shouldn't be a problem for you, then,' Douglas said jovially. 'Come on, I'll show you around the ward.'

Douglas picked up his coffee and Roland followed.

'We do ECT on this ward every Monday morning. Do you have a problem with that?'

Roland shrugged.

'Mr Fitzpatrick manages that. You can sit in today and observe. I think your girlfriend's escorting the patient round this morning.'

'Who, Sophie?'

'If she's still your girlfriend?' asked Douglas, mischievously, winking as he led Roland into the day room.

'Yes,' said Roland, wondering why there was any need to question.

'Here we are then,' said Douglas, presenting the worst of the worst, the patients beyond redemption.

It was just as Roland feared, just as he had heard. In

the central circle of mumbling dementia, a pale, shorn-haired torso, all skin and bone, rocked and swayed in an adult-size highchair. Roland was transfixed by the twisting, gawping woman, dressed only in a green T-shirt and baggy checked shorts, wriggling in a criss-cross system of leather belts. He looked at her face, into her eyes. What madness (or perhaps sanity) had driven her to achieve such a state?

'She's a bit of a tragic story,' said Douglas, as she continued to rock back and forth, grunting at their presence. 'She managed to escape and head straight for the railway line. She threw herself under a train and got mangled. They saved her, minus her peripheries of course. She didn't stop there, though. God knows how she did it, but she later swallowed enough acid to remove most of her stomach and tongue. Anyway, because she can still bite, it was agreed to use restraints on what is left of her.'

If the shocking figure of the limbless woman was not enough for Roland to contemplate how hideous life could be, Douglas provided a short and introductory precis of another case: a petite, fragile form, curled up in a ball in a chair, who offered up a pained, anguished cry which Roland recognised as the voice which greeted his arrival.

'This one has an infected vagina,' said Douglas, 'due to the obsessive insertion of various unsuitable objects.'

Great, thought Roland, as he surveyed it all: the full scope of sadness, a manifestation of purgatory, all rolled into a putrefying mass, a rotting, hopeless corpse. He had been crazy to think he could ever make a difference to these poor, helpless creatures. He knew nothing about their terror, what had driven them to the ends of absurdity. And he was a useless cog in a useless machine, which churned around the bile of human suffering. He was no better than anyone else and he had nothing more to give than what the institution prescribed.

'Just keep an eye on them,' said Douglas. 'I've got a few things to finish off in the washroom. Shout if you need me.'

Douglas disappeared down the corridor towards the dormitory.

Roland was left on his own and wished he had a coffee now, something to do with his hands, something to be preoccupied with, because he could not keep his eyes off the limbless woman. Roland was morbidly fascinated by the notion that she had been destroying her physical being; the consequences of her suicidal drive had left her as a living yet powerless head and torso, with little or no chance of completing her journey, a captive of the institution. She could do nothing for herself whilst they carried on her meaningless life and she was the perfect patient for Wellington Park: a powerless, everlasting patient.

*

Sophie rang the bell whilst waiting with Mrs Sandy, who was dressed in a fluffy white nightgown with a thin nightie underneath. She was attractive for her age, thought Sophie, as she ran her fingers through the front of Mrs Sandy's hair, but her illness (and the debilitating effects of her "therapy") had reduced her to a hunched and huddled shadow.

The ward door was pulled back on its heavy hinges.

'Hello, Student Nurse Smith, I presume?'

'You…' said Sophie, surprised to see Roland. 'What are you doing here?'

'Eh… I'm training,' said Roland, less than impressed with Sophie's greeting.

'Is this your new placement?'

'Yes,' said Roland, even more annoyed because he had told her quite a few times.

'Mrs Sandy's for ECT this morning,' she said, in formal nurse mode.

'Right, Douglas did mention it.'

'Oh…'

'I don't know where you go or anything,' said Roland apologetically.

'Typical…' said Sophie, as she let go of the quivering Mrs Sandy. 'Just take her round to the dormitory.'

Roland took the docile arm of Mrs Sandy.

'Is Fitzpatrick here yet?' Sophie asked, as she turned to leave.

'Yes,' said Roland, pleased he had managed to avoid the tyrant.

This time Sophie frowned.

'Okay, I'll see you later.'

'Yeah…'

Roland watched Sophie wander back down the corridor of humming ductwork. She was pissed off with him, that was for sure. *And I bet*, said Roland to himself, *it is all about that bloody petition*. Fuck, what was he supposed to do? He said he would do it, he said he would get all his intake to sign it.

Roland led Mrs Sandy through the day room and along the corridor. On one side was a vast expanse of window, patterned with condensation from the winter cold and heat pumping from the radiators. Halfway down there was a large open washroom, perfectly clean from the morning washes, and as he got closer to the bottom of the dormitory he could see Douglas talking to Fitzpatrick, preparing (no doubt) the hideous instruments of therapeutic intervention.

'Not just yet,' instructed Douglas. 'You can sit with her in one of the rooms.'

Douglas then levered open a large green metal door.

'We used to use them,' he said, 'for solitary confinement.'

Roland had no choice but to walk Mrs Sandy into the cell, sitting with her on a wooden bench. There was a small, round window above them, and thin black twigs slapping against the porthole due to a rumbling wind. As they waited in the green-painted interior, it reminded Roland of the police cell he had once sat in before being interviewed for his pot-smoking misdemeanour.

'The devils,' whispered Mrs Sandy, holding Roland's hand.

Yes, thought Roland, *the real and the imagined*.

'Don't worry,' he said, 'there are no devils here.'

But Mrs Sandy was hallucinating: the devils were coming for her, the fat git goblins; the menacing, mendacious demons were banging on the window, trying to get in. Exhausted and fearful, Mrs Sandy flopped forwards and rested her body on her legs. Roland tried to lever her back up as Douglas came in.

'What's happened to her?' he asked distrustfully.

'Nothing,' said Roland, sitting her upright.

'Okay,' Douglas said, 'we're ready for her now… you can bring her in.'

As Roland helped Mrs Sandy stand up, he felt he was leading her to an execution. Perhaps he should be reading her the last rites, benignly supporting the judgement of the state for crimes as yet indeterminate.

They entered the dormitory and Fitzpatrick and Douglas clinically accepted their patient. Roland was ready to leave, partly in order to avoid the potential scrutiny of the domed-foreheaded Fitzpatrick, but it was impossible to escape once the white-coated anaesthetist invited him to observe, and Roland was now trapped between trainee participation and principled opposition.

In between various medical tasks, Roland received intermittent explanations on the apparatus, the tubing and ventilation. Roland pretended to sound interested, whilst debating in his own mind whether he should grab Mrs Sandy and run out of the ward to save her from the insanity about to occur. He also speculated on the possible ulterior motives of Fitzpatrick or Douglas. Why did they keep him here? Were they trying to prove to the new president of the student council that wards took their training responsibilities seriously? Or were they just trying to test Roland's resolve, as it was well known that most of the students were against ECT?

Fitzpatrick settled the agitated Mrs Sandy, whilst Douglas stood by Roland's side and continued to provide further commentary.

'There's very little apparatus required for ECT,' he explained, 'just some electrodes and a charging box.'

'Right,' said Roland.

Mrs Sandy was administered a general anaesthetic and soon drifted off with the devils she had come in with. Fitzpatrick took charge, wetting the cotton-coated electrodes, placing them around Mrs Sandy's head and flicking the switch to release the voltage. Mrs Sandy began to convulse with her first dosage; her frail body jolted into an epileptic seizure. It seemed ridiculous, thought Roland, as he watched Mrs Sandy's shuddering body. But they looked happy, Fitzpatrick and his ECT pals... they thought they did a good job. Did it matter if Mrs Sandy had a load more brain cells blasted into oblivion? The prevailing logic was, if it works then there's nothing wrong with it. And as far as everyone was concerned, ECT worked for the patient; it jolted them out of their stupor, whatever the unintended consequences.

★

Once Fitzpatrick was off the ward, the washes were started again, just before dinner. Douglas had told Roland to bring each patient into the washroom, walking or wheeling. He expected to be mucking in, but Douglas had said, 'No, no, just bring them to us for today... bring that one, yes, that one in front of you.' Roland pulled at the reluctant, terrified patients, woken from their slumber, levered into wheelchairs, pushed along the corridor and left outside the washroom.

With all six basins full of hot water, Douglas and his two nursing assistants set about undressing, wiping and cleaning the bottoms of the confused and distressed. The institutional underpants flew into the laundry bins, incontinence pads heavy with urine or runny faeces were piled in the middle, whilst words of encouragement punctuated the cries of the non-compliant: 'Come on, it's not that bad… yes… pull those pants down… you can do it… there's nothing wrong with you.' The shivering limbs and wrinkled flesh hung on to the rims of the basins, hung on to their Zimmer frames, wobbling on their barely muscled pins as large flannels whipped and wiped with experience and expediency.

There was no denying this was an accomplished operation. Perhaps this was the way to do it, thought Roland. Perhaps he had failed to understand the pressure and needs of patient care? Perhaps it could only be met through taking large short cuts through the manuals and policies of decency?

Then the cry went out for Amy. Who was Amy? Oh, she was the crumpled one with the infected vagina.

Roland again pulled and tugged to lever her from her chair.

'You'll need a wheelchair with that one. Also, you need to be quicker. We're almost finished in there.'

Should he not be gentle? Should he not care… just for a second?

He could not move her.

'She won't budge,' he said, rather feebly.

The nursing assistant grabbed the frail mouse and threw her into the wheelchair.

'She'll have you doing everything for her, that one.'

And off Amy went, into the bowels of the washroom. Then there was another cry, the same pained, anguished scream, which shot through the whole ward. Roland walked back to the washroom. He watched as Douglas, with his wet, hot cloth, came slashing down on to Amy's vagina. Hung up by her legs, like an animal ready for the slaughter, Douglas again brought down the flannel to rip into the infected wound.

This was pernicious and spiteful, abuse borne out of the treadmill of hard labour, the thankless task of dealing with all the bits of humanity no one gives a fuck about. How much more was Roland supposed to put up with before he did something about it? Enough was enough! He was president of the student council... he had a vehicle, ways and means to do something about it. They had the petition and it would soon be time to make their move.

CHAPTER 17

IF YOU GO DOWN TO THE WOODS TODAY

Jas knocked on Terry's door and dragged him out of his room. He had a new method of consumption which he needed to trial. He drew a diagram and they both eagerly set about assembling the apparatus. Once constructed, Jas hit the switch. The Hoover began pumping the amber nectar down the fibre of the loaded joint, into the plastic bag Terry had over his head. As the balloon filled, Terry was instructed to avoid breathing in until the bag was full of succulent smoke.

'Are you sure this won't kill me?' asked Terry, his voice muffled by the plastic.

'Only a few brain cells,' replied Jas.

He retracted the hose and closed the small hole in the plastic bag with his fingers. Terry began sucking down the smoke surrounding his head… down into his lungs. At first he was enthusiastic, but as the plastic bag began to sink around his face, he started tugging at the tape around his neck.

'Hang in there,' said Jas encouragingly.

'I can't, I'm dying!' squeaked Terry.

'But there's loads of smoke left,' said Jas, failing to comprehend the lack of air Terry now needed.

'Fuck this!' said Terry, ripping open the plastic bag, coughing and convulsing.

Jas laughed hysterically.

'Water…' said Terry, in between coughing fits.

'Water… oh yeah… no problem.'

As Terry drank, regaining his composure, Jas waited expectantly for the result.

'Intoxicating hell,' said Terry.

Jas was disappointed.

'If only Dr Jonas was here,' he said. 'That mad fucker would try anything.'

'Well, it's your turn now.'

'No way,' said Jas. 'Do you think I'm a fucking idiot?!'

'We need Roland.'

'I don't know,' said Jas. 'He's always shagging Sophie.'

'He'll be here,' said Terry. 'You can't keep a pixie away from the amber nectar.'

★

Roland had always agreed to respect Sophie's beliefs, specifically, respecting her veganism. He agreed not to consume dairy products, meat, fish and assorted other banned foodstuffs in her presence. Two or three times a week Sophie would cook one of her vegan specials of spaghetti, lentils, beans, sweetcorn, peppers, onions, cabbage, courgettes, carrots and curry powder. So, whilst Jas and Terry were absorbed in the Hoover experimentation, Roland hoovered slowly through his plate of vegetation and eventually retired to the communal toilets.

Sat in contemplation, he heard a harsh scream, followed by a cry of pain seeking help. He knew he should probably rush off the toilet, but he needed to concentrate on his task and was ambivalent about getting involved in a nurses' hostel melodrama. He waited. Then there was noise… things were happening in the corridor outside. Perhaps it was time to emerge?

He found Cranfield full of wide-eyed shock.

'What's happening?' asked Roland innocently.

'It's Dave,' said Cranfield, nodding in the direction of Dave's room.

Suddenly, at the bottom of the corridor, the fire exit door swung open and a green boiler-suited paramedic rushed towards them.

'Just wait out here,' said the paramedic, before diving into Dave's room with a large cylinder of oxygen.

'Fuck, that looks serious,' said Roland.

'It is,' replied Cranfield.

One or two doors began to open and a few residents congregated at a respectful distance.

Dave's door opened as the same paramedic shot off down the corridor and disappeared. This enabled Roland to just see into Dave's room through a crack between the hinge and the door frame. Only for a second, a brief glance, but he could see a bed coated with the thick veneer of blood. Then the door slammed shut.

'Fuck,' said Roland, looking again at Cranfield, whose eyes were still bulging.

Cranfield nodded, acknowledging the seriousness of the situation.

'You must have heard the screams,' he said. 'Why didn't you come out earlier? He could die, you know.'

'I was stuck on the toilet,' said Roland, in a tone that was less than convincing.

Cranfield was not impressed, and turned to indulge the gathering crowd.

'I hope they save him,' he said. 'I kicked the door down. He tried to kill himself with a scalpel.'

Fuck, thought Roland, so Cranfield was a fucking hero! He could also hear fevered activity inside the blood-red room.

Another paramedic opened Dave's door and asked everyone to move away. Roland decided to stand on the periphery of the small gathering of concerned residents, listening to Cranfield describe his heroic role: how he had seen everything and phoned the emergency services. The same paramedic appeared again and this time requested everyone to go back to their rooms... there was nothing to see.

Well, that was good advice, thought Roland, deciding absence from the scene was the best available option. But as he left he received a funny look from Cranfield. It was as if Cranfield wanted to apportion blame for Roland's inaction.

Anyway, he checked the communal kitchen and looked outside the window. Shit! Just as he had feared... police!

Roland crossed back into the corridor and knocked on Sophie's door.

'Let me in,' he whispered, as Sophie opened her door.

'Where have you been?'

'Lock it again,' he said, slipping through the thin space Sophie had made for him.

'Why, who's out there?' she asked, speculating that this was probably another nurses' hostel crisis.

'There's a police car outside,' said Roland, in hushed tones.

'Is it a raid?'

'Don't know, but Dave's just done himself in.'

'What, suicide?'

'Yeah, I saw his bed,' said Roland, pacing around the room. 'I've never seen so much blood.'

'Is he dead?'

'Don't know.'

'Christ!'

'I know... heavy shit.'

Roland paused.

'I was in the toilet and heard these screams,' he said, as he tried to control his adrenaline. 'I knew it didn't sound right, but your ex is out there playing the hero. Cranfield thinks he saved the guy's life. He thinks I should have done something.'

Sophie kissed him on the lips in order to reassure him.

They both now stood in Sophie's room, calculating the ramifications, variables and consequences in regards to Dave's suicide attempt. They decided, at the end of the day (and neither of them had anything against Dave... they both hoped he lived), the incident was bound to invite intrusion.

'I'll open the window,' said Sophie. 'There's a good chance the police might come knocking on people's doors to get statements.'

'Fuck, I can't speak to them, I'm too stoned.'

'That doesn't matter right now. We need to get rid of the dope. It's too big a risk to have anything on us.'

'You're right,' said Roland. 'Let me get Jas and Terry.'

'You don't need to tell them.'

'What do you mean?' said Roland. 'Of course we do.'

'Well, don't get stuck round there and get even more stoned.'

'No, no, don't worry.'

*

Initially, the two Pothead Pixies persuaded Roland to trial their new Hoover experiment. Neither was bothered about Dave; he was always going to kill himself, he was just as fucked up as the patients... plus, you have to be fucked up if you "want" to work on the locked ward. This was true, but the matter was urgent: there were risks, dangers, paranoia... they needed to get rid of the shit, the dope, the smoke – everything! Why? Because there's a police car!

Roland now had the attention of the pixies. But there was one caveat, before they went round to Sophie's.

'If Sophie says anything about the petition,' said Roland, 'you've got to say you've signed it.'

'What petition?' asked Jas.

'The one about how crap this place is,' said Roland, squeezing out his words as he sucked on a joint.

'Oh yeah, we've signed it,' said Jas, levering his stoned body from the sofa bed.

'No you haven't,' said Roland, 'but you do have to sign it… but if Sophie asks, you have to say you've signed it.'

'Where's the pen?' asked Terry.

'Why do I need a pen?' asked Jas.

'So we can sign the petition or else his girlfriend is going to get rid of him.'

'I'm not going to sign a petition,' said Jas. 'Those fuckers will fuck me over if I sign something like that.'

'No, you are going to sign the petition,' said Roland, frustrated, 'when I ask you to… but I haven't yet.'

'Why haven't you asked us to sign the petition?' asked Terry.

'Because… because I was going to, but I haven't yet.'

'Do you know what he's talking about?'

'No… and I don't care,' said Jas. 'So, where are these fucking pigs then?'

'Outside, sitting in a police car.'

'Shall we go then?' asked Terry, smirking.

'Yeah, let's get out of here and find out what's going on,' said Jas, pulling his jeans and pants above his hips and then watching them slip back down again.

It was quiet in the corridor, as all the activity Roland had described was around the corner and out of sight.

'There's nothing happening,' said Jas, locking his door.

'It doesn't matter,' said Roland. 'We need to go back to Sophie's and decide what to do with the shit.'

'Well, are the pigs out there?' asked Jas, as they walked along the corridor.

'Yes,' said Roland, 'but don't go near the kitchen window.'

'Why?'

'Because they might see you.'

'But they can't arrest me for standing by a window.'

'For fuck's sake,' said Roland, 'come on!'

'I think he's angry,' said Terry.

'Why, what the fuck have I done?'

'Exactly, what the fuck have you done?' said Terry.

'Come on,' said Roland again, whilst guiding them along the corridor.

Roland knocked quietly on Sophie's door.

'Quick, come in,' she said, pulling Jas by his T-shirt in case he continued on his way round to Dave's room.

'We brought everything we had,' said Terry, throwing his dope and Lizra on to Sophie's bed.

They all copied Terry and then stared at the bed, calculating the significance of the events outside and the implications for themselves.

'Cranfield's a faggot,' said Jas, associating Dave's suicide and Cranfield's lifesaving with the threat of a police raid.

'Shut up,' said Sophie, annoyed by his usual derogatory language.

'What did Cranfield say?' asked Terry, seeking clarity.

'He didn't say anything,' said Roland. 'But he thinks I should have helped Dave, but I couldn't because I was on the toilet.'

'Having a shit?' asked Jas.

'Don't answer that,' said Sophie.

'Is Dave dead?' asked Terry.

'I think he's still alive,' said Roland. 'But I've never seen so much blood…'

Roland's voice faded. He was beginning to shut down. He was very, very stoned.

'Fuck!' said Jas, annoyed he had missed the full horror. 'I bet he didn't do it properly.'

They all looked at Jas.

'You need to do it here,' he said, carving a groove with his hands on the inside of his groin, 'the femoral artery… slashing your wrists is for pussies!'

'Do you think about it a lot, then?' asked Terry.

'Yeah, all the time…'

'Right,' said Sophie, who was keen to focus minds. 'Roland thinks we should get rid of the gear.'

There was a moment's silence, as they all tried to fathom the level of risk. Then, the pixies all laughed spontaneously.

'Shit, I'm so stoned! That's good stuff,' said Jas, confessing they had been smoking all day.

There was general agreement on quality, but they needed a plan because there might be a knock on the door at any minute, and they needed to think… quick.

'Why don't we smoke it all now?' said Jas.

'That will take all night… there's half an ounce there,' said Terry, who could always estimate quantity.

Roland had a better idea. Even though he had lost the ability to speak, he pointed towards the window and out into the dark woods. They all understood his meaning.

'No way,' said Terry. 'I'm not going out there. What are we going to do with it out there anyway?'

'Bury it,' said Jas, warming to Roland's silent suggestion.

'What about the horse?' said Terry. 'I can't stand horses.'

'Terry,' said Sophie, 'no one's ever seen the horse. It's probably Starr and he's not going to be in the woods at this time of night. He'll be tucked up in bed.'

'Okay, so what about the goat?'

'There are no goats,' said Sophie.

'So you say,' said Terry.

'Yes, I do say,' said Sophie.

'Listen, those woods are creepy at night,' said Terry, who hated the prospect of leaving the nurses' hostel and stepping out into the dark and cold.

'I think,' said Sophie, 'Roland's right.'

'What do you mean? He hasn't said anything!' exclaimed Terry.

'That's because he's stoned,' said Jas, adding sympathetically, 'and he's seen a lot of blood.'

Roland's temporary catatonia began to fade. He smiled and began to recapture some lost synapse.

'See, he's coming round,' said Jas, meaning they should move on to Plan A. 'So, let's fucking do it!'

They decided to stand in a line behind the door with the dope stuffed down their pants.

Jas let a fart rip through his buttocks.

'See if the coast is clear,' said Terry.

'My bottom is,' said Jas.

'Clear of what?' asked Sophie.

'Police, of course,' said Terry.

'Are you saying my arse is clear of police?'

'Shut up!' said Sophie. 'Just open it.'

Jas turned the doorknob and tugged gently.

'Shit, it's locked!'

'Are we locked in?' asked Terry.

'Turn the key in the door,' said Sophie despairingly.

'Oh, right, why didn't you say that?'

'What was I meant to say?' said Sophie, struggling with the stoned idiocy.

Jas poked his head round the door and led the pixies along the corridor. They all tuned into the muffled sound of TVs and music systems emanating from the rooms of residents who were presumably unaware of the suicide drama. Jas stopped outside the door of room forty-four.

'Why have we stopped?' whispered Jas.

They all suggested it was because Jas had stopped and he was leading.

'Oh yeah…'

'Jas,' said Sophie, 'we look really suspicious like this.'

'And what makes you think we're going to look any different outside?' asked Terry.

Sophie punched Jas in the bum, in reply to Terry, then they all moved forwards again.

They filtered down the concrete stairs, out through the fire exit and into the night. Doing their best to look casual, they sauntered across the lawns and up to the fence which defined the border with the deep, dark woods. They peered into the bleakness.

'I told you,' said Terry, 'there's a society of wildlife out there.'

'There's no such thing as society,' said Roland.

'You must be joking; there's plenty of wildlife in there,' said Terry, keeping his hands in his pockets, fondling the precious nectar in his pants.

They all listened intently, watching the grey and dark shadows define the distorting woods.

'We all agreed to it,' said Sophie, trying to ensure there was some collective responsibility.

'Did anyone think to bring a torch?' asked Terry, peering once again into the blackness.

'We don't need a torch,' said Sophie, 'because that will draw attention to ourselves.'

'Great,' said Terry, 'but that also means we can't see anything. How are we going to bury our shit in there and know where we put it so we can find it in the morning?'

'What's wrong with you girls?' said Jas, eager to confront the unknown rather than deal with logic.

'Well, technically speaking, Sophie is the only girl,' said Terry, happy to delay stepping into the alien brew.

'It's not technical,' said Sophie, pushing out her chest.

'Can you testify to that fact?' asked Terry, looking at Roland.

'Yeah,' said Roland, who sensed he might be held accountable for what was beginning to look like a bad idea.

'I'm going in,' said Jas, as he grabbed the top of the fence and balanced his leg on the wobbling wire.

'You can, but no way am I going in there,' said Terry defiantly.

Jas kept his leg balanced, looking back at the hesitant troops.

'Come on, you pussies,' said Jas, reluctant to step alone into the morass of nothingness.

'How do we know Dave isn't dead?' asked Terry, rather obliquely.

'What's that got to do with it?' asked Jas, who was beginning to lose his balance.

Terry turned to face Roland.

'Did you actually see Dave alive?'

'No,' said Roland, mystified.

'Exactly,' said Terry.

'Exactly what?' asked Sophie, who felt she might need to defend Roland.

'And did you not fail to help in his hour of need?' said Terry.

'I was in the toilet,' said Roland.

'He was having a crap,' said Jas, who had now removed his leg from the wire fence.

'Dave doesn't know that,' said Terry, who stretched out his hands towards the wooded interior. 'It's weird, but I can feel his spirit.'

'He had no spirit,' said Sophie, who thought that was sufficient to resume Plan A.

'What if he's got it in for Roland?' asked Terry.

'Who, Cranfield?' asked Jas.

'No, Dave,' said Terry.

'Why, what's Roland done?' asked Sophie, preparing to support Roland against any obscure inquisition.

'Yeah, what have I done?'

'Nothing… that's what you've done,' said Terry, delivering his mock accusation, stretching his arms into the mystifying abyss of the woods. 'I bet he's out there, the spirit of Dave…'

'Bollocks!' said Jas, losing patience.

'Well, if his dead spirit is out there he's going to go for Roland,' said Sophie, trying to counter the obscure reasoning. 'So, you've got nothing to worry about.'

'It's by association… he won't discriminate,' said Terry, satisfied he had planted the seed of paranoia.

'I was in the toilet,' said Roland again, exasperated.

Crack!

'Shit!' said Terry, beginning to believe his own nonsense. 'Did you hear that?'

'Hear what?' asked Jas, who knew he had heard the same disturbing noise.

'Listen!'

All four listened, confused by reality, spooked by their own playfulness and straining to detect any mysterious forces.

'Okay,' said Sophie, seeking to reassure them, 'there's bound to be things out there. It's a wood, full of lots of creepy-crawly things.'

'Yeah… and what if Dave is creeping around?' said Terry, adding fuel to the fire. 'That's a vengeful spirit.'

Sophie turned to Roland, looking for a response to end Terry's teasing.

'Dave's alive, isn't he?'

'Yeah, as far as I know,' said Roland.

'As… far… as… you… know,' said Terry, punctuating every word.

'Look,' said Jas, 'aren't we missing the point? We need to get rid of the shit.'

There was another loud crack.

'Fuck!'

'What was that?'

'That's fucking Dave, man, I'm telling you.'

'Bollocks!'

They all stared again into the darkness.

'This is definitely freaking me out now,' said Terry.

'You're the one freaking everyone out,' said Sophie.

There were a few more cracks, a few twigs breaking; it, whatever it was, was getting closer. They all acknowledged there was definitely something out there.

'Look, you idiots, I bet it's the fucking police,' said Jas, retreating from the fence.

Then panic gripped them all, as a loud crack and the unmistakable sound of feet on the ground were almost upon them.

Jas and Terry were the first to run.

'It's the police. You guys go the other way!' shouted Jas, who had left Sophie and Roland standing.

'Come on,' said Roland, grabbing Sophie's hand and pulling her along.

Roland was convinced the police were on their tail as they ran together through the cold, wet grass hugging the border of the wire fence. Roland was not going to take any chances and threw his dope into the woods. That was a relief; even if they got caught, there was no way they would get busted.

They stopped and crouched down in the shadows.

'I got rid of the shit,' said Roland breathlessly. 'The police can't bust us now.'

'We don't know if it was the police,' said Sophie, rationalising.

'But Jas said he saw the police.'

Sophie raised her eyebrows.

They continued to crouch, surveying as best they could the lawns lit by the lights from the windows of the nurses' hostel. Then they noticed two figures walking along the line of the fence. They braced themselves for interrogation, but it was only Jas and Terry, laughing hysterically.

'It was nothing,' said Jas, as Sophie and Roland stood up.

'You're kidding,' said Roland. 'Why did you say it was the police?'

'Did I say that?'

'Yes, you did, I threw my fucking dope away!'

'That's not my fault,' said Jas, laughing.

'You can look for it in the morning,' said Terry, slightly more concerned about the loss. 'Do you know where you threw it?'

'He threw it into the woods,' said Sophie.

'You didn't chuck yours?' asked Roland, regretting his impetuousness.

'No way, do you think I'm crazy?' said Terry. 'You should never get rid of good shit.'

'What about the police?' asked Roland.

Jas and Terry both shrugged and started walking back towards the nurses' hostel.

'Where are you going?' asked Roland.

'Inside,' they said collectively. 'It's too cold out here.'

'It doesn't matter,' said Sophie. 'We don't want to take the risk.'

'What a bloody farce,' said Roland. 'And all because of that fucking idiot Dave... I knew I should've stayed on the toilet.'

'Hey, Roland!' shouted Jas across the lawns. 'Don't forget to bring that petition round so we can sign it.'

CHAPTER 18

THE MORNING AFTER

Roland came across Dave and Cranfield sitting together outside the nursing office. Cranfield looked severe, but at least Dave was alive.

'I thought you were dead,' said Roland, smiling.

Dave looked sheepish, his skin a pasty grey-white.

'They let me out this morning,' he said contritely.

'Really? I mean… that's good,' said Roland, surprised, thinking he shouldn't really be surprised. 'I mean… they think that's alright?'

'It was just a mistake,' said Dave. 'I was fed up. Lucy dumped me.'

'Oh, right,' said Roland, feigning some sympathy.

'You'd be upset,' said Cranfield forcefully, 'if Sophie left you.'

'Suicidal,' said Roland, trying to bring some light relief.

Cranfield's face resumed the look of disapproval which had permeated last night's intervention.

'I hear you chucked your dope away,' said Cranfield, sneering.

Roland blushed slightly and then frowned.

'I did,' he said.

'I'll help you look for it later if you want,' said Cranfield jauntily. 'Where did you throw it?'

'No, it's alright, I know where it is.'

'Up to you,' said Cranfield.

Bloody vulture, thought Roland, whilst regretting the rash act.

'Why did you throw it?' asked Dave, distracted for a moment from his own predicament.

'They got paranoid,' said Cranfield, almost gloating, 'because they thought the police were going to raid the place.'

Roland momentarily looked above his head, following the line of square metallic ductwork, hoping he could avoid any further humiliation.

'We heard something in the woods,' he said, trying to demonstrate he was not the only stoned pixie. 'Anyway, are you feeling better?'

'It's just a hangover,' said Dave, seemingly oblivious to the consequences of his actions.

'Right...' said Roland, judging Dave looked a little anaemic. 'Shouldn't you be in bed or something?'

'I can't, they won't let me back into my room.'

'I suppose it's a bit of mess in there,' he said, thinking back to all the blood he had seen.

'Is it?'

'Well, yeah, that's a lot to replace,' said Roland, who managed to stop himself from describing the bed soaked in blood. 'You must have had a few pints then?'

'I was rat-arsed.'

'I think he means blood,' said Cranfield, who was

happy to listen whilst Roland struggled to connect with the penitent Dave.

'Yeah, I had plenty,' he said, grinning.

'You know,' said Roland, who wanted to prove to Cranfield he was really on Dave's side in all of this, 'that's probably the best form of rehydration for a hangover.'

Dave failed to respond and took on a sullen melancholia.

'Listen,' said Roland, attempting to be more consoling, 'you can use my room if you want to crash. I'm in Sophie's all the time.'

'They won't let him back in,' said Cranfield. 'We're just waiting to see Fitzpatrick.'

'Shit, but where's he supposed to live?'

'Don't know,' said Dave, speaking up for himself.

Cranfield leaned forward, indicating he had some confidential information.

'When they broke into his room they found some dope. They arrested him in A&E. He's just been suspended.'

A remorseful Dave nodded.

'You'd better watch yourselves,' said Cranfield.

'What do you mean?' asked Roland.

'Just be sensible,' said Cranfield.

Roland knew that... he did not need to be told that.

'Look,' said Roland, facing Dave, 'good luck in there.'

Dave acknowledged the semi-heartfelt support.

'See you later...'

Roland headed off down the corridor, cursing Cranfield. *What is wrong with that man? Just because one of his cronies is going to get the boot we're all supposed to feel sorry for him. Plus, it's Cranfield's bunch of fucking pixies who are now going to get the police interested in what goes on. Fucking Cranfield, he's the problem, yet he makes out that we're to blame. And I bet*, thought Roland, *I bet that fucking bastard grasses on us just to take the fucking heat off.*

The bumbling Starr was roaming towards him as he got closer to the exit of the main reception. Starr's fat face was covered in saliva from his incessant dribbling. He uttered a simmering giggle, a mix between a braying horse and hysterical hyena. Something had obviously tickled him, thought Roland.

'How are you?' he said, wondering if he would get a coherent answer.

Starr buried his head bashfully.

'Are you going to the ark?'

Starr remained rooted to the spot. Then he thrust both his arms and hands forward. Roland stepped back and looked more closely at a bulging fist. Starr loosened his grip. There was something there, in his hand, a gritty piece of stone or mineral.

'Oh, that's nice,' said Roland. 'Did you find it in the woods?'

'Six... one-five... one-five... one-two,' replied Starr.

Okay, thought Roland, *off his rocker...*

'Well, I have to go now. Bye-bye.'

Roland moved around the static Starr and rapidly out into the bright winter sunshine. He had no idea what the fuck that was about, but it seemed to have meaning... for Starr.

Roland leapt up the stairs of the nurses' hostel, expecting to fall into Sophie's room and tell her how he had found Dave alive and Starr consumed with a little bit of stone. He turned the doorknob, but it was locked. That was odd, he thought, she couldn't have gone out.

'Sophie, it's me!' he shouted through the door.

He could hear a faint shuffling, but no response.

'Sophie, it's me, Roland...'

Again, no response.

'Sophie, are you there? Is everything alright?'

'No,' said Sophie, whimpering.

'Come on, let me in.'

'I can't...'

'Why, what's wrong?'

There was another silence.

'Come on,' said Roland anxiously.

'You can't come in.'

'What do you mean?'

'I'm ill.'

'I know you're ill,' said Roland jokingly. 'We're all ill... that's why we're here!'

There was another pause.

'I've changed,' said Sophie.

Roland laughed.

'What do you mean, you've changed?'

'I've got something and you can't look at me.'

'Why can't I look at you?'

More silence.

'Sophie, you need to let me in... I can't stand out here, can I?'

Roland heard Sophie move to the door.

'Wait a minute,' she said, as she unlocked the door. 'Don't come in till I say so.'

'Okay,' said Roland, still bemused as to what terrible fate had befallen her.

'You won't like me any more,' she said, as a final warning.

Roland waited, then opened the door. Sophie was standing by the window with her back to him.

'Are you alright?' he asked, still baffled.

'No,' said Sophie, continuing to look out of the window.

'What's wrong with you?' asked Roland, as he stood in the narrow room feeling helpless.

Sophie began to cry. Roland moved forward, ready to comfort her.

'Wait,' she said.

'Sophie, what is it?'

'I've got a disease.'

'A disease... it's not the bubonic plague is it?' said Roland, trying to lighten the mood.

'It is, a bit.'

'Come on... what is it?'

'Will you still love me, whatever?' asked Sophie, remaining by the window.

This is getting stranger by the minute, thought Roland.

'Of course I will... look at me.'

Sophie turned her head to reveal a mass of blazing red infection. Roland stared, determined to maintain his gaze... but it looked really bad...

Sophie stared back.

'Okay,' said Roland, trying to remain composed, 'what's happened?'

'It's chickenpox,' said Sophie.

'I thought you only got that as a kid? How do you know it's chickenpox?'

'I asked Dr Jonas to come over and have a look. I thought it was, I just wanted him to confirm it.'

'Look, that's not so bad, is it, that it's chickenpox?' said Roland, relieved. 'It will go, won't it, in a couple of weeks?'

'I'm hideous…' said Sophie, as she burst into tears.

Roland laughed as he sat on the bed.

'Come here,' he said.

Sophie rushed over and wrapped her arms around him. Roland let Sophie cry, whilst also making sure he avoided any contact with her scary pus-balls.

'Listen,' said Roland, as he moved Sophie's head back to prove he could look at her again. 'This is temporary, right… and even if it wasn't, I would still love you. That's what love is, isn't it? So, don't worry, I'm not going to walk out on you just because you've got chickenpox. True, it's not nice to look at, but it's just an infection.'

'Oh,' said Sophie, still crying, 'I don't deserve you.'

'Don't be silly. Look, we're both the same. We want the same things in life. That's why we're meant for each other. You trust me and I trust you. Whatever happens, we will stick together… alright?'

'Yes, okay.'

Roland could feel Sophie relaxing as he continued to hold her. It was a shock; obviously a shock.

'Right,' said Roland, 'maybe avoid the mirror for a while. Think about it like this: you'll be off sick for a few weeks, which is a bonus…'

Sophie laughed.

'Good,' said Roland.

They held each other tightly, reaffirming their closeness, their bond, their togetherness. Everything was alright, thought Roland. In fact, things couldn't be better. And perhaps this was a good time just to say something… something about himself… something he had kept hidden, kept secret, not really lied about, but something that would help bind them together, so Sophie could see that by being honest and open they would always be together.

'I know it's an odd thing to say, but I've been wanting to say something to you for a while. Anyway, you know about honesty and everything, so you know everything about me, and I know everything about you…'

'What do you mean?'

There was no other way to say it, thought Roland, but it seemed to make sense, to get it off his chest.

'Well, I'm going to say this to you just so you know…'

Roland paused. Yes, now was the time to say it, he thought, it seemed right.

'It's just that – and this might come as a bit of a surprise to you, but when we first met… well… I was…' Roland paused again, before shrugging his shoulders, 'a virgin. When we did it… you know… the first time.'

There, he had said it.

'I know it sounds a bit weird… and I wanted to say something…'

'But how did you… ?'

'You mean on the night?'

'You seemed to know what you were doing,' said Sophie, whilst clearly retracing in her mind the first night, trying to remember what it was like.

'I know,' said Roland, almost proud of his deception. 'I read a lot of books.'

'Are you joking?'

'No, I was a virgin.'

Sophie was struggling to comprehend – her preconception, her recollections, her understanding of the truth.

'Well, anyway,' said Roland, 'I'm not now.'

Shit! That did not go down well. He could tell Sophie was really surprised, shocked, a double whammy with his little confession. But it wasn't a big deal. Surely it was better? No more pretending about girlfriends in the past who did not really exist. No more lurching into fiction when they had to swap notes.

But Sophie was shaking her head, still trying to fathom how Roland had managed to falsify his sexual experience.

'What's wrong?' asked Roland, feeling relieved he had at last got rid of the awkward truth.

Sophie was struggling.

'But you said you had girlfriends?'

'They were white lies.'

Sophie puffed out her cheeks. She did not know what was worse, her disfigurement or Roland's capacity for acting… lying?

'You amaze me,' she said, rather negatively. 'How long were you going to keep this a secret?'

'It's no big deal… I was a virgin. You were a virgin once. We're all virgins once. What was I supposed to do? "Hi, I'm Roland, I'd like to sleep with you, but by the way I'm a virgin." I don't think that would have impressed you very much.'

Sophie was silent, thinking, filtering, going over in her head the first night they had been together. It did not seem possible. But what did that make her? Was she so sexually naïve that a virgin had fooled her?

'I'm just a bit shocked, that's all,' said Sophie.

'Well, you know now,' said Roland, who was regretting saying anything.

'I've just got to think about it,' she said.

'I'm still me,' said Roland, as a plea of mitigation.

'Yes, I know…'

And then there was silence.

CHAPTER 19

THE MILITANT

Roland and Gobi sat opposite each other in the main teaching room, waiting for Fitzpatrick to appear as representative of the senior management team. It was the first meeting of the reconvened student council, and unfortunately for Gobi, Roland Cauldron was the only representative from the student body.

'Oh, you know, Sophie…'

'She's ill,' said Roland.

'Oh, yes, you know, that's a shame.'

'That's she's ill, or not here?' asked Roland, acutely aware of Gobi's preference.

'Oh, you know, I thought you were a team,' said Gobi light-heartedly.

'We are,' stated Roland, whilst reflecting he should probably have done more to help Sophie in preparing for the meeting.

For instance, Sophie had done all the paperwork, carefully putting together an agenda with appropriate documentation, including copies of the petition, which she had forwarded through the internal post to Gobi and Fitzpatrick. It provided all the proof they needed to support their case: students were fed up with being exposed to unnecessary risk, fed up with covering staff shortages and appalled at witnessing nursing care which was either negligent, abusive or barbaric.

Gobi looked at the clock.

'Oh, you know,' he said, 'it is unusual for Mr Fitzpatrick to be late.'

'Well, we are on time,' replied Roland.

'Yes, you know, he is a busy man,' said Gobi in mitigation. Then, referring to the petition, 'Well, you know, we also need to remember the issues, you know. Does this come from every student, you know?'

Roland frowned.

'Yes,' he said, simply, because there was also no point in engaging in fruitless debate with Gobi.

So they sat in silence whilst Roland watched the second hand move and the minutes tick by.

Then the door to the teaching room burst open. It was Fitzpatrick, his eyes almost blood red with rage. He scrutinised Roland and Gobi with an X-ray intensity, before sitting down in a chair with three or four desks between them. He had the petition in his hand, poised, ready to launch into a tirade.

'What is this, then?' he said, waving the photocopy in the air.

Here we go, thought Roland.

'I was shocked that students from this school,' continued Fitzpatrick, looking directly at Gobi, 'could take so much time to complain in a manner I can only describe as... militant!'

'Militant?' intervened Roland, laughing incredulously. 'It's a petition!'

'And who are you?' asked Fitzpatrick.

'I am president of the student council.'

'And what's your name?'

'Roland Cauldron,' said Roland, irritated because he knew Fitzpatrick was fully aware who he was.

'You know, I think,' said Gobi, attempting to regain some control of the situation, 'we should have a meeting based on some procedure before we get into the detail.'

'I'm sorry, Mr Gobi, but this,' said Fitzpatrick, waving the petition again, 'has forfeited any right to a discussion or a meeting. Trust me, Mr Gobi, I am here to voice our profound dissatisfaction on behalf of the senior management team and the board.'

Roland decided to wait, to see if Gobi had a slither of backbone to stand up to the dictator.

'Well, Mr Fitzpatrick,' said Gobi, moving uneasily in his chair, 'you know, I had no idea this was what the students were going to do. You're right, you know, we should never let things get to this kind of thing. But, you know, perhaps we should let the young man tell us how he feels, you know, rather than let the method get in the way.'

Roland looked to the ceiling: why did Gobi not just tell him to have some respect?

'Well, young man,' said Fitzpatrick, 'why have you set out to ruin the reputation of this hospital?'

'How have I done that?' asked Roland, warming to the notion he was now a "militant".

'You need to realise,' said Fitzpatrick, as he set out

his main charge, 'that the complaints you make on this bit of paper are a direct assault on the management and staff. We deserve better than this from students who we take on to our wards and give them a chance to practise on our patients.'

'I don't understand,' said Roland, rising to the occasion. 'How does highlighting serious issues as a student body ruin the reputation of the hospital?'

Fitzpatrick bristled, but Gobi interpreted on his behalf.

'You know, I think, Roland, Mr Fitzpatrick is trying to make the point, you know, that these things can be taken out of context.'

'Do you realise,' said Fitzpatrick, 'that this is exactly what the local press is looking for? They are all waiting for something like this to come to the surface. You do not seem to understand the hard work and dedication required from nurses and doctors to keep this place going. By publishing this, you could bring the hospital down!'

'You know, I don't think you had any intention of doing that,' said Gobi, glancing anxiously at the president of the student council.

'No,' said Roland, 'but now that you've mentioned it, I will give it serious consideration.'

This ignited Fitzpatrick's fuse.

'There you go, Mr Gobi – as I said!' he boomed.

'Look,' said Roland, determined to make his point, 'we're fed up with raising it through the school and nothing being done about it. The point of this petition is to make you realise that all – and I mean all – the students feel the same way and we're serious about wanting to change things.'

'Mr Gobi,' said Fitzpatrick, almost spitting out his words, 'what sort of students do you have here? A student's role is to learn, not to question the running of a hospital.'

'Of course we can question it,' said Roland. 'As students it is our role to question… and there's a lot to question about this place.'

'How dare you?!' said Fitzpatrick, genuinely affronted. 'Who do you think you are?'

Oh dear – Gobi's worst fears had been confirmed, but he needed to ensure this did not lead to irreparable damage for the school.

'You know,' said Gobi, seeking to mediate, 'I am sure Roland is only trying to emphasise some of the frustrations he feels. You know, expectations are always high.'

'To be quite honest with you,' said Roland, easing into his role of dissenter, 'I think we have very low expectations. There's not enough qualified staff on the wards for us to learn anything, because of understaffing we put ourselves in danger and the patients are also then put at risk. We know patients are drugged up to their eyeballs because there is not enough staff to manage the wards as it is.'

'That's it!' shouted Fitzpatrick, pushing aside his chair. 'I have never been so insulted! Mr Gobi… to be lectured to by a student… I'm no longer going to sit here and listen.'

He leant forward with his hands on the desk.

'And as for this,' he said, waving the petition again, 'as for this… I do not expect to see anything like it again from your school, Mr Gobi.'

Fitzpatrick then turned, with the same flourish with which he had entered, pushed through the door and marched swiftly across the velvet green grass.

Result, thought Roland, *we now have a war!*

Gobi was less than enthusiastic.

'Oh, you know, that is a shame, he behaved like that, you know.'

'He seems to take a rational discussion as a threat to his authority,' said Roland, feeling a great deal of satisfaction.

Gobi remained pensive. He certainly was not about to side with Roland.

'You know, we will have to be careful from now on,' he said, identifying joint responsibility as a tactic for appeasement. 'We do not want to get on the wrong side of a man like Mr Fitzpatrick.'

'I think it's a bit late for that,' said Roland, relishing the whole episode, exposing the authoritarian as unreasonable and intolerant.

Gobi remained far more circumspect.

'Well, you know, what will you do with the petition?'

'I don't know,' said Roland, happy to be keeping Gobi guessing.

CHAPTER 20

THE PSYCHOPATH

Sunlight began to drape its last thin veins over the wards of Wellington Park and into the office of Morten Slaney. The close of day meant he could relax in his much-loved home from home, quality time in his own personal space. He spun his leather chair round and gazed at his own distorted window reflection. There was enough clarity to admire his stretched pink skin, boxed jawline and curled hair-flick above his brow. He flexed his oversized shoulders as he stared through into the old abandoned courtyard, which had been sealed off before his time as interim chief executive. There was a mouldy green bench, fibrous ends of shrubs and a waterless concrete fountain in the centre of a broken stone. It was an odd space, thought Slaney, a perfectly meaningless space.

However, overall, he had implemented all the changes he intended since his appointment. Initially, he had moved his PA, Mrs Flamey, into her own little cupboard around the corner and then set about restoring the rather neglected staff gym, which was conveniently located next to his office. As soon as Slaney's connecting door was fitted staff usage dropped significantly because no one wanted to be in the same room as a man who was infused with a depth of incalculable menace. Those that did enter, if Slaney was present, ran the risk of being a target of his unfettered libido, overwhelmed by his steroid-driven, muscular build, which housed an impenetrable psychopathy. With his favourite pastime secured (rigorous exercise and bodybuilding), Slaney found time to fit a bespoke drinks cabinet in his office, removing a fridge from one of the wards and filling it with a wide selection of beers and spirits. There was little else, he decided, which needed changing: after all, there was no point in making improvements to a hospital which needed closing.

Slaney's rule was from a distance, but his influence was all-pervasive. He would occasionally make an appearance in the corridors and attempt to awkwardly engage patients or staff. They all viewed him with suspicion, a large degree of antipathy, as someone only mildly tethered by societal rules. He relished the fact nobody liked him, and he liked not being liked. He had the power of a controlled bully, who rarely, if ever, needed to act on his propensity for intimidation which oozed from every pore.

Not only was he hated within the wards and corridors of Wellington Park, but also at home, where his wife hated him for being an unfaithful husband and his children hated him for not being a dad. If there was any ambivalence towards Slaney it came from the hospital management board, grateful for his efficiency and his readiness to take on the task of deinstitutionalisation.

His objective, if he did a good job of shutting down Wellington Park, was to capitalise on any benefit he could accumulate personally and professionally. He just needed to keep a firm hand on the tiller, steer and command, using the day-to-day control of Fitzpatrick and the clinical authority of the self-interested Dr Caldwell.

He looked at the clock next to the empty coat stand and detected some movement in the staff gym. He would have to wait for Fitzpatrick to deliver his end-of-the-day report before he could check in on his assignation. He picked his nose and wiped his finger underneath his desk just as Fitzpatrick knocked and entered.

'Good evening, Michael,' said Slaney, relaxing in the comfort of his chair.

'Mr Slaney,' replied Fitzpatrick, as he slid efficiently on to a hard plastic chair, separated by a vast desk space which Slaney always kept clear of finished paperwork.

'All is well, I hope?' said Slaney, levering his hydraulic suspension to ensure equality with Fitzpatrick's domed forehead.

'In general, yes,' said Fitzpatrick, who had never reported under his watch that things were not under his control. 'There are just a few things we need to cover. The day returns, a rather unpleasant meeting at the school of nursing this morning and a request in regards to the suicide of Mr Vilnous.'

'Ah, yes, our Falklands veteran,' said Slaney, who paused, appearing to reflect.

'Indeed...'

There was a sudden thump next door as the exercises in the staff gym took on a greater momentum. Slaney waited, as Fitzpatrick flicked through the papers on his A4 size clipboard, before he found the figures for the inflow/outflow of patient numbers. As soon as Fitzpatrick had confirmed the capacity level, incidents and risk items, Slaney hastily moved things on.

'So, our militant friends...' said Slaney, inviting Fitzpatrick to summarise his meeting at the school.

Fitzpatrick sighed before offering a brief precis: he felt the meeting was all rather unpleasant, unprofessional, which was disappointing considering Mr Gobi was fully aware of the decommissioning of the hospital. With the school going against the hospital in this way it put into question the commitment of the students to patient care on the wards; this was particularly regrettable when there was already a strain on staffing levels, and if the school chose to respond by supporting actions which effectively undermined the hospital, there would obviously be implications.

Slaney articulated his neck and shoulders.

'Do we know if any of this has gone outside?'

Fitzpatrick shook his head; he doubted it, because there was not a great deal of coherence to their campaign.

'And do we know who is behind all of this?'

'A young man called Roland Cauldron,' stated Fitzpatrick.

'Ah...' said Slaney. 'Was he not involved in some incident with a patient last year?'

'That's my understanding... we gave him a chance but he has failed to appreciate it. Unfortunately, we think there is also a third-year student, Sophie Smith, who has got involved. She will have to watch her step. I've already indicated to Mr Gobi that his school has a responsibility for the attitude and behaviour of their students. If he cannot restrain disruptive elements, then it will fall to us to do the job for him.'

'How many students are involved?'

'Just Cauldron and Miss Smith. However, they are part of a rather unsavoury group coalescing in the nurses' hostel.'

Slaney leaned forward, eager to hear of the latest antics of his "beloved flock".

'We have anecdotal reports of drug use,' said Fitzpatrick. 'We already know most of the other individuals involved and will be liaising with the police.'

'And this involves Cauldron and Miss Smith?'

'Oh, yes... and a Mr Jaswinder and a Mr Alcock... and potentially an issue for Dr Caldwell in regards to one of his juniors.'

'As and when...' said Slaney. 'Inform me of your progress and I'll update the board if the petition gets raised. Our little friends are clearly exposed, but we should bide our time and measure our responses to meet our own interests. To draw attention to these issues now could potentially provide further exposure, which we need to guard against. Our strategy should be to decouple any support and effectively leave Cauldron isolated.'

Fitzpatrick was in agreement, and fully understood the direction in which to take things. Slaney leant back into his crumpled cow skin.

'And Mr Vilnous?'

'We could consider a minute's silence,' said Fitzpatrick. 'This has been suggested by the staff who had responsibility for his care.'

Slaney was cautious.

'That's something that we should do on Remembrance Day, later in the year, for those who want to remember him. Highlighting the issue is not good practice. We don't want to encourage any more hanging from trees if it can be avoided. Have I seen the final report yet?'

'I'll ensure you get a copy… it exonerates key staff. We may have some recommendations to follow, but Mr Vilnous was determined and ultimately successful.'

'That's military training for you,' said Slaney wistfully.

Fitzpatrick remained impassive.

'Okay, thank you, Michael,' said Slaney.

As swiftly as he had arrived, Fitzpatrick lifted from his chair, wished Slaney a pleasant evening and returned to the nursing office to supervise the changeover.

With the day's business completed, Slaney locked his office door. He undid his shirt and tie, neatly hanging them on the coat stand. He untied his shoes and removed his belt and trousers, before placing his trousers on a hanger and suspending them from the same hook. From inside his filing cabinet he pulled out a pair of shorts. He rubbed his naked torso as he opened the connecting door to the staff gym.

Imogen Clough was already levering weights and thrusting her pelvis.

'Miss Clough,' said Slaney, checking all four corners of the room.

'Mr Slaney,' she said, smiling.

Imogen continued to push the weights, snapping her arms into a fixed position and then moving them back on to the safety bar. Every female nurse in Wellington Park always sniggered at her flirtatiousness, but it was not a turn-off for Slaney, who responded positively to the "Imogen lips", thick-cake foundation and maximus buttocks.

He walked over to the staff gym door, flicked the handle a few times and then locked it with the single key he kept in his gym shorts. He wasted no time and straddled the prone Imogen. She responded by lifting and pushing up into Slaney and running her hands over his bare chest.

'I heard you next door,' she said, straining to feel Slaney's bulge between her legs.

'We heard you in here,' said Slaney, pushing enthusiastically.

'Oh, so that's why you had a short meeting.'

Slaney would not have spent any longer with Fitzpatrick, but it did not hurt to let Imogen think he was impatient to fuck her.

'So,' said Slaney, placing Imogen's hands on his pecs, 'did you find out any more about our pot-smoking anarchists?'

Imogen pouted and sighed. Slaney and Fitzpatrick knew everything without the need for her supplementary information.

'You know I know Jas...' she said contritely.

Slaney raised his eyebrow.

'Are you still friends?'

'No,' said Imogen, beginning to feel Slaney's small but talented penis.

'Has he got anything against the hospital?' he asked in one breathless gasp, as he thrust up into Imogen's tracksuit bottoms, whilst hanging on to the lifting bar.

'He'd be lost without this place,' she said.

'Wouldn't we all?' said Slaney, as he let out a faint, sexualised grunt.

'They hang out together... Jas, Sophie and her boyfriend... there are a few others. As far as I know, they just smoke pot... lots of them do it...'

Imogen wriggled her hips so she could receive a bit more stimulation. Slaney stopped his gyration, held her hips and adopted a serious tone.

'Just so you know, I need to protect the interests of this hospital and I will not tolerate drug use by any member of staff, especially student nurses.'

Imogen narrowed her eyebrows. She was not a snitch, as such, and she certainly had nothing against Sophie; she knew nothing about her boyfriend and still had a soft spot for Jas, even if he did go around ruining her reputation.

'Look, Fitzpatrick knows everything that goes on in this place,' she said. 'He'll know what they're up to.'

Slaney let go of her hips and relaxed. She was right, but he always liked to check things out for himself.

'Why don't you do some more weights?' he said, elevating his body and avoiding a kiss as he looked sideways at the door.

'I can't lift those,' she said, pointing to the large discs on the floor.

'Lift some weights,' he said into her ear, 'and then I'll fuck you.'

Oh well, whatever turned him on, thought Imogen. Slaney began to unwind the clamps. She removed her tracksuit top so that he could see her nipples harden. Slaney was impressed, as he slipped the first clamp off and let it clunk on to the floor. He then lifted off the weights on one side and placed a thick plate back on.

'How heavy is that?' she asked.

'Don't worry, a mouse could lift it,' he said, moving round to the other side of the bar to remove the other clamp.

Imogen thought for a moment.

'They all think there's going to be a police raid,' she said.

Slaney laughed.

'I think that's the least of their troubles,' he said, whilst assuming his most threatening gaze. 'But you... say nothing.'

CHAPTER 21

A RED RASH WITH THE UNION MAN

After the first few weeks of Sophie contracting chickenpox there was a strange transformation and a red rash forming all over her body. She saw Dr Jonas again and then kept quiet about it. But soon Sophie's red rash had turned into something far worse, and eventually she had to confess to Roland it had a name: psoriasis.

Her beautiful body, her dark brown Amazonian skin, was caked in raised plateaus of flaky, dry scales. It was not, if Roland was honest, an easy thing to look at. The Sophie he had fallen in love with, the Sophie who was probably out of his league, had a flawed, disfigured appearance. Which, in the great scheme of things, was no reason to question his commitment, but anyone, surely, would question exactly what this meant? Or at least, Roland had decided to think, reasonably, what did this mean for their relationship? He certainly sensed Sophie's recent frustrations with him were now a distant memory. It was now Sophie who needed confirmation and affirmation of their love. And he said he still loved her, of course he did; he genuinely did. *But I bet*, thought Roland, *there*

*can't be too many people who have to wake up in the morning
and use a dustpan and brush to sweep the dead skin out of the
bed.* Or make love in a reduced, almost non-tactile way,
perhaps no more than a form of mutual masturbation.
How long, he wondered, was this supposed to go on for?

It was not a question he was willing to ask Sophie,
who required unconditional love and devotion. Roland
knew, if he was to pose the question he would be exposing
a potential ambivalence, which was best left hidden. And
in truth, he was deeply, deeply in love with Sophie. But
this was certainly a challenge, a test of Roland's resolve.
He needed to find a way through and come to terms
with Sophie's disease. No rational person, he thought,
could pretend things did not need some re-evaluation.
Which meant he had to talk to somebody, and the only
person he could trust was Jas.

What would he do, Roland had asked, if he was in
his position? At first Jas was unequivocal: no way could
he do it! But then qualified his response: he was not
Roland, and for someone like Roland maybe it was
something he could do and stand by his girlfriend. In
fact, according to Jas, Roland was in a bit of a no-win
situation. If he crapped out on her, he'd definitely be
seen as the villain who, at the slightest adversity, failed to
meet the minimum obligation.

Fuck, Jas was right: there was no way out, not that he
wanted a way out, but there certainly was no way out.

So, given he loved Sophie, there was a simple answer:
adapt to the new condition because love conquers all.
See beneath the surface… in this case quite literally!

It was obvious… why had he ever questioned it?

There should be no question. He loved Sophie, and part of loving somebody is to stand by them, not walk out just because they happen to be ill. It was all part of the package and he should never, ever have questioned it.

Sophie was keen to get things going again after the fallout with Fitzpatrick and had contacted Bob Jacobs, the full-time union official who had agreed to come down and "have a chat". Roland was far less eager to engage with the "union man" (as he liked to call him), suspicious he was no better than management, part of the same thing, the same corrupt system. Sophie said they needed all the help they could get, especially after Roland had raised the temperature and effectively ruined any chance of using the student council to change anything. No way, Sophie had said, would they ever be able to get management to attend another council meeting.

With Gobi on annual leave, Sophie had managed to get one of the tutors to put aside a room in the school to meet with Bob Jacobs. As they waited, Roland reiterated his "political dialogue" on the failings of unions to change anything. They were "dinosaurs from another world", a dying, irrelevant world, especially after the way things had gone with the miners.

'The only way to change things is to be even more radical, because if nobody is listening then there is no point in talking. Only blood will get people to stop and listen and take notice.'

Sophie merely reminded Roland of the reality of their situation, as they were not taking on the might of the British state, but trying to help people, students and patients who were being badly treated. It was all part of the same thing, according to Roland, who was about to make a further point when the doors flew open and a lumbering, jovial voice intervened.

'You must be the two militants I have heard so much about…'

Sophie stood up, self-consciously pulled her sleeves down in order to hide the marks of her dermatological disease and extended a handshake.

Roland nodded his greeting. Immediately, instinctively, there was something Roland did not like about Jacobs. Maybe it was his grubby moustache, his thick black hair which just covered his ears, or something that wasn't quite tangible. But whatever it was, he knew he wasn't going to get on with him. Yet Sophie seemed completely enamoured with the oversized git. In fact, he looked a bit like Douglas without any of the mischievous glint in his eyes; typically, thought Roland, in his mismatched blazer and trousers… like a retired teacher, another "Professor Franks".

They soon got down to business as Sophie filled in some of the background. Bob Jacobs nodded knowingly, informing them that as long as they were both members of the union he would be happy to give his advice and support. Then Roland confessed he hadn't joined the union but had his membership form with him. This wasn't going to stop Roland saying his piece. Things came pouring out of him: there was only so much people were prepared to take… there had to be something done about it… students, nursing staff and patients were at risk… wards were being manned by unqualified nurses… there were never enough staff to do more than just the basics… there were bound to be more incidents unless management were held to account.

'Okay, okay…' said Bob Jacobs, releasing the strap of his bruised brown leather satchel. 'We need to take a step back before rushing into something here. Rome wasn't built in a day.'

'It's not Rome we're trying to build,' said Roland, 'just some basic bloody humanity!'

'You know what I mean,' said Bob Jacobs. 'I'm on your side. I wouldn't be meeting you if I didn't think there was a cause, but it is one thing to say it and another thing to prove it.'

'What do you think we should do?' asked Sophie, who genuinely wanted "professional" advice.

'So,' he said, 'you've had some run-ins with Michael?'

'Who's Michael?' asked Roland.

'He means Fitzpatrick,' said Sophie. 'We've had one meeting and he walked out.'

'Sounds like Michael,' said Bob Jacobs.

'Well, I had the meeting,' said Roland. 'And he's a wanker.'

'He rules through fear,' said Sophie.

'Oh, I know that,' said Bob Jacobs. 'He's from the military and hasn't forgotten those old habits. He's not a bad man underneath, but he doesn't really control this place.'

'You mean Slaney does,' said Sophie.

'Morten Slaney has a lot of influence,' confirmed Bob Jacobs. 'I think he also makes himself popular with the… ladies.'

Sophie blushed.

'Well, we can't do him for adultery,' said Roland,

wondering why Sophie was red-faced. 'We need to know what to do next – basically, what we should do with the petition?'

'Let's see…' said Bob Jacobs, with a sleepy sigh. 'If you have a meeting with management, based on what you've told me, they just won't listen. It's as simple as that. You've got a petition against dangerous levels of staffing on the wards… you say students are being used to fill the gaps and I don't doubt that for one minute, but to be honest with you, that's nothing unusual.'

'Yeah, but it's wrong,' said Roland.

Bob Jacobs gave a wry smile.

'What you are going to have to do to prove your case,' he said, raising his voice slightly, 'is provide some evidence, otherwise someone like Morten Slaney won't take you seriously. Can you get access to the records of staffing levels on the wards?'

'Staffing levels?' wondered Roland, turning to Sophie. 'How are we going to get something like that?'

'I know,' she said enthusiastically. 'Each ward submits a day return to the nursing office and that shows the number of staff on the ward for each shift. They also keep a copy on the ward. That's how we get the evidence, from all the copies they keep on the wards.'

'Can you get access to them?' asked Bob Jacobs.

'I don't know,' said Sophie, beginning to think it through.

'There's no way we'd be able to get hold of them,' said Roland, who could just see where all this was going: a long, drawn-out process which added up to nothing.

'You know,' said Sophie, anticipating what needed to be done, 'I think all we have to do is ask.'

'Ask who?' said Roland unenthusiastically.

'We can get permission off the sister or charge nurse on the ward,' she said, looking sternly at Roland to ensure he did not undermine the solution.

'Do you really think they'll do that?' he asked sceptically.

'I don't know,' said Sophie, 'but we've got to do something. Have you got a better idea?'

'No,' said Roland. 'I would need time to think about it.'

'Well, what you will need,' said Bob Jacobs, intervening, 'is solid evidence to support your case and people who are prepared to support you.'

'I just can't see sisters and charge nurses doing that,' said Roland, imagining how it would go down on the wards if he started turning up uninvited.

'You don't know that, do you?' said Sophie. 'I think Bob is right: without any evidence someone like Slaney will walk all over us.'

'But how long is it going to take?' asked Roland.

'You're going to need at least three months,' replied Bob Jacobs.

'Three months!' said Roland in exasperation.

'It's the only way to do it,' Jacobs said, revealing all of his union experience in a short, unexciting phrase.

'I think we can do it,' said Sophie, beginning to think about the practicality of such a campaign. 'We'll have to go round every ward and see if they are willing to let us photocopy the day returns. If we can get them, we can prove we are not just making it up.'

'I don't see it,' said Roland, shaking his head. 'I can't see sisters putting their careers on the line.'

'We're only asking them to help,' said Sophie. 'We're not asking them to confront management or go on a march with us!'

'You will have to be careful,' said Bob Jacobs. 'If management find out what you're up to they will try and stop it.'

'How?' asked Roland.

'Well, you know,' he said, easing back in his chair, 'just don't make yourselves an easy target.'

It's a bit late for that, thought Roland.

'Listen, guys, don't forget to keep your eyes on the bigger picture. We've got the bitch in power and we've taken a big hit with the miners.'

'We know that,' said Roland, who had no intention of being patronised by the dinosaur.

'I think what Bob's trying to say is that we're all part of a bigger fight,' said Sophie.

'Listen,' said Roland, keen to put his credentials on the table, 'I can't stand the bitch! Do you think I haven't suffered? There was fuck all for me when I left school and by the time I was nineteen they told me I would never work again... which was a joke because I hadn't even fucking worked by then anyway. You don't have to tell me about the bigger picture.'

'Well, there are brothers – miners with no job... whole communities have suffered,' said Bob Jacobs, less than impressed with Roland's experience of Thatcherite structural adjustment. 'They are devastated and don't know how they are going to keep a roof over their heads or feed their families.'

There was an uneasy pause; Roland appreciated

his bitterness was not equivalent but he still thought it worthy of recognition.

'Hey!' said Bob Jacobs, trying to lighten the mood. 'Have you heard the one about Thatcher and the fire station?'

'No,' they said together.

'Well, the story goes she was offered a cup of tea on a visit to a fire station, which of course she couldn't refuse. So the guys that went back to the kitchen wiped their dicks all around the mug before giving her the tea. And of course, she had to drink it!'

Bob Jacobs burst out laughing.

'Was that before or after they put the tea in?' asked Roland, still smarting from Bob Jacobs' put-down.

'What do you mean?' asked Sophie.

'Well, you know, it's hot…'

Sophie raised her eyes to the ceiling.

'Anyway, they need our support,' said Bob Jacobs, feeling increasingly antagonistic towards Roland. 'Just don't concentrate on one thing and try and broaden your campaign.'

'You mean the miners,' said Roland dubiously.

'Yes, that's what he means,' said Sophie.

Bob Jacobs flipped the flap of his bulging satchel and started to extract a pile of leaflets held loosely together by an elastic band.

'It's important,' he said, 'where we have activists, we raise awareness and help the trade union movement. Trust me, with the miners defeated there are going to be tough times ahead. It will be a real struggle to recover… and at the moment no one knows how the movement will adapt.'

'Well, there are still issues for us,' said Roland. 'We have a fight on our hands... and not just what we've told you. We're also concerned about the impact of community care.'

'I thought you'd be in favour of it?'

'We are, in principle,' said Roland, 'but what if the community doesn't care?'

Bob Jacobs spread out a pile of leaflets in front of him.

'So, you don't want to see a place like this shut down, then?'

'We do,' said Roland. 'It's a barbaric hellhole, but not at the price of shoving everyone from one hellhole into another... the heartless one out there...'

'What are they planning to do?'

'We don't know yet,' said Sophie. 'We'd support the closure, but not without adequate support for the patients. For some of them this is all they've known. They've lived here for years and are completely institutionalised. There's no programme to rehabilitate or integrate into the community and we're sure they will start shutting down wards soon.'

Bob Jacobs breathed in deeply.

'I tell you what I'll do,' he said. 'See how you get on with gathering the evidence and I'll speak to the board about what their plans are for moving patients into the community.'

'You sit on the board?' asked Roland incredulously.

'We're invited along. At the end of the day, Roland, you always have to sit down and negotiate.'

You mean with the enemy, thought Roland.

'Are those leaflets about the miners?' asked Sophie, stretching out her hand.

'We're all involved in this,' said Bob Jacobs. 'They need all the support they can get, the lads up there, and money to keep their families going.'

He pulled out a blue plastic collection pot from his satchel.

'It's every trade unionist's duty to support the miners, given the sacrifices they've made. When you go round talking to staff, you need to ask if they can make a contribution.'

Roland laughed.

'Do you know how many people here are in the union?' said Roland assertively. 'I bet I could count them on one hand. It's going to be an uphill battle just to get them to give us some day returns!'

'You don't have to be in the union to support the miners,' said Sophie.

'Yes, I know that, I'm just saying people here live in their own little world. We'll be pushing it just to get them to hand over some basic information without them pissing their pants!'

'That's no reason not to try,' said Bob Jacobs. 'You shouldn't underestimate people.'

'I'm just trying to be realistic,' said Roland, frustrated by the prospect. 'If you ask me, no one gives a damn about the miners.'

'We're fighting for the heart of the labour movement,' replied Bob Jacobs, staring animatedly at Roland. 'There is no room for dilettantes!'

'Well,' said Roland, struggling to think what a

dilettante was, 'people here don't even know what a trade union is!'

'I don't know if that's true,' said Sophie.

'Of course it is!'

Bob Jacobs laughed, deciding to draw back from confrontation.

'You two must be an item then?'

Sophie blushed again.

'I thought you were... nothing wrong with that. I met my wife at a trade union conference.'

'Oh, you're married?' said Sophie.

'Not any more,' said Bob Jacobs, winking.

'Well, yes, we're going out with each other,' said Roland. 'And we don't believe in marriage.'

'I think you'll find it's the same thing,' said Bob Jacobs.

'Really?' said Roland, whilst turning to look at Sophie. 'Do you want to marry me?'

'No,' she said, taken aback by Roland's mock proposal.

'You see,' said Roland, almost triumphant.

Bob Jacobs smiled, a nauseating, self-knowing smile.

★

'You know Fitzpatrick will find out what we're up to,' said Roland, as they walked along the tarmac path back to the nurses' hostel.

'So?' said Sophie. 'We can't stop now.'

'I know... I'm just thinking more about the implications.'

'I don't care,' she said, rather dismissively. 'I don't want to work here after I qualify, so there's not much they can do to me in the time I've got left.'

Roland was silent. Sophie had touched on a subject which had implications for their relationship.

'You didn't like Bob Jacobs, then?' asked Sophie.

'No,' said Roland, still thinking.

But like Roland, Sophie wasn't really thinking about Bob Jacobs. She was thinking at last she had sown the seed, in Roland's mind, as to their future. She wasn't going to say any more, as she wasn't entirely sure herself, but she would let the seed grow, the seed of doubt.

'I can't see what's wrong with him,' she said.

'Who, Mr Union Man? I don't trust him. And what's a dilettante? That was a put-down!'

'I think it means someone who is not really committed, or a poser, or something like that,' said Sophie, preparing herself for Roland's rage.

'What?!'

'I knew you wouldn't like it,' she said, wondering if Bob Jacobs might have put his finger on something.

'Too bloody right… what a fucking cheek!'

'Well, he's probably focused on bigger things.'

'What do you mean?'

'I don't think he meant to insult you. He's just concerned about the labour movement. It's under attack.'

'You mean he's afraid he might lose his job.'

'He's not bothered about his job,' said Sophie.

'I bet he gets paid a packet,' said Roland. 'The only thing I liked was the story about the firemen.'

'It was a good story,' said Sophie, 'but I have heard it before.'

'Yeah?'

'My brother… I think it's a bit of an urban myth.'

Bullshit, in other words, thought Roland.

'Anyway,' he said, anxious to know what Sophie really thought about Bob Jacobs' strategy, 'I can't see why we have to do this evidence-gathering. And what was the point of pushing the whole bloody miners thing? That's only going to make things worse.'

'We're doing a small collection… people support the miners.'

'Do they?'

'Of course they do,' said Sophie.

'Nobody believes in unions any more,' said Roland, who still had a point to make. 'We're the only ones here who know what a trade union is. We're the only ones who are active in the student council. In fact, we're the only ones who are active!'

'Look, I thought you wanted to change things?'

'I do,' said Roland, 'but there's something about Bob Jacobs I don't like. I don't trust him. As I said, I mean, he sits on the board with Slaney, for Christ's sake!'

'That's his job,' said Sophie. 'He has to do that, but it doesn't turn him into management. You should have a bit more respect for people instead of always running them down.'

Roland was silent again. He relied on his gut instinct, that was all. He had respect for people – people he liked… and he did not like Bob Jacobs. And the unions didn't change anything. You needed to do things now, not wait;

you needed to smash the door down, not knock and wait to be called in.

'I just feel as if we're playing their game,' said Roland.

'Well, sometimes you have to do that,' said Sophie, sure of the need for a coherent approach. 'The point is, once management know we've got the union behind us, they'll be scared to touch us.'

Well, that might be right, thought Roland. In fact, that was a good point. They needed some sort of backup, some sort of default, a powerful body behind them. Not that he thought Bob Jacobs would do anything if they got into trouble. But it wouldn't do any harm to let management know they had the union involved. If the battles started, they were digging trenches, defining their position; they were getting serious, they were not going to be dismissed, walked over and ignored. Yes, perhaps Sophie was right; it did make sense.

'Well,' said Roland, trying to think about what lay ahead of them, 'I think it's going to be hard for me to convince a sister to hand over the day returns.'

'What do you mean?'

'You've been here longer than me,' said Roland. 'People know you… they're probably going to be more willing to hand over things to you than they are to me.'

'I'm not going to do this on my own,' said Sophie assertively.

'I know… I'm just saying I know what people think of me here. As soon as I walk on a ward they think I'm trouble.'

Sophie was guarded. Roland had to accept things as well, such as a bit of hard work, a bit of hard labour… getting his hands dirty instead of all this posturing.

CHAPTER 22

A LESSON IN STRATEGY FROM THE KUNG FU CHESS MEN AND A HAIRY BOLLOCK

With an agreed strategy for the two leading members of the student council (and token trade union representation), Roland, just like Sophie, still had to face the daily trauma of student placements on the wards. He had become numb to the daily routine of heaving decaying flesh, feeding, washing and putting it to bed on Rose Ward. He consoled himself with providing what little comfort he could to the afflicted Amy, but the limbless torso he avoided as much as possible. The sight of the tortuous, gyrating tragedy pricked Roland's underlying sense of self-doubt: there was surely little purpose to life in such a physical, self-inflicted condition. Roland even had some admiration for Douglas and his nurses who attended to her needs, putting aside the fact that the leather contraption which restrained her probably violated the remainder of her human rights.

Interspersed with his time on Rose Ward, Roland was required to enhance his "learning experiences" by providing occupational therapy, or OT, on a designated ward. Scheduled as a taster for students to gain insight into other therapeutic professions, Roland had been assigned to the male-only locked ward: Sunflower. He loathed the prospect of spending a second, let alone an hour, on the notorious ward, because there was always the threat of violence, whether it was patients on staff, patients on patients, or staff on patients.

Perhaps subconsciously, in anticipation of his OT session, he had overslept and was fumbling around in Sophie's room with time working against him. He desperately needed to find some clean pants, and realised they were back in his own room. He checked the clock again and he was already late. Shit! He pulled his jeans on and then noticed the crotch was frayed (a result of Jas using the hot knife as a deadly weapon). He put his hand on his scrotum and could feel the slight hint of testicular flesh beginning to poke through. He looked at the time again. Fuck it, he was always in trouble for being late. Did it notice? He pulled apart his legs and tried to examine the fraying material. Actually, it did not look too bad. He'd take the risk. Well, it wasn't for long and they could probably survive.

He ran along the corridor, levered back the fire exit door, jumped two, then three steps at a time, out into the bright winter sun, running across the lawns, before finding a quick access into the main hospital. He shuffled at a hurried walking pace through the humming, domed corridors, turned the corner and leapt up a short flight of stairs.

He stood panting outside and rang the doorbell.

He was feeling rough, probably looked rough and was desperate to get the whole thing over and done with. But there was something odd, a strange breezy feeling about his nether region. He put his hand on his crotch again and felt his bulging bollocks. It felt weird, but he could just detect his naked scrotum pushing through his jeans.

The keys in the lock turned and Cranfield's blonde wisps of hair appeared.

'What are you doing here?'

Roland raised his eyebrows, fully aware Cranfield would only laugh at him.

'I've got to do the lunchtime OT,' he said, appealing for a little understanding.

'You're not an OT,' said Cranfield, stating the obvious.

'I know,' said Roland. 'It's part of my placement, to gain the experience.'

It was Cranfield's turn to raise his eyebrows.

'Well, you'd better come in.'

He provided just enough space for Roland to slip through the thick white door and then hear it firmly locked behind him.

'You look like shit,' said Cranfield, leading him towards the day room.

'I feel like shit,' said Roland.

Cranfield looked at him mischievously.

'I thought you'd come to see your mate.'

'What do you mean?' asked Roland.

Cranfield laughed, leaving it up to Roland to figure it out.

'You can make yourself a coffee if you want,' he said,

pulling open a couple of cupboard doors and looking for mugs.

'Thanks, I need something.'

'The coffee's in there,' he said, pointing to another cupboard. 'Milk's in the fridge.'

Thwack!

'Fuck!'

Roland stumbled forward, lifting his arms to protect his head.

'What the fuck?!'

'Heh, you!' asserted Cranfield in a commanding tone. 'What did I tell you? No hitting people round the head.'

Roland turned to face his aggressor, a rotund middle-aged man, almost bare-chested, with a striped light blue dressing gown hanging off his shoulders.

'That's Sam-the-Taxi-Driver,' said Cranfield, as if his occupation served as a suitable introduction. 'Never turn your back on him… he tends to creep up on you.'

'Thanks,' said Roland, rubbing the back of his head.

Sam-the-Taxi-Driver stared menacingly at Roland, his grey stubble and stocky build filling the space of the door frame.

'Don't worry,' said Cranfield, 'he's harmless.'

But Roland took a few steps back, just in case.

'Sam,' ordered Cranfield, 'move away from the door.'

Sam-the-Taxi-Driver maintained his intransigence, continuing to fixate on Roland.

'Sam,' said Cranfield, issuing the command, 'you know what will happen if you don't move away from the door.'

The threat appeared to disrupt Sam-the-Taxi-Driver's thinking. There was a faint flicker of his eyelids and a brief shuffle of his feet. In recognition of this, Cranfield offered further encouragement, by pushing Sam-the-Taxi-Driver back into the day room and out of sight.

'Thanks for that,' said Roland. 'I thought he was going to go for me.'

'It's not him you need to keep an eye on.'

'Really?' asked Roland, beginning to have visions of a tortuous hour ahead of him.

Cranfield smirked.

'We'll keep an eye on things… better rustle up some patients for you.'

Cranfield stepped out of the kitchen and headed off down to the dormitory at the end of the ward.

Roland turned the kettle on and waited for the water to boil. He had no idea what he was meant to do with the extreme end of madness, off-the-deep-end patients whose violent unpredictability meant they were maintained on high doses of antipsychotic drugs.

Roland poked his head around the kitchen door and could hear Cranfield herding and cajoling reluctant patients to join in the lunchtime activity.

'Come on… yes, you… yes, you are… no, not that… leave that there… and you… you get off your arse.'

In quick time, Cranfield had three unwilling playmates, verbally pushing them away from the haven of the dormitory and towards the day room. Among them was Franks.

Roland turned back into the kitchen and resumed making coffee, dreading what faced him next.

'Right,' said Cranfield, as he entered the kitchen, 'I've managed to find a few for you.'

'Cheers,' said Roland half-heartedly.

Cranfield smirked again, only too pleased to wallow in Roland's unease.

'Come on then,' he said, turning back into the day room.

Roland followed Cranfield. At least Sam-the-Taxi-Driver had disappeared.

'I think you know him,' said Cranfield, pointing at the forlorn figure of Franks.

Roland nodded, acutely aware everyone knew about the day Franks had slashed his throat on the lawns of the hospital.

'He likes to play chess,' said Cranfield, pointing at a large wooden games box by the window. 'There's a board in there.'

In the middle of the day room, a suspender-belted giant, balding and frothing at the mouth, walked in a mumbling circle.

'That's Alan-the-Robot,' said Cranfield. 'He thinks he's a robot.'

'What am I supposed to do with him?'

Cranfield shrugged his shoulders.

'Down there,' said Cranfield, pointing his head back down the corridor, 'is Charlie… you'll probably have the same problem of engagement.'

Charlie was slinking along the side of the corridor walls, rolling an empty Lizra paper.

'That's the one you have to watch for,' said Cranfield. 'He likes to do his kung fu drop kicks when he's pissed about something.'

'I've heard,' said Roland.

'He's a bit crusty,' said Cranfield. 'Apparently, he joined the army to learn how to shoot so he could sign up with the Black Panthers. However, by the time they chucked him out it was all over for the urban guerrillas. Still, he's prone to occasional acts of violence. He comes and goes between prison and here and fakes his psychosis.'

Charlie gazed back and chuckled ominously to himself.

'I've got handover now,' said Cranfield. 'We'll keep an eye on you so don't press the alarm or else we'll have everyone piling in here.'

'Where is the button?' asked Roland, looking around for the panic alarm.

'Don't worry, we can see you… just don't leave the day room.'

Through a large shatterproof window of the ward office, previously unseen staff waved to Roland from behind the protective screen. Roland waved back with two fingers, circumvented the mechanical motions of Alan-the-Robot and approached Franks sitting on the ledge of the bay window.

'Hi,' said Roland, 'would you like a game of chess?'

Franks turned to face Roland and offered a withering, disdainful look.

'It's just a game of chess,' said Roland, hoping Franks would offer him the chance to be occupied.

Franks raised one eyebrow, implying there was an opportunity, a slight easing of his usual intransigence. Roland gratefully fumbled through the wooden box and unearthed a chequered board and a plastic bag full of chess pieces. He also noticed Charlie had become more attentive. Roland was aware of a fixed grin. This was designed to unnerve him. Then a bent forefinger wagged up and down, ticking Roland off. *Fuck, that's all I need*, thought Roland, *the nutter has got his eye on me*.

Roland unfolded the board on to a small round table, checking Alan-the-Robot was content to continue his set of roundabouts.

'Do you want to put the pieces out?'

To Roland's surprise, Franks began extracting one piece after another, placing them correctly on the board.

'I'll just get my coffee then,' said Roland.

He walked back into the kitchen and could feel the calculating eyes of Charlie follow him. On his way back to Franks he glanced at the protective screen, hoping to see someone watching. There was a leg hanging out from behind a metal filing cabinet, but no vigilance, as Cranfield had promised.

'There's a piece missing,' said Franks, as Roland sat down, realising he probably relied on Franks for protection.

'A white horse, you mean,' said Roland, studying the board.

'No,' said Franks emphatically, 'you need a white knight.'

'Oh, yeah,' said Roland, thinking this was going to be one of the most bizarre chess games he had ever played.

'How's this?' said Roland, picking up a matchstick from the tinfoil ashtray and placing it on the empty square.

Franks scowled.

'Don't worry,' said Roland, desperate to keep Franks engaged, 'as soon as you take my knight we can replace it.'

Franks grunted.

'Who goes first then?' asked Roland, trying to remain positive. 'White, I think, isn't it? Or do you want to go first?'

Franks sighed with impatience, grabbed a white and a black pawn, hid them behind his back and stretched out his clenched fists. Roland pointed and Franks revealed a white pawn.

'Okay,' said Roland, 'I'll go first then.'

Roland decided to concentrate on the game and moved a pawn forward. Franks countered with a pawn and Roland trotted out a few basic moves. Charlie began to strain his neck in order to follow the play. By the third or fourth move, Charlie was laughing knowingly to himself. Alan-the-Robot appeared less concerned, indulged in dribbles and word association before he suddenly diverted his attention and hovered over the board. Roland looked up as saliva dripped.

'Kung fu chess men and the hairy bollock,' said Alan-the-Robot. 'Kung fu chess men and the hairy bollock. Kung fu chess men and the hairy bollock.'

'If you say so,' said Roland, trying to make light of the intrusion.

Alan-the-Robot continued to hover, then restarted his motor, sipping back his drool and returning to his circular track.

Roland was feeling distinctly uneasy. Perhaps the only way to calm his nerves was to play Franks seriously?

Franks moved his bishop. Was this a cunning sacrifice? He checked as best he could all the possible permutations and could see no obvious advantage black could gain. Should he question Franks' thinking? Should he be playing Franks as an equal? Or should he let Franks win?

He moved his bishop forward and extracted the piece. Franks remained enigmatic, his steely thought processes undisturbed. He must have meant it, thought Roland, as he sat back to try and estimate where this could possibly lead. Was there a significant price to pay, a checkmate even? He could not see it. But perhaps it was in Roland's best interests to let Franks win? After all, it was hardly necessary to compete with an old professor drugged up to his eyeballs.

Franks moved another pawn forward, which left it isolated and stranded. Roland was tempted to ask Franks if this was what he meant, because it was all too easy. Clearly, he was playing someone who had lost the capacity to think logically. But there it was: the little black pawn. Roland could not see any possible disadvantage from immediately moving his queen and sweeping the piece off the board. To ensure this would not cause a riot, he looked back again at Charlie. He had lost interest and was rolling the same Lizra paper he had fondled since Roland's arrival. There was no point in patronising Franks. He would just have to beat him.

He removed the black pawn with a clear opening to checkmate in the next few moves. Without hesitation, Franks moved another pawn forward, just as vulnerable as before, just as kamikaze as his last few moves. Roland could bide his time a little and remove the pawn. On the other hand, he could launch his queen right next to the king and declare checkmate. It seemed so obvious. Magnanimously, he took the pawn instead, calculating the longer the game went on, the less time he would have left to occupy the psychotics.

Franks seemed unperturbed and moved his horse (knight) forward for Roland. *He's given up*, thought Roland, *it's probably too much – too much of a challenge for someone who is ill, psychotic and preoccupied*. He should do the decent thing and end it. Roland moved his queen forward.

'Sorry,' said Roland sheepishly, 'check.'

Franks' eagle-like forehead pulsed. He leant forward, grabbed his queen and smashed Roland's king halfway across the day room. Surprisingly, the rest of the pieces remained on the board.

'Checkmate,' said Franks, puffing out his cheeks.

Roland was startled by the sudden burst of petulance, but immediately scrutinised the move which Franks now claimed as victory. It did not make sense. There was no distinct line available for the black queen to follow.

'Asymmetric victory,' said Franks, leaning back with a firm, obdurate stare.

'What's that?' asked Roland, as he attempted to locate the distressed chess piece on the floor.

Franks folded his arms, communicating the game was over and implying he had no further comment. Alan-the-Robot kicked the white king from under his feet and it scurried across the lino, rolling ominously towards Charlie.

'You cannot see, can you?' said Franks. 'You only see the surface... what is in front of you! Look beneath the surface and you will see the lines!'

Charlie raised himself up from the chair.

'It's not three-dimensional,' said Roland.

'Pah! Command from above, on top of the hill, but learn from below. Always be with your men and they will follow.'

Charlie flexed his head from side to side in a slow, muscular stretch. The kung fu king was winding up. At the same time Roland felt a competitive urge to claim Franks' victory invalid... just for the record.

'Well, you are bound to win if you make up the rules,' said Roland.

'It's all about strategy,' said Franks. 'With the wrong strategy you will fail. See, look at the consequences, the consequences of failure, for me, for Napoleon, for you.'

Roland did not know what to say, and was acutely aware of Charlie twisting his torso and sending a muscular spasm rippling through his whole body. Roland had to focus, to look Charlie in the eye. Show no fear.

But where the fuck was Cranfield?

Charlie ground his teeth and hissed, preparing to launch a deadly arrow of feet and legs.

Roland needed help, now, and glanced towards the ward office.

Where's the fucking panic alarm?

'Kung fu chess men and the hairy bollock,' reiterated Alan-the-Robot, dribbling more excitedly. 'Kung fu chess men and the hairy bollock.'

240

Fuck! Fuck! Fuck!

Here it comes…

Roland braced himself to avoid the blow at the last minute, to run for the door, to get the fuck out.

But Charlie's face turned from a deep, dark, brooding cauldron to a hysterical laughing hyena. His hand and finger pointed and he almost fell over as he slid down the side of the wall.

What the fuck is that about?

Charlie's finger continued to point. *What the fuck's so funny?* Roland looked down. It was (praise be to the benign idiocy of Jas) his pink and hairy bollock poking through his jeans. Fate, no more than fate, but the madness of destiny! Roland did not care because Jas had inadvertently saved his life.

Cranfield appeared from around the corner.

'Where the fuck have you been?' asked Roland, seething at his abandonment.

'Listen, you shouldn't try and beat patients,' said Cranfield. 'They'll only get pissed with you.'

CHAPTER 23

THE "BACK WARDS" OF COLLECTIVE DEMENTIA

If he could, he would have left all the work to Sophie, because, as he said, he did not exactly agree with Bob "the union man" Jacobs. And Roland did suggest some alternatives: writing a collective letter of protest to the local press with the petition; occupying the school of nursing; refusing to do any work on the wards if staffing was insufficient. But according to Sophie, it was all unrealistic, and as Roland had already pointed out, there was very little enthusiasm to do anything among the staff and students. Bob Jacobs' strategy was the only option.

Roland hated such stark realism, but perhaps Sophie was right: trying to be too radical would only make them more isolated. It doesn't help change things; you can be satisfied with yourself but the world around you is still just as bad… and if you want people to follow you have to walk with them. Perhaps he was running too far ahead, especially as Sophie had also heard people say he was an anarchist and was just trying to cause trouble. Well, thought Roland, at least people were right about one thing! He was just frustrated because nobody seemed to care and everybody just buried their heads in the sand. Were they the only ones who could see what was wrong with this place? Sophie said most people probably did see it, they just did not think there was anything they could do about it.

Well, Sophie had drawn up a list of wards and put her name or Roland's against each one, a fair split, fifty-fifty, to visit and persuade the sister (or charge nurse) to supply copies of the day returns. At the end of the day, if they could just get some, they would have enough evidence to implicate Slaney and his crew in running staffing levels below thresholds for patient safety. Also, by implication, it would prove there were no resources (i.e. staff) to support student learning on the wards.

So, as per the schedule, Roland headed off to one of the dementia-ridden "back wards", hidden away in the fibrous tentacles of the hospital. It was here that the drudgery of nursing took place, capacity stretched to breaking point, where the senseless and useless tasks of feeding and washing achieved their epitome of meaninglessness. It was a last resting place, to be locked away in bleak, overcrowded, unforgiving regimes; patients who could no longer be looked after by their husbands, wives or partners, rejected by the private nursing homes and dispatched to the elderly mentally ill (EMI) wards of Wellington Park Psychiatric Hospital. It was a barbarous sentence to end their final months and years with their shrinking brains in a miserable denouement, an unsympathetic retreat to an institutionalised purgatory, with no cognition left to comprehend the world. They were hollow shells, all flesh and bone, all personality extinguished in an elongated death phase.

As Roland trudged reluctantly from the nurses' hostel to the ward, he tried to rehearse his opening lines to the sister, convinced he would immediately be eyed with suspicion, questioned about his legitimacy and sent away, admonished for his presumptuousness. Still, he must try and demonstrate to Sophie he was not just all talk but was prepared to put some work in.

Roland rang the doorbell of the ward and waited. After a few minutes a young female nurse opened the door.

Roland mumbled incoherently.

'Who did you say you wanted to see?' she asked, her hands full of a sodden incontinence pad.

'I wonder if I could speak to the sister or charge nurse, if they're on duty,' he said, assertively this time.

'Oh, come in,' she said cheerfully.

He followed the rustle of her plastic apron down the corridor.

'Can you wait five minutes?' she said, whilst skilfully manoeuvring her foot to open the lid of a bin and drop the wet pad in. 'Are you a relative?'

'No, I'm a representative from the student council and trade union.'

'Oh!' she said, surprised. 'We're just finishing off the washes. You can wait over there.'

She pointed to the remnants of dementia, washed, dressed and prepared in a circle of armchairs.

'Don't worry, they don't bite,' she said, sensing Roland's apprehension, before swiftly returning to her work in the dormitory.

244

He would have preferred to have waited in the ward office, away from the sad and forgotten human waste.

He looked down the corridor into the day room at the half-dead morass of patients. A few wandered aimlessly, all hanging on to their last vestiges of humanity. In the centre of the day room, like positioned mannequins, there was the resemblance of a genteel gathering – a coffee morning; a meeting of the WI. Everything was normal, apart from the interaction, the interrelationship which would normally flow from having so many facing each other in a circle. These were patients who knew only one thing: what they used to do, what they used to be, with only a grip on their past and their once regular functional routines.

A subdued silence was broken by a groan, a slow, distorted ache. Perhaps the Grim Reaper had visited, thought Roland, to suck out the final part of who they were. A patient diligently rubbed the Formica dinner tables, her hands moving round and round over the surface, repeating her embedded cleaning routines. Another patient dusted with her bare hands the edges of the white-painted window ledges. In front of Roland, an old man, bent over double, diligently moved in his own personal space. Odd, he thought, male patients on an all-female ward, but to be expected. Roland studied his movements like a game of charades, trying to fathom the occupation of the mime act. The hands appeared to be using a needle and thread, moving in and out, threading and tightening, whilst he circled around in a graceful dance. A shoemaker, thought Roland, or maybe a tailor.

Feeling self-conscious, Roland walked over to the large bay window at the back of the day room. There was no recognition among the patients of his presence as he perched awkwardly on the semicircular window ledge, facing the old women sat in their chairs, their eyes shut, like drifting, dreaming human vegetables. Plant life, thought Roland, well-watered but drying out.

He noticed another male patient sitting in one of the high-backed armchairs. Roland watched the scaly, withered hands grab hold of the armrests as they lifted themselves forward. Slight and pale, he steadied himself on his frail pins. Concentrating his energy, he needed to turn and swivel, holding his chair as a method to prop his pint-sized body into a standing position.

Roland waited as the old man smiled and took a few deep breaths.

'I was in the civil service, you know,' he said, his throat dry and croaking.

Roland acknowledged this self-important fact as the old man shakily moved a few feet forward. Roland stood up, ready to grab him in case he fell. To his credit, thought Roland, he stood unaided.

'Do you work here?' the man asked.

'Not on this ward,' said Roland, 'but I work in the hospital, as a student.'

The old man looked down at his feet, then rushed forward to reach up with his eyes so his head was almost nuzzling against Roland's chest.

'Can you help me?' he asked urgently.

'In what way?' replied Roland, feeling a mild degree of uneasiness.

'I need help,' he said, 'with my washing… and I need someone to help dress me in the morning… and I need someone to cook me some meals and keep the fireplace going.'

'The nurses do that,' said Roland. 'They look after you here.'

The old man wobbled, waiting for his thoughts to assemble.

'I can pay you,' he said earnestly. 'I have a civil service pension.'

'You don't need to pay for things here,' said Roland. 'We're paid to look after you.'

There was the *clip-clop* of shoes emerging from the dormitory.

'Clive, leave the man alone, will you, please? He hasn't come to see you.'

It was the sister, who even though she had probably been in the depths of piss and shit, looked remarkably clean. She must have ironed her dark blue uniform with a powerful steam, thought Roland, not a crease in sight. But she was young enough, Roland hoped, to be persuaded.

She took hold of Clive's arm and helped him sit back down in his chair.

'I'm sorry,' said the sister, 'he's one of the livelier ones. Thinks he's still living at home. Always pestering any new faces. Shall we go to my office?'

Roland followed, feeling a bit sorry for poor old Clive and his desire for a personal servant. The sister inserted a key in the ward office door and opened it with a swift flick of her wrist.

'Jackie said you were from the council or something,' she said, as they walked inside.

'The student council,' said Roland, in case she thought he was an aspirant member of the local government.

'Oh, I've not heard of that before.'

The sister sat on a swivel chair and looked thoughtfully at the desk covered in patient files, specimen bottles and a large box of surgical gloves. Roland helped himself to the only other available chair by the side of the desk, whilst explaining he was the president of the student council and a trade union representative.

'You look familiar,' she said, squeezing her eyes. 'What can I do for you?'

'We're running a campaign to try and address the problems of staff shortages on the wards.'

'I'm with you there!'

'Great!' said Roland, wishing he was better rehearsed in his response. 'Well, that's good… and…'

'And… ?' she said expectantly.

'And we need to get evidence to prove the wards are understaffed. It's a joint campaign with the trade union and the student council. Also, we want to prove students are used to fill the staffing gaps on the wards.'

'That's probably true,' she said, continuing to sound amenable. 'Although we don't get students on this ward. But the staffing is bad here. There's only me and Jackie on this morning. All of the patients are doubly incontinent. It's a crying shame for these poor things to end up like this. I wish we could do more, but we just don't have time to do anything but the basics and even then we struggle, to be honest with you.'

Roland was encouraged.

'Well, that's what we want to try and address,' he said. 'We want management to accept that conditions on the wards are dangerous for patients and staff.'

'I wish you luck,' she said, swivelling on her chair, 'but I can't see things ever changing.'

'They can change,' said Roland, slightly animated. 'As long as we get people to support us.'

The sister looked quizzically at Roland.

'What sort of support is it?'

'We need evidence of the staffing levels from as many wards as possible.'

'How are you going to do that?' she asked, picking up a ballpoint pen and drawing a swirling semicircle on a large, tattered sheet of green blotting paper.

'Well,' said Roland, ready to test the sister's commitment, 'we're asking all the wards to provide us with copies of the day returns, because they show the number of staff who actually worked on the ward for each shift, which is always lower than the figure they have for staff booked on to a ward.'

The sister stopped swirling her pen.

'Do you have permission to do this?'

'Permission?' said Roland, wondering if she had fully understood.

'Yes,' she said. 'You just can't go wandering on to wards asking for that kind of information. The day returns are confidential. I would need approval from Mr Fitzpatrick.'

Roland paused. How far, he wondered, did she really understand the point of his request?

'We can't ask for permission. That's the whole point of our campaign: to gather evidence to show the true picture of staffing levels on the wards. If we asked for permission, they would only say no.'

'You're asking me to take a risk.'

Would she do it? Roland wondered, as she began again to twirl her doodle into a deeper mix of ink.

'I think the risk is minimal,' he said, in order to reassure her. 'The more people who do it, the less risk there is.'

'Who else has signed up?'

'You're the first ward I've visited, but we've only just started.'

This was clearly not what the sister wanted to hear. She arched her back in her chair.

'Why don't you come back to me,' she said, 'when you've got more people involved?'

Just as Roland had thought: a reluctance to commit, a fear of the consequences, a fear of making just one little step towards trying to change things.

'Can I put you down as a possible then?' he asked.

'Oh yes,' she said, relieved Roland was not going to pile the pressure on, 'but I don't want to be on any list.'

'Don't worry, there's no list... but we'll put you down as a ward to come back to once we've got others committed.'

'Of course,' the sister said. 'Let me know how it's going because things are pretty awful here.'

Perhaps that was the best he could expect? But she had confirmed all his worst fears. They were never going to get people to embrace any form of protest, or anything which was a threat to their interests.

'We're also doing a collection for the miners,' said Roland, more in hope than expectation of getting a positive response.

'Do they need our help?' she asked, rather cynically.

'Well, it's the wider issue, about helping fellow trade unionists who are fighting for their jobs.'

'Would they do the same for us if I lost my job?'

'They're fighting for all our jobs,' said Roland, realising this sounded vague and abstract.

'I don't like that man…'

Roland knew who she meant.

'Scargill?'

'That's the one… there's something about him.'

'Well, it's the miners we need to support, even if you don't like him.'

'Yes, but he represents them, doesn't he? He's the one who's created all this mess.'

'I think it's Thatcher who decided to take on the miners,' said Roland in a corrective tone.

'I like Maggie – she's a woman!'

'But she's a woman who's declared war on us!'

'Not on me.'

Roland was ready to launch into a tirade against the vile ideology of Thatcherism, polluting his life and distorting every known concept of humanity. But what was the point? She was just like everyone else.

'Okay,' said Roland, 'I'll put you down as a possible.'

'I wish you luck,' she said, without any real meaning.

'Yeah…'

Roland stood up. He just wanted to get out; out of the stupid ward office, out of the stupid ward, away from all the stupid people. He thanked her, but it really, really was a waste of time.

He strolled back along the corridors, feeling defeated. If he was honest with himself, he hated the whole process; he hated having to convince people of the righteousness of their campaign. It should be self-evident, plain to see. Plus, he was useless at it. It was not really him. Sophie was far better at it – talking to people, convincing them, persuading, coaxing. All Roland really wanted was a box to stand on: let them listen and make their minds up, then it's up to them. But the grind, the hard work, that wasn't really what Roland wanted to do because it was not really him.

He was supposed to visit two more wards, but instead headed straight back to the nurses' hostel. He was angry – angry with himself, angry with complacency, angry with the way the world was, powerless to reverse the tide. That sister had no awareness of the world she lived in. It was not just the back wards of Wellington Park that had dementia, it was the whole fucking society… collective dementia, insensitive to the actual world; the real world. It was society that was going backwards in time. That's what Thatcherism was doing, bludgeoning every mind into amnesia, making people forget what it was like to be human, promoting selfishness and greed as if they were virtues, ripping out the core of conscience and morality.

Roland despaired. He had no faith in people, in their ability to be anything but unthinking machines. He despaired at their lack of depth, their thoughtlessness. What made them tick? What went around in their heads? They were in love with the daily routine, grounded and secure in the drudgery of life, in its clockwork turning, tick-tock, tick-tock. Round and round they went, not searching, not seeking, not metaphysical. In fact, thinking for them was dangerous, like a disease or virus. *Help, I think I had a thought!*

There must be more to life than just this, thought Roland, *than just being, just alive, just working, a slave to the machine. How can people live without ideas? Why not have big ideas? Why can't everyone see, in a moment, in a flash, what is plain to see, what is obvious: how everything is wrong, how the world is unfair, an unequal world of exploitation and oppression? Why, why, why… why can they not see?*

As he got closer to the nurses' hostel, he composed in his head a story for Sophie in order to demonstrate he had gone to the wards and had tried his best. But what he really needed now was a joint to soothe his anxiety, for the amber nectar to soothe his frustrations, to be back where all was well, in a warm, self-medicating blanket.

CHAPTER 24

TOWERS OF FEAR AND DOUBT

Roland travelled down by coach to Brighton with Jas, Terry and over thirty long-stay patients on board. It was a grey, chilly spring day, as they parked and stepped out underneath the green-painted promenade. The qualified nurses divided the patients up into manageable groups, agreeing to meet back at the pub at the end of the East Pier. Roland, Jas and Terry headed off into the town to do some shopping with Starr, the fidgeting Mr Andrews and the hallucinating Mr Creely. Within minutes the latter two had become disturbed and anxious. Terry offered to return them to the main group, allowing time to go off and do some "business". This left Jas and Roland with Starr, stood by a zebra crossing.

'Alright, Alan,' said Jas to Starr, 'let's get you some clothes. Would you like that?'

Starr nodded, dribbling down his stained institutional shirt.

'They'll be pissed that there's two of us with him,' said Roland, in reference to the qualified nurses supervising the bulk of the patients.

'Nah, it'll be alright,' said Jas. 'What are they going to do about it?'

'I thought the point was to try and get into Gobi's good books, not be caught wandering off doing nothing.'

'Look,' said Jas, 'no one else is bothering to do anything for him. Anyway, they'll all be heading off to the pub. At least he'll have some proper clothes to wear for once.'

Starr was happy to remain compliant.

Jas led the way, holding Starr's hand and pulling the distracted man-child along. Roland trailed behind, impressed with Jas and the rapport he had with Starr.

'They've got good stuff in here,' said Jas, pushing open the doors to a large department store.

They travelled in single file up the escalator, checked the categories of items on the floor listing before heading off to the sports department.

'What do you think of this, Alan?' asked Jas, picking up a grey flannel tracksuit bottom and holding it against the front of Starr's legs.

Starr looked down at the grey cloth.

'Do you like that?' asked Jas, standing back a little to get a better view. 'I think he likes it.'

'I don't know,' said Roland, trying to gauge if Starr had cognition.

'I think that looks cool,' said Jas, returning to the shelf and hunting for a matching top.

'Do you like the tracksuit?' asked Roland.

Starr nodded and responded with a quiet, barely audible, 'Yes.'

'Christ, I think he understands us,' said Roland, as

Jas returned with the top and put it against Starr's chest.

'Of course he does,' said Jas. 'You know what's going on, don't you, Alan?'

Starr looked down again at the sportswear, admiring and touching the logo.

'How do you know what size to get him?' asked Roland.

'I know sizes,' said Jas. 'That's one thing I'm good at. He'll need some trainers to go with that.'

'Right,' said Roland, who regretted his initial reluctance.

Jas picked out a pair of bright white trainers, suggesting Starr tried them on. They explained to an uneasy shop assistant they needed to stay with their patient in the changing room and "not to worry, he isn't dangerous".

Roland, Jas and Starr stared back at their image in the mirror. For a moment there was no difference… nothing separated them.

'Do you like that, Alan?' asked Jas, whilst preening his hair.

Starr chuckled and looked down at the floor.

'Amazing,' said Roland, shocked at the simplicity of the transformation.

'Not bad,' said Jas, still admiring his own reflection.

'One thing, though…' said Roland, who tried to lever Starr's head up so he would look at himself again. 'How are you going to pay for it?'

'That's not a problem,' said Jas, talking to Roland via the mirror. 'He's got loads of money… they all have.'

'You're joking?'

'No, they're loaded.'

'How?'

'Benefits… the wards ration it out but they hardly spend any of it. I've seen the accounts… they've all got thousands.'

'Fuck!'

'I know,' said Jas. 'They let me take some money out for him.'

'You're not going to spend it on yourself, are you?'

'I wish,' said Jas, moving back into the changing cubicle, 'but I've got to show receipts, haven't I?'

Starr continued to refuse to look up.

'Blimey,' said Roland to Starr, 'you're a rich man.'

'I'll just go and pay for it,' said Jas, picking up Starr's old clothing. 'Might as well keep him in it.'

Roland guided Starr out of the changing room. There was a display case full of watches which caught his eye.

'Do you want a watch? You could buy yourself a watch if you wanted.'

Starr shook his head vigorously.

'Come on,' said Roland, who wanted to make amends, 'no harm just having a look.'

Starr remained rooted to the spot.

'Come on,' said Roland, 'they're only watches.'

'No,' said Starr adamantly.

'Why?' asked Roland, surprised by Starr's assertiveness.

'Time.'

'They tell the time,' stated Roland. 'All watches tell the time.'

'No,' said Starr firmly. 'My brother said if you know the time it can send you mad. Never look at the Clock Tower.'

Roland was taken aback. This was the same Starr who every day wandered the corridors and lawns of Wellington Park, lost in another world, yet had the insight to say something of an abstract rationality... even a metaphysical rationality.

'Alright,' said Jas, holding the shopping bag with Starr's old clothes.

'You know what,' said Roland, 'I think I've just had a conversation with him.'

'Yeah, he's not stupid, you know.'

Roland was keen to develop this new connectivity with Starr and looked him straight in the face.

'You told me about the Clock Tower in Wellington Park, didn't you, Alan?'

'Oh, that thing,' said Jas. 'It doesn't work.'

'What? You're kidding.'

'No!' said Jas, laughing. 'That thing hasn't worked in years.'

'Are you sure?'

'Yeah... why, have you been using it?'

'Yeah, I'm sure it tells the time.'

'Only in your head, mate.'

Roland was dumbfounded. He couldn't work it out. He was sure, definite, the Clock Tower told the time. He had used it to get to work – late, obviously, but it was still close to the correct time.

'Forget about it,' said Jas. 'Is that what Alan told you: never look at the clock? He's right... it can send you mad!'

'I can't believe it,' said Roland, still trying to recall the number of times he had looked at the Clock Tower to check the time.

'Listen, mate, you're not a patient, so trust me, it's not important.'

'There's something going on in there, though,' said Roland, nodding in the direction of Starr.

'Of course, you used to have a job, didn't you, Alan?'

'Christ, he had a job?'

'Yeah,' replied Jas, explaining, 'you worked in a call centre, didn't you?'

Starr ignored the comments as he tugged on the logo of his tracksuit top.

'Hard to believe, I know,' said Jas, watching the preoccupied Starr. 'Not that I think he took any calls. I reckon that's what did him in. Working in a call centre would do anyone in. Anyway, I've got to leave you now.'

'What? You can't do that,' said Roland, feeling he had been left with the kid who was too young to play with.

'Got to, mate, need to buy some clothes while I'm here. You'll be alright. Take him for a walk along the beach and I'll meet you back at the pub.'

And before Roland had a chance to respond, Jas was off, slipping away to start his shopping trip.

★

Roland and Starr walked along the promenade, observing the swirling brown sea and pebble beach. There were a few brave souls who now and then ran into the freezing water before jumping back out again. The cafes and bars below trundled through a dribble of trade. Starr seemed happy enough, repeating his standard phrases interspersed with minor exclamations. Roland would have tried to talk to him, but he was also self-absorbed.

They came to the end of the other pier, which seemed a suitable point to head back and join the others.

'You alright?' asked Roland, who had wrapped himself in his coat against the cold sea breeze.

'Yes,' said Starr, who was always content in his own world.

'I like your tracksuit,' said Roland, 'it looks really good on you.'

'Thank you,' said Starr, who then hummed, chuckled and tried to eat the air.

'Aren't you cold?' asked Roland, as Starr billowed against the prevailing wind.

'No,' said Starr, who was sweating profusely.

'Shall we go to the pub then?'

'Six... one-five... one-five... one-two,' replied Starr.

'Why do you use those numbers?' asked Roland, as they headed back. 'Was that the number of your call centre?'

Starr remained inscrutable.

Oh well, who is the fool? thought Roland. *I can't even tell if the clock is working.* There was something about Starr, something which said that there was more to him than he let on. But then, that would be true of a lot of them. For all the madness, the bizarreness, there were moments, pure moments of lucidity. But it was impossible to cross the boundary into "their world". As much as Roland wanted to, as much as he thought it was how he should care, he knew there was no way he could cross over, because to cross over meant no going back… you would become "one of them".

They walked through the entrance to the East Pier, staring through the gaps in the timber board at the brown muddy sea below, before venturing along the white-painted benches which combined with the souvenir outlets, doughnuts and candyfloss. There was a damp drizzle in the air which distorted Roland's view of the couples who walked past them, hugging tightly against the wind.

'Shall we walk all the way down?' asked Roland.

'Yes,' said Starr assertively.

At the end of the pier the seagulls lurched and manoeuvred over the cold sea, then swooped in, hovering above the small fairground attractions. The wind whipped up the guide ropes of green and black tarpaulins, slapping the straining material. It felt desolate, the dull horizon falling down on their long view out into the sea. Then Roland felt a strange sense of closeness, some link between them which lay beneath the surface. Perhaps, if there was not so much rubbish in the way, they would normally be friends. But instead, Roland was Starr's "keeper", looking after a man who was no more than a child.

'We should go back,' said Roland.

Starr did not move.

'Would you like a drink? We're going to meet the others in the pub.'

Starr's eyes lit up.

★

It was standing room only. Any patron who opened the door to the pub seemed to understand this was not the usual drinking congregation and made a hasty retreat. Roland had bought the tracksuited Starr a fizzy drink and left him at the bar, a figure who could be considered less a part of the patient population and almost a member of "normal" society. A few of the qualified nurses came over to Roland and said what a good job he had done in buying the new clothes. Roland accepted the compliment but said it was Jas who deserved all the credit, who was also on his way (Roland hoped).

While they all waited, Roland sat by the window surveying the mass of long-stay patients. They sat gurning, grinning, fidgeting, smiling and occasionally singing. Roland perceived a collective sense of anxiety, removed as they were from the comfort of the ward, the hospital and the grounds. If a process of eviction from Wellington Park would soon be starting for all of these patients, did they know what lay ahead of them? Perhaps that was why they appeared to struggle with their newfound freedom, even if it was just for a day? Most of them would just become victims in a heartless, disinterested world, thought Roland, if more was not done to help. Perhaps they all knew something was coming? Perhaps that was why they all appeared subdued, as if shot down by a virulent virus, a poisonous gun from out of nowhere, smashing their world with deadly accuracy. Was something rampant, nasty, pernicious polluting the air, an unfettered epidemic of callousness and intransigence? It was as if reality had hit home, a signal their world was coming to an end. Their dysfunctional comfort zone housed in the rundown Wellington Park was going to be extinguished, evaporated, vaporised and exterminated.

Mr George didn't have his dancing feet on; gone was the perpetual motion and the imitation soft shoe shuffle. For frozen, catatonic Mr McCarthy, the therapeutically drug-damaged Mr Andrews, the vividly hallucinating Mr Creely, the carpet was going to be taken from underneath their feet. Someone, or something, was rolling back the frontiers and forcing them to stand on their own two feet… even if they had no feet to stand on.

'Where are your mates?' asked one of the qualified nurses. 'We're going in a minute.'

Roland shrugged. He knew Jas was coming, but he had no idea what Terry was up to.

'We'll give it five more minutes and if they're not here by then we're going without them. Wasn't it you lot who organised this trip anyway?'

'Yes,' said Roland, with a pained sense of failed obligation.

'Well, we can't hold them here forever.'

But just as Roland was acknowledging time was against them, Jas pushed open the door, with two large bags swinging from both arms and a broad, apologetic smile across his face.

'Hi, guys,' said Jas, 'sorry about that.'

Roland looked at Jas so he understood immediately it was not a good idea to start bragging about his purchases. Jas' arrival was the signal to instruct the patients to return to the coach. They began gathering the troops, counting each one as they left through the door.

'Do you know where Terry is?' asked Roland, as Jas stumbled along the wooden planks of the pier.

'Not a clue,' said Jas, weighed down by his plastic bags.

They did a final count on the coach and asked the driver to wait a few more minutes. This was not going to look good if Terry did not make it, not least because there was no account of Terry doing anything with the patients while they were out and about.

The hydraulics of the coach sounded and the door shut.

'He'll be alright,' said Jas, seated next to Roland. 'He can get the train home.'

As the coach pulled off there was a thud on the side and then the figure of Terry waving at the driver through the front windscreen.

'Don't let him on!' shouted Jas.

Terry apologised profusely and strolled down the main aisle and sat in front of Roland and Jas. Jas leaned forward and tapped Terry on the shoulder.

'How did you get on?' he asked, whispering through the V-shaped gap in the seats.

'No problem,' said Terry, raising his eyebrows.

'You're kidding me,' said Roland, who immediately drew the right conclusion.

'Don't moan about it,' said Jas. 'You won't be complaining later on.'

CHAPTER 25

WITHIN THE SYSTEM

Roland walked along the circular tarmac path towards the school of nursing with his head down. He had spotted Fitzpatrick striding towards him with his usual sense of military purpose. It was the last thing Roland needed. Should he say hello, or grunt some form of recognition? As much as he hated the authoritarianism, he still wondered if he should be demonising him so readily... enough people had said he wasn't all bad. It was with this in mind that Roland let his guard slip.

'Hello,' he said distinctively.

It was a mistake. Fitzpatrick ignored him, delivering a calculated snub.

What a bastard! Learn the lesson, Roland said to himself, *always trust your instincts.*

He pushed open the door to the school and made his way up the rickety stairs to the open door of Gobi's office. Gobi was seated behind his desk and indicated with a nod of his head where Roland should sit whilst he finished a phone call. Roland did his best to ignore the conversation, looking out of the open window, across the vast manicured lawns and as far as the ominous Clock Tower. Fuck, Jas was right: the clock did not work.

This was ostensibly just another tutorial, with the added component of Gobi providing "protective guidance". But Roland knew it was a barely disguised attempt to keep tabs on what he and Sophie were up to.

'How are you, young man?' asked Gobi, replacing the receiver and grimacing at the accumulation of dust on his phone.

'Fine, thank you,' said Roland, his tone of voice betraying a lack of interest in their meeting.

'Good. Now, you know, let me see,' said Gobi, as he fumbled with various bits of paper on his desk. 'Let me just find what I need.'

Roland waited.

'So, you know, what are you doing at the moment? You know, more trips to the seaside and all that?' said Gobi, as he continued to search for the appropriate papers.

'I've just finished my placement.'

'Oh yes, good,' said Gobi, as he lifted a large stack of papers and extracted what he needed. He scrutinised Roland's ward placement report and nodded to himself.

'What did you think of it?' asked Gobi.

'The placement? Surreal…' said Roland sarcastically.

Gobi raised his eyebrows, which was usually a sign he needed to offer something corrective.

'Oh yes, you know, but not a word we would use…'

Gobi dipped his head and continued to examine the report. Roland knew it contained little Gobi could use to contain or control him. He stared out of the window, looking again across the vast lawns towards the sandstone entrance to Wellington Park. That was where it had all begun, he mused, reflecting on his first day, bumping into Sophie, nervously wondering what he had let himself in for.

'Oh, you know, you had a good report,' said Gobi, confirming it for himself.

Roland smiled.

'They say you performed well... under difficult circumstances.'

'Short on staff, I think they mean.'

Gobi ignored the sarcasm again.

'Where were you?' he asked, inspecting the report for more detail.

'The death ward,' said Roland succinctly.

Gobi hesitated.

'Oh yes, we had discussed this before you went.'

'Yes,' said Roland.

'And you did not get into any trouble then?'

'No,' said Roland. 'It was just your average dose of institutionalised barbarity.'

There was a disapproving silence as Gobi raised his eyebrows.

'You coped,' said Gobi, in an effort to avoid Roland's baiting.

'I like to think so,' said Roland, ready to confront Gobi with the reality of his experience.

But Gobi did not need the grim detail... he knew what went on.

'You know,' he said, anxious to reveal his own heartfelt beliefs, 'even in a perfect world things are bound to go wrong.'

'I know that,' said Roland, 'but things here are the opposite of perfect... this place is perfect at being imperfect.'

'Well, how do you think we can change things?' asked Gobi, raising his head from scouring Roland's report.

'By smashing the whole corrupt system... starting with this institution.'

Gobi blinked a few times as he considered how he should assert his authority.

'You know, you could do a lot of damage to this school if you want to play with fire...'

'I'm not playing,' said Roland. 'I'm well aware of how things can get... so is Sophie.'

Gobi wiped his brow, clearly antagonised.

'You know,' he said, leaning forward to add weight to his words, 'we took a risk with some of you, you know... we gave you a chance...'

'I know that,' said Roland, partially grateful, 'but you only took that chance because you had no choice.'

'No, no, no, no, no... we have lots of people who want to come to this school. It's not easy...'

'Really?'

'Oh yes, you know, you have some ability... but, you know, you need to learn how to channel it. Sometimes, you know, you might have to accept you cannot change some things. You know, even some of us here are not happy with the way things go on.'

Roland looked out of the window again at the robust sandstone columns standing guard over the main reception, keeping everything in its place. He looked back at Gobi.

'But what if the system is wrong?'

'I'm not sure what you mean by "the system",' said Gobi, confidently controlling his response. 'Do you know?'

Roland hesitated. He hadn't anticipated a combative Gobi.

'Well, the system is everything,' he said falteringly.

'Oh, you know, are you against everything?'

'No, but... well, there is this system,' said Roland, raising his voice. 'I can state quite clearly exactly what is wrong with this hospital and the school... if you want me to?'

'No, no, no,' said Gobi hurriedly. 'You know, there's no need for you to do that.'

No, I bet there isn't, thought Roland.

'We would need all day,' said Gobi, rather disarmingly. 'However, you know, you should try and be a bit more constructive. I think, you know, it's always easy to find negatives, you know, a lot harder to find solutions.'

'Is it negative to be critical?' said Roland. 'Is there any point in offering solutions when they are not going to be accepted?'

'You know, you should always try to find some good in people,' said Gobi. 'You might find they are more willing to listen.'

'If I see any good I'll let you know,' said Roland dismissively.

'Oh, you know, it's not all bad... you can still make things better. I've always found you can change things over time. But you have to win people over, you know, to do that.'

269

Roland shook his head. He knew where this was going.

'You become part of the system,' he said. 'You don't really change anything.'

'But you will fail,' said Gobi sincerely. 'You know, you have to be part of it, in order to change it.'

'But what if the system can't change?' said Roland. 'And what if, in trying to change it, you just help in keeping the whole rotten system going?'

Sweat appeared on Gobi's brow, either due to the heat or coping with Roland's intransigence.

'You know...' said Gobi, searching for his words. 'You know, this institution has been here a long time, as have many of the people in charge here. And you know, you cannot win... they will not roll over.'

'I wouldn't expect them to,' said Roland, laughing. 'The point is, what goes on here is just plain wrong. So I have no choice, I have to try and do something about it.'

That, surely, was the point.

'The care here is not as bad as you think,' said Gobi, feeling a trickle of sweat drip into his eye socket.

'If you mean drugging people up to their eyeballs and hoping that somehow they'll get over it—'

'You know, it's more than that,' said Gobi, interrupting.

'Is it?'

'There was a time, you know,' he said, stretching out his legs, 'when Wellington Park was internationally renowned.'

'You mean, when they were cutting bits of brain out?'

'Oh yes, you know…'

Gobi did not rise to the bait. He was getting nowhere, he decided, and instead looked down again at Roland's report, searching for something else to move the conversation on.

Where is this going? wondered Roland. *He really is wasting his time if he thinks I'm just going to roll over.*

'Hmmm… you know, that's a better report than I thought you would get,' said Gobi, folding the last page and putting it on top of another pile of papers. 'You know, you could easily have been in trouble on a ward like that.'

'Well, it's nice to know I'm not in trouble.'

'It's not something you should wish for,' said Gobi, taking off his glasses and rubbing the sweat from his forehead. 'You still have a long way to go in your training.'

'I know,' said Roland unenthusiastically.

Gobi wiped his finger across his thick-rimmed spectacles.

'Is it what you expected… on the ward?' he asked, squinting.

'That's a good question,' said Roland, reflecting. 'I kept my mouth shut, just as Douglas told me to…'

'You know, as I've said to you before, Roland,' said Gobi, increasingly frustrated by Roland's provocation, 'if you want to improve things here you will have to do it within the system.'

'But that means no change,' said Roland. 'Pretending to change things when there is no intention of changing anything.'

'You know, you need to think about yourself,' said Gobi. 'You need to think about your career. Otherwise, you know, you're going to find it very difficult.'

'I know that,' said Roland, feeling Gobi was close to being overly paternal. 'But I have to be myself, I can't be someone I'm not. I would rather try and do something about it and fail.'

Gobi smiled.

'One of my sons is like you,' he said thoughtfully. 'And like you, he doesn't listen.'

'No, I do listen,' said Roland, 'I just don't agree.'

Gobi fumbled with his glasses and put them back on his face.

'You're sharp, you know,' he said. 'You know, that can irritate certain types of people.'

'You mean someone like Fitzpatrick? He can't even say hello to me, so there's little chance of anything changing there.'

'Mr Fitzpatrick has his way of doing things. He'll do anything for this hospital, but I'm afraid if you cross him, you know, he can be unforgiving.'

What could Roland do? Such an implacably authoritarian figure was hardly going to suddenly embrace him even if he did turn into a compliant robot.

'Okay, so, you know, what are you and Sophie planning?'

Ah, thought Roland, Gobi had got to the point of their conversation.

'I'm not sure that's something I can discuss,' said Roland, sitting upright.

'Well, you know, I need to know, if it's something to do with the school.'

'We're not exactly doing anything,' said Roland, trying to recall as best he could how far Sophie had got with the day returns.

'But you would let me know before you did anything?'

'We'd let you know if the student council wanted to raise anything with you.'

That was not what Gobi wanted.

'You know I would not want you to do something without my knowledge.'

'Why is that?'

'Because, you know, you still represent the school.'

'I represent the students… they elected me.'

Gobi was going to clarify that Roland was nominated, not elected, but decided to get straight to the point.

'I will tell you, you know, so that you know about these things,' said Gobi, preparing to take Roland into his confidence. 'I've had Mr Fitzpatrick threatening to close down this school, you know…'

Roland shrugged.

'He's not going to do that,' he said, offering Gobi a grain of comfort. 'We're his best source of cheap labour. Without us he couldn't run the place.'

'Well, you know, we will see,' said Gobi. 'You will let me know if you do anything, you know, which could have an impact on the school?'

'Of course,' said Roland, lacking any sincerity.

Gobi's phone set buzzed and he flicked a switch. It was his secretary, reminding him of his next appointment, and he also had a caller on the line.

'Shall I go, then?' asked Roland, keen to seize the opportunity and escape.

Gobi stretched out his arm, trying to indicate Roland should stay.

'Put them through,' said Gobi into the phone.

Roland sat back down, but he could tell from Gobi's face there was a degree of seriousness involved. Hopefully, Gobi would not want him to overhear. He was right. With a wave of his hand Gobi signalled Roland could leave.

Roland smiled and slid effortlessly from the office, down the stairs and out on to the tarmac path.

Man, what a dick, he said to himself, *all that bullshit about sucking up to the system. I don't give a fuck about the system. Smash the system. The system's fucked. Why keep the bullshit thing? Who wants it? Who needs it? Hanging on to some fucked up pile of shite. The system doesn't work. It's on its last legs. It's dying.*

It's fucking dead.

CHAPTER 26

UNDER THE OLD OAK TREE

Sophie had decided her psoriasis was something she would embrace: women were not objects (good, bad or ugly), and people could stare, but she did not care – she was not going to hide it and she was not going to hide away, she was going to be out and proud; if something she wore showed her scaly arms, so be it, it was not her problem but the people who were staring. It was a renewed self-confidence and assertiveness which did not stop there; Sophie wanted to be sexually adventurous too, because they had moved on, because there was no need to be shy or limited just because of her disease. They should try it out in the open, in the great outdoors.

For Roland, sex in the room, in the bed, was sufficient. Together, they had overcome the scaly, dry flesh and had resumed penetrative pleasure. He couldn't see the logic, the reasoning, the need to have sex anywhere else other than in the comfort and privacy of Sophie's room. But Sophie was adamant, they should go for a picnic and try it out for once. What was Roland's problem?

So, on a blisteringly hot summer's day (having made

sure Jas and Terry were on shift to avoid the risk of being spied on), Roland reluctantly headed off with Sophie into the woods behind the nurses' hostel.

'The plan,' said Sophie, as they followed a dry track, 'is just to see how we feel... but we should also walk towards the old abbey.'

'What about people?' said Roland, who was desperate not to be caught in the act, by patients, staff or strangers.

'Well, of course there are people about,' said Sophie. 'But we can't avoid people, especially on such a lovely day. You need to stop worrying, relax and stop trying to avoid something just because you've never done it before. At the end of the day, everyone does it. We're a couple... Having sex in the same room all the time is okay, but it's not... liberating.'

Liberating... liberating... that was an odd word, thought Roland: the sex they had was somehow not right, not free? What was not free about having sex together?

'Why, is there something wrong with the sex we have?' he asked cautiously.

'Of course not,' said Sophie, 'but we should try out different things, experiment. We're supposed to be young! Christ, everyone has had sex in the woods... even the patients!'

That's that, then, thought Roland.

He walked behind Sophie, brushing aside the rich growth of stinging nettles and ferns jutting into their path, looking furtively through the trees for other walkers. He carried the rucksack and watched Sophie trek along the tracks in her short-sleeved T-shirt, with her red, flaky psoriasis arms exposed. Clearly, it was like a badge of honour, a point of principle, a statement she was not going to be intimidated or forced to run and hide because people couldn't cope with the way she looked.

Sophie glanced back at Roland, making sure he was still following, still a willing partner. She couldn't understand why he was so reticent. But there were also other things she wanted him to do. What's the point in being together if you don't try different things? But when it came to it, Roland always stood back. He said a lot, but he was always reluctant to follow through. Perhaps he was all talk? Perhaps he was just a dilettante?

Roland was concentrating, trying to open the gate of sexual desire. But there was nothing natural, nothing relaxing, nothing that made him feel he could make love to Sophie out in the open. Did Sophie now expect him to take the lead? Was it down to him to initiate the whole thing, to grab her, kiss her and fuck her?

Sophie stopped in a small clearing.

Okay, so maybe it was up to him to make the first move?

He wrapped his arms around her, watched her eyes, her beautiful blue eyes which still captivated him. They kissed and it began to feel natural, it began to feel almost right. He pushed forward, and Sophie stepped back. He wanted to press against her, to lie on the floor, but as he tried, Sophie laughed.

'What?'

'Not yet,' she said. 'I don't think it will work here.'

Roland stopped as instructed. He was relieved.

Putting it off, finding the right spot, that was okay with him.

They moved off again. Within a few minutes they could see, through a web of branches and leaves, the soft brown tones of the stumpy walls of the old abbey. It might make sense to picnic there, perhaps hidden by the oak tree?

As they emerged from the wooded foliage they circumvented the walls, examined the levelled stumps and peered through the remaining windowless rectangles into the interior. Rather than just climbing over the foundation stones, they entered the old abbey through the remains of a doorway. There really was, thought Roland, not much left of the place, just the great big old oak tree growing in the middle of it. They looked up into the thick branches of the star green leaves of the old oak, blinking against the blazing sun forcing down its rays. Sophie pointed to one of the thickest branches and identified the wearing away of the bark: that was the hanging branch, the one where they swing. Perhaps it was not the best place to be, but there was one bonus: it was shaded and discreet.

They walked around the old oak, searching for a patch of ground which was smooth enough to sit down on. Sophie also wanted the sun, whilst Roland always tried to stay out of direct sunlight as it induced a severe headache.

Eventually, they sat slightly apart on a blanket, drinking from a bottle, both wondering if this was the time when they should "do it".

'Can I ask you...?' said Sophie, a little sheepishly. 'Can we do something different?'

'Different? This is different.'

'Yes, but… don't you want to try out different things?'

'I don't mind,' he said, looking around at the eroded flint stone walls and beyond into the surrounding wood.

'Can you do it differently?' she asked self-consciously.

Roland was bemused.

'What do you mean?'

'Well…' she said, pausing. 'You know, there is more than one hole down there.'

Sophie's eyes widened, trying non-verbally to complete her sentence.

The penny dropped… something different. Christ, that was different!

'Everyone does it,' said Sophie.

What choice did he have?

'Yeah, let's do it,' he said, with the minimum of conviction.

Was this the way things were going, he asked himself? A tick in the box: *I did this, I did that… I've now done it all!* Surely, it was not everyone doing it which should be the reason for them to do so. It should be that this was something they both wanted to do; it should be part of what they would both want to explore. But the truth was, Roland did not want to do it.

And this was his failing – failing to come up to scratch; failing to be all the things Sophie wanted him to be. Failing to be a grown-up?

★

Sophie slept and Roland wandered into a bad dream. He was lost, drifting through a vaulted hall, Romanesque, the walls glistening with a secret light source, a sparkling, crystalline form. But his time was short: suddenly he was thrust down, pushed into the belly of the soil, into the bowels of the undergrowth and in amongst the fibres of tree roots and plant. The air was stagnant, full of the rotting corpses of mud and vegetation. He fumbled around, struggling to reveal the surface above, but it was like quicksand. He thrashed about, beating his arms and legs in order to break free, but his movements forced him down deeper into the darkness.

Then, from nowhere, he re-emerged within the strange vaults again. He felt the heat of the carnivorous surroundings warm his skin, and his heart beat faster. He began to navigate the hall and alcoves, all of which were empty, until he came across a door, a dazzlingly bright white door. It was obvious: push the door open. The other side of the door was different, in another colour, or not really a colour. He could make out the grains of the wood and he stared deeply into the grains, into the very heart of the grain; into the very veins of the wood. Did it have meaning? Would it reveal something he did not know, or he needed to know?

Whoosh!

He was elevated at speed, rushing through, back where he started, back in the old vaulted hall. There was a wide stone plinth, and on it stood a tall, proud bird. He did not know why he knew, but he knew it was a golden phoenix. As he studied the bird it turned and spoke to him.

'Fight for your life,' said the golden phoenix. 'Fight for your life!'

The golden phoenix began to break free, thrashing its wings and penetrating the ceiling above. *This is my way out*, thought Roland, *I need to follow*. He grabbed the creature's feet as it rocketed upwards. He could feel the surface breaking, the pressure relieving as they fought their way up, onwards and upwards, all the way to the top.

Was he awake? Was he still dreaming? His heart was beating.

He felt the presence of the golden phoenix. It was now a threat. Roland lashed out, his arm and fist flying, making contact with the head of the bird. Was he awake? He was sure. He waited. Yes, it was real, and he was in real time. God knows what would have happened if he had not lashed out, so vivid was the experience, so real and tangible.

He looked down at Sophie, blinking in the dappled light wafting over her half-naked body, her breasts angled to both sides. He was going to wake her, to tell her how this bird, a golden phoenix (and he did not know why it was, or why that word had come to him), had been real, beside him. Then he noticed, the miracle, the magic, the cure. And just as he was going to wake her, so Sophie stirred, rubbed her eyes, licked her lips and raised her hand to her eyebrows to look at Roland.

'What?' she said, lifting her head.

'I don't believe it!' said Roland, spreading his arms wide, indicating it was something about Sophie.

Sophie did not answer. Instead, she quickly inspected herself.

'Can't you see?!' said Roland. 'Look, it's almost gone – the psoriasis!'

Roland was expecting Sophie to scream with delight, to praise God (even though he didn't exist), to scream at the joy of a miracle. But Sophie was composed, gazing down at her arms, which were almost free of the ugly, scaly disease.

'I can't believe it,' said Roland again, trying to fathom why Sophie was so calm about her sudden curative transformation.

'Don't worry,' she said, 'that's normal.'

'What do you mean, normal?'

'It's the sun,' she said. 'It usually gets rid of it.'

'What do you mean, it usually gets rid of it?'

'I've always had psoriasis, but I didn't know if the sun would make that much difference.'

'You've always had psoriasis?'

'Yes, but never this bad.'

'You mean you always get it?'

'No, not all the time, but usually in the winter, especially on my scalp, and sometimes on my arms and legs. I didn't know whether it would go away this time because of the chickenpox.'

'But...'

Roland was struggling. Sophie was going to get better. But he was frustrated: he had invested all his energy into thinking he was going to be living with a devastating disease, Sophie's disease, but all along she probably knew it could easily be cured by sunlight.

'But aren't you pleased?' he said.

'Of course,' said Sophie, reaching for her top.

'Well, I think it's great news! We should celebrate!'

'Okay.'

'Don't you want to?'

'Of course,' said Sophie.

But for Roland it was all odd. Sophie's behaviour was strange.

'Shall we go?' she said, standing up and looking around.

'Yeah, if you want to…'

But Roland wanted to wait. He wanted to hold the moment as something special, far more meaningful, as a moment when the virtue of standing by Sophie, of helping her and being prepared to live with the disease should mean something for both of them. In a way, he wanted to be rewarded, to be told he had been a good person.

But perhaps he was being selfish? It was, after all, Sophie's life, Sophie's body which had suffered all the damage.

As Roland began packing the rucksack, Sophie explored the edges of the old abbey. It did not feel right for Roland, but Sophie was distant. In a moment they should share, Sophie was not there, she was separate, wanting to be separate. It was peculiar, but Roland felt alienated and pushed out.

CHAPTER 27

THE LAST SUPPER

Jas decided to organise a special dinner in celebration of Sophie's cure and cook one of his famous dry Indian curries. It was to be served in the communal rooms downstairs in the nurses' hostel. Jas had highlighted which room they were going to use by sticking a sign on the door, which said:

FUCK OFF!
DINNER AT 7.30
DO NOT ENTER
YOU ARE NOT INVITED

Surely, no one could complain about that?

Preparations were underway with guitar-based music flexing from Jas' room, all the way down the corridor and into the commandeered kitchen. It was also going to be one heavy, smoking, doping session, and he had roped Sophie in to prepare a substantial space cake in her honour.

Sophie, conscious of the connoisseurs' watchful

supervision, crumbled hashish into a pre-prepared cake mix.

'How much more should I put in?' she asked.

'Who knows? Put it all in,' said Jas nonchalantly.

'What?!' said Sophie, initially surprised. 'You want to use a whole ounce?'

Jas paused.

'How much have you put in, then?' he asked, with the intention of calculating how much should be smoked and eaten.

'This much,' said Sophie, holding up the brown lump of hash, her fingers and thumb covered in oily crumbs.

'Okay, cool,' said Jas.

He then grabbed a kitchen knife, scored a line through the lump of amber nectar, roughly equivalent to a further quarter, and instructed Sophie to put that portion in… and no more. Jas now refocused, running between his room and the kitchen, smoking a joint, resuming work on his culinary masterpiece and verbally abusing anyone who happened to ask, 'What's going on?' In between these gaps, "the guests" (as Jas fondly decided to call Terry, Roland, Dr Jonas and Maria), made periodic stoned visits in order to query how long it would take and whether Sophie had appropriately prepared the cake.

'How much have you put in?' asked Terry, dipping his finger into the semi-liquid mixture and having his hand slapped.

'Eh… about half an ounce,' Sophie estimated, sniffing her saturated, oily fingers.

'I'd put in more,' said Terry, asserting his Pothead Pixie membership status.

'How do you know how much to put in?' asked Sophie. 'It's not as if there's a recipe…'

'Experience.'

'Okay, how about this much then?' she said, showing him half of the remaining hashish.

'That'll do it,' said Terry, turning his back, anxious to return to his room to smoke another joint.

Sophie burnt and crumbled more hash into the cake mix.

Jas returned from his room, his eyes glazed and (according to his own estimate) his mind focused.

'This is for you,' he said, dancing like a bizarre headless chicken to the syncopated rhythm pumping from his room. 'It's called Lick-my-Dick.'

Sophie ignored him and Jas decided to concentrate.

'Basmati rice is the best, you know,' he said, pouring the grains into a large saucepan.

'How long is dinner going to take?' asked Sophie.

Jas paused, as he tried to calculate.

'What's the time now?'

'The big hand is pointing to the twelve and the little hand is pointing to the four,' said Sophie, directing his gaze to the kitchen clock above their heads. 'So, that means it's four o'clock.'

'Fuck! I didn't see that there,' said Jas, laughing.

'This isn't going to take forever, is it?' she asked, suspicious of how stoned Jas appeared to be, and liable to elongate the cooking process.

'Listen,' said Jas, regaining his composure, 'you work on the cake and let me do the cooking!'

Sophie rolled her eyes.

'What?!' exclaimed Jas.

Right, he needed to get a grip; things were beginning to feel a bit off-plan and he needed to configure his cooking brain. He opened the oven door a couple of times, turned on some gas rings, poured water over the rice, pulled out some baking trays and turned things over. It was an impressive display, if slightly disjointed. Sophie would be none the wiser, he thought, as she was the one who had burnt the kitchen down last year. In response, Sophie complained about how tired and worn her fingers were from burning and crumbling the hash.

'Hmmm... that smells good,' said Dr Jonas, who appeared in the kitchen doorway.

'I'm making a cake,' said Sophie, who picked up her bowl and showed it to him.

'A special cake,' said Jas.

'Ah... excellent,' he said. 'I hope it is sufficiently fuelled?'

'Of course,' said Sophie. 'I've got this much left from an ounce.'

She held up what was left of the hashish.

'Why don't you put it all in?' said Dr Jonas.

Sophie looked at Jas in despair.

'Did I say something wrong?' asked Dr Jonas.

★

The communal rooms on the ground floor had a lower level of usage as most of the residents lived on the upper floor. There was one large room which had a delegated huddle of armchairs around a raised television, occupied in the evenings by the soap addicts. Next to the "TV room" was the dining room, which Jas had designated with his impolite notice. It had a degree of ornateness: a fireplace (real stone, marble or slate), a fake but realistic chandelier dimming the worn, absorbent red carpet, and bleached yellow wallpaper from cigarettes and sunlight.

By the time dinner was served Sophie's space cake had been eaten to fill the gaping hole in everyone's stomachs. As they assembled downstairs with the various dishes ladled hot and steaming on to their plates, they could all feel the effect of the cake reducing their ability to consume what was now in front of them. Having earlier declared how ravenous they all were, it was only Jas who appeared to relish, munch and chew through his rice, spinach, chickpeas and chicken. Roland and Sophie, Dr Jonas and Maria sat subdued in their chairs, picking like fussy children at their plates, while Terry mumbled about how heavy his head was feeling.

'You lot of lightweights,' said Jas, as he sat back in his chair surveying the chemically strangled gathering.

'What d' you mean?' asked Maria, who had not touched a thing.

'I've gone to all this trouble and none of you are eating it,' said Jas, whilst anticipating the substantial leftovers.

'But you took so long we had to eat the cake,' said Sophie, who raised her fork and stabbed at a chickpea.

'Don't blame me,' said Jas.

'It is a lovely meal,' said Maria, 'but I just don't think I can eat it.'

They all agreed it was a lovely meal. Out of respect for all his effort, they valiantly began tackling the dry, hot curry.

'So...' said Dr Jonas, after a few mouthfuls, projecting his voice towards Sophie and Roland sitting at the other end of the table. 'How goes the revolution?'

'What revolution?' asked Roland wistfully.

'Yeah!' said Terry. 'When's the revolution? I want to put it in my diary.'

'Terry,' said Sophie, keen to reduce the puerile input, 'you're not interested.'

'You won't beat the bastards,' said Maria. 'I mean, I'm all behind you, but yous'll never get enough support in this place to change a thing.'

'Even if they don't change anything,' said Jas, his mouth full of rice, 'at least they had a go!'

'We've got a lot of support,' said Roland, feeling slightly insincere, as the support he referred to had been garnered by Sophie's tireless legwork.

'We've got over half the wards giving us information on staffing levels,' informed Sophie.

'They'll let you do that,' said Maria, sceptically, 'but it won't make any difference.'

'I don't know,' said Dr Jonas, 'they do lie about the figures. Maybe if you show them something different they would have to try and explain it.'

'It's not the figures you need,' said Maria, flexing her Irish accent. 'Yous need people supporting you.'

'People are supporting us,' said Sophie, thinking she had already stated the obvious.

'Yeah, they will now, but not if you ask them to put their names to anything,' countered Maria. 'Not if you ask them to stand with you and take action.'

'You can't expect people to change all of a sudden... overnight,' said Sophie. 'If we called for a strike tomorrow nobody would follow us.'

'That's my point,' said Maria.

'Is there a point to any of this?' asked Terry, who found the conversation and food tiring.

'Yeah, there is a point,' said Jas, who also preferred to avoid any intense dialogue. 'I've cooked this dinner and none of you fuckers are eating it!'

They all looked guiltily at their plates.

'Oh, that's the point,' said Terry, disappointed he would have to try again to plough his way through.

'Do we have to eat it?' asked Maria, who just wanted to lie down.

'Well, I'll have it if you don't want it,' said Jas. 'Just let me finish my plate.'

'I think he's got the munchies,' said Terry.

'How can he have the munchies and we don't have them?' asked Roland.

'Did you have any cake?' asked Dr Jonas.

'No,' said Jas, 'I've been cooking.'

'Ah...'

'You know, I am finding it difficult,' said Terry, staring above Jas' head, 'but you see that picture? I'm sure it moved.'

Above the fireplace, a partially soiled biblical scene looked down upon the gathering.

'What moved?' asked Jas.

'John the Baptist,' said Terry, now fixated.

'How do you know it is John the Baptist?' asked Dr Jonas, noticing the picture for the first time.

'I don't,' said Terry. 'Or is it Judas?'

'Why did you say it was John the Baptist then?' asked Roland.

'I don't know,' said Terry, beginning to feel his mind sinking towards mild psychosis.

Jas stopped eating and looked behind him.

'It says...' said Jas, pointing with his fork at the lettering beneath. 'John the Baptist.'

Terry let out a deep sigh.

'That's alright then,' he said. 'I thought I was losing it for a minute.'

'How much did you put in the cake?' asked Roland, looking at Sophie and surprised by the colours emanating from her face.

'An ounce,' said Sophie, confident she had done no wrong and had merely followed instructions.

Jas chuckled to himself.

'You put a whole ounce in?!' said Roland, realising the potency.

'Don't worry,' said Dr Jonas, 'it's fun.'

'You guys look really out of it,' said Jas, as if administering a word of caution.

They all observed each other, examined each other's faces and came to the same conclusion: they were all "out of it".

Jas cleared his plate, scraped Maria's food on to his own and continued to devour his favourite meal. He was, after all, psychologically at an advantage.

'I would laugh,' said Jas whilst chewing with his mouth full, 'if there was a raid right now... you guys would be fucked!'

'Do you know if there's going to be a raid?' asked Sophie, who knew Jas had the best ear for hospital gossip.

'There's bound to be one,' said Maria. 'Yous guys can't carry on and think there won't be... that's one way they can get back at you.'

'But I've got nothing to do with it,' said Terry, looking at Sophie and Roland. 'I like the world the way it is. What's wrong with exploitation and oppression?'

'We're all involved,' said Jas, 'just by association.'

'I don't know you,' said Terry to Roland and Sophie.

'There will be consequences,' said Dr Jonas. 'Although, I'm all in favour of what you guys are doing.'

There was silence, as they all tried to determine what might be required to avoid the consequences of a police raid.

'Fuck it!' said Jas. 'We've been here before. Take away the dope and we'll end up going mad in this place.'

'He has a point,' said Terry, relieved.

'Right on!' said Dr Jonas, punching the air with his fist and raising his glass. 'To the Pothead Pixies!'

'Yeah!' said Jas, jumping up in support. 'And to Sophie, who has received the miracle cure and can now fuck whoever she wants!'

'What?!' exclaimed Roland.

'He means you,' said Terry.

'I am here,' said Sophie.

'Oh, right,' said Terry. 'Then you can fuck whoever you want.'

'Okay,' said Jas, rising to the occasion. 'I have another toast... to the Pothead Pixies!'

'Yous guys are going to get yourselves into serious trouble,' said Maria admonishingly.

'Jas,' said Sophie, who was keen to move the topic of conversation on, 'you need to be less open about it.'

'What do you mean?'

'You know what I mean,' said Sophie.

'No, we don't know what you mean,' said Terry.

'Well, you're too daft to know any better,' said Sophie. 'Look, we should all try and calm it down... the smoking. It's all down the corridors at night – everyone can smell it... you can't hide it. We need to be careful with everything that's going on.'

'I think we're all getting a little bit paranoid,' said Dr Jonas, who also thought he should be excluded from any reproach.

'It's the cake,' said Terry. 'And that picture's still freaking me out. I'm sure there's a fucking Judas in there...'

'Then don't look at it,' said Maria.

'I'm not looking at it... it keeps looking at me,' said Terry, confident of his stoned rationality.

They looked again at John the Baptist, stripped to the waist and blessing a suitably pious believer.

'Didn't he lose his head?' asked Roland.

They all nodded in agreement.

'Shouldn't that mean he should be headless?' wondered Dr Jonas.

'Eventually, you'd think,' said Terry.

'I object...' said Dr Jonas, leaving a pause which remained unanswered before filling the void. 'I object to this religious symbol hanging over my head... passing judgement!'

'How is it passing judgement?' asked Sophie.

Dr Jonas arrowed his finger towards the offensive print.

'That bastard wants to cleanse us of our sins… but I love sin. I love the ability to sin and we should take that picture down and burn it!'

'Yeah!' said Terry in agreement. 'How dare they put John the Baptist in front of me while I'm having my dinner!'

'Sit down,' said Maria to Dr Jonas, aware he was more than capable of carrying out his threat.

Dr Jonas fell back into his chair, slightly exhausted by all his efforts and overcome by the deadening effects of Sophie's cake.

'You know, it's weird, but this is like… biblical,' said Terry.

'You mean as in… the Last Supper?' asked Roland.

'But there's only six of us,' said Terry, who also started counting.

'Anyway,' said Jas, 'why would it be the last?'

'Yeah, you agent of paranoia,' said Dr Jonas.

'I blame John the Baptist,' said Terry.

'I don't think he was at the Last Supper,' said Roland.

'You're trying to freak us out,' said Sophie.

'I think I've freaked myself out,' said Terry.

'Good,' said Sophie.

'This is not the Last Supper,' said Jas, partially trying to reassure himself. 'Don't let the bastards grind you down!'

'That's easy for you to say… but you're not on medication,' said Terry.

'You're not on medication,' said Sophie correctively.

'No, but I should be.'

'What you all need,' said Jas, licking his lips, 'is a great big fuck-off joint!'

'Yeah!' said Dr Jonas. 'I like the thinking.'

'Guys,' said Maria, intervening, 'I think I need to go to my bed.'

Maria pushed back her chair and stood up abruptly, waited a few seconds to cope with the sudden rush of blood to her head, then bolted for the door. She thanked Jas for a lovely meal, levered the hinges and disappeared with a chorus of 'See you later'.

'I think that's your girlfriend who's just left,' said Terry to Dr Jonas.

Dr Jonas shrugged. He was enjoying himself far too much to chase after Maria.

'There is one thing…' said Dr Jonas, leaning forward. 'You guys need to watch out for that psychopath Slaney.'

'It's Fitzpatrick,' said Roland. 'He's the real nutter running this place.'

'Believe what you want…'

'We will,' they all said in chorus.

'What can I say?' said Dr Jonas, who intended to say just a bit more.

'You mean the bullshit…' said Jas.

'Surprise us,' said Terry.

'Heh, I like you guys, but you need to know who the real enemy is… just don't focus on the hatchet. They will and can go to any lengths. Remember Annie Buchanan?'

'She's still here, isn't she?' said Jas.

'You're the one who locked her up,' said Terry.

'I had to,' said Dr Jonas, 'based on what I saw that night.'

'You were out of it that night,' said Jas.

'He's always out of it,' said Terry.

Dr Jonas ignored the comments.

'I never put her on a six-month section… that was done after I had assessed her.'

'By who?' asked Roland.

'Caldwell, I bet,' said Jas.

'You mean Dr Caldwell?' said Roland. 'But he has nothing to do with the main hospital.'

'Don't you believe it,' said Jas. 'He's the most senior consultant here and pretty much does what he wants. You watch, they'll close this place down but they won't touch Chaolla House.'

They all remained silent, digesting the proposed reality.

'Look,' said Jas, 'you're even freaking me out and I'm not as stoned as the rest of you.'

'Yeah!' said Terry, looking at Dr Jonas. 'And wouldn't it be funny if you were shagging Sophie as well?'

Dr Jonas stared back, momentarily off guard before quickly regaining his composure.

Roland looked keenly at Sophie, at the same time completely confused by the sudden change in atmosphere.

'I just thought I'd ask,' said Terry, easing back into his stoned stupor.

'Why would you ask that?' said Sophie, determined to remain composed.

'Well, there's always gossip,' said Jas.

'That's ridiculous,' said Sophie.

'It's a smear,' said Dr Jonas. 'Stuff we have to deal with.'

Not you, thought Roland, *you're nothing to do with us.*

'An ugly smear,' stated Terry ironically.

'That's what we're up against,' said Sophie, looking directly at Dr Jonas.

'I can't believe it!' said Roland, suddenly convinced this was a malicious rumour to undermine them.

'You'd better believe it!' said Terry.

Roland looked quizzically at Sophie. *No, no way*, he thought.

'Heh!' said Jas. 'Who's for hot knives?'

Roland needed to get a grip. Could she really be shagging Dr Jonas? It seemed impossible... improbable... unlikely. After all, he reasoned, how could she have time to do anything like that? They were always together. If she wasn't working she was with him, or... well... getting the evidence and going to all the wards.

★

He sat with her in their room on the bed, still feeling the full effects of the space cake. He wished, as he battled in his mind with the unthinkable deceit and betrayal, that he was straight in his head, just this once, so he could deal with the emotion of the situation.

'That was weird, wasn't it?' he said, trying to remain calm.

'What?'

'At the dinner... Jas and Terry.'

'Jas and Terry?' she said, feigning a lack of understanding.

'Yeah,' said Roland, 'why did they say that about you and Dr Jonas?'

Roland looked at Sophie's face, staring at her eyes, trying to look into her mind so he could detect the lies or the truth.

'That's what we're up against,' she said, keeping her head low. 'This place is full of malicious gossip, as you know.'

Why did she not look at me? thought Roland. But she was right about the gossip.

'That's really bad,' he said, if he was to believe her.

'What?'

'Gossip, designed to be destructive.'

Sophie laughed.

'Why?' she said.

'Well… it is,' said Roland, taken aback by Sophie's continuing lack of concern.

'It's not a problem.'

'What do you mean?'

'It doesn't matter,' she said, now looking directly at Roland, 'if I was, or wasn't having an affair with Dr Jonas.'

Roland repeated the phrase in his head: if she was, or wasn't having an affair with Dr Jonas. That's what she said. Was that code? Was that something he should understand as meaning something else? Was she saying she was having an affair? But he had to trust her. He knew Sophie wasn't like that. She wasn't someone who would be deceitful and go behind his back. But it did matter, of course it mattered if she was having an affair.

'Well,' he said tentatively, 'it would matter, if you said you were having an affair.'

Sophie let her head drop to one side, looked down at the floor and then back at Roland.

'I'm not having an affair,' she said, with her eyes wide open.

Roland looked intently for the truth, the undeniable, unassailable truth. And he could tell this was the truth.

'I know,' he said, wanting to ensure she realised he was on her side; he was not falling into the pit of gossip which would destroy everything.

'Jas and Terry are just playing games,' she said.

That was true, he thought: Jas and Terry were always playing games. After all, it was only Jas and Terry who had said it. He hadn't heard it from anyone else.

'You're right,' he said.

Roland was feeling guilty. Jas and Terry would be laughing now: laughing at him; laughing at freaking him out. He had fallen into the trap, the trap of paranoia, the trap of distrust and lack of faith. Yes, you definitely had to keep your wits about you or else you'd get lost in the mist of madness, sucked in, and become prey to tensions, distractions and distortions.

'I wonder what Dr Jonas thought?' asked Roland, as he sought to eradicate all nagging doubt.

'Why?'

'Well, I bet it freaked him out. Lucky Maria wasn't there.'

'Look,' said Sophie, in a tone of frustration, 'it's not that important.'

No, she's probably right, he thought. *If it's not true, it's not that important*. Anyway, he now knew there was no way she was having an affair with Dr Jonas. It was impossible.

'We should get back at them,' said Roland.

'At who?'

'Jas and Terry.'

'It's not worth it.'

'I'd love to get back at them,' said Roland, trying to think how he could fix it.

Sophie dropped back on to the bed with an exaggerated sigh.

'What?'

'Roland…' said Sophie, who then paused, contemplating her next words but failing to complete her sentence.

'What?'

'Nothing,' she said reflectively.

Nothing? What had he done wrong?

'If it's only a game, let's play the game,' he said. 'Let's get back at them.'

'We haven't got time to play games,' said Sophie, sitting up. 'I've been running around like crazy trying to get all the day returns in from the wards. I've been compiling all the figures, I've got my finals coming up in a few months and then I've got to find somewhere to live at the end of all this.'

'You mean, *we've* got to find somewhere to live,' said Roland, seeing Sophie's last point as the most pertinent.

Bang! Bang! Bang!

'Fuck! What was that?'

They both feared it was the much-anticipated police raid.

Bang-bang! Bang-bang!

'It's in the corridor,' whispered Sophie.

'Do you think it's the police?'

Sophie bent down to pick up the ashtray with its mixture of roll-ups and roaches.

'Quick,' she said, as she searched for somewhere to hide the evidence.

'What should I do with this?' asked Roland, pulling out a small lump of hash from his pocket.

'Just get ready by the window.'

Roland looked anxiously at the hash. Sophie bagged up the roaches and then instructed Roland to throw the whole package out of the window if their door was targeted. Then she stealthily rested her ear against the door, before kneeling down to see if she could view anything through the keyhole.

There was another faint bang, almost futile and exasperated.

'Can you see anything?' asked Roland.

'No,' said Sophie, putting her finger to her lips.

There was a long pause.

'I don't think it's the police,' she said. 'Should I have a look?'

Roland frowned, unsure of the consequences.

'Just wait a bit,' he said, watching out of the window.

'I don't think the police would do a raid at this time of night,' said Sophie. 'They're not going to catch anyone out.'

There was a faint tap on the door. Roland jolted, ready to drop the incriminating evidence.

'Who is it?' asked Sophie quietly.

'It's me, Jas,' said Jas, whispering through the keyhole.

Sophie took out her key and unlocked the door.

Jas swept in, his face a mixture of fear and laughter. He looked at Roland, with his arm hanging out of the window.

'Don't panic,' he said, 'it's not the police.'

'Then who the fuck is it?' asked Roland, angry he had scored a plus ten on the Richter paranoia scale.

'Fuck knows… but it freaked me out.'

Jas sat in the middle of the room, pulled out a packet of Lizra and started to roll up (panic over). But Sophie was not ready to so easily abandon their state of vigilance and decided to wander the corridor in search of the cause.

With Sophie out of the room, Roland seized upon the opportunity to confront Jas.

'You know,' said Roland, 'you're a right fucking bastard.'

'What do you mean?' said Jas, smirking.

'Why did you say Sophie was having an affair with Dr Jonas?'

'Oh, that… it was just something I heard.'

'Who told you?' asked Roland, ready to confront anyone who had spread the malicious gossip.

'Don't waste your time on it.'

'But it's wrong.'

'That's all that matters then.'

'What do you mean?'

'Look,' said Jas, 'all that matters is what you guys know to be the truth. It doesn't matter what other people say. We were just warning you – letting you know it's out there.'

'Oh, I see.'

Roland felt guilty again. He was jumping to conclusions, letting the stoned paranoia get to him. Jas was right: he must trust Sophie. Just because his friends in the past had let him down, kept secrets, didn't mean

Sophie would do the same. Sophie was right, it was just a wind-up. He needed to move on, forget about it.

'Here,' said Jas, handing him the speedily rolled joint, 'get your lungs round this.'

Sophie had returned with Janice, whose puffed and anxious red face harboured greater anxiety than usual.

'She needs our help,' said Sophie, as they all sat uncomfortably on the bed.

'Alright, Janice,' said Jas, who had thought about shagging her if he ever got desperate.

Janice told her story to reveal how things had gone wrong. Tom, her boyfriend, had been down the social club drinking and someone had said to him they had seen her (Janice) coming out of Greg's room, and then he had got into a jealous rage and come over to sort out Greg, and it was Tom banging on Greg's door and he was going to smash him to a pulp. Greg was in his room but he wasn't going to open the door, and so Tom had gone back to the social club to have another drink and Janice was really afraid that he'd do something stupid, and that if he attacked Greg then she was sure he'd end up in trouble, probably lose his job, and she did not want any of that to happen. Plus, it wasn't Greg's fault, she wasn't doing anything with Greg… they were just chatting.

'I'll see if I can speak to Greg,' said Sophie, who left the room again.

Sophie had a soft spot for the quivering adolescent, and tapped delicately on Greg's door to assure him the aggressor was no longer in the vicinity. Janice, on the other hand, hoped to galvanise a coordinated approach to the return of Tom.

'You've got to help me,' said Janice, appealing to Jas rather than Roland (who she considered to be distant and less amenable). 'Tom's so mad and so drunk and he won't listen to reason.'

'There's only one solution, then,' said Jas. 'We'll have to isolate him until he calms down… but after that it's down to you.'

Janice nodded, her ringlet curls swirling in agreement.

'At the end of the day,' said Roland, 'we don't want things kicking off. We don't want the police.'

Janice nodded again, although she only had faith in Jas coming to her rescue.

'Go to Tom's room,' said Jas, 'and then let us know how much stuff is in it.'

'But he hasn't got much,' said Janice, as she stood up to accomplish her mission.

'Have a look anyway because we need to move it,' said Jas.

'Oh,' said Janice, as she tried to visualise the removal of Tom's institutional furniture.

'Don't worry,' said Jas, 'I know where there's an empty room. We just need to leave the bed.'

Janice blushed.

'You don't have to shag him,' said Jas, 'just talk to him.'

'Oh,' said Janice again.

'We're creating a safe environment for you and him to talk,' said Jas, who had a visualisation of the action ahead.

'Won't he be violent?' she wondered, hoping her part was to avoid rather than engage.

'We can restrain him, but it's only you who can calm him down,' said Jas.

'Oh,' said Janice.

They recruited Terry and Cranfield to act with them as self-appointed police, swiftly removing Tom's furniture and placing it in an empty room (made available through the use of Jas' master key). Sophie then persuaded Cranfield to give up his cycle helmet and it was donated to Greg for protection. Janice was instructed to return to her room and prepare to either console, apologise or rebuke her errant boyfriend.

They all sat in Sophie's room, calculating when Tom would reappear to finish what he had started. They also agreed on a plan of restraint by dividing Tom's body into equal portions: Jas and Terry would hold his arms, Roland and Cranfield his legs. Sophie was to act as a point of distraction before they jumped him.

As each clatter of the doors signalled a returning resident they listened for the anticipated *thud-thud* of the marauding Tom. Cranfield, who resented his outsider status amongst the puffing clique, observed they all looked "out of it" and ordered Jas to restrain from rolling another joint. This prompted Jas to state he would only commit to their collective response within the next five minutes, otherwise he was returning to his room. Sophie told him to be quiet in order to prevent further discord.

'Look,' said Terry, 'we'd hear him even if we were having a party. In fact, what happened to our party?'

'Quiet,' said Sophie, pressing her head against the door.

'Is he there?' asked Roland.

Sophie shook her head and pulled a face.

'I want this as overtime,' said Terry, turning to face Roland. 'I want to get paid for protecting a virgin.'

'Be quiet,' said Sophie. 'If we don't stop this from kicking off it will give them another excuse to bring the police in.'

There was a brief agreement that Sophie was probably right, as they all nodded sagely and thanked her for reminding them of the main issue in hand.

'Listen!' said Sophie, who had heard something.

'That sounds like him,' said Cranfield, who had also picked out the heavy clump of feet.

'Get ready, lads,' said Jas, suddenly animated by the prospect of hauling down a six-foot-five-inch drunk.

They all piled out of Sophie's room, walking in single file towards the heavily burdened Tom, his head resting against Greg's door.

'You... fucking... wanker!'

Bang!

'Shit,' said Terry, 'he's really mad.'

Bang-bang!

'Hiya, Tom,' said Jas, ignoring the plan that it was meant to be Sophie who distracted him.

'I'm going... to fucking... kill him,' said Tom, slurring his words.

'Why's that then, mate?' asked Jas superficially.

'Wanker...' said Tom.

'Greg hasn't done anything wrong,' said Sophie, who felt she should assume her role, but was blocked by the four figures ready to bring Tom down.

Bang!

Tom's fist thundered on to the wooden panelling of the door.

'Right, that's it,' said Jas, grabbing Tom's arms and pinning them to his sides.

Cranfield kicked the backs of his legs and then all four leaped on the flailing limbs as Tom crumpled to the floor.

'Hold him down!' shouted Jas, as pressure restricted Tom's movement.

'This is for your own good,' said Cranfield, who could be relied upon to patronise without any hint of self-consciousness.

Tom struggled, but he was unable to resist. He was instructed as to his fate, with no choice but to comply, and was carried away to his empty room. Handcuffed to his iron bed, his belt removed, his shirt half undone, he looked a chastened figure.

Janice was ushered in and reassured they would wait around in case he erupted again. It was only Cranfield who maintained a degree of watchfulness as the others returned to Sophie's room to roll up.

'I hope he appreciates what we've done for him in the morning,' said Jas.

'And Greg,' said Terry.

'Oh yeah…' laughed Jas. 'Where's Greg?'

'Probably still shitting himself,' said Terry.

'Leave him alone,' said Sophie. 'It wasn't his fault.'

'Well, he shouldn't go messing with another man's girl,' said Terry, in mock machismo.

'I don't think he did anything wrong,' said Roland.

'Well, you never know,' said Terry.

'You never know what?' asked Sophie.

'What you never know…'

CHAPTER 28

AN EXTRAORDINARY BOARD

Mrs Flamey had prepared coffee, tea and biscuits and sat silently in the boardroom for the extraordinary board meeting. As she waited she occasionally touched her face, which was layered with a thick foundation (most notably around her nose, because she hated the fact one nostril was bigger than the other). She knew Slaney had kept her on as his PA because she could be relied upon to be discreet, although she never forgot he had unkindly referred to her once as the "flame that never rose from the fire". In response, she had told Slaney her husband had died young (although she had never had a husband), in the hope this would at least help him understand why she led a fairly solitary life, content to turn up for work and not socialise beyond her required hours.

Fitzpatrick was the first to arrive, striding purposefully to the end of the table and reaching across to grab a coffee cup before pushing his chair with the backs of his legs.

'Mrs Flamey,' he said in recognition. 'How are you this morning?'

'Very well, thank you, Michael,' she said, as she liked to refer to all the managers by their first name.

'Good, good, good,' he said, without a second thought.

He sat down on the soft cushion seat, bowed his head to stir his coffee before looking for the customary agenda and minutes. Mrs Flamey pushed two piles of paper in Fitzpatrick's direction.

'Thank you, Mrs Flamey,' he said, as he twirled the upside-down text the right way up.

He began to scrutinise the minutes of the previous board meeting, huffing slightly at decisions he may have disagreed with or were inaccurately recorded. Then he looked at the clock to ensure he was on time. Mrs Flamey was about to apologise for her boss' lateness, when Slaney, along with Dr Caldwell, made their belated appearance. They levered their chairs, sat down and wasted no time with the coffee or biscuits.

Slaney acted as chair and was keen to get down to business for the:

EXTRAORDINARY BOARD MEETING
Wellington Park Psychiatric Hospital
16th June 1985

Attending: Mr Morten Slaney, Interim Chief Executive (MS); Brian Caldwell, Senior Consultant (BC); Mr Michael Fitzpatrick, Nursing Manager (MF).

Agenda & Minutes

Introductions

Approval of minutes for last meeting is deferred to a full board.

Item 1: Response to the findings of the Vilnous Serious Incident Report.

Item 2: Maintaining clinical standards.

Item 3: Strategy for decommissioning wards, relocating services to the community and maintaining flagship services. Note: this also requires ratification by a full meeting of the board.

Full discussion of:
Item 1:
Noted MF had intervened in an incident late last year in regards to patient care and special observation guidance on Lilywhite Ward. In addition, MF stated the report in other aspects had complemented the actions of the senior management team. MF stated the hospital had effectively locked down in order to support other patients who were at risk. Where there were legal sections in place restrictions to movement was applied to individual patients and allowed inward and outward access to 'open wards'.

MS stated the loss of Mr Vilnous was a tragedy, for the family and the staff who cared for Mr Vilnous. He had been referred by social services and was under assessment at the time of the incident with an initial diagnosis of acute depression related to a post-traumatic stress disorder. The section he was under had elapsed the day before so he was free to come and go as he pleased. The nursing staff had very little contact with him while he was on the ward and the last person to see him was Dr Jonas. MF understood that Dr Jonas had gone against the advice of the nursing staff and judged a further section inappropriate.

BC stated Dr Jonas would have to account for his assessment and he had no intention of prejudging the outcome.

MS stated all recommendations from the report will be communicated back to all board members, although it was unlikely any further actions would need to be taken.

Item 2:

MS stated there was a link between Item 1 of the agenda and Item 2. In summary, student militancy, clinical errors and deviant and illegal behaviours among students.

MS stated known individuals as posing a risk to the hospital's reputation and a potential liability in clinical areas. In addition, there was a political motivation not dissimilar to the character of militancy in a section of the wider society. In particular, he had reports that Dr Jonas mixed socially with student nurses Roland Cauldron, Sophie Smith, Jas Jaswinder and Terry Alcock. These four students were close to being dealt with in regards to breach of contract of residency in the nurses' hostel.

BC stated that in nursing matters he would not necessarily get involved, but he appreciated poor quality of nursing had an interrelationship with diagnostic judgements and he would be concerned if these individuals were a known factor in compromising clinical excellence.

MF stated Roland Cauldron had recently been on a

one-day placement to Chaolla House. MF queried if BC had found anything about the student which merited further investigation. BC stated Roland Cauldron's demeanour. BC also stated he would check with his staff and act on any information which could be considered detrimental to the therapeutic environment, disturbance of clinical interventions or ignoring codes of conduct required of staff while on duty and observation.

BC enquired as to the nature of the deviancy and MF explained they had consistently identified behaviour which had a strong lifestyle element, mainly the use of cannabis. This particular group had formed in the nurses' hostel and they had duties under tenancy and residential management which they needed to enforce. In addition, it would be remiss of management responsibilities if students were allowed to qualify whilst it was known that their behaviours demonstrated a social dysfunction.

MF stated the causes reflected a casualness in recruitment to nurse training driven by the school of nursing's need to maintain its own existence at a cost to quality and professionalism. Whilst similar mistakes had been made in the past, this particular group of student nurses combined deviancy, political militancy and alternative lifestyles that were not compatible with a future nursing career.

MS agreed that whilst it was not their job to discriminate against a diverse population, the line had to be drawn in regards to what the hospital accepts as permissible within a clinical setting. However, it was acknowledged that it would be unfortunate to harm an individual's career as well as their future job prospects.

This was particularly the case with Sophie Smith, who had demonstrated a high degree of excellence on the wards. BC was also of the opinion that Sophie Smith was known to him in a positive capacity and hoped this particular disruptive group be dealt with on an individual basis. Slaney advised Sophie Smith would not necessarily suffer disciplinary action as he considered her to be under the influence of others.

MS stated management were aware of reports which linked these individuals with illegal drug use within residency; further investigation would be needed as to the veracity of these reports. If confirmed it would be acted upon.

MS stated there was an active campaign by the militant student group previously mentioned above to undermine the hospital and its day-to-day operations. Roland Cauldron and Sophie Smith were conducting a highly destabilising activity during a difficult transition period for the hospital. Until they had robustly addressed these issues it would be necessary to tactically delay any disciplinary action. They had spoken with the union representative and he was in agreement. They would then be able to act effectively to address a number of concerns.

MS also stated any record of Item 2 will be redacted if publication beyond those attending today's meeting was required, on the basis of the highly sensitive and confidential issues involved.

Item 3:
MS invited BC to introduce his proposals for the transition of Wellington Park Psychiatric Hospital from

an institutionalised setting to a community-based mental health service.

BC stated this was an historic turning point. A step change was required, significant as the dismantling of the walls that used to surround the old asylum. It was an opportunity to change the face of psychiatric care and capitalise on the freedoms psychotropic therapy had given patients. No longer would the mentally ill run the risk of being incarcerated as the inevitable cost of illness. Institutional care was an anachronism and an outmoded model of care.

BC stated the principle established by central government of moving mental health provision from the institution to the community was a correct one. Whilst it would mean the demise of Wellington Park Psychiatric Hospital as an institution, the benefits far outweighed the costs to patients' well-being. There would be a difficult period during transition, not just for the patients, but also for the staff. It was also the case central government had assumed this change could be managed through a reduction in funding before the cashable savings had a chance to be fully realised. In addition, unless they were to meet the government deadlines for ward closures, they would see a further reduction in budgets which could potentially compromise the delivery of care. Working within tight timescales, BC suggested this should be mitigated by bringing forward the closure of long-stay wards.

BC stipulated Chaolla House was already an established community service and did not fall within the remit of the government's closure policy. Once the main hospital is depopulated, the land will realise a value which could be redistributed to a wider range of community services.

MF enquired if this realisation of capital assets by the sale of land on which Wellington Park Psychiatric Hospital stood would also benefit Chaolla House?

MS clarified that Chaolla House was a designated community service and therefore it would be able to receive community funding. It was incidental if the funding was supplemented by the sale of capital assets. In addition, this was also dependent on the transfer of funds between capital and revenue and there was no indication so far if this would be sanctioned by the department.

MS stated a narrow focus on one unit within a range of community services blurred the vision BC had outlined and it was important to move forward on this strategy. None of these changes usually proceeded at the pace envisioned. The need to retain beds for the transition to community care would mean that Wellington Park Psychiatric Hospital remained open for a number of years, but the institution had come to a natural end and had served its purpose.

MS concluded they would take forward BC's proposals to a full board meeting at the earliest opportunity.

Meeting closed.

CHAPTER 29

TEA, DREAMS AND FORGIVENESS

Roland lay in bed thinking about last night, because Sophie had told him she was leaving once she qualified because she couldn't stand it for another minute. He had said, 'What about us?' and Sophie was ambivalent; she just said she thought it was important he finished his training and he shouldn't give up his career, and anyway, she wanted some time on her own, to live on her own and get away from all the small-mindedness. That was alright for her to say, Roland had said, but what about their relationship… was it over? Was that what she meant: did she want to finish it? Did she still love him? Yes, she had said, after a pause.

Well, thought Roland, perhaps that meant things with Sophie were solid. In fact, he did not doubt that… but then, sometimes, she would just go into one; distance herself, cut him off as if he was in her way or crowding her out or something. He did not know what it was, really… he wished he knew. But if she said she still loved him (which was good), then how would it work out from here? Where could they go from here?

But Sophie wasn't interested last night; she did not want a long conversation about it. Anyway, she said, she thought he was all about non-oppressive relationships, or was that all talk?

No, no, no, he believed in it. She should be free… she was free! But you couldn't just neglect people's feelings; it didn't work like that… you couldn't just toss people aside, Roland had said. Did Sophie really understand? But then, what did she need to understand? She would soon be free of this place; free to go and work somewhere else and find something better out there. He would still be stuck here… a marked man. He could just imagine the likes of Fitzpatrick and Slaney sharpening their knives, ready to cut him up like a great big piece of salami. It wasn't just a matter of their relationship… it was everything.

Roland pulled himself out of bed, pulled the curtains open and looked out across the lawns and down to the boundary of the woods. He wondered if Starr was out there galloping around like a nutter, or perhaps another patient had slipped out and was hanging themselves from the oak tree in the old abbey? There was certainly something weird about the woods out there… ever since he'd done that thing with Sophie he'd been drawn to them at times, but never felt confident enough to go walking on his own.

Fuck it, he needed something to get himself going, to wake himself up.

He picked up the kettle and ran some water, put it back on its electric plate and switched the red light on. He listened as the power surged through. And then his mind went back to it – he couldn't keep his mind off it, what Sophie had said… it was like all their time together meant nothing. There was a risk she just wanted to throw it all aside. (*And I bet she would if she could.*) But there was the investment – his emotional investment – and he couldn't just end it there as if nothing had happened; as if… *okay… let's just move on.*

The kettle boiled and he picked up a mug and rinsed it with the hot water. A brown residue still remained on the rim of the cup. He swilled the hot water around and used a grubby bit of cloth to remove the last stubborn stains.

Perhaps, he thought (although he knew it was a bit crazy to think it; a bit paranoid and unfair on Sophie), but perhaps she had found someone else? But he couldn't understand it. How could she be having an affair? That didn't make sense. There was no time to have an affair.

He opened the cupboard door and pulled out a jar of decaffeinated coffee (which he really hated but put up with), unscrewed the lid and dropped two large teaspoons into the mug and poured the hot water in. He'd have it black, which he usually did, but also because he couldn't be bothered raiding someone else's milk in the communal kitchen. He topped it up with a bit of cold water to cool it down. He needed two sugars, but they were out of sugar as well.

Fuck it! There was a deep sigh as he lay back on the bed. He was certainly not prepared to give up on their relationship. He would fight for it; fight to keep the whole thing going. But he just didn't get it – how Sophie could end it all once she had finished her training… just fuck off like that? Perhaps he was wrong... perhaps she hadn't said that? *Be rational... think it through.* All she had said was she wanted to get out of this place. But why couldn't she wait? If she loved him she'd wait, just for a year or so; that's all it'd take. Then they could both leave together. *Why can't she do that? What's wrong with that?*

Roland took a sip of his coffee. It was still hot, so he closed his eyes again.

He was losing her... he was sure of it. He could tell... not that he could *really* tell. He'd never been in this situation before. Never been in a relationship before. Never known feelings like this before. He was out of his depth. He knew it and he had no control over it. It was a mind-fuck and he couldn't see any way forward. The thing was, he needed to get a grip... yes, he must get a grip on things. He needed to have it out with her. He needed to know for sure what the future was. But she was so bloody vague: maybe this, maybe that, maybe something. He needed certainty; he needed to know. But what if she was finished with him... then what? Could he cope? Could he cope without her? His whole world would fall apart. She was the one thing that meant something. He needed to find a way to keep her. If she left then he'd go with her. He did not really care that much about his so-called career. *I mean, who wants to stay in a madhouse, in a fucked up institution?* He did not want to be part of it any more. It just hadn't worked out. He'd probably done it for the wrong reasons. He was in the system, working for the system, an agent of the system... and he wasn't going to make a difference to anybody. Whether he liked it or not he was part of it, delivering the same inane thoughtlessness which kept everything going for the sake of keeping it going. He could give up his career, start again, go back to the beginning and find something else.

He opened his eyes.

That's good, he thought, *this place doesn't really matter, when it comes down to things that really matter. Who gives a fuck about a stupid fucking career based on treating human beings like processed fucking meat?*

He stretched his arm out to lift his coffee cup and sipped the hot black water. It certainly tasted better this time, less heat fusing through his lips. He levered himself up from his bed, moved a few steps to the window and stared out at the unforgiving misery of grey, a fine drizzle of rain getting in the way of summer.

So, he said to himself, the logic of what he'd just thought, if he put it all together: he had no future, back to square one, and all for the sake of... well... for love. And he desperately loved Sophie. Everything else could be put to one side. He had never had love, never felt its strength and power. To be without it, to be without Sophie, was the worst thing he could imagine. And he wasn't going to let that happen. She needed to hear him, rationally hear him. It was simple really, just a matter of explaining: the bonds, the links had all been signed, sealed and delivered. They couldn't be broken overnight. They couldn't be smashed on a whim; on a half-thought-out plan that was not really a plan... not anything.

He undid the latch and pushed open the window so it sat a few notches out into the drizzle. The wet air whisked through and shivered his body. Not a good idea, he thought, and shut the window.

Yes, he was probably right, he needed to get control of the relationship. He was not going to be dictated to. She needed to hear what he wanted. Alright, he could not force her into staying with him, but she needed to hear how he felt, what he thought.

But she did say she wanted to be on her own... he remembered that from last night. *That means something... that does mean, in essence, she wants to end the relationship, doesn't it?* Was Sophie trying to say something, but she did not know how to say it? Was she trying to say she did not love him any more... that it was over?

He just didn't know. Perhaps it was all ending? But why should he give in? Why should he just lie down and let her walk all over him? Fuck it! If it was over, he might as well tell her exactly what he thought. He might as well tell her that she'd be throwing away something that hadn't really finished... there was still life in it... plenty of life! He wouldn't insist on anything. If and when she felt ready, then fine, they'd split up. But give it time. Let the relationship move to its natural end; just don't cut it off... just don't leave with no option, or only one option.

★

Sophie needed to avoid Roland for a bit longer after finishing her shift, and called on Terry. His room was essentially in the same condition from the first day he took up his residency. There was no sign of personalisation, no concession to humanising the stark interior. Perhaps, Sophie thought, as she sat on his bed sipping a cup of tea, by avoiding creature comforts it reminded Terry that all was temporary, that it was only a matter of time before he too would go.

'How are things with you and Roland then?' he asked, leaning back in his chair by his desk and arching his back.

'Why?' asked Sophie, blowing into her mug.

'Just wondered, that's all,' he said impishly.

'Things are okay.'

'That means they're not.'

Sophie frowned.

'So,' said Terry, pleased with his own insight, 'how long have you been going out with each other?'

'About six months,' said Sophie, refraining from adding it was probably long enough.

Terry paused, scrutinising.

'You know, I had a funny dream last night,' he said. 'You and Roland were smoking, round mine… and then out of the blue you announced you were getting married.'

'What?!' said Sophie, choking on her tea as she sipped.

'Don't worry, it's not a prediction.'

'Why would you dream a thing like that?'

'Well,' said Terry mischievously, 'according to dream theory, it's because secretly *I* want to marry you.'

'Hmmm… why do people want to marry me when they don't mean it?'

'Why, who else has proposed to you?'

'Oh, no one…'

'So, you wouldn't marry Roland then?'

'Nooo…' said Sophie, extending the vowel to emphasise her resolve.

'He's a nice guy, you know,' offered Terry, 'but a bit angry about things.'

'That,' said Sophie, 'is what I like about him. At least he cares and he's passionate.'

'I know, but is he consistent? You can only be angry for so long.'

'What do you mean?'

'Well, we all calm down eventually.'

'Don't you get angry about things?'

'No, I just freak out.'

Sophie sipped her tea again and judged it was an insipid offering.

'Did you use any teabags in this?' she asked, holding her mug up in the air for inspection.

'I thought you liked my tea.'

'I can make better hot water!'

'Right, that's it!' he said, faking hurt pride. 'You're lucky that it isn't a special one!'

Sophie nearly choked before she managed to scramble a few words.

'You haven't spiked it, have you?'

'No, it's not the season for magic mushrooms,' said Terry slyly.

'Christ, are you sure?' asked Sophie, looking suspiciously at her cup again.

'Well, there's only one way to find out… see how you feel in a minute.'

'It doesn't take long, then?'

'Well, a bit longer than that. Tea makes it palatable and gets rid of all the impurities.'

'God, Terry… it's a shame I think you are capable of doing something like that.'

'You're not the only one…'

'Well, none of that is an excuse for a poor cup of tea.'

Terry shrugged. Admittedly, he had not provided her with one of his quality brews (they were stashed away in the cupboard).

Sophie surveyed Terry's sparse, soulless room again and noticed he still had a suitcase on the floor stuffed full of clothes.

'How long have you been here?' she asked.

'The same time as Roland.'

'But you've done nothing to your room!'

'Neither has he…'

'That's different.'

'Don't you like it then?' said Terry, spreading his arms and inviting more comment.

'It's cold and empty. What do girls think when you bring them back?'

'I don't.'

'I thought you had a girlfriend?'

'I do, but not here. Too much gossip.'

'Hmmm… I know what you mean.'

'I thought you might.'

'And what does that mean?'

'That there's always a lot of gossip.'

'Terry, why don't you ever say what you really think?'

'Where would the fun be in that?'

'Does there have to be fun at other people's expense?'

'If possible.'

'Terry…' said Sophie, preparing to rebuke him. 'You and Jas… when Jas cooked that meal… what were you up to?'

'Were we up to something?'

'You remember, don't you?'

'No, remind me.'

'Stop it, Terry! I'm not in the mood.'

'Oh, why not? I like games.'

'I know you do, but it's not funny.'

'Surely it was a bit funny?'

Sophie offered Terry her serious face.

'Oh, perhaps not, then,' said Terry. 'It was just a little bit of fun.'

'Fun?! I nearly had a heart attack!'

'Listen,' he said, prepared to play it straight for a minute, 'what you do is none of my business, but you wouldn't come in here if you didn't want to tell me something.'

'Like what?'

'Okay, then,' said Terry, rising to the challenge. 'Either you tell me why you don't want to go out with Roland or I'll tell Jas that you're available.'

'Who said I didn't want to go out with Roland?'

'Nobody, I was just guessing. Anyway, do you?'

'Do I what?'

'Want to go out with Roland?'

'Of course I do! I am going out with Roland… we live together!'

Terry raised his eyebrow in order to pose the question again.

'Terry,' said Sophie, trying to regain her composure, 'that's really cheeky.'

'I was only asking,' he said. 'These things usually come up after six months. All that lust stuff goes and then you have to ask yourself…'

Sophie blushed.

'Aha!' said Terry triumphantly.

'Don't say anything to Roland,' she said, pleading.

'No, no, no, I won't say a thing… but on one condition: tell me more.'

'I love him,' she said spontaneously. 'But it's not what I want. I don't want it to go on and on.'

'Ah,' said Terry, in a mock erudite tone.

'Did you really dream we were getting married?' asked Sophie.

'Of course,' he said, rather unconvincingly. 'But when are you going to tell him?'

'Tell him?' replied Sophie, slightly frustrated.

'That it's over, of course!'

Sophie sighed.

'I can't,' she said.

'Of course you can,' said Terry, more than ready to offer a way out.

'How can I?'

And just at the point when Terry felt he could persuade Sophie of a rational perspective, he too, had no answer.

'I assume you've done this sort of thing before?' he said, thinking he had best turn the emphasis back on to Sophie.

'No, Terry,' she said, 'I've always been dumped.'

'You're right, it's never easy.'

'See!'

'You know Roland would be devastated if you told him it was over.'

'Do you think?' wondered Sophie, feeling the reality beginning to cast a shadow again.

'One hundred per cent,' said Terry emphatically.

'I know…'

'I mean, you guys are both in this fight with management… things could fall apart if you split.'

'But isn't honesty the best policy?'

'You're right, but that's not how the world works. I think Roland would take it really bad if you chucked him.'

'What do you mean… do you think he wouldn't speak to me?'

'And the rest…' said Terry, laughing. 'You have to think about the consequences of stabbing Roland through the heart… things like that…'

Sophie was deflated.

'Oh, why do things have to be so complicated?'

'What you need is a strategy,' said Terry optimistically. 'If you're sure you don't want to carry on with him.'

'What do you mean?'

'Well, you haven't got long left. When do you finish – Christmas? Why not carry on until you leave this place?'

This was Sophie's own fateful calculation, the one she wanted to avoid, but the most sensible, realistic conclusion.

'I know,' said Sophie, 'but I didn't want to do that.'

'Yeah, but it will make things easier for you.'

'I don't want this to go on forever,' she said, trying to reinforce her own determination.

'It won't go on forever… not if you don't want it to. But if you know what you want, a few months won't be such a bad thing. It will give you time to let him down gently.'

Terry had said what she thought, what she knew in her heart of hearts to be the only possible scenario. She was trapped, even if she still loved Roland. Perhaps she could suppress her thoughts and feelings and just get on with things? What harm would come from carrying on with Roland for just a bit longer… as long as he didn't focus on what they were going to do together once she finished her training? The best strategy, as Terry had called it, was to avoid the issue, let it swim in the stew and don't indulge or offer anything permanent. All relationships come to an end, that was obvious, self-evident, the undeniable truth.

'You know,' said Sophie, sipping her tea, 'I think you might be right for once.'

'I like to think I'm always right,' said Terry. 'As long as that's all there is to it?'

'What do you mean?'

'That there's nothing else?'

'Of course, why should there be anything else?'

'I don't know… should there be anything else?'

'No, there isn't anything else.'

'That's alright then.'

Sophie paused.

'If you want to say something then just say it,' she said.

'If you want to say something, then you just say it,' said Terry.

'No, I don't.'

'Then that's alright then.'

★

The key in the door turned. It was Sophie.

Roland looked at her, unable to hide his bitterness.

'What are you doing here?'

'It's my room,' she said, her face flushed.

'I know,' said Roland, ready to let loose a volley of vitriol.

But Sophie's eyes were red. He could tell she had been crying. She bent her head down.

'Do you forgive me?'

'Why do I need to forgive you?' he said, betraying his desire to confront her.

'I'm sorry,' she said.

Sophie reached forward and wound her arms around him. They remained silent as she hugged him tightly, hoping her grip would ensure forgiveness. She lifted her head and kissed him on the side of his neck.

He did not know whether he should turn his head and kiss her on her lips, whether he should make her suffer for turning their relationship upside down, or whether he should just give in.

Sophie pulled his head round so he had to look at her face.

'You do forgive me, don't you?'

What else could he do? He had no choice. He wanted the relationship more than anything. He needed her more than anything.

'You know I love you,' she said.

'Yes,' said Roland, resenting his weakness.

He wanted to question her, to pick up on all the points he had gone through in his mind. But she was back, full of regret and she had said she still loved him.

CHAPTER 30

IN THE ARK OF ZOMBIE PARK

Jas and Roland stood outside the double doors to the art therapy unit, reassuring each other that they did not look stoned. Above their heads hung a bright, rainbow-coloured sign, with the word *Ark*. This perfectly illustrated the Portakabin's purpose, which was a haven and oasis from the rigours of the wards.

'Perhaps we should go back?' said Roland, feeling the paranoid effects of their session. 'She's bound to notice.'

'Fuck it,' said Jas, 'she won't care.'

And before Roland had time to consider any further backtracking, Jas pulled open the doors and stepped into a small porch. Roland reluctantly stepped forward and felt the doors behind him slam against the back of his head.

'Fuck!' said Roland, as he stumbled forward.

Jas responded with a stoned laugh.

Through the second set of doors they could see Ms Colgate cheerily waving them through.

'She's seen us,' said Roland, acutely conscious of their narcotic state of mind.

'Come on,' said Jas, who pushed open the doors, forcing Roland to follow.

'Hello, you two, I hope you've come to help?' said Ms Colgate, already assuming they were willing volunteers.

'Yeah!' said Jas, his voice raised with stoned enthusiasm.

Ms Colgate tightened the elastic band tied behind her silver hair, bit down on her lip and rubbed her weathered face. She looked just like the art teachers from his school days, thought Roland, flaky and behaviourally younger for her age.

They clumsily made their way around scattered tables with plastic bottles of acrylic paint left abandoned on them. On one side of the wall hung oversize paintings and papier mâché face masks, interspersed with a stack of metal drying frames. Along the other side of a long windowscape was a large open space which was being used for therapeutic self-expression.

Ms Colgate opened her arms in the direction of her three "special patients": Franks, who sat in the corner staring out of the window; Starr, who followed a circuit (possibly as a motorised vehicle); and Mrs Sandy, once again draped in a thin white nightie and dressing gown.

'It's lovely to see you both,' she said, to the silent disinterest of her patients. 'We like having visitors, don't we?'

Roland watched Mrs Sandy. It was clear after all the electricity pumped through her brain she was still preoccupied with devils, witches and goblins, as she dribbled, moaned and meandered.

'Look what Grace is doing,' said Ms Colgate, drawing

their attention to her walking in bare, painted feet on a rolled-out sheet of wallpaper. 'Why don't you go and help Grace?'

Jas jumped at the opportunity, probably calculating she was the best of a bad bunch. This left Roland facing Ms Colgate, who scrutinised his glazed eyes.

'How would you like to join us on a journey?' she asked, which Roland interpreted as an instruction rather than a request. 'Why don't you go and see if Julius would like to travel with us?'

'Julius?' asked Roland, wondering if there was a patient hidden somewhere else.

'Yes,' she said, directing Roland to look at Franks.

Fuck, why did he not know Franks was called Julius?

Ms Colgate then turned her attention to Starr, slowing him down and encouraging a walking pace around some of the tables and chairs.

Roland tried to get his brain in gear. He watched Jas leading Mrs Sandy along the rolled-out paper, clearly stoned and having fun with the Salem-orientated psychotic.

'Eh... where are we going on this journey?' queried Roland, as he watched Ms Colgate manoeuvre Starr.

'Wherever you want to,' she replied. 'Ask Julius and he'll lead you.'

This was awkward, thought Roland, who knew stubborn old Franks would be unwilling to do anything, especially after his lesson in chess and strategy.

'Is this a journey with paints?' asked Roland, seeking reassurance.

'It can be with anything,' said Ms Colgate, beginning

to lose control of Starr as he accelerated. 'There are no boundaries or limits.'

He looked again at the isolated Franks, sitting cramped against the wall and staring out of the window at the overgrown shrubbery. *He's bound to make another scene*, thought Roland, as Franks tightened his folded arms, securing his personal territory from the impending intervention.

'Ms Colgate,' said Jas, leaving Mrs Sandy to wander off the paper, 'have you got a minute?'

'Of course,' she said, then asking Roland, 'Are you alright keeping an eye on things? You should try and talk to Julius.'

'Yeah…' said Roland, thinking he would avoid Franks. 'I can manage.'

'We can watch from the office,' said Jas, 'if anything kicks off.'

'Thanks,' said Roland mockingly, as Jas and Ms Colgate disappeared into her small office at the back of the Portakabin.

As much as Roland wanted to know why Jas had to speak exclusively with Ms Colgate, he had more pressing concerns with the three psychotics. Not ideal, especially stoned out of his head. Mrs Sandy continued to meander with her painted feet. Franks stared intensely through the window, and Starr continued to spin round and round, sounding more and more like a sports car on a racetrack. Peculiarly, just for a second, Roland could smell petrol.

Mrs Sandy came to a stop. *As long as she stays there and doesn't fall over*, thought Roland, *there's no need for me to intervene*. He looked over at Franks, just to check on him

333

again. He did not stir, did not blink, fixed in his obsessive, depressive bind. Poor old Franks, a victim of his idealism, his spirit pummelled into madness. He must know what it was like to go up against the system, he must have thought he had some answers, to be a Communist. Now he was mute, lost in a maze of grandiose delusions.

'Six... one-five... one-five... one-two!'

Starr was standing beside Roland.

'Six... one-five... one-five... one-two...'

Roland expected the same old mantra to go on for a few more minutes, but instead Starr wandered over to Franks, tilted his head and stared inquisitively into his face. Franks ignored the intrusion. There was a kind of empathy there, perhaps an understanding of Franks' tortured soul. But the humanity only lasted a few seconds. With a horse-like laugh he was off again, brum-brumming around the tables and chairs. Fuck it, what did Ms Colgate really expect of him... surely it was enough just to keep an eye on things?

He could see through the office door Jas mouthing stuff he would love to hear. Still, it was none of his business.

He should try and do something. He walked over to Mrs Sandy and touched her lightly on the arm.

'Would you like to walk on the paper again?'

Mrs Sandy turned her head, puzzled, answering voices in her head. Roland gestured to the rolled-out wallpaper.

'Would you like to carry on painting with your feet?'

Mrs Sandy appeared to comprehend and shook her head.

'Okay, why don't you sit down?' said Roland, walking her towards a chair. 'Would you like me to sit with you?'

Mrs Sandy did not care. She was struggling with her heavy dosage, her eyelids dulled into submission. What was the cure for Mrs Sandy? wondered Roland. How could anyone so psychotic ever have a chance of getting better? Perhaps the only cure, so Sophie had said, was time. Time for what, though? thought Roland. Time was a curse in Wellington Park, double-edged, where everyone got lost in some forgotten world.

From out of the corner of his eye he detected Starr leaning again into Franks' face and causing him to growl.

'Come away, please,' said Roland, getting out of his chair. 'Come away from Mr Franks.'

Franks stood up abruptly. Then, with a sudden snap of his arm, released a punch which glanced off the side of Starr's shoulder.

'Oi!' asserted Roland, rushing to pull Starr away.

Franks extended his neck, with an intense, eagle-like stare. Roland immediately stood between the two, facing Franks.

'Okay, Julius,' said Roland, glad now he knew his first name. 'If you do that again you know what will happen. I would suggest you calm down, take a deep breath... there's no need for this. No one wishes to do you any harm.'

Starr emitted a low, cajoling noise, a timbre of disapproval and understanding.

'Okay, okay,' said Roland, his adrenaline beginning to pump, unsure how he could restrain Franks if he lunged forward again.

Starr was unperturbed, cooing incongruously, before heading off again. Roland followed his circuit. As he passed Mrs Sandy she let out a deep, inconsolable cry. Roland glanced over at the office, but Jas was talking and Ms Colgate was listening. Starr started to shout. The words were indistinguishable at first, but as he passed by at an accelerating speed, Roland heard the phrases.

'Zombie, Zombie, ZombiePark…Zombieeeeeeee…'

Franks let out a deep-throated groan.

'Owlllllllllllllllllll…'

'Not you as well,' said Roland.

'Zombie, Zombie, Zombie Park… Zombie, Zombie, Zombie Park.'

'Ehhhhhhhhhhhhhhh…'

Things were getting out of hand. Roland had no choice. He rushed to Ms Colgate's office and knocked on the window, gesturing at Jas to come to his aid.

'Alright, mate,' said Jas, as he opened the door, 'need a little help?'

'If you can,' said Roland. 'Franks had a go at Starr.'

Jas decided immediately on the action required. He cut off Starr's circular route, standing in between the clutter of tables and chairs. Starr got the message (as if he had faced Jas in the past) and made an immediate detour for the exit.

'Problem solved,' said Jas cheekily.

Ms Colgate rushed to Mrs Sandy's side, although she was the least troubled. Franks went quiet.

'Franks tried to hit him,' said Roland, as they both approached him.

'He seems alright to me,' said Jas.

They both stood over Franks, who stared out of the window again.

'Well, he is now,' said Roland, irritated.

Jas bent forward, looking directly into Franks' face.

'Do something like that again and you know what will happen,' said Jas.

Franks remained unmoved.

'Can we go?' asked Roland, desperate to end their stoned voluntarism.

'Yeah,' said Jas, 'I could do with a joint right now.'

'Are you boys off then?' asked Ms Colgate, still comforting Mrs Sandy.

'Yeah... we'd better go,' said Jas. 'Thanks for the chat.'

'Don't be afraid to pop in any time,' she said.

'Come on,' said Roland, whispering, 'let's go, for fuck's sake.'

'Bye-bye,' said Ms Colgate, waving with Mrs Sandy's hand.

Roland glanced back at Franks; weird, but he felt that was the last time he would see him.

'What were you two talking about, then?' asked Roland, as he pushed Jas towards the door.

'Nothing,' said Jas, closing the point of enquiry down.

That, thought Roland, was not true, as they made their way outside into the bright sunlight.

'We should never have done that,' said Roland, as they started on their walk back to the nurses' hostel. 'Starr was screaming out, "Zombie Park... Zombie Park!"'

Jas laughed, as they walked by the side of the boiler house and the potting sheds.

'That's all about McEmery,' said Jas.

'What do you mean?'

'That's what McEmery used to call this place. Think about it: all the patients are dosed up to their eyeballs and most of the staff get wasted on drugs and alcohol just so they can cope. We're all zombified. Just look across the lawns every morning and it looks like some scene from a fucking zombie film.'

'But why was Starr saying it?'

'Oh yeah, fuck… McEmery taught Starr to say it. He used to look after him on the old ward they closed down, the one near the cricket pitch.'

Roland paused, reflecting.

'That sounds good… Zombie Park,' said Roland. 'Everything about this place is dead.'

'Too right,' said Jas, who then pointed towards the arched opening into the patients' graveyard. 'That's where the real zombies live, the poor bastards who have been fucked over and left to rot. I bet they would like to take revenge for what happened to them.'

'That's a good reason to close this place down, isn't it?' said Roland. 'I mean, I know patients like Starr will struggle to survive when they get thrown out of here, but perhaps it will be better for them.'

'Are you fucking kidding?! This is all they know. They are the zombies who will get shot in the fucking head when they leave here.'

'But don't things need to change?'

'No, they fucking don't. If they didn't run this

place down, then there'd be nothing wrong with it.'

'Are you sure?'

'Yeah, don't fall for the bullshit. Trust me, mate, we live in a fucking Zombie Park because that's the way they want it. But what you and Sophie are doing is going to put the shits right up 'em.'

'Thanks,' said Roland, grateful for the support, 'but I don't think we will change much.'

'Of course not... that's not the point, is it? It's just about letting them know that we know they are fucking bastards for presiding over all this fuck up. It's worth it just for that!'

CHAPTER 31

THE EVIDENCE

It was midsummer and the opportunity had arrived: the meeting with the authoritarians, the great dictators, the heartless scabs of a failing system. Roland was up for the fight, the confrontation with Fitzpatrick and Slaney, to make them squirm, crawl and beg for forgiveness.

'We've got them by the balls this time,' said Roland, whilst scanning Sophie's bookshelf and reading some of the titles in his head.

'I'm nervous,' she said, sitting on the bed with the evidence on a spreadsheet in front of her. 'It won't be easy confronting Slaney and Fitzpatrick.'

'But we've got them now,' said Roland. 'They can't deny it any more. We've got the proof. That was the whole point, wasn't it?'

Sophie nodded and checked the time. It was a bit early to go over there just yet.

'I can't wait to see their faces, Slaney and Fitzpatrick,' said Roland, who had moved over to the window. 'Those bastards have been getting away with it for so long. I mean, how many patients have to die before they do something about it?'

Sophie shrugged her shoulders. She did not want Roland going in there all guns blazing and making things worse. It was important they remained calm so they could get their points across. It was a meeting, not a war.

'We've got to be different this time,' she said.

'What do you mean, different?'

'You know... we need to use the evidence. We've got to prove our point.'

'Of course we will.'

'So, perhaps it is best if I do the talking.'

'You mean, I'm not to say anything?' said Roland, offended.

'No, that's not what I mean, but you know what you're like. I don't want it to be a fight... I don't want them to walk out on us again.'

'Look,' said Roland, 'Fitzpatrick walked out of the student council meeting because he couldn't cope with someone standing up to him.'

'You made him walk out.'

'No I didn't!' said Roland, laughing at his moment of triumph. 'Anyway, he wanted to walk out.'

'Exactly, that's what I mean: don't give him an excuse. I haven't done all this for nothing.'

'Don't worry... we're going to get the fuckers!'

And Roland raised his hand, squeezed it, crushing the imaginary balls of Slaney and Fitzpatrick.

'Bob Jacobs will be there to help us out,' he said, thinking this would reassure Sophie.

But Sophie just gazed, thinking.

★

Roland and Sophie sat in the boardroom waiting, watching the clock tick by. Sophie kept in front of her the meticulously produced copies of the spreadsheet to ensure everyone could scrutinise the same evidence. It showed, ward by ward, how the number of qualified staff, as a ratio to patients, was consistently below the hospital's own safety standards. It showed a correlation between student nurses left in charge of wards and an increase in recorded incidents, all backed up with a thick file of copies of the day returns.

'I hope they turn up,' she said, flicking through her paperwork.

'Of course they will,' said Roland, his left leg moving up and down rapidly. 'They can't not turn up… they invited us to a meeting.'

Sophie was not so sure.

'What should we do if they don't turn up?'

Roland shrugged.

'We'll go to the local press,' he said.

'That won't work… we'd both get sacked.'

'I think it's a bit late for that.'

Sophie paused.

'I am not wasting three years in this place and coming out with nothing… although this is just as important.'

'But then what are you going to do when you qualify… are you leaving?'

'I don't know…'

Roland looked to the ceiling.

'Don't be like that,' she said.

'Like what?' he protested.

'You know…'

The door to the boardroom flung open.

'Hello, you two,' said Douglas, as he let the door swing back and walked crab-like along the opposite side of the table.

They both stared at Douglas.

'What's wrong?' he said, as he pulled back his chair.

'Why are you here?' asked Sophie.

'Why shouldn't I be?' said Douglas. 'I am part of the management team.'

They were both suspicious, calculating the implications.

'Well, don't forget to speak up for us,' said Sophie.

'That's agreed, then,' he said, putting his hands together, stretching his arms out flat across the table and winking at Roland. 'But I like to speak for myself.'

He pointed with his head at Sophie's collection of data.

'What have you got there then?'

'It's our evidence,' said Roland.

'Good,' said Douglas, 'you'll need that… but don't expect too much.'

'We never do,' replied Roland.

'Do you know where they are, then?' asked Sophie.

'They're on their way, I would think,' said Douglas, as he leant back to view the clock behind him. 'What time is the meeting meant to start?'

'Ten minutes ago,' said Roland.

'Don't worry, Slaney's always late.'

Douglas was being his usual affable and inscrutable self, thought Roland. But something was up... Roland was sure of it. He wanted to whisper in Sophie's ear: *He's here to smooth things over.* But it was too late. Slaney and Fitzpatrick suddenly appeared through the boardroom doors.

Neither of them said a word as they sat directly opposite the two protagonists and stared intently. There was no way Roland was going to be intimidated, and so he stared back with equal measure.

Sophie broke the silence.

'Should we start?' she asked, looking to Douglas for some guidance or reassurance.

Douglas remained impassive. Slaney smiled, loaded with his usual psychopathy.

'What about Bob Jacobs?' asked Roland, weighing up the forces ranged against them and feeling already at a disadvantage.

'What's Bob Jacobs got to do with this?' asked Fitzpatrick, whose tone was as aggressive as his stare.

'We need Bob Jacobs to be here in order to start the meeting,' said Roland.

'You called the meeting,' said Slaney to Sophie. 'I suggest you have the meeting.'

'We didn't call the meeting,' said Roland. 'And we can't have the meeting without Bob Jacobs.'

Slaney sat back in his chair.

'Well,' he said, 'I will consider the issue closed if you don't want to go ahead.'

'No, no,' said Sophie, 'we want the meeting. Bob said he wanted to be here, but we can start without him.'

'Really?' said Roland to Sophie, feeling immediately undermined.

'This is your opportunity to make your case,' said Slaney. 'You won't get another chance. Otherwise, we have more important things to get on with.'

And there was Sophie telling me to be calm, thought Roland. *The bastards are pushing us into this… and where the fuck is Bob Jacobs?*

'How long can we wait?' asked Roland, looking at Sophie.

'I don't think we should,' she said.

'Shall we start?' said Slaney, issuing the instruction.

'Shouldn't we have an agenda?' asked Sophie.

'Do you have one?' replied Slaney.

'We didn't know we had to provide an agenda,' she said.

Slaney maintained his intransigence.

'What about minutes? We need someone to take some minutes,' said Sophie, anxious everything was recorded.

Again, Slaney stared back.

This was going to be their tactic, thought Roland: low-level intimidation.

'Let's get on with it,' said Roland to Sophie, feeling they were already weakening their position. 'We can write something up after the meeting, can't we?'

'Well, who's going to chair?' asked Sophie, still determined to drive home her point about protocol.

'I think,' said Douglas, 'that Mr Slaney is here to listen to you and so you should use this opportunity and not waste it.'

'You don't need to worry about that,' said Roland, keen to fire the first bullet.

'Listen, young man,' said Fitzpatrick, 'think about who you are talking to.'

'Excuse me,' said Roland, rising to the challenge, 'but we know exactly who we are talking to and we would also like to be referred to by our names.'

'Who are you, then?' asked Slaney, who sounded as if he might not know.

'You know who we are,' retorted Roland.

'Let's have at least one formality,' said Sophie, fearing the worst, 'and introduce ourselves.'

'I think we all know who everyone is,' said Douglas, intervening as the unofficial arbitration. 'Let's drop the temperature a little.'

'Well, we haven't got very far, have we?' said Slaney, grinning pointedly at Sophie and Roland.

'That's not our fault,' said Roland, who was now ready for the battle.

'Sophie,' said Douglas, 'don't you have something to show us?'

Hesitantly, Sophie leaned over to begin her analysis of her spreadsheet.

'We've got the evidence,' said Roland, stealing Sophie's thunder, 'that proves you've been understaffing wards and putting students and patients at risk.'

There, thought Roland, *I've said it. What's wrong with Sophie? All this protocol shit! Get the bastards against the wall and let's see what they've got to say for themselves!*

Slaney and Fitzpatrick sat upright in their chairs.

'I…' said Sophie, falteringly, then pausing to ensure

she had an audience. 'I have compiled a body of evidence which shows that over the last three months a number of wards have been staffed below acceptable levels... and...'

'What evidence is this?' interjected Fitzpatrick.

'Proof,' asserted Roland calmly, 'in front of you...'

'Evidence,' continued Sophie, 'that there is a direct link to low staffing levels and incidents on the wards.'

It was meant to be a bombshell, but Slaney was unmoved. Sophie lifted up her photocopied sheets and stood up to distribute her documentation.

'If everyone has a copy of the evidence we have been gathering I can begin to explain where there is a correlation.'

Slaney turned Sophie's paperwork the right side up and began to study what was in front of him. Fitzpatrick refused to handle such incendiary proof and resumed staring intently at Roland. Douglas seemed to appreciate Sophie's work and began to smile, rather disconcertingly. Sophie gave them a few more minutes to absorb the details.

'As you can see,' she said, 'if you look at—'

'Okay, thank you, Miss Smith,' said Fitzpatrick, cutting her short. 'We can see for ourselves what you're seeking to do.'

'I think Sophie has some points she would like to make,' said Roland, convinced they could now ram the nails into the management coffin.

'If you look down column one...'

'Excuse me, young lady,' interrupted Fitzpatrick, 'but how did you get this information?'

Sophie was taken aback... they were meant to be listening.

'What does it matter how we got the information?' said Roland, realising what Fitzpatrick was up to.

'There are statutory regulations governing the confidentiality of such information,' said Fitzpatrick, briefly scanning Sophie's documentation. 'Have you made any of this public?'

'No,' said Sophie.

'Well,' said Slaney, 'I think you've produced an excellent set of figures.'

Sophie and Roland were caught off guard. Did they just hear right?

'I think you'll find, Mr Slaney,' said Fitzpatrick, who lacked any sense of humour or irony, 'that I do not produce figures to undermine this hospital.'

'Of course you don't, Michael,' said Slaney, soothing the uptight ego of his lieutenant. 'And you're right, there is certainly a need to consider how this information was obtained.'

'It was done with the full cooperation of the staff and under the instruction of Bob Jacobs,' said Roland, who had no compunction about naming their useless full-time union official.

The room was silent; a pause for thought... a pause to consider.

'I think it's true,' said Slaney, looking across at Fitzpatrick and Douglas, 'that we've always had difficultly filling posts. It's a struggle to get the right people to work in our little reservoir, our little oasis... cut off from the rest of the world, so to speak. How many vacancies do we have at the moment, Michael?'

'We've just filled two more staff nurse posts during

a period of sustained recruitment and over the last three months we are almost up to a full complement,' said Fitzpatrick.

'So, we could say, then,' said Slaney, 'that the difficulties we've had with staffing levels are now resolved?'

'We've always coped,' said Fitzpatrick.

'Coped!' coughed Roland, realising this was going to be some management fudge if they did not say something now. 'How can you say that?'

Slaney narrowed his eyes, before responding in a measured, self-assured tone.

'Whilst I will acknowledge there have been times when we have called on nursing staff and students to cope with very demanding circumstances, we are no longer in that situation. Bob Jacobs had made us aware of these concerns and I think we have successfully addressed them. The excellence, commitment and hard work of our staff should never be underestimated. We rely on people who are prepared to go that extra mile.'

'Are you seriously saying,' said Roland, his voice raising an octave or two, 'that none of what has happened on these wards is relevant?'

'Okay, Roland…' said Douglas, in an attempt to either protect Roland from himself or smooth over the resolution. 'I think this is the time when you need to listen.'

Roland looked at Sophie, his rage obvious to all, but she was passive. *You can't accept it? Not you as well?*

'There are serious incidents that have occurred here,' said Roland. 'We know that for a fact.'

'Is there a case that has not followed procedure?' asked Slaney. 'If there is, I would be very concerned—'

'Procedure?' said Roland. 'What does that prove? Procedure is a whitewash here!'

'Well, if it is,' said Slaney, 'I would not be happy. But then, you are questioning the integrity of me and my staff by saying that.'

Good, thought Roland.

'I think you have to accept you can't expect everything to change overnight,' said Douglas. 'You've done a great job in highlighting these issues. I think it's spurred us on to do something about it. At the end of the day, Roland, you have to get around the table and come to some agreement. We certainly feel we've done our best to accommodate the students on the wards, and I hope you do too.'

We're fucked, thought Roland, *just as I fucking predicted… we gave them time to sort it out whilst we ran around like fucking idiots.*

'Okay,' said Slaney, 'I'd like to thank you both for bringing this to our attention. However, I would prefer it if you raise these matters first through the school or directly with me or Mr Fitzpatrick. That would give us a chance to do something about it before it gets to such a situation.'

Smug git, thought Roland. He looked at Sophie again. *Why doesn't she say anything?* But it was over. Slaney and Fitzpatrick stood up and left the room as swiftly as they had entered.

'Well, that was a waste of fucking time,' said Roland. 'What the fuck happened there?'

350

Sophie was close to tears.

'You did your best,' said Douglas, 'but I would suggest you keep your heads down for a while.'

'Why?' asked Roland.

'Just be careful, that's all,' he said.

'Great,' said Roland, 'now we're really fucked!'

★

Sophie let out a long, deep sigh. As far as she was concerned it was all over.

'Have you spoken to Bob Jacobs?' asked Roland.

'Yes,' said Sophie, sitting down on the bed.

Roland was standing by the window of her room. She knew he was angry, fuming. He stared into the woods at the bottom of the long lawn, watching the green trees move silently in the breeze. He wanted to shout into the woods about the injustice of it all, about the vile betrayal of Bob Jacobs, about the two-faced git who made out he was the only one who knew anything about struggle and sacrifice, about how you can only be working class if you work in a fucking mine or something…

'Why wasn't he there?' asked Roland, turning to face Sophie.

'He couldn't make it.'

'Why not?'

'He had to go to another meeting.'

'Another meeting?!' said Roland, his voice rising in disbelief.

What could she do? She was not Bob Jacobs.

'He wanted to know how we got on…'

'Great,' said Roland sarcastically.

'It was not his fault,' she said, breathing in deeply.

'What do you mean?'

'He had to go to a tribunal, to defend somebody.'

'Yeah, right…'

'I don't know why you're so against him.'

'Come off it,' said Roland, 'he never had any intention of turning up.'

'You don't know that.'

Wrong – I do, thought Roland.

'He should have been there… he was the one who got us to do all this bullshit.'

Roland paused, so angry he could barely think straight.

'So what did he say?'

'Who?'

'Bob the-working-class-fucking-hero Jacobs?'

'About what?'

'When you told him what happened?'

'He said it was a good result.'

Roland snorted.

'For who?'

'He said,' said Sophie, who was going to do her best to remain objective, 'that at least things had got better on the wards, that we now had more staff, that we'd run a good campaign and done the right thing.'

'We had a five-minute meeting where they said everything's alright now and we just accepted it!'

'There wasn't much else to say.'

'You don't think so?' said Roland, turning to gaze out of the window and then back at Sophie.

'No,' she said, 'I didn't think there was.'

'So, all this,' said Roland, pointing at Sophie's evidence on the bed, 'wasn't a waste of time, then?'

'No,' she said, indignantly. 'Why, do you think it's a waste of time?'

Roland paused, infuriated at his own powerlessness.

'What can we do?' she said. 'They increased the staffing and so they're not breaking guidelines any more.'

'And are things any better on the wards? I haven't noticed any difference.'

'We've got a new sister on our ward,' said Sophie awkwardly.

'What does that prove? We wanted to do more than that, surely? We wanted to change the way things were done around here. We were supposed to challenge management, prove their authoritarian methods were killing patients. That was the point of it: to have a go and make them realise there were better ways of doing things... but instead we've lost!'

'We didn't lose. Why does everything have to be a battle with you?' said Sophie, determined to put things in perspective. 'I think Bob Jacobs is right when he says we made a difference. We got them to change things a bit even if it didn't come out the way we wanted.'

'They had it all figured before we even went in there,' said Roland. 'What was it they said about Bob Jacobs – that they'd already spoken to him? Why was Bob Jacobs talking to them? I bet he was giving them time to sort things out while we ran around like fucking idiots. We're the suckers for going along with it!'

'But that's the way things work,' said Sophie. 'I felt

awful at first, like you, I thought we had wasted our time. But you can't argue if they've done something about it.'

'They've done one thing, that's all,' said Roland. 'There should be loads more happening.'

That might be true, thought Sophie, but realistically the campaign had come to an end and Roland needed to let go (in more ways than one).

'I'm not sure I can put any more time into it,' she said. 'It's getting hard… I've got my last assessments coming up and I need to pass them all.'

'I have stuff to pass as well you know.'

'I know you do,' said Sophie. 'That's why we probably can't do much more.'

There was one thing they could do, thought Roland: they could pin Bob Jacobs against the wall and make him confess to being a slimy toad, a liar, a traitor…

'I'll write a newsletter or something,' said Sophie, 'to the students and staff.'

'They'll say we've lost.'

'Who will say that?'

'You know what people are like here,' said Roland. 'They'll say, "I told you so, nothing's changed, nothing's happened, same old shit, same old crap, same old bullshit!"'

'Well, there's nothing we can do about that.'

But Sophie was acutely aware people would be stopping her in the corridor, whispering in her ear, 'How did you get on with Slaney? Did you make him squirm? Did he give in? Are we going to see things change around here?'

'Okay, do the newsletter,' said Roland, resigned to

the disaster which he felt he had predicted from day one.

'And there's another thing,' said Sophie. 'Because of what Douglas said, there's one thing we need to be careful of and that's a police raid. That means I don't want the smoking in my room any more.'

'You don't want to smoke?'

'Not at the moment,' she said. 'I need to keep my head clear. Plus, it means we're not at risk then. We could lose everything if we got caught.'

Sophie was right, it was their big vulnerability, but there was no way he was giving up. Roland would need to get stoned... it was the only thing that kept him sane.

'That's a hard one,' he said.

'It will be good for you. To tell you the truth, I'm just a bit bored of it.'

'What do you mean, bored?'

'It's just a bit boring, that's all, night after night, unable to speak and being paranoid all the time.'

'Well, I don't find it boring.'

'Let's just watch what happens,' she said. 'Not do anything for a while. Things are changing.'

'What is?'

'Well, things change...'

'Why, what's changing?'

'You get used to things in here and we never go outside these walls.'

'There are no walls.'

'The metaphorical walls!'

'Oh, those...'

'Exactly,' said Sophie. 'And things are changing. Things are getting worse.'

'Why, what's got worse?'

'The miners,' said Sophie, as an initial proposition.

'The miners? That's over, and they were fucked from the start!'

'No they weren't,' said Sophie. 'Anyway, Bob Jacobs says Thatcher's won at the end of the day… it's just a matter of time now.'

'So?' said Roland, feeling belligerent towards anything that came from the mouth of Bob Jacobs.

'We don't know what the implications are yet,' confessed Sophie. 'But it's a defeat.'

'Not my defeat,' said Roland.

'Don't you have any understanding of the broader movement?'

'No,' said Roland, laughing, 'it's an old farts' movement.'

'You're wrong,' said Sophie. 'These are people's jobs and livelihoods.'

'I know that… I just mean the unions and all that stuff. God, it's just so…' Roland struggled to find the word.

'It's what?'

'You know…'

'No, I don't.'

'Christ, it's just playing along with everything. It leads everyone up the garden path. A little bit of this, a little bit of that, like pissing in the wind, but it just doesn't change anything.'

'You don't understand, do you?' said Sophie. 'That's not what they are about.'

'Of course I do!' protested Roland.

'This is a defeat,' she said. 'Everything will change.'

Roland did not see it like that.

'So, what's going to change?'

'We don't know what it's going to be like,' she said, using a "Royal we" again, which Roland had never heard before. 'But we know it's going to be all about business now.'

'Business... what does that mean?'

'Bob Jacobs said they are going to have to be a lot more like a business.'

'What?' said Roland, laughing and confirming in his own mind that trade unionism was like a "dead parrot".

'If we don't, we can't survive.'

'You mean unions can't survive?'

'Yes, that means us.'

Roland did not care. If unions meant someone like Bob Jacobs they could go fuck themselves; they were all a bunch of lying, bullshit traitors.

'Anyway,' said Sophie, 'Bob Jacobs has invited us for a drink.'

'Fuck that... I'm not going for a drink with him!'

'What's wrong with him?'

'He's a fucking traitor.'

'Don't be ridiculous.'

'He should have been there today. He knew exactly what was going to happen.'

'You can't blame him for what happened.'

Well, Roland did.

'When does he want to go for a drink?'

'I thought you weren't interested?'

'I'll go,' said Roland.

'You don't have to go.'

'No, I'll go if he's paying.'

'You don't have to go,' said Sophie again. 'You'll only end up arguing.'

'So, what's wrong with that?' said Roland, posturing, beginning to relish the thought of an evening with the great Bob Jacobs, full of tales of struggle, sacrifice and strife.

Sophie sat up straight.

'Do you mind,' she said, in a softer tone, 'but I'd rather go on my own.'

'I thought he'd invited us both?'

'Well, not really,' she said guiltily.

'Then why did you say he'd invited us both for a drink?'

'Well, he did, but only after I said that you would probably want to come as well. But you don't want to go.'

'Sophie,' said Roland, feeling he needed to get to the bottom of this immediately, 'what's going on?'

'There's nothing going on,' she said, annoyed that Roland (as usual), should jump in with both feet.

'Yes, there is,' said Roland, not sure what he should think. 'Tell me what it is.'

Sophie frowned. This was why she wanted out of the relationship. She could not do anything by herself.

'You won't get annoyed, will you?'

'It depends what it is,' he said, his voice croaking a bit, wondering if this was the moment when Sophie said it was all over.

'It's nothing to worry about,' she said, sensing Roland

was fearing the worst. 'It's just that… there might be an opportunity.'

'Go on,' he said.

'There's a job, a post going in the region… a full-time post as an organiser for the union.'

'Is that a job… a proper job?'

'Yes.'

'Right,' said Roland. 'Why didn't you say that in the first place?'

'So, you don't mind, then?'

'No, why would I mind?'

'I thought you would.'

'If that's what you want to do I can't stop you, can I? I don't want to stop you.'

Sophie bowed her head.

'Okay,' he said, 'good luck to you.'

Why did he say that? She wasn't going away; she was just seeing that fuckwit Bob Jacobs for a drink. Well, Sophie was right about one thing: everything was going to change, and none of it for the better.

CHAPTER 32

THE ILLUSION OF THE FOUNTAIN

It was a hot end to the summer, with the window wide open to catch the breeze and cool the room in Dr Jonas' hospital accommodation. It was a bit more palatial than the nurses' hostel, on the basis the standard three bits of furniture (a bed, table and chair), were built from a dark hardwood. As Sophie pored over her final assignment, she drew some comfort from the fact that she had done quite a good job, albeit with the help of the good Dr Jonas, who was growing increasingly impatient sitting next to her on the end of the bed.

'Haven't you finished with that?' he asked, his hands moving over the back of her neck and moving forwards so he could kiss her close to her lips.

'Almost,' she said, pulling away slightly, her shoulders curling inwards as she partially resisted.

'Good… because time is running out.'

Sophie ignored him, concentrating on scanning her assignment. Dr Jonas let out a sigh of frustration.

'Don't do that,' she said. 'You're distracting me.'

So, Dr Jonas let out an exaggerated deep sigh, designed to be childish and irritating.

'And don't do that,' said Sophie. 'You're as bad as the rest of them.'

'I can roll one if you want,' said Dr Jonas, continuing to tease.

'That's the last thing I need. Plus, I've banned Roland, so that would make me a hypocrite.'

'And how does that make you feel?'

Sophie stiffened her body; she was not going to rise to the bait. Dr Jonas leaned forward again so he could scrutinise Sophie's face.

'I just get so bored of it all,' she said, stretching her back. 'Roland, Jas and Terry, every night… stoned out of their minds. Then they get paranoid about a raid! What do they expect?'

'You ought to be careful,' said Dr Jonas.

'What do you mean?'

He rested his hands on her shoulders.

'You've only got a few months left,' he said. 'It's not worth taking any risks.'

'I don't take risks,' said Sophie, only too aware he could be just as much one of the Pothead Pixie gang.

Dr Jonas leant back, staring at her bare shoulders. He would have to work a bit harder in order to get his way.

'I can't believe you're still reading that assignment,' he said. 'Trust me, it's good. I should know… I wrote it.'

'No you didn't!' said Sophie, turning to face him.

Dr Jonas waited, to see what concession he could extract.

'Okay, so you helped me,' said Sophie, faking annoyance. 'But you're not helping now.'

'Good, I don't want to help… I want to fuck you.'

Sophie grimaced. She would have preferred something a bit more romantic.

'Why don't you just say, "I want to make love to you"?'

'Because I don't… I want to fuck you.'

Sophie smiled and turned her back on him.

'If you let me get on with it,' she said, glancing at the alarm clock next to his bed, 'I'll be finished in ten minutes.'

Dr Jonas also looked at his clock.

'Okay,' he said, 'I'll start timing you.'

'That's approximate,' she said, as she put her head down to scrutinise the analysis at the core of her text.

Dr Jonas put his arms behind his head, put his feet under her buttocks and flexed his big toes. Sophie would let him play but she was determined she would finish the assignment before the deadline later today.

'You know Roland's naïve,' said Dr Jonas.

Sophie ignored him.

'I was just wondering,' continued Dr Jonas, 'whether you thought he was a socialist, an anarchist, a nihilist, or maybe all three?'

'He's training to be a psychiatric nurse,' said Sophie assertively.

'Perhaps he is an environmentalist opposed to the environment he is in,' said Dr Jonas, chuckling.

Sophie ignored him again, so he bent his toes more pointedly into her buttock.

'Well, clearly you don't believe in anything,' she said, shifting herself from side to side to avoid the pointed toes. 'I think Roland wants to change the world, to make it a better world. It's also what I believe in.'

'You'll never change it,' said Dr Jonas dismissively. 'People only want change if there's a crisis. Once the crisis is over they just go back to their old ways.'

Sophie pushed herself forward so she was eventually free of Dr Jonas' invasive feet and grabbed a pen hidden in the creases of the duvet waving it in front of his face.

'I know what you're trying to do and it's not going to work!'

Sophie continued to hold her pen as a symbolic gun pointed at his head.

'You know I love you,' he said, with a small amount of sincerity.

'That's no excuse,' she said, wagging her pen.

'You're right,' he said. 'I am a naughty boy and I deserve a good spanking.'

'You mean, if you behave you'll get a good spanking.'

'Oh, yes please!' said Dr Jonas, mimicking a child. 'And will Mummy let me suck her tits?'

'When Mummy has finished her work,' said Sophie, going along with the role play. 'But you must promise to be a good boy until then.'

Dr Jonas panted like a good dog, elevated his forearms like paws, imitating a grateful pet.

'You see,' he said, 'I can be very obedient.'

'When you want to…'

However, Sophie kept one eye on Dr Jonas, in case he made a sudden move.

'I think it must be fun being a dog,' he said, ready to demonstrate he had genuinely thought it through. 'All you do is run around pissing and shitting all day, licking your bollocks and shagging anything with an orifice.'

'You don't have to be a dog to do that.'

'You must be thinking of Morten Slaney then…'

'No, he is an orifice.'

'A much-maligned man,' said Dr Jonas, in a pseudo-legal tone.

'And all of it justified.'

'Now that would be interesting,' said Dr Jonas, pondering, 'to be Morten Slaney for a day…'

'Depressing.'

'Well, wouldn't it be great to be your average managerial psychopath, casually disguising your incompetence whilst compensating for an overwhelming sense of emptiness through aimless adultery?'

'He's a ruthless, heartless son of a bitch,' said Sophie, who had a low tolerance of anything that might pass as an apology for Slaney's behaviour. 'He lets Fitzpatrick run this place like the bloody army camp, shags anything in a skirt and cares only about his career and position.'

'As I said,' said Dr Jonas, 'that's a man who you could almost admire. Is it a man who *you* could admire?'

Sophie scowled.

'Why would I admire him? I've put my career on the line confronting the bastard. Nobody else has done that!'

'Apart from Roland…'

'Stop it!' she said, pointing her pen again, reloaded. 'You said you would behave.'

But she knew she was being sucked into one of Dr Jonas' little games.

'Look,' she said, 'if I don't get this done Roland will be suspicious. He'll wonder what I've been doing all this time.'

'You can lie…' said Dr Jonas, letting his words slip out slowly.

'Yes, I can lie,' said Sophie, with increasing annoyance. 'If you mean I do lie, then yes I have to, just like you lie to Maria.'

'I don't lie to Maria,' said Dr Jonas, in a highly controlled manner.

'You mean you've told her about us?' asked Sophie anxiously.

'Maria doesn't care what I get up to.'

'Really?' said Sophie doubtfully. 'That's what you say…'

'No, that is what she says,' said Dr Jonas emphatically. 'And she can also shag whoever she wants as far as I am concerned.'

Sophie spotted a spelling mistake and circled the word.

'Maria has feelings for you, you know,' she said, admonishing the self-satisfied Dr Jonas.

'Oh, let me guess,' he said. 'Is that based on a woman's intuition?'

Sophie eyed Dr Jonas.

'Does Maria know about us?'

'Why?' replied Dr Jonas. 'Why should I lie to Maria? Secrets are not good for you – they are unhealthy. They act like a cancer and turn you into a basket case.'

'She doesn't know, then,' said Sophie, out to regain control of the issue. 'If she did, she would have said something to me.'

'Why do you think she would say anything to you?' said Dr Jonas dismissively.

Sophie was going to say exactly why and then

realised she wasn't sure. In fact, she didn't really get on with Maria.

'You see,' continued Dr Jonas, 'the first rule of deceit is, never let your loved ones know what you are doing.'

'But you said you told Maria...'

Dr Jonas cleared his throat in order to elucidate.

'The second rule of deceit is denial,' he said, thoroughly enjoying his devised distraction. 'Even in the face of overwhelming evidence.'

'I wouldn't deny it if Roland confronted me,' said Sophie. 'What's the point?'

'So, you're ready to tell Roland, then?'

Sophie groaned and rubbed her forehead.

'Maybe not,' she said. 'It's just not the right time. Not with the end of the campaign and getting through my finals.'

'The third rule of deceit, if the secret is out,' resumed Dr Jonas, 'always ensure you control the truth once it is known.'

'What does that mean?'

Dr Jonas scratched the side of his neck, inspecting his fingernail to see if he had scraped off any loose skin.

'Have you ever heard of the Illusion of the Fountain?'

'No,' said Sophie, knowing she was now going to hear all about the Illusion of the Fountain.

'I learnt this in a lecture...'

'You went to a lecture?' said Sophie mockingly.

'I thought I should before I got qualified. Anyway, this was a case about a woman who was mute, depressed and catatonic. However, they were able to establish the following facts about her: apparently, she had come home at the wrong time and disturbed her husband shagging another woman. So, you'd think she would go ape-shit, catching her husband in the act, so to speak. But no – as she looked at the other woman starkers in the bedroom, the husband told her she was looking at a beautiful fountain.'

'So?'

'Well, he knew, or speculated, his wife would struggle to take it all in. So, by creating the illusion, suggesting she was looking at a beautiful fountain, he was exploiting her emotional trauma. There was reality and his suggested reality, which confused her and sent her into a fugue-like state.'

'What did she do?'

'Well, she was sectioned, with suicidal depression.'

'I don't believe it.'

'It's true, as far as I know.'

'You don't say… and your point is?'

'Roland,' said Dr Jonas, 'is like that woman. You could take a photo of us shagging and he still wouldn't believe you were going behind his back.'

Sophie blushed, her red face an innocent contrast to Dr Jonas' cool, calculating logic. He remained silent, staring mischievously.

'You're making me feel as if I'm doing something wrong,' she said, angry she had been separated out from their combined deceit.

'That's only in your head,' said Dr Jonas. 'You said you wanted to be liberated, to get away from the straitjacket of sexual convention.'

'Yes, I do. I am and I have… with you…' she said, stumbling over her assertion.

'But I'm not enough, am I? I thought I was just for starters, your hors d'oeuvres…'

'I don't want to be trapped,' said Sophie, restoring her composure.

'We're all trapped,' said Dr Jonas. 'My trap is just the stench of a little privilege.'

'That's not a trap,' said Sophie, laughing. 'You can do what you want with your life.'

'That takes confidence,' said Dr Jonas, indicating it might be absent.

'You are confident,' stated Sophie. 'After all, most doctors are egotistical arseholes who think they should be worshipped.'

'Oh, it's nice to know you worship me.'

'Well, perhaps you're the exception.'

Dr Jonas paused.

'It's just about knowing how to play the game,' he said, 'in order to portray that confidence.'

'And what's the name of the game?'

'Knowing where you come from,' said Dr Jonas craftily. 'In order to know your destination.'

'What do you mean?'

'You'll work it out.'

'You're patronising me. And you're stopping me from doing this!' she said, pointing her pen at the assignment.

But it had become a meaningless task. She might as well give up and do what she had come to do with Dr Jonas.

'You like playing games, don't you?' said Sophie, resigned to talking. 'But it can cause damage, you know…'

Dr Jonas shrugged.

'Don't you think you got it wrong with Annie Buchanan?' she asked.

'Hmmm… you mean the mad fucking music therapist. But it's too late for her – she can't row back… she's gone too far out to sea.'

'She didn't deserve what happened to her.'

'She fucked with Slaney… quite literally, probably, which is why he had her locked up.'

'And you are willing to be part of it?'

'She broke the rules… I had no choice. I have bosses as well, you know.'

'But you sectioned her.'

'Look, she was pretty mad, but it might have been temporary. I mean, she is mad now: a full-on manic depressive! Problem is, it's all a bit messed up for her because of this place and Slaney.'

Sophie blinked. She felt adrenaline rush through her body. There was something she had to grasp, something immediate, something pertinent. A powerful self-realisation came shooting through to the front of her mind: if she wasn't careful, she too could end up just like Annie Buchanan.

'The thing is,' said Dr Jonas:

'When we spin a spider's web
And make revenge the only pledge
Our deeds will seem quite merciless
To those above the surfaces.'

'That's not funny,' said Sophie, the light-hearted banter now draining into an acute sense of paranoia.

369

It was always difficult to get to the truth in Wellington Park and Dr Jonas was as opaque as the rest of them... but she had heard rumours, just like everyone else. It was crazy to think anyone could end up a patient on the wards just because you crossed Slaney or Fitzpatrick... but maybe, just maybe, there was something to it. And it wouldn't surprise her if Slaney had been shagging Annie Buchanan. The question she had to ask herself: would Slaney turn on her after all this time? It was just too risky. Why risk it and put everything on the line? She had tried her best to get back at the adulterous piece of shit, and she had never meant Roland to become a pawn in all of it, but it was time to escape and move on, just in case Slaney really resented what she had done: introducing a little instability into his grand plans for Wellington Park and his personal profit.

'Listen,' said Dr Jonas, 'there are all sorts of rules – understand what the rules are and you can play by the rules and get what you want. Fail to understand those rules and you can fall foul of them, have an extremely difficult and unrewarding life and become a patient in an institution like this.'

'But the people here are ill,' said Sophie. 'They haven't particularly broken any set of rules.'

'Oh, they have,' said Dr Jonas. 'They have broken the rule that thou shall not be a weak and pathetic victim of an unfair and unequal society. They have broken the rule that thou shall not be an over-sensitive human being incapable of taking responsibility. They have broken the rule that says they do not have the ability to adapt and survive. Once they have become mentally ill they are evolutionary rejects, unfit for the demands of our system. They are put to one side, put in a human dustbin, the doors locked and the key thrown away.'

'You don't believe that,' said Sophie.

He gave Sophie a steely glance in order to appear inscrutable.

'Wait a minute,' she said, stretching across the bed and grabbing from her small rucksack an A4-size pad. She then turned her back on Dr Jonas and began to draw and write something.

'Do I get to fuck you at the end of this?' asked Dr Jonas, as Sophie continued with her creativity.

Sophie ignored him. Then with a flourish, she ripped the sheet of paper from its perforated binding.

'There,' she said, 'that's for you!'

Dr Jonas read it, intrigued and bemused, before bursting out laughing.

'You know me only too well,' he said, as he threw the piece of paper in the air, grabbed Sophie by her arms and pinned her to the bed. 'For that, I will have to punish you with two – no, maybe three – uncontrollable orgasms.'

'I'll hold you to that,' said Sophie, as Dr Jonas tried to kiss her lips.

'Make sure you do,' he said, as he pushed the piece of paper off the bed.

'Hang on,' said Sophie.

She pulled her precious assignment from underneath their bodies and let it drop on the floor, resting on top of the improvised Certificate of Arseholes she had just given Dr Jonas.

CHAPTER 33

NOW IT STARTS

Just as Roland feared, the retribution for failure had started. He knew he was innocent of the crime (the disgrace, the effrontery to etiquette), but Dr Caldwell had made the complaint, a handwritten letter in scrawling black permanent ink, that on said, date, time and place, Mr Cauldron had attended the clinic of said godlike presence, Dr Caldwell, inappropriately dressed. How did he plead? Innocent! Is a man not innocent until proven guilty? Is it not the inalienable right of all men (women and children included) to be judged by his peers, in the light of all evidence, before pronouncing judgement? Roland would have his day in court. Or in this case, a meeting with Gobi to explain himself, relishing the opportunity to confront such an obvious injustice and setting about devising his defence.

Firstly, he needed to rebut the accusation that on said, date, time and place, he had failed to wear a tie, as the good Dr Caldwell had stated in his letter of complaint. This would be a simple rebuttal based on the fact Dr Caldwell had provided no evidence in support of the minor indiscretion (if it were true, and it was not).

Secondly, once he had disproved the accusation, or the alleged transgression, he would seek to characterise the complaint as a move by management to ensure he felt constantly under threat, pressurised, monitored, with the intention to drive him into an all-pervasive mindset of paranoia. It was not a question of whether Roland had failed to adhere to the requirements laid down for student nurses when on duty in Chaolla House, but the pernicious motivation of management to suppress all dissent. This was clearly what lay at the heart of Dr Caldwell's letter of complaint. A classic, tried-and-tested method to undermine views and activity which served as opposition to their autocratic rule.

Unfortunately, all of this only seemed to matter to Roland and no one else seemed particularly bothered. Not Jas or Terry, his best and only mates, not anyone he worked with on the wards, or anyone he met in the social club. No one stopped him in the corridors, in the canteen, in the nurses' hostel and said anything to support him. 'You'll be alright' was as much as they offered in support. He was, he realised, isolated, cut-off and forgotten. Although no one said it, the lack of sympathy said his troubles had been brought upon himself; he had made his own bed and he now must lie in it.

What had he done wrong? Where had he gone wrong? He had put his whole career on the line to help people and to fight for a cause and what thanks did he get? Looks of "told you so", looks that said, "We could see it coming… we could have told you it was a waste of time going up against management."

Therefore, not only did he hate the known enemy, their accomplices and collaborators, he hated everyone he came into contact with because at a minimum everyone was two-faced. He had lost faith in any faith he might have had in the human spirit, in the notion there was some good in people. No, none of that applied now. He was going to face whatever came his way all on his own. And worst of all, Sophie did not seem to care either.

Gobi knew only too well how Roland would react once he had received Dr Caldwell's complaint. As much as he would willingly pretend the matter had been dealt with in order to satisfy the powers that be, a meeting with the angry young man was inevitable. He also knew Dr Caldwell's letter was a product of a need to deal with the troubling activism of his own students, a warning shot and the beginning of a concerted effort to extinguish the so-called militancy. This was only to be expected, since he had heard that the campaign to address staffing shortages had been extinguished with the connivance of the trade union. It had all the telltale signs of a management tolerance threshold being crossed. The gloves were off and they were beginning to resolve these problems, with or without Gobi's acquiescence.

Roland sat in Gobi's office with the window shut due to the chill autumn breeze.

'So, you know,' said Gobi, resting his head on his hands with his elbows on his desk, 'did you wear a tie or didn't you?'

'Yes, of course I wore a tie,' said Roland, agitated in the chair of interrogation. 'There's no reason for me not to wear a tie. I knew I had to wear a tie and so I did.'

Gobi lifted his head.

'So, you know, why do you think someone of Dr Caldwell's status, you know, and standing, has gone to all this trouble to say that you didn't?'

'You mean, why has he complained about me?'

Gobi moved his head backwards and forwards.

'You know, I think… you know what I mean,' said Gobi.

'You mean, why would someone of Dr Caldwell's standing make something up?'

That was not what Gobi meant.

'Roland,' said Gobi, 'you know, who do you think is going to be believed?'

'Who do you think should be believed?'

'You know, do you have any proof you were wearing a tie on that day?'

'Proof?!' blurted out Roland. 'How am I supposed to provide proof? Are you saying I should take a photograph of myself every time I go on to a ward in case someone complains about my dress code?'

'No, no, no,' said Gobi. 'You know, no one's suggesting that.'

'Then what are you suggesting?'

Again, Gobi thought he knew what he meant.

'It may help, you know, if you could find someone who would be willing to confirm you were wearing a tie on that day.'

'Look,' said Roland, 'there was a staff member called Felix who saw me wearing a tie but I am not going to ask him to prove anything. Do you know why? Because a) he might have to lie to protect himself, and b) it gives credence to something which should be dismissed and laughed at.'

'Oh, you know, why don't we speak to this Felix?'

'You can, but I am not. I'm sure Sophie would willingly say that before I went to work that day I was wearing a tie. But I'm not going to do that because it's absurd.'

'I would not want you to make things up,' said Gobi.

'No, I don't want to make things up,' said Roland. 'You should believe me.'

Gobi paused.

'Did anything happen that day?' asked Gobi.

'No.'

'You know… nothing at all?'

'Not to my knowledge.'

'Are you sure?'

'Yes.'

Gobi paused again. He was in a dilemma.

'You know, I will need to write back to Dr Caldwell,' he said. 'I will need to be able to reassure him the school will continue to adhere to the guidelines for attending these placements. You know, we don't want to jeopardise the opportunities for all the other students. I think I will have to say that I have spoken to you, and that… you know…'

But Gobi had run out of words to describe what he was thinking, what he intended, what he needed to do to ensure he was acting in the best interests of the school. However, Roland knew what Gobi wanted to do.

'Are you going to say that I was in the wrong?' asked Roland tensely. 'And is this going on my file?'

'No, no, no,' said Gobi, attempting to reassure. 'You know, there's no need to admit anything. You know, these doctors get into a position where if they think they are not given enough respect, they can, you know, be a little bit awkward. The letter can go on your file, but it won't mean anything.'

Roland raised his voice.

'I'm not having that letter on my file!' he said, physically rising a few inches at the same time.

Gobi's hands were tied.

'I can't pretend this hasn't happened,' he said.

'If the letter goes on my file that's the beginning of it,' said Roland. 'I know how it works: building up evidence, keeping up the pressure, making life difficult, the drip-drip-drip effect...'

It was not something Gobi was going to deny.

'There's no need to worry,' he said. 'You know, nothing will come of it. Perhaps you just need to take this, you know, on the chin, and keep your head down for a while.'

'Why should I?' said Roland. 'Conformity is a disease, a living death, a sapping of the life force. That's not me. I can't be something I am not. I have to be myself. I have to be true to myself.'

'Well, you know, there will be consequences.'

'I am aware of that,' said Roland, pointing at the handwritten scrawl of Dr Caldwell's letter on Gobi's desk. 'Which is why I don't want things like this going on my file.'

Gobi had hoped Roland would accept he had been equitable in his dealing with the matter, as he had no intention of pursuing any disciplinary action.

'You know, what would you consider a satisfactory outcome?' asked Gobi.

This is what I've been waiting for, thought Roland.

'I would consider a satisfactory outcome a letter of apology from Dr Caldwell for making false and inaccurate accusations against me, on the basis he has no evidence that I was inappropriately dressed. Secondly, if he does not withdraw the complaint, then I will pursue with my union a grievance for bullying and harassment, on the basis that this is maliciously motivated because of my role as president of the student council and a trade union rep.'

As Gobi had suspected.

'Of course, you know, you are perfectly entitled to use whatever means are available to you. However, from my experience, you may just want to consider the impact it will have on your career, if you were to take such a course of action.'

'I don't care about my career,' said Roland, angry Gobi had in essence made an indirect threat. 'I care about justice!'

Gobi leaned forward.

'You know, you don't want to get into trouble over this,' he said, still hopeful he could persuade Roland.

'It's a bit too late for that,' said Roland defiantly. 'He shouldn't be making up stories about me. Am I supposed to bow down and say, "Sorry, sir, three bags full, sir" and all that deference bullshit?'

'You know, there's no need for you to do anything,' said Gobi. 'As I said, leave it with me and I will respond to his letter. You know, it's my duty as head of this school to address the complaint. All I needed to do was to hear your side of the story.'

'Is... it... going... on... my... file?' asked Roland, singling out each word, his frustration beginning to boil over.

Was it worth it? thought Gobi. He knew Fitzpatrick would expect to see it in Roland's file. He knew this was just part of a strategy to rid them of yet another troubling soul. They would succeed, with or without the letter.

'Okay,' said Gobi, 'I won't put it in your file. You're probably right.'

'I know I'm right,' said Roland, feeling sure his threat of making life difficult had been the deciding factor in Gobi backing down.

'You know, perhaps Dr Caldwell has always been a bit too fussy over things, but I will need to keep him sweet.'

'Fine,' said Roland, in a tone of disgruntled satisfaction.

'But, you know... none of this will go away.'

Roland nodded. He knew that. He knew it had started.

CHAPTER 34

A LOGICAL CONCLUSION

Annie Buchanan had come to a final, logical conclusion, because there was no way out, no route or path which offered hope. They had taken away her freedom, incarcerated and deleted her soul, and left her to rot in a nonsensical world. With no end in sight there was no hope of her returning to the way she used to be.

So, what was the point in carrying on living? The light at the end of the tunnel, the exit sign, directed her to say goodbye, to put to bed the pain, anxiety and despair which drove a spike into the core of her very being. There was one simple, single thought, the only thing which gave her peace: death at the end of it all, and sooner rather than later. Otherwise, the terror raged inside her brain, the air congealed into a thick strangulation, sapping the oxygen, sapping the energy to breathe, dissolving in a medicated dream of dribbling incoherence and constipation.

How, she wondered, had she slipped from the sane music therapist into a bipolar depressive? Had it always been there, this madness, depression, psychosis, or whatever they wanted to call it? Did she have some predisposition, a genetic time bomb waiting to go off? Was it really all her fault? Or was it Slaney's mean and psychopathic tendencies which kept her trapped in this false and unjust prison? It was self-evident before any kind of jury, any kind of tribunal, she would normally be found innocent and released. But of course, they would never let her go, whatever they might say about the legitimacy of her section. The hope of salvation had evaporated. No one was going to save her. Annie was undoubtedly abandoned and alone, and knew she was going nowhere.

But sleep was good. It stopped her mind from working in the real world, a false world, a world full of illusions where truth was never tangible. It meant reality did not exist in there, in sleep, swimming in the realm of dreams. *Why would I want to come out and shake the hand of some nasty, ugly goblin who does not believe a single word I say? Better to be in the non-world and pass over to the new universe. Perhaps I should say to myself, 'No, Annie, don't be stupid: suicide is a coward's way out, the wrong way out – it is for the defeated, giving in to all those who are against you.' But then, most days, I am standing alone, categorised and isolated, with some useless, feckless, poorly trained idiot keeping an eye on me and asking how I am feeling. But no one really knows how I am feeling. Would they really want to know how I am feeling? Unlikely...*

Ironically, I was once part of the system, the system that knows nothing about pain; treated as a thing, one more thing to be managed, ordered and kept out of harm's way. But at least I stood up to the system, challenged Slaney before being smashed into the ground by their insane protection of their unthinking machine.

Well, what did it matter? She had made her decision. A rational decision, a well-thought-out decision. All that was left was the execution. This had to be her focus. It would require all her energy, all her concentration to finish it once and for all, to bring to an end the circle of misery.

Tonight, she lay on her bed, still in her clothes and the partition curtains open so she could watch what was going on. There was her usual smile, which was enough for the night staff to assume all was well. The good thing was, no one really noticed; she was part of the furniture now, here to stay. But it would be difficult to slip beneath the radar at night because the ward doors were always locked and the windowpanes nailed down.

However, now her mind had been flipped, the short time left for existence was relatively peaceful. All the stress and anxiety fell away. All the things which had kept her body taut and tense became the wasted past. Relief was in the recognition of dominion over herself; resolution and destiny had returned. She was no longer under the control of others. She had the ultimate weapon. By her act of free will, she would regain her power. Moving from life to death, she would feel the enhanced pleasure of being completely free to die as and when she chose. This was the ultimate act of power, restoring what the institution had stripped away.

As she listened to the coughs, snorts and snoring of the dormitory, there was no haunting tonight, no vicious paranoia chasing after her thoughts, no vivid torture in her mind, no cold, fibrous ends biting and gnawing at her periphery. Tonight was her first night of sanity. *Who cares now about budgets, truth, honesty, virtue, goodness and caring?* Her head was no longer banging against the brick wall, trying to make sense of it all, no longer putting sticking plasters on gaping wounds, no longer going along with it just to keep her job. The dam had burst. The floodgates were open. The succinct conclusion had been reached. The blindingly obvious staring in her face: all she had to do was end it.

Morning had come and Annie was ready to leap off her bed, run as quickly as possible out of the ward and head to her chosen destination. But she needed restraint, calmness, patience. She must not raise suspicions, otherwise they would clamp her in irons, drug her more than she was already drugged and invent more sections to prolong her insanity. She lay on her bed until she was asked if she wanted breakfast downstairs, crawled meekly to wash her face in the basin and smiled to reassure the nurses that everything was okay. Downstairs, the smell of sulphurous boiled eggs filled her nostrils. She declined everything: no toast, bacon or boiled tomatoes (just tea because she had such a dry mouth). Then she slipped out unnoticed.

This is it… it has come to this. Did I always think this was the best way out? Perhaps I did. Thinking is not good for you. Caring about others is not good for you. Mother always used to say it would only end in tears – in my tears, because I am crying now… not because I don't want to die, but because I will hurt my mother. I hope she will understand my predicament and see it from my point of view. But there has never been a time when anyone has understood me. What can I say? There is nothing good about life. There never was much good. There is only so much emptiness one can take. The void, the chasm, the great big hole, all its darkness, all its fetid reason for existing has swallowed me up, sucked out all my hopes and wishes, laughed and mocked me and washed me away. I am a pale and insignificant shadow, a nothing. I cannot make a difference, not for myself, for others or the world around me. This is the point: I am at the point of nothingness.

Annie kept her head down low, her eyes drawn to the moving pavement, the long curves of her dress flapping along with her determined steps. She hoped to make it before anyone spotted her, before anyone stopped to think someone like her should not be out and about. But it was easy, so easy to get to the nurses' hostel and drift seamlessly through the fire exit door and into the side of the building. *Am I really going to die? Or am I just all talk and no action? This is the true test of my courage. Will I go up these stairs or will I stay here too long? Am I waiting for someone to see me so they can stop me?*

I am breathing, so fast…

The doors upstairs on the top floor swung open and Annie darted underneath the concrete steps to hide. The person above jumped two, then three, then one, then a few more steps, then jumped again and landed with a loud clump of their feet next to the door. They stopped and arranged something on their body, then flung open the swing-back heavy door and hurried out into the morning. Probably late for their shift, thought Annie.

She looked closely at the one thing which had been left underneath the stairs: a bicycle wheel with a few forks bent inwards. She reflected for a moment on the possible story behind how it had got there, imagined the person whose bike it was; who had to walk because someone had come along and kicked in their front wheel. Why was this wheel important? It wasn't. It was just there, that's all, an insignificant, useless object.

Focus. She must maintain focus, keep her eye on the prize, the ultimate goal, the most important statement.

Death was in sight and control was coming back.

The doors swung open on the ground floor again and someone ran up the stairs. Perhaps it was the same person? Maybe they had forgotten something? Better to stay still, stay here, crouched with the bent-forked wheel. But for a flitting, lucid moment, it did not really make sense. Maybe she had made the wrong decision? Maybe there was some hope? But why would she think that now? This was just doubt, understandable doubt, fear of the big decision, the big unknown. Once it was done, everything would stop. No more pain, anguish, shame, agony and torment. The push must come now. The actions required must be implemented. There was softness, a gentle pillow to lay her head down, a soothing quietness, a sacred chamber, a cool, calm cavern of pleasantness and respite.

There were footsteps again, clattering down: clomp, clomp, clomp; the same footsteps leaping down and out again into the day. Her body shook and shivered. She felt the onward rush of nerves and energy pulse through her muscles. There was reflux, acid… sick.

Annie, you are going to die. Is this what you really want? Think about it. This is your last chance to say no. Let's go back,

back to the ward, talk it through with somebody, find a way through all this cloudiness, puzzle and confusion. But I am not confused. I am clear in my mind and my thinking has choice. It does seem right, somehow, to say goodbye, to get it over and done with. I am just one of those that needs to go, to put a termination notice into practice. It's not bad, it's not wrong, it is part of life.

Annie stood up and her body shook again. She shut her eyes.

Come on, you must do this.

And then, all of sudden, her shaking stopped and a warm blanket covered her thin, pale body. An opening appeared, a blessing, a friendly angel wrapped their wings around the troubled soul of Annie Buchanan. There was light, a glimmer of opportunity. She knew now that it could happen without difficulty, without question, without people getting in the way.

She walked to the top of the stairs and let herself fall. There was a loud crack as her head hit the concrete floor. But there was still consciousness. She went back up the stairs with the taste of blood in her mouth and stood again in position. Her eyes shot back into their sockets as she flew like an arrow with the same amount of force. Her neck broke and her skull shattered, blood rushing from her wound and swimming on the concrete floor.

CHAPTER 35

URBAN MYTH

The impact of Annie Buchanan's suicide rippled throughout the hospital, sending shock waves through the institution. It was the one thing which prefaced every conversation: had you heard about Annie Buchanan?

For the Pothead Pixies it was a difficult time as they navigated the occupation of the nurses' hostel by the police over the first few days, waiting to see if they would be interviewed, before finally settling down to some sense of normality. They debated endlessly into the night, in Sophie's room, in Jas' room: why had Annie Buchanan done it in the nurses' hostel? Roland decided not to reveal Annie's little visit. After a great deal of intense debate, they settled on the following rationale: Annie Buchanan killed herself because she was kept against her will, with no constructive therapeutic solution for her, even if she was ill; the blame for her suicide rested squarely with Slaney, who was more than capable of keeping someone locked up if he thought they posed a threat to his authoritarian regime. In addition, there was now a heightened risk the authorities would take a keen interest in what went on in the nurses' hostel, and they would definitely target dope-smoking. It was up to each individual to decide how they should deal with it, but they would stop the big smoking sessions, be as discreet as possible and wait and see what happened.

Sophie seized on the chance to declare she had given up pot-smoking. Roland did not dispute her decision because he sensed their relationship was on rocky ground. He would hang on to his dope, though, and sneak in a smoke whenever he could. Jas and Terry were not going to be intimidated, although Jas seemed to understand the need for less overt displays of stoned pixie behaviour. The only outstanding issue, one raised at the end of all their convoluted conversations: had anyone heard from Dr Jonas? No, they all replied, and wondered what was going on with the "mad fucker".

Once Dr Jonas had been informed of Annie Buchanan's suicide he decided his doctoring days were over. Her death was the final straw, the wake-up call he needed, a sign all was not well, either in his personal or professional life. He did feel guilty and partly responsible for her incarceration. And he knew that they (the authorities) would be eager to point one or two fingers his way. As a consequence, he fell into a mild depression, something which had always threatened to bubble up to the surface.

His dalliance with Sophie Smith had been a temporary distraction and had failed to mitigate his profound sense of existential tedium. He was fed up and needed to make some radical changes, put words and thoughts into action to ensure a decisive turn for the better. Self-medicating his way through the dreary procession of his existence, ambling through his middle-class parental expectations, was no cure for his underlying sense of futility. He certainly felt a dramatic statement was needed. Just as Annie Buchanan had found it within herself to hurl her fragile body over the edge, to send a message (although a sad and lonely one), so Dr Jonas needed to make a similar dramatic statement before he journeyed on.

His opportunity, his "Annie Buchanan moment", meant no limits, no boundaries, everything or anything was possible. Dr Jonas would turn the world upside down in his own little way. Why should he go quietly when he could make a real arse of himself, sail away into the distance, release the chains which had bound him to a life less meaningful?

It all started when he was conducting an initial assessment on a new admission to Lilywhite Ward.

'Are you sure,' asked Dr Jonas, isolated in the bland clinic room, 'you are hearing voices?'

The young man, who had arrived with his parents, howled at the top of his voice.

'I see…' said Dr Jonas, less than impressed. 'Why did you feel the need to do that, Christopher?'

'I am a wolf,' Christopher said, his eyes glistening with a watery sheen.

'Do you imagine yourself to be a wolf?'

'No,' said Christopher, narrowing his eyes, slumping back into his chair and pulling his metallic, heavily badged leather jacket around his waist.

Whilst the adolescent behaviour annoyed Dr Jonas, he had some sympathy with the disaffected teenager, remembering he had once also suffered from a pale white pallor and randomly spread pimples.

'What would you think if I did something like that?' asked Dr Jonas.

'Like what?'

'If I howled at the top of my voice?'

'Why would you do that?' asked Christopher, smirking.

'I could do it for a number of reasons,' said Dr Jonas, maintaining his composure. 'I might be frustrated, unhappy, or just bored.'

'Go on then,' said Christopher.

This was a challenge Dr Jonas could not refuse. He stood up, arched his back and let out a full-throated howl which reverberated around the tiny anaesthetised room. He then fixed a stare at the belligerent Christopher, before sitting back down and calmly picking up his pen.

'You're fucking mad!' said Christopher, in response to the provocation.

'Maybe,' said Dr Jonas. 'The thing is, are you?'

Christopher shrugged and tilted his head.

'Do you know the reason why you are here?' asked Dr Jonas.

Christopher shook his head.

'Your parents brought you, didn't they?'

Christopher used his face to say, *so what?*

'They're waiting outside to see if you need help,' continued Dr Jonas. 'So, do you need help?'

'I don't know,' said Christopher.

'Would you like me to help you?'

'How do I know... you're the doctor, aren't you? They all say there's something wrong with me.'

Dr Jonas knew there was very little wrong with the young man. He drew a three-dimensional cube (his favourite squiggle) on his patient notes.

'You're not writing anything,' said Christopher. 'I can see.'

'Would you like me to write something?'

'That's what you're meant to do, isn't it?'

Yes, it probably was what he was meant to do, but this time (and perhaps forever), he had no inclination to write.

'It's far too easy to make clinical judgements,' said Dr Jonas. 'Especially in your case, when no judgement at all might be in your best interests.'

'What does that mean?'

'I'm not sure,' said Dr Jonas, laughing.

Christopher looked around the room, either through dissatisfaction or a desire to avoid further probing. Dr Jonas remained silent, deliberately staring at the confused and unhappy young man.

'Is that what you do?' asked Christopher.

'What do you mean?'

'Stare at people all day… try and freak them out?'

'Yes, I do,' said Dr Jonas.

He decided to wait, to let Christopher spend time in silence. And as he waited, he reflected on how he had spent so much time going through the motions, ticking boxes for schizophrenia, depression, anxiety, mania and obsessive compulsive behaviours. Perhaps now was the time to make things more equal, stop the rot before the rot went any further, disengage from the process and answer a human being's call for understanding? After all, Christopher had no concept of what a bleak and desolate future lay ahead of him if he continued seeking symptoms which would put him in a box, a box he would never, ever be able to climb out of: medicated, categorised and abandoned.

'Do you know what my mum thinks?' said Christopher, who needed to bring the silence to an end.

'No,' said Dr Jonas. 'You'd have to tell me.'

'She says I'm the Devil.'

'Does she say that when you've done something wrong?'

'No,' said Christopher, slightly animated and leaning forward, 'she actually thinks I am the Devil.'

'Are you?' asked Dr Jonas, unmoved by such a revelation.

'No!' said Christopher, raising his voice in frustration. 'Of course I'm not. Don't you see…? She's the one who's off her head! You don't know what she's like… she's a religious nut.'

'Would you like me to talk to your mum?'

Christopher leant back in his chair, sneering with a sense of fatalism.

'Look,' he said, 'she's not going to admit that to you. Do you think she's going to bring me to a place like this and then go, "Oh yeah, right, it's not my son that's mad, it's really me because I think he's the Devil incarnate"? That's not going to happen, is it?'

'No,' said Dr Jonas, rather calmly.

'Don't you see?' said Christopher. 'I'm trapped. There's no one going to believe me.'

'You're right,' said Dr Jonas. 'You're in a sticky situation.'

392

This was not what Christopher expected to hear.

'So, what… you're going to say I'm mad?'

'No, not if you don't want me to.'

'Are you going to tell my mum there's nothing wrong with me?'

'Well, you see this bit of paper?' said Dr Jonas, sliding the form on the desk towards him. 'This is where I fill in details about the assessment I've made of you. So far, I haven't filled it in. And to be honest with you, I don't want to fill it in.'

'You're on my side, then?'

'No, not really, but you might be the last patient I see. It would be a shame to section you, lock you up just because you're having a bad time of it.'

Christopher was perplexed. He thought he had the measure of Dr Jonas, but now he was not so sure.

'You don't care, do you?' he said. 'You don't give a fuck about people like me, do you?'

Dr Jonas grinned. He was enjoying this.

'The thing is,' said Dr Jonas, 'you just don't know. And even if I said I don't care, I still might care. It might just be that I'm not allowed to tell you.'

'Well, I don't care if you did care.'

'Okay,' said Dr Jonas, 'let's say I do care. Let's say I care so much about what happens to you that I'm prepared to put my job on the line for you, to throw away my whole career, to fail my parents… even risk serious consequences.'

'This is fucked,' said Christopher, looking around the room again, hoping there might be a small hole in the wall he could climb through.

'That's what I often think,' said Dr Jonas.

Christopher laughed.

'Man, you're more fucked up than me!'

'Probably…'

'Yet you're the one that does all of this,' he said, pointing at his blank patient notes on the desk.

'Oh yes, I'm the… lucky man.'

'But you don't want to do it?'

'Not any more.'

'That's really crazy.'

Dr Jonas nodded, conscious of a mild sense of depersonalisation sweeping through his body, as he began to realise he was at the beginning of his metamorphosis.

'Are you sure you're not one of the patients?' asked Christopher, who was wondering whether he should get out of the room as quickly as possible.

'No, but there's a close correlation,' said Dr Jonas. 'What you find in a backward, rundown institution on the verge of closure is there is not a lot of difference between, say, a doctor or a nurse or a patient. It all tends to merge into one. It's the institution that probably does it. These four walls, they suck you in and leave reality outside the gate.'

'So, there's no difference between you and the patients here, then? Is that what you're saying… that you're all mad?'

'That's right,' said Dr Jonas, standing to attention, 'we're all mad in here!'

'Cool,' said Christopher, who was feeling he might just be able to fit in.

'No, no, no. No. No! Not cool! Not cool at all!'

said Dr Jonas, wondering why he had ever bothered to indulge the little fucker.

'Where do I sign?'

'No!' said Dr Jonas, his pupils widening. 'You don't sign anything!'

'Oh man, you're a bummer.'

Dr Jonas screamed, an ear-crunching, deep-throated, diabolical scream. It punctured the clinic room door and ran helter-skelter through the ward.

★

'You will not believe what I've just heard,' said Jas, as he knocked and entered Sophie's room.

'I think we have,' said Roland, grinning and sitting up from the bed.

Sophie remained lying on her back and lifted her arms behind her head.

'Why, what have you heard then?' asked Jas, annoyed he may not have been first to get the gossip.

'About Dr Jonas,' said Roland.

'What's wrong with you, then?' said Jas, wondering why Sophie looked so morose. 'Is it your time of the month?'

'Fuck off, Jas!' replied Sophie.

'That answers that, then,' he said, standing in the room ready to reveal all. 'Are you making a coffee?'

'I'll do it,' said Roland, 'but it will have to be black.'

Jas eased himself down on to the floor and pulled out a Lizra packet. Sophie was about to remind him of her no-smoking rule when Jas pre-empted her.

'Don't worry, I am just going to roll it, then smoke it back in my own gaff.'

'Thank you,' said Sophie.

'So, what have you heard, then?' asked Roland, as he filled up the kettle.

'About Dr Jonas?'

'That's why you came round, isn't it?'

'Oh yeah… he's gone crazy.'

'Because?' asked Sophie, who was now pretending she still did not care.

'Because he is a mad fucker,' stated Jas.

'He always was,' said Roland, as he switched the kettle on.

'And now he's proved it,' added Jas.

'Exactly,' concluded Roland.

'That's nothing to crow about,' said Sophie, turning her head back to stare at the ceiling.

'Yeah, but it's funny.'

'You mean what he did?' said Roland, cleaning the dirty mugs in the basin with a wedge of green plastic cloth.

'Yeah – why else whip out your penis, take out a pair of scissors and cut it off right in front of an acute admission on Lilywhite Ward?'

'Is that what you heard?' asked Roland.

'Yeah,' said Jas, now taking the opportunity to describe all the gossip he had garnered. 'This kid was screaming and ran out of the clinic room, ran past his parents who were waiting for him, out of the grounds and jumped on a bus which was just pulling off. The police were alerted and they found him in a state of shock curled up on the back seat. One of the nurses who heard all the commotion in the clinic room rushed in to see what was going on and found Dr Jonas laughing his head off with blood all over his hands and something lying on the floor. She picked it up and realised it was a penis. She asked Dr Jonas what had happened and he said it was just a joke. She thought at first he'd been wounded, but he said he was fine and then said he was leaving. He then walked out and no one has seen or heard of him since. He must have got hold of some dead guy's penis, one from a post-mortem, stuck it down his trousers and made it look like he'd cut it off.'

'That's not what we've heard,' said Roland, mildly gratified he had a different version of events.

'No? Why, what have you heard then?' asked Jas, eager to add to his tapestry of emerging mythology.

'Well, the story I heard was this,' said Roland, as he poured hot water into the mugs. 'Dr Jonas had been acting really weird after Annie Buchanan had killed herself. I think he thought they were going to come down on him heavy. Maria had chucked him... she'd had enough. Anyway, he was doing some admission on a young kid, then he came out and started shouting abuse at the parents, saying there was nothing wrong with their son and they were the real problem. One of the nurses had to intervene and Dr Jonas just walked off the ward. Well, all this was reported and Slaney got to hear about it. Anyway, they were desperately trying to track him down – Dr Jonas – because the parents straight away put in a formal complaint. Once they found him they called him in, in front of Dr Caldwell and Slaney, and they suspended him there and then. That's when he did this really outrageous thing. Apparently, he got up in the meeting, took out a pair of scissors and cut off his penis. They were like, "Fuck, this guy's gone crazy" and tried to jump on him and everything, but he ran out of the office. But the crazy thing is, they thought at first, this guy's really gone mad and he's going to bleed to death if they don't catch him, but then when they looked on the floor they realised that it was a joke… a crazy, sick joke. I tell you, I wish I had seen their faces when he'd done it. But he's in a lot of trouble now. Well, he's fucked basically. There's no coming back from a situation like that. I wonder what made him do it?'

'You know, I don't believe either of you,' said Sophie, sitting up. 'I've heard a story like that before.'

'Yeah, what's that?' asked Jas.

'All the doctors tell the same story. The one I've heard is, this doctor gets hold of a penis from the mortuary and wanders up and down the high street flashing it at people. They call the police and then he whips out the scissors and cuts it off in front of a police officer, who faints as she's trying to arrest him.'

'So, you don't think Dr Jonas did any of that?'

'Well, all we know is he's gone AWOL. I reckon he's freaked out about the Annie Buchanan thing… but that's all.'

'They haven't proved anything,' said Roland, handing Jas his coffee.

'Yes they have!' said Jas. 'He's a mad fucker.'

CHAPTER 36

WHAT HAVE I DONE?

Jas slipped on his tracksuit bottoms, a thin white vest and his sand-coloured Woodlands. After all the serious shit going down he was in desperate need of a session with Ms Colgate. He headed out towards the ark, meandering along the circular tarmac path, studying the ground and then looking up over the edge of his shades. It was not long before he spotted a potential target and distraction, the rounded figure of Imogen Clough, wobbling ungracefully in her high heels, her nurse's uniform half-shrouded by a pink cardigan.

'Oi, shag bucket!' he shouted after her, without running to catch up.

She knew she would have to stop, if only to prevent further insults booming across the hospital lawns.

'You know your name, then,' said Jas, smiling mischievously as he approached.

Imogen glared.

'Who have you been screwing lately?' he asked unapologetically. 'Are you still at it with Slaney?'

'Why does everyone think I've got anything to do with that man?' said Imogen, half-convinced she was genuinely entitled to be puzzled.

'Oh, I've just heard you shag him in the gym after work,' said Jas casually.

'I can't believe it!' she said, fully aware of the gossip. 'Just because I use the gym.'

'Well, why else would you go in there?'

'To work out,' she said, as she always said.

'He has got a nice gym,' Jas conceded, 'but I bet you shag him when he's in there.'

'We're not all like you,' she said, determined to maintain her pretence of integrity.

She was, thought Jas, who was eager to continue teasing.

'So, do you still do a good blow-job?'

'Don't be disgusting!' she said, rebuking him.

'So, that's a no then?'

'God, Jas, what's wrong with you... are you constantly on heat or something?'

Jas mockingly acknowledged this with a sly grin.

'Have you ever heard of romance?' sighed Imogen.

'Is that what Slaney does, then... is he romantic?'

Imogen pulled a face and stuck out her tongue.

'You should be careful,' she said, comforted by the implied malice.

'I am careful,' said Jas. 'I never come inside.'

'Oh, you're so gross.'

'Girls like it.'

'You mean, young and naïve girls.'

'I'm not complaining.'

'No, but I bet their parents are.'

'Why bring them into it? At least I don't fuck with somebody else's family.'

Imogen paused. She had to assert herself and stop feeling she was the wrong side of Jas' distorted moral compass.

'Slaney's a powerful man,' she said. 'You don't want to cross him.'

Jas laughed. He had no fear; at least it was important to project that to someone in Imogen's position.

'Still smoking your pot, are you?' she retorted.

'Why, does Slaney want some?'

Imogen scowled. Jas was in a combative mood.

'You know,' she said, calmly measuring her words, 'they like you, but they will only put up with so much.'

Jas laughed again, this time rather defensively. What "they" liked, thought Jas, was him being in his little Indian box.

'So,' said Jas, determined to pursue his prey, 'are you sleeping with him then?'

'Do you think I'd tell you if I was?'

'No, but I think you just have.'

Imogen tried to maintain a look of inscrutability, and not to explicitly admit anything.

'Come on, you can tell me,' said Jas, desperate to see if she could keep up the charade. 'I won't say anything. It's just between you and me.'

'Why do you need to know?'

'I just like to know what's going on. If you don't want to tell me, I'll eventually find out from someone else.'

Imogen paused, with the thoughts of her assignations on the tip of her tongue.

'If I tell you something, you'll have to keep it a secret,' she said.

'Okay,' said Jas nonchalantly, wondering why Imogen would think he would want to keep it a secret.

'You mustn't tell anybody.'

'So, are you fucking him?'

Imogen smiled briefly.

'You are fucking him!' squealed Jas triumphantly.

'I haven't said that,' she said coyly.

'No, you haven't said that… but you are fucking him.'

'Maybe…'

'You dirty whore,' said Jas, as a kind of congratulation he knew Imogen would appreciate. 'You'll be able to make sister soon.'

'I don't care about promotion,' she said insincerely.

'No, of course not… why else shag the interim chief executive?'

'God, you're wicked!'

Jas shrugged his shoulders. He knew all along what she had been up to, he just wanted to see if she would admit it.

'So, no chance of a shag then?'

'Sorry,' said Imogen. 'I'm late as it is.'

'Just remember, the offer's always there,' said Jas, which was as close as he could get to affection for the "dirty slag".

'Oh, that's sweet,' she said, stretching out her hand to stroke his cheek.

Jas was disarmed.

'Do you still hang out with Sophie?' asked Imogen, feeling they had now got the Slaney thing out of the way. 'I hear she's got a boyfriend.'

'Yeah.'

'They don't like him,' she said gravely, adding in a withering squint of impatience. 'They think he's a bad influence on Sophie and he's turned her against them.'

'You're joking?!' he said, raising his voice.

'No,' she said, confident it would unsettle Jas.

'What the fuck's wrong with them?' he said, calculating at the same time the consequences of his association.

'You've got to be careful,' she said. 'They're going to get serious.'

'I haven't done anything!' said Jas, declaring his innocence, even if it was to Imogen as a third party.

'They won't see it like that. You think you can just do what you want... well, you can't.'

'Why, what have I done?' pleaded Jas, who genuinely thought his only crime was getting stoned.

'Come on,' said Imogen incredulously, 'look what's happened after that girl's suicide and Dr Jonas... they know you all hang out together.'

'Why pick on me?'

It was Imogen's turn to laugh at the compromised Jas.

'Because you picked a fight with them. You lot must be mad... too much pot-smoking in there,' said Imogen, pointing at the faceless nurses' hostel.

'Well,' said Jas, taking a step back, because he had an announcement to make, 'we're metaphysicians.'

Imogen burst out laughing, her loud cackle startling

the odd wandering patient as they hoovered the lawns with their gaze.

'That's your problem,' she said, 'you think you're something that you're not, whatever it is supposed to mean. So, what does it mean? You're not doctors, you're just student nurses.'

'It doesn't mean we're doctors,' said Jas, who regretted having said anything.

'Well, come on, what does it mean? Or don't you know what it means?'

'It doesn't matter,' said Jas, feeling embarrassed, desperate to move the subject on.

'Oh, Jas, you poor thing, you've really got yourself mixed up again.'

Jas ignored Imogen's patronising statement.

'I bet it's the dope-smoking Slaney's pissed about.'

'They know all about that,' she said, rather dismissively.

'They can't stop it,' said Jas, searching weakly for mitigation.

'Well, you're all on their radar.'

'Who is?'

'You, Sophie and her boyfriend… and that other one.'

'Terry?' suggested Jas.

Imogen nodded.

'Don't worry, it probably won't come to anything,' she said disingenuously.

'Look,' said Jas, rather hopefully, 'if you know there's going to be a raid, you will tell me?'

'Sure, if I can,' she said, anxious to move on. 'Listen, I have to go… take care.'

Then her round arse turned and wobbled defiantly away, the click of her heels strutting forward, leaving Jas behind.

He waited.

What a slut, he thought, *but a nice slut*. He'd always have time for her even if she'd sell her mother, brother and sisters to get whatever she wanted. He kind of liked that in her. But she could always see through him, though... through to his core. He knew she looked down on his fallibility, his grain of humanity, his softness. It meant it was easy to dump him when they were shagging. But this time she had left a nasty taste in his mouth, a reminder there was a sinister force, a dark force which had the power to intervene at any time, disrupt his playful antics and destroy his little kingdom.

He knew they hated his cocksure attitude, his childlike defiance, but they were all hypocrites as far as Jas was concerned. They were all at it, treading the moral tightrope, up to just as much deviancy (if not more). His only fault was he was just open and honest about it. They preferred to hide behind the façade of being grown-up and serious, when all along they were pissing on each other, stabbing each other in the back and lying through their teeth. Jas couldn't be like that. And Imogen was just putting the shits up him because that was the way she operated.

With enough distance between them, he started walking. He needed to see Ms Colgate, he needed to talk, he needed the ark.

CHAPTER 37

BUSTED!

'Guess what?' said Jas, as he walked into the room, his face showing a mixture of humour and seriousness.

'What?' asked Roland, who had got out of bed to answer the door as Sophie pulled on a top.

'I've been busted!'

'You're joking!'

'You're kidding!'

'No,' said Jas, his face flushed red.

'How?'

'When?'

'This morning,' he said, his shocked eyes revealing the truth.

'This morning?' queried Roland, immediately wondering how such an event could pass unnoticed in the nurses' hostel... if it was in the nurses' hostel?

'Do you want coffee?' asked Sophie, composed, as she filled the kettle.

Jas propped himself up against the wardrobe, needing the support.

'Shit!' said Roland, beginning to calculate the full ramifications.

'I know,' said Jas, appearing to stand outside his own trauma for a few seconds, 'I've just got back.'

'From the police station?' asked Sophie.

'I don't get it,' said Roland. 'Where were you this morning to end up getting busted?'

'In my room.'

'You mean there was a raid this morning... here in the nurses' hostel?'

Jas nodded.

'But I've got dope on me,' said Roland.

'Good,' said Jas, who had come round not just to tell his story. 'Those bastards have all my stash.'

'Here, you can have it,' said Roland, pulling out the soft black hashish from his pocket.

'Cheers, guys,' said Jas, as he dropped to the floor. 'Got any skins? They've taken everything.'

Roland searched in the same pocket and pulled out some crumpled Lizra. As Jas got to work, Sophie made the coffee.

'What are you going to do?' asked Roland.

'He'll have to resign or get dismissed,' said Sophie factually.

'At the moment,' said Jas, 'I just need to get stoned.'

They both watched respectfully in silence as Jas expertly worked on his conical joint. It was the end: the end for Jas and the end of an era.

'Here,' said Sophie, as she placed the coffee on the floor next to Jas.

'Thanks,' he said, as he paused to sip.

'I can't believe it,' said Roland. 'I mean, we didn't hear a thing.'

Sophie sat next to Roland on the bed.

'What time was it,' she asked, 'when the police raided?'

'Seven,' said Jas. 'I was like, in my bed, heard this knock on the door and then, bang – the bastards kicked it in.'

'You know, I can't believe we didn't hear it,' said Roland to Sophie.

'I was like,' continued Jas, 'trying to find my stuff so I could throw it out of the window, but this great big fucker was all over me, had my arm behind my back and my face in the bed. I was like, "I can't breathe, I can't breathe." Then they were going, "Where's your stuff, where's your stuff?" and I was like, "I can't breathe... I'd tell you if I could breathe!" Then this fat bastard let me up and says, "We know you've got drugs on you, so show us where it is and then we won't have to turn your place over." I thought, *What the fuck... I'm busted!*'

'How many pigs were there?' asked Roland angrily.

'There were only two of them.'

'So, what happened next?'

'Oh, they were alright after that.'

'What do you mean, they were alright?' asked Roland in disbelief.

Jas laughed.

'I asked if they wanted a cup of tea.'

'What did you do that for?'

'Well... I thought, why not? I was parched.'

'So, you made them a cup of tea?'

'Yeah, we had a bit of chat… said they had to take me down to the station to be charged and that they'd drive me back afterwards.'

'That's nice,' said Roland ironically.

'Well, it is better they do that than beat the crap out of me. Anyway, I knew it was all over.'

'Are you sure you are alright?' asked Sophie.

'No sweat,' said Jas, full of his usual bravado. 'At least I can get out of this place. The only thing keeping me here was the training and now that is fucked.'

'Have you told Gobi, then?' asked Roland.

'No, not yet, but I'm sure he knows. I'll go and see him later and hand my notice in.'

'Do you have to do that?'

'Of course he does,' said Sophie.

'If I resign I can avoid getting dismissed, as long as Gobi agrees to it.'

'Which means he can get a reference,' she said.

'So, you're going to resign,' said Roland, in an attempt to grasp the next steps. 'But where are you going to live?'

'I'll go back to my parents.'

'But what are you going to tell them?'

'Well, I'm not going to tell them I got busted. I'll think of something. I don't think they'll be that bothered… they can marry me off instead.'

'You're going to get married?' said Roland, struggling to understand the link.

'That's what Indians do,' said Jas.

'I think he means an arranged marriage,' said Sophie.

'Yeah,' said Jas, who sparked up and breathed in deeply, 'might as well do it now… there's money in it.'

'You can't do that,' said Sophie. 'You'll be exploiting some poor woman for financial gain.'

'How is there money in it?' asked Roland.

Jas watched a stream of smoke pour from his mouth.

'You get two Indian families,' said Jas, blowing gently on the end of the joint in order to even out the burn rate, 'they get together, show me some pictures, I'll choose a decent-looking one and then we'll get married. After that, I'll get set up in business, still carry on shagging whoever I want and everyone's happy.'

'Promise me you won't do that,' said Sophie.

'Why? I think it's a great idea myself,' said Jas, looking at Roland. 'You don't mind if I smoke all of this?'

'It's oppressive,' said Sophie. 'You will be the agent of male oppression.'

Jas raised his eyebrows.

'You don't have to do it,' said Roland. 'You are… anglicised.'

'You don't understand,' said Jas, pressing his shoulders against the wardrobe. 'If I have to go back to my parents, that's the price I have to pay.'

'I can understand that,' said Roland, who knew only too well the psychological power of parental control.

'You're not like Jas,' said Sophie pointedly.

'No,' said Roland calmly, 'but I can understand the pressure.'

'Thanks,' said Jas appreciatively.

'We all feel the pressure to conform to what our parents want,' said Roland. 'Why do you think I have nothing to do with mine? It's because they tried to beat me into submission.'

'Why, what did they do to you?' asked Sophie sceptically.

'I was always under pressure,' said Roland, who thought he did not need to explain himself.

'To do what?'

'I've told you before what they were like…'

'Guys, guys,' said Jas, 'have your arguments after I've gone, please. I need peace and calm to recover.'

'We're not arguing,' said Sophie.

'No, we're not arguing,' said Roland.

'Okay, puff on this,' said Jas, handing over the joint to Roland.

'Aren't you going to work this afternoon?' said Sophie.

Roland hesitated before taking the joint. Jas held up the oily hash.

'You're alright if I have this then?' he asked.

'Take it with you,' said Roland, squeezing out the last word as he sucked in the amber nectar. 'There's no way I can smoke it after what's happened. I just don't understand why they didn't do us as well.'

There was a few seconds' silence as each pondered the significance of Roland's question.

'Who knows?' said Sophie.

'All I know is,' said Jas, 'the fuckers got me.'

'Perhaps you were just too open about it,' said Sophie.

'No,' said Roland, 'I think they've picked on Jas because of his association with us.'

'Maybe…'

'Listen,' said Jas, 'it's not your fault. No one else stood up to those bastards.'

'Yeah, but it's all over now,' said Roland.

As he handed back the joint to Jas they heard a quiet tap on the door. Jas stubbed the joint out in the ashtray. Was it the police again? There was another tap.

'I'll get it,' said Jas. 'They can't bust me twice in a day.'

It was Terry.

'Fuck,' said Roland, sounding his relief.

Jas laughed, almost hysterically.

'Alright?' said Terry sheepishly.

'Have you heard?' asked Roland.

'They got you, didn't they?' said Terry to Jas.

'How do you know?'

'I saw them taking you away.'

'Why were you up so early?' said Jas.

'They busted me as well,' said Terry.

'You're joking! Fuck!'

'Well, I was lucky,' said Terry, who knelt cross-legged on the floor next to Jas, shaking his head and demonstrating his relief. 'I'd just scored last night and got back with a slab and was so stoned I fell asleep. Then in the morning they knocked on my door. I thought I was going down big time.'

'What were you doing with a slab?' asked Roland.

'I have a large appetite,' said Terry, who then paused for a moment.

'Tell us what happened, then,' said Jas. 'Did they bust you?'

'No,' said Terry, 'but it was so weird, I couldn't even remember where I'd put the stuff. There were loads of coppers in my room...'

'I only had two,' said Jas.

'What did they do you for?' asked Terry.

'An eighth.'

'Shit… that's really unlucky.'

'How,' interrupted Roland, slightly frustrated, 'did you get away with it?'

Terry shook his head from side to side, smiling with a sense of disbelief and satisfaction.

'Is that a joint?' asked Terry, pointing at the roach sitting in the ashtray.

'Look,' said Sophie, 'if you don't mind, I really wish you wouldn't smoke.'

Terry laughed.

'How do you think I knew you guys were in here?' he said. 'I could smell it all the way down the corridor.'

'That's the last time,' said Sophie, who was beginning to feel exasperated. 'I don't want them to find anything on me.'

Terry looked at Roland.

'You shouldn't let them freak you out, you know.'

'That's easy for you to say,' said Sophie. 'Jas has just lost his career.'

'What are you going to do?' asked Terry.

'Resign,' said Jas.

'Shit! Where are you going to live?'

'My parents' house,' said Jas, still trying to make it sound like a good idea.

'That's a bad move,' said Terry.

'I've got no choice.'

'He's going to get married,' said Roland.

'Wow! That's drastic.'

'Tell me about it…'

'It's at these times when you really need it, though,' said Terry, pointing at the joint in the ashtray.

'Don't,' said Sophie, as an instruction and an appeal to respect her wishes.

'So, why aren't you locked up then?' asked Jas.

'God knows,' said Terry, who again shook his head from side to side, appearing to recall this morning's raid for his own benefit.

'So, what happened?' asked Jas, beginning to feel a tinge of injustice, as it was clear he had become the only victim.

'You won't believe it,' said Terry, shaking his head.

'Did they break your door down?' asked Jas.

'No, I was like, "Hang on a minute" and as soon as I opened the door they all piled in.'

'So, then what happened?'

'Nothing, I just stood there and they started going through everything. This policewoman was asking me questions – I think she quite fancied me – and then they started going through all my coats hanging on the door. That's when I thought, *Shit… they're going to find it and I'm really fucked.*'

'How come they didn't find it?'

Terry once again shook his head from side to side.

'You won't believe this,' he said, 'but this copper got to the coat where I'd left the dope – I've got so many coats they were taking them off the door and going through them one by one – but instead of looking in the pockets of the coat I had the dope in, this copper just threw it down on the bed. I was like, result, I don't

414

believe it. Then another copper picked it up and goes to this other one, "Have you searched this one?" and so this copper goes, "Yeah, there's nothing in it." I could hardly control myself. I was like, desperately trying to hold back a smile and pretend everything's cool and it's not a problem. Yet, there it was, sitting on the bed in the pocket of my coat.'

'I know what it is,' said Roland. 'I reckon if you'd hidden it somewhere they would have found it, but because you just left it in the coat pocket they weren't expecting to find anything.'

'No,' said Terry, 'it's a sign.'

'It's a sign you're a lucky bastard,' said Jas, who was beginning to feel he was the only one to pay the price for all their deviancy.

'How is it a sign?' asked Sophie.

'It's a sign that I can carry on,' said Terry.

'You're joking!' said Roland.

'No, man, it is! They're not going to do that again. There's nothing stopping us now!'

Roland and Sophie looked at each other to confirm there was one thing they now agreed on: Terry had lost the plot. But Jas was swallowing the bitter pill of being the martyr; the scapegoat.

'I can't believe you got away with it,' said Jas.

'Don't worry,' said Roland, 'I'm sure there is something we can do.'

'Like what?' asked Sophie, who had no doubt Jas had brought it upon himself.

'Well,' said Roland, shrugging his shoulders and looking directly at Jas, 'just make sure you don't get married.'

'Listen, mate,' said Terry, 'if they throw you out I can put you up in my room for a bit.'

'Thanks,' said Jas, who now realised he was on his own, 'but it's all over really.'

'You'll be alright,' said Terry, 'as long as you don't kill yourself or cut off your penis.'

CHAPTER 38

IT'S ONLY A MATTER OF TIME

Roland sat on one of the wooden benches outside the breeze-block visitor centre. He watched Jas, wrapped in a shiny blue Puffa jacket, stroll across the lawns with a few bits of paper fluttering in his hand. Roland had agreed to wait whilst Jas handed in his resignation, which was probably why Jas jauntily punctuated his walk with a few sideways glances back at the school. He felt he owed Jas something in return for taking the hit, the police raid, but there was little he could do now that could make a difference. But unlike Sophie, he did not believe Jas had brought it upon himself. Yes, Jas was indiscreet, but so was everyone else.

Creely, who had been in the hedge talking to Adam (and who was notorious for pestering staff and patients for cigarettes), hovered near Roland.

'No,' said Roland assertively, before Creely had a chance to speak.

Undeterred, Creely offered his hands as an artificial begging bowl and bowed his head.

'Cigarette?'

'No,' said Roland again, in a stern and non-negotiable manner.

Creely waited (because it was always worth waiting, as persistence was sometimes rewarded), but Roland was determined not to give in.

'Alright?' said Jas, as he arrived.

Roland nodded.

'What's Creely want?' asked Jas.

'What do you think?'

Jas put his hand in his coat pocket.

'Here,' said Jas, as he pulled out a packet of cigarettes and handed over an extra-long.

Creely moved nervously forward.

'Thank you,' he said.

'Do you want one?' asked Jas.

'No, I'm alright,' said Roland.

And Creely walked off, triumphant.

'You've made his day,' said Roland.

'Why not?' said Jas. 'The poor bastards don't get much in here.'

No, that was probably true.

'You saw him, then?' asked Roland.

Jas angled his leg on the paving steps, stuffing the paperwork back in his pocket.

'Yep, that's me finished with,' he said.

'What was Gobi like?'

'He was okay about it.'

'So, he let you resign then?'

'Yeah, he doesn't want the hassle of going through a disciplinary.'

'No, I bet he doesn't.'

'Yeah, it's a result for me,' reflected Jas.

'So, what you going to do now then?'

'Get stoned.'

Roland smiled… that went without saying.

'What I mean is, what are you going to do for the future?'

Jas shifted backwards and forwards on his angled leg, looked over at the sandstone-columned façade which boldly stated the entrance to the reception.

'There's a way out,' said Jas.

'How's that?' asked Roland, who was convinced Jas would be barred from ever working again.

'Social work,' said Jas.

'Social work? But you're not qualified. Plus, you'll have a criminal record.'

'It didn't stop you, did it?' said Jas.

'I think that was different,' said Roland. 'Gobi himself said they would never normally have taken me on.'

Jas was undaunted.

'I've already looked into it… I can't hang around and wait. I've got the bank on my case about my overdraft and I've got to have some money coming in.'

'Yeah, tell me about it,' said Roland, who did not need convincing about the reality of being fed and watered.

'I've got an interview next week,' asserted Jas.

'An interview? Blimey, that's quick… to be a social worker?'

'With an agency. I found out that with the time I've done here I can convert it into being a residential social worker.'

'What's that?'

'You know, working with kids in care homes.'

'Crazy kids?'

'Yeah, really fucked up kids… but I don't mind that. I'm fucked up so I think I'll fit in. Plus, it's good money compared to what we get here.'

'Is that proper social work?' wondered Roland.

'Yeah, it's just different. It's not the same level.'

'So, you're not training to be a social worker?'

'No, I couldn't face doing any of that. Anyway, I'm going to get married so it's only until I'm sorted.'

Roland pulled a face.

'You're not really going to get married, are you?'

Jas laughed.

'Yeah, why not? Nobody thinks I am Indian. Everyone seems to think I am just someone who crossed over to being English.'

'It's your life,' said Roland, as he shrugged. 'It just seems a bit drastic. Maybe you should see how things work out?'

'I can't,' said Jas, 'I've already spoken to my parents. They said they'd let me move back but my mum was straight in about the marriage thing. Anyway, I knew it was going to happen at some point so it might as well happen now.'

'But… well… you know…' said Roland, struggling to find the right words. 'You're such a rampant… hedonist…'

'That's just one side of me,' said Jas, frustrated with having to explain himself again. 'You don't see the whole Indian thing.'

'No, I know that, but we all have pressures, especially from our parents. That's why we break away from them: to be ourselves. If we did what our parents wanted all the time we'd end up like the zombies here.'

'It's my choice,' said Jas defensively.

'Yeah, but you might be choosing something that ends up a disaster!'

Jas flicked his cigarette on to the paving and watched it bounce. The force of the propulsion knocked out the flaming embers. It was a skill Roland admired and had tried to emulate without much success.

'I can't see anything worse than the situation I'm in at the moment,' said Jas. 'I've got a court case for possession, I've had to resign from my training and I'm basically homeless and broke.'

'Is that all?' said Roland, struggling to make light of the dilemma. 'Look, I know it's bad… but do you really have to move back with your parents?'

'I've got a week's notice on my room,' said Jas, pulling out the paperwork he had stuffed into his pocket.

'Shit,' said Roland, as he squinted sideways at the paper and scanned the eviction notice.

'Those bastards aren't going to let me stay.'

'No,' said Roland, reflecting on the finality of it all.

'If you've got any better suggestions,' said Jas, feeling vindicated, 'I'd like to know.'

'You can't rent then?'

'I haven't got a penny,' said Jas, pausing. 'In fact, I was wondering if you could lend me some money?'

'Money? Shit!'

'Just a tenner would do,' said Jas.

'Oh, yeah, a tenner's okay,' said Roland, barely disguising his relief.

'Cheers, I need it to get some fags.'

'Oh, right,' said Roland, reaching inside his pocket.

'I'll be back in a minute,' Jas said, jumping up the paving stones and into the visitor centre.

Jas did not deserve to be treated so badly, thought Roland; it was not really his fault. *I should be the one who is losing his career, especially after the meaningless campaign.*

Roland looked out across the lawns, ruminating on the overwhelming sense of defeat. The blank green canvas always disguised so much, he thought, always portrayed a thin veneer of normality. But beneath the surface – in fact, *on* the surface – there was the constant parade of insanity, madness, craziness. There they were, the zombies of Zombie Park, strolling aimlessly through their undead routines.

Out of the corner of his eye he noticed the hovering Creely. Roland gave him a stern rebuke as he moved closer.

'Don't waste your time,' he said.

Creely stared at the floor, his hands eager to clasp more nicotine.

'You know you're not meant to smoke,' said Roland.

'Fuck it,' said Jas, who appeared from behind the bench, 'there you go.'

Jas unwrapped the cellophane and pulled out a fresh-smelling extra-long. Creely gratefully grasped the cigarette and headed back out across the lawns whilst replying again to the voices in his head. They both watched him meander, checking to go one way and then the next, avoiding obstacles ahead which were invisible to everyone else.

'You never guess who I've just spoken to,' said Jas, lighting up.

Roland thought for a second. 'Fitzpatrick, and all is forgiven?'

'Mrs Sandy,' said Jas.

'Sandy?' said Roland, wondering how a conversation could ever have happened. 'You mean Mrs Sandy who sees devils and witches wherever she goes?'

'Yep,' said Jas, rather proudly.

'You're kidding,' said Roland, who turned to look back into the visitor centre to see if she was still there. 'How can you have a conversation?'

'I know,' said Jas, grinning.

'You mean she's cured?' said Roland sceptically, unable to spot Mrs Sandy in amongst the patchwork of patients and relatives.

'Sounds like it,' said Jas. 'She's going home next week.'

'Blimey, I don't believe it!'

'Said she was looking forward to being a mum again, back with the kids and her husband... how she was so grateful for what everyone had done for her while she was here.'

'You know what that means?' said Roland, with the strain of disappointment in his voice. 'Something actually works.'

'She said she can't remember a thing. She just woke up one day and felt better again.'

'Now that is a miracle!'

'I mean,' said Jas, following his last train of thought, 'she was zapped more than Frankenstein but she's come out of the end of it and is back to normal.'

'Well, maybe she cured herself,' said Roland, who studied Creely, statuesque in the middle of the lawns.

'It's time which is the cure for some of these mad fuckers,' said Jas, looking up at the broken Clock Tower. 'It gives a few of them the chance to heal and recover… and at least it means a few of us make it out of here alive!'

'Thanks,' said Roland, who did not need reminding of his encroaching sense of abandonment.

'Listen,' said Jas, as he moved closer to Roland, 'I know you think this place is a real basket case and I wouldn't disagree with you, but it's done a few good things for me.'

Jas paused. Roland could tell he had a few last things he wanted to say.

'You know I like to see Colgate in the ark?'

'Yeah?'

'Well, there's a reason for that.'

'I had worked that one out.'

Jas drew hard on his cigarette.

'You see,' said Jas, 'we are all here for a reason. Like you said, we could be like, metaphysicians, looking for answers, the root cause of things… looking for meaning in a crazy, fucked up world… but all I needed really was to be cured, and I am now.'

Roland waited, ready for his own suspicions to be confirmed.

'It all came out when I was talking with Colgate… how I was… well… sexually abused…'

424

Roland remained impassive. He wanted to say he had put two and two together but waited to see if Jas was going to say any more.

'It's taken me ages,' said Jas, 'but once I'd said it to Colgate, once I'd got it out of my system what those cunts had done to me, I felt cured.'

'Okay,' said Roland, 'I must admit, I always thought there was something behind it… your behaviour…'

'Heh,' said Jas, 'I ain't changing anything, it's just that I can accept it now.'

'Who did it, if you don't mind me asking?'

'It was two of my uncles… and you know how heavy it is with all the family shit and being Indian. Well, there was no way anyone would've believed me if I'd said anything. I still ain't going to tell them now… not with all the marriage stuff.'

'Won't you see them again?'

'Nah… they've both fucked off back to India.'

'Right…'

'I know… crazy stuff,' said Jas, ruefully, as he flicked his cigarette ash. 'Anyway, I know you're stuck here but you'll be alright.'

'I can't see it,' said Roland, who was now reluctant to say anything about himself after such a disclosure.

'You shouldn't give up.'

'I don't know…'

'You shouldn't let the bastards grind you down. At least you've got Sophie.'

'Well, I don't know about that…'

'Why, are things a bit rocky?'

'I think she wants to finish it.'

'No, mate,' said Jas, 'you two are really good together.'

That's what Roland thought, but he was tired of trying to convince Sophie.

'She's going to go her own way,' said Roland, as a matter of fact.

'That's no surprise,' said Jas fatalistically.

'No?'

'Ad… am!'

It was Creely who had interrupted them, who then wrenched from his vocal chords a deep-throated roar. They could also see Starr wandering meaningfully around the disturbance.

'He's off again,' said Jas.

'Yeah,' said Roland, who was preoccupied with his own thoughts about Sophie.

'I could talk to her…'

'No, it's alright, you've got enough on your plate.'

'I don't mind,' said Jas. 'Me and Sophie go back…'

'Yeah, I know,' said Roland, sensing fate was one step away.

'Have you talked to her about what she's going to do, then?'

'What?'

'When she finishes here – this place, her training?'

'Well, we have,' said Roland, adding as an afterthought, 'but not really.'

Jas paused for a moment.

'Does Sophie know what she wants to do?'

'Yeah, leave,' said Roland dogmatically.

'Well, you can understand that. So, what are you going to do then?'

'Leave,' said Roland, wondering if it still made sense.

'What, give up your training?'

'Why not? I'm not going to make it here... they're not going to let me finish. Remember what Dr Jonas said: how they always get you in the end if you criticise anything. I can see myself being set up on one of the wards – you know how they do it: put you in an impossible situation so you make a mistake. Why wait for that to happen and have a bad reference when like you, I can get out of here?'

'But I had no choice... I would have stayed if they hadn't busted me.'

'They were never going to let you qualify,' said Roland unequivocally.

'If I'd been a bit more careful they never would have caught me.'

'No,' said Roland, 'they wanted to get back at me by getting at people who I associate with... that means you. They know with you gone and Sophie going I will be even more isolated and easy pickings.'

'There's still Terry...'

Roland put no value on knowing Terry. As far as Roland was concerned, Terry believed in nothing except himself.

'He's not interested,' said Roland. 'Never has been.'

'Well, don't give up your training,' said Jas paternalistically.

'I don't give a fuck about the training!' said Roland, becoming more animated. 'The only good thing to come out of this place is meeting Sophie. That's the only thing that really matters... I love her.'

'Does she love you?'

'She says she does,' said Roland, 'but I don't think so.'

'That's not good,' said Jas.

'What d' you mean?'

'You need to know for sure, don't you?'

Roland frowned. How could he know for sure? It was never something he could ever pin her down on, and he was always hanging on to the relationship by his fingernails.

'Listen,' said Jas, 'you need to look around you and don't think too much about Sophie.'

'What does that mean?'

'She'll go her own way. You should try and look at things differently.'

Roland was confused. What oblique message was Jas trying to convey?

'You see those mad fuckers out there?' said Jas, pointing at Starr and Creely. 'They can see things differently.'

Roland stared, annoyed with Jas, annoyed with Jas thinking he understood anything.

'Do you mean I have to go mad in order to see things differently?'

'Isn't that what the metaphysician stuff is about?' said Jas.

'I don't know. We didn't do anything about it... we just got stoned.'

'Well, that's part of it, if you think about it... seeing things differently. I think going mad is the easy bit... it's coming back from the craziness that's difficult.'

What was Jas trying to say? Roland did not get it… any of it. Jas was going and everything was going wrong, everything was going downhill, and his world was yet again falling apart.

'Anyway,' said Jas, 'it's been good while it's lasted.'

'Yeah, I suppose you're right. But how is it going to end?'

'Fuck knows, mate. But it's ended for me.'

CHAPTER 39

DECEIT AND BETRAYAL

Roland was crying. Sophie had said the one thing he had dreaded: 'I don't love you any more.' He couldn't get his head around it. Why… why did she not love him any more? What was wrong with him? What had he done wrong? And to say it, as if she didn't care. The phrase was swimming around in his head like a violent mantra, boring into his brain, banging nails into his aching, crushed heart. Fuck it! She had stabbed him right between the eyes, struck a blow at a time when he needed her most, when everything was falling apart. She was not just ending their relationship, she was abandoning him. She could go now, live her life and get out of the place, but he was stuck here, left to cope, left with nothing, left with the vultures ready to fuck him up.

That was at the heart of his grievance, he decided: he had been there to support her with her psoriasis, but oh no, when it comes to giving back a little: thank you very much, I'm out of here. Think I'm waiting around for you? No, no, no – "I'm off!" That's what hurt, that's what stuck in his gullet, made him mad, made him mad and angry; the betrayal – yes, that was it: the complete betrayal.

Or, was he being fair? Was he being rational? Perhaps he was at fault? Perhaps he was in the wrong? Perhaps he was being oppressive? Yes, that's what she had said: he was holding her back, oppressing, preventing her from being who she wanted to be. He was holding on, holding on to something that did not exist any more. And she had said she did not want to end up like her parents. That was bizarre... why would they end up like her parents? It's not as if he was asking to marry her. He did not want that, he just wanted the relationship, but she was terminating it because she was ready to move on. She had the power, the power to end it, because she had her head together. Well, fuck you!

Okay, enough. He was weak. He had to stop crying. He was alone again, in his old room, banished from the joys of a relationship. He had nothing again, just his clothes stuffed in the bag he had retrieved from her room. It was too much. It was so embarrassing. He was being humiliated, put in his place. He was a loser, that's what they would say about him; a no-hoper...

There was a knock on his door. Perhaps it was Sophie?

'Who is it?' asked Roland, as he wiped his eyes.

'Terry.'

Fuck it! He needed to talk to someone – anyone; even Terry.

'Alright?' said Terry, as Roland let him in.

'Yeah, sort of,' said Roland, sitting back down on his bed.

Terry nodded awkwardly.

'You've heard, then?' said Roland.

Terry dropped on to the floor and crossed his legs.

'Yeah,' he said, with a genuine sigh.

'I can't believe it,' said Roland, hoping he might find a sympathetic ear.

'No,' said Terry, 'it's always a hard one to take in.'

He then maintained a respectful silence whilst Roland rubbed his face.

'Do you need a spliff?' asked Terry.

'No, no,' said Roland; he needed a clear head for once. 'Are you still smoking then?'

'Yeah,' said Terry, 'they won't do anything now they've got Jas.'

'I don't know… I think I'm going to have to watch it myself.'

'You can smoke in my room if you want.'

'No, it's alright, I'm on a late shift anyway.'

'Phone in sick,' offered Terry.

'No, it will take my mind off things.'

'Okay. Horrible rooms, aren't they?' said Terry, looking around the sparse interior which matched his own.

'I hate it,' said Roland.

'Yeah, you two had a nice set-up.'

'It was all Sophie's stuff.'

'Well, yeah, I suppose she has been here longer. Back to basics, then,' said Terry, pointing at Roland's half-opened suitcase.

'Back to fuck all!' said Roland, who could feel his bitter bile rising again.

Terry waited, wondering if Roland was going to inflate his acute sense of anger.

'Listen,' he said, keen to refocus Roland's thinking, 'you probably don't want to hear this right now, but it was going to happen at some point. I mean, it wasn't going to last forever.'

'Yeah,' said Roland, ready to expand on his sense of grievance, 'but she's ended it on her terms. I'm completely fucked, but she can just fuck off out of this place as soon as she's finished her training.'

'She was never going to stay once she finished.'

'I know that,' said Roland, full of his boiling frustration, 'but did she end it because she'd had enough of me, or did she end it because she wasn't going to be here any longer?'

'It's the same difference, isn't it?'

'Not really,' said Roland, who needed Terry to understand.

'You should know,' said Terry, implying he had something else to reveal, 'she had been thinking about finishing it for some time.'

'Really?'

'I mean, she did talk about it,' said Terry hesitantly.

'You mean,' said Roland, wanting to ensure he understood Terry exactly, 'she talked to you about it?'

Terry raised his eyebrows, acknowledging he had been a confidant.

'Fuck!' said Roland, shaking his head, accumulating more reason to hate her.

'Sorry,' said Terry.

'Fuck it! It doesn't matter now.'

Although it did: Sophie must have always been talking to other people. He must have looked a right dipstick...

'I just feel like shit,' said Roland, trying to find the words for his indescribable pain. 'It's like she has died or something. But I can't get this feeling out of my head that she's just laughing at me.'

'Heh, you shouldn't give yourself a hard time. Of course you're going to feel like shit... it's natural.'

Yeah, Terry was right. All these feelings were right.

'I suppose I should've seen it coming,' said Roland. 'Well, I knew it was coming, but the worst thing is, she's made me feel I was in the wrong, as if it's something I have done. But I don't know what I've done wrong.'

Roland held his arms out, appealing for reason.

'That's probably just Sophie's way of coping,' said Terry.

'That's okay for her, then!' said Roland, full of resentment. 'I don't think she's got a problem with it... she couldn't wait to get out. It's like she's been released and I was the oppressor, holding her back, preventing her from being herself.'

'Maybe you were,' said Terry.

'What?!' responded Roland, glaring at Terry. 'I am the most liberated person here! I would never dream of stifling Sophie – I didn't, but she makes out I did. For me to be an oppressor is absolute bullshit!'

'What I mean is,' said Terry, remaining calm, 'she may have felt you were holding her back. You know, you are both different. You might not see it now, but

434

you have very different ideas about relationships. But if it's any consolation, I'm sure she's hurting in her own way.'

'I haven't seen it,' said Roland, whilst trying to assimilate what Terry had just said. 'It's like, she's got a new lease of life and the way I feel doesn't matter.'

'What would you want her to do?'

Roland paused. He knew what he was going to say was unrealistic, but he felt he just had to say it.

'I just don't want her to get involved with anyone. I know it sounds stupid, possessive, but if she's only here for a little bit longer, can't she just hold off and wait? It's like rubbing salt into the wound.'

'Have you told her that?'

'No,' said Roland, grimacing at the thought of such an unreasonable request. 'I know it sounds bad. It's just that, this is such a small place... everyone will be gossiping about it and I know there'll be people queuing up to...'

'Well, if it's any comfort, I would never do it,' said Terry. 'Never shit on your own doorstep.'

'Thanks,' said Roland disdainfully.

Terry feigned an unapologetic smile.

'The thing is,' said Terry, 'you won't be able to stop Sophie. I know what she's like.'

'What do you mean?'

'There are some people,' said Terry, rather obliquely, 'who find it difficult to think what it is like to be in somebody else's shoes. They only know what it is to be who they are and struggle to imagine anything else apart from themselves.'

'You mean empathy? Are you saying Sophie only thinks about herself?'

Terry raised his eyebrow.

'What does that mean?'

Terry looked down and then back up at Roland. 'You know,' said Terry, 'you are a bit too trusting of people.'

'Am I?' said Roland, desperate for Terry to make his point.

'You can't go through life with blinkers on,' he said. 'You need to open your eyes a bit… not be so naïve.'

'Naïve?!' roared Roland.

Terry nodded, in a sage-like manner.

'I'm not naïve,' Roland spluttered. 'I've done more in my life than most of the useless fucking idiots who live here… and I am not naïve!'

'Are you sure you know everything about Sophie, then?'

'Why, what do you know?' demanded Roland, ready to insist Terry stopped playing games.

'Maybe,' said Terry, 'she's already living the life she wants to live.'

'How's that?' asked Roland, still trying to grasp Terry's coded message.

'I think you should ask her.'

'Ask her what?'

Terry sighed, a knowing, encouraging smile.

'I don't think it's for me to tell you, but for you to find out.'

'Oh, come on!' Roland blurted out in exasperation. 'I really don't know what it is I am supposed to be getting here…'

'I like Sophie,' said Terry, 'don't get me wrong, but she may have been a bit rough on you.'

'I know that! She fucked me over!'

'But do you *really* know?' asked Terry pointedly.

'No!' said Roland, holding up his hands in mock despair. 'Not unless you tell me!'

'I can't say,' he said. 'It's probably best if it came from her.'

'Well, it isn't going to come from her, so you might as well tell me.'

Terry paused.

'Sophie had an affair,' he said. 'Sorry to have to tell you this, but it's better you found out now that it's finished.'

'She had an affair?' said Roland, almost to himself, barely able to grasp the where, when and why.

Terry remained respectfully silent, to give Roland more time to absorb.

'How?' asked Roland, trying to imagine when Sophie could have found the time and place to do it.

There was little more Terry was going to add.

'How could she have an affair?' continued Roland, his heart sinking at the reality of such infidelity, falseness… betrayal. 'I don't believe it! I just can't see how she had time to do it.'

'Listen,' said Terry, thinking he had better reinforce the message, 'I know you won't want to hear this – and we did try and tell you once – but it was Dr Jonas.'

'Dr Jonas?'

Terry shrugged his shoulders.

Roland's face went red. This was worse, far worse than anything he could have imagined.

'When did you know?' asked Roland, fuming beneath his shattered ego.

'Look, that's not the point, but we did try and tell you. I just thought it was better you knew.'

'I really can't believe what you've just told me,' said Roland, feeling his throat go dry. 'She's been going on at me as if I was the one at fault when all along she was fucking Jonas behind my back... she was the one making me feel guilty, as if I was in the wrong... as if I was the one to blame for everything!'

'I don't know it was like that,' said Terry. 'But I know it will hurt. At least he's gone now, so you don't have to worry about that happening...'

'Fucking hell!' said Roland, falling back on to his bed.

He shut his eyes. He wanted to cry again. Yes, Terry was right: the fucking meal and the lies Sophie told then! What had she done? Why had she done it? He just couldn't understand. How had he missed it? Why did he not listen to the truth, the obvious truth, the bare statement of facts? How had he been so fucking naïve?

'You okay?' asked Terry, wondering if he had done the right thing. 'I know it's a bit of a shock but I thought it was better you knew... you know, get all the crap things over in one go.'

'You're telling me,' said Roland, pulling himself up again.

'So, there is one more thing,' said Terry awkwardly.

'What?' said Roland, with an overwhelming sense of emotional fatigue.

'I'm transferring.'

'Shit... you're not! You're going as well?'

'Yep!' said Terry, in a tone which expressed a profound sense of relief.

'Fuck! Where are you going?'

'I've put in a transfer to Brighton. I need to get away from here… this place is fucked up.'

Roland dropped his head. Terry laughed.

'It's not been a good day for you.'

'No, not really. That means I'll be the only one. I'll never survive. Those bastards will carve me up.'

'Look,' said Terry, 'if things don't work out for you, get in touch. I've got a few things planned.'

'Like what?'

'This and that…'

'What's this and that?'

Terry tapped his nose a couple of times.

'I know it's shit right now, but honestly, I've been there myself and you do get over it.'

★

Betrayal… lies… deceit… liar. She was a liar, that was for sure. So, now he knew. He knew what it was all about, what had been going on. What a bitch! What a lying, selfish, fucking bitch! All that bullshit about how she had to be free, about how she did not know, about how she was not sure… all a fucking lie! She knew alright, she just didn't want him knowing the truth, so she could avoid his anger, avoid his justice. He couldn't believe it; he couldn't believe how he had been taken in. What a mug. He had been thoroughly used, sucked in and spat out. He did not know what was worse: the humiliation of losing her or the humiliation that she'd been shagging Dr Jonas behind his back. No wonder she was so fucking vague all the time. No wonder she could never spell out the reason why she wanted to finish it. It was because she couldn't face telling him the truth, owning up to being a deceitful fucking cow. But at least he had her now. He had the ammunition. He couldn't wait to make her squirm, to let her know he knew the truth. He would have his day. She couldn't pull the wool over his eyes... not any more.

But what did it mean? Was she just using him all along? When they had sex, was that just a thing she had to put up with? Was he crap in bed; was that why she was fucking Dr Jonas? She was always impressed by that: older, so-called more mature men. He couldn't compete with that. And who else was she shagging? Fuck! Anything was possible now.

He hadn't listened. He hadn't seen the warning signs, but they were all around him. He had been naïve, as Terry said, he had been so fucking naïve about everything.

CHAPTER 40

QUID PRO QUO

Morten Slaney was back in his office with the door firmly shut. It had been a testing time, reporting to the board on the Annie Buchanan suicide, the bizarre behaviour of Dr Jonas, plans for closing down the hospital, the militants, and the related issues over at the nurses' hostel. One way or another he had skilfully manipulated, edited, deflected and separated cause from effect. He was entitled, so he thought, to feel reasonably satisfied with his overall performance. After all, his art and craft was negotiating his way through a web of tortuous conflicts of interest, whilst providing reassurance the accumulation of incidents was effectively managed and mitigated. In fact, he allowed himself a brief moment of self-congratulation: still interim chief executive with little sign of a permanent replacement being sought by the board. He leant back in his chair and closed his eyes, with only one task left open: he needed to get hold of Dr Caldwell.

Caldwell's non-attendance at today's board meeting had undermined his ability to garner support for the proposals in his report, *Care in the Community, Deinstitutionalisation and a Centre for Excellence*. Some board members had raised concerns in regards to the prospective sale to the preferred bidders which Slaney had so assiduously drawn up. Not that the board had any choice in the matter, it was just a question of timing and positioning. The potential to realise value from the sale of Wellington Park was a gift, a capital asset which could flow with liquidity into entrepreneurial hands. The quid pro quo enabled Dr Caldwell to preserve his empire at Chaolla House, leaving Slaney free to exploit the commercial opportunities at the heart of the closure plans. As he had explained to the board, the legal transfer of the "purpose of land" to commercial development and the establishment of a limited company to oversee the venture were all in the interests of patients and the community. It ensured the board fulfilled the government's objective of community-based care, and significantly reduced the expensive institutionalised failings of Wellington Park, whilst attracting private investment into an area historically dependent on central government funding. But some board members had resisted endorsement unless Dr Caldwell explicitly voted for the plans... and the snake had failed to appear!

But first things first, he needed to masturbate. He stood up, pulled down his trousers and rubbed his penis vigorously, aiming his deposit on a blank sheet of A4 paper. Slaney was compulsive about his ability to come within a minute, kept an eye on the second hand of the clock and worked hard to deliver in double quick time. Thirty-one... thirty-two... thirty-three...

Slaney released an anguished gasp as he squeezed out the seminal fluid. With a flick of his hand he flipped his come on to the paper. He stood gazing for a few seconds, enjoying his orgasmic moment, then grabbed a tissue on the desk and wiped the tip of his penis. He crumpled up his product and threw it in the waste-paper bin. He paused for a second and sniffed his hand. He tightened the belt around his trousers a further notch, flexed his arms, shoulders and torso. He could feel his muscles bulge inside his jacket before sitting back down in the comfort of his leather chair. He was focused now and ready for business.

Slaney checked the time, punched the extension number on his phone and held the receiver one foot away from his ear. Dr Caldwell's secretary answered.

'Hi, Angie,' he said, with the receiver still some distance from his mouth, 'Morten Slaney here.'

'I'll put you through,' she said, always keen to avoid any delays when it was Slaney on the line.

He waited, tilting his head from side to side.

'Oh, hello, it's Angie here again. I'm afraid he's still in a clinic, but that should be over shortly. Shall I get him to ring you?'

'Yes, please,' said Slaney, 'on my office number… thanks, Angie.

'Slimy toad,' said Slaney under his breath, as he tapped his finger twice on the desk.

He checked the clock again as the door handle to his office moved a couple of times with a few swift twists. It was probably Imogen, but he was not going to let her in. He heard the clicks of her shoes before she opened the door to the small gym. He had a few minutes to spare so he fumbled in his drawer and pulled out his gym key.

Imogen was just removing her shoes as he popped his head round.

'Oh, hi,' she said, with an innocent smile. 'It doesn't matter if I change in here, does it?'

Slaney shrugged.

'You alright?' she said, removing her stockings, seated on a hard plastic chair against the wall.

She pulled from her gym bag her tracksuit bottoms and T-shirt. Slaney smiled insincerely, continuing to stand in silence, watching her undress.

'So…' she said, as she looked Slaney in the eye, expecting there to be more of a response.

Oh well, she thought, there was no point in going on about anything. She glanced over with a few more smiles before commencing on her exercises, placing her back on the bench and picking up the dumb-bells. She would have asked Slaney to help but he seemed intent on just watching. It was peculiar, unnerving, but typical of Slaney, as she pulled her arms in and over her head.

'Have you been busy then?' asked Imogen, squeezing out the words as she pushed upwards and together.

'Yes,' he said, with no intention of elaborating.

'There's been so much going on it's difficult to keep up.'

Slaney retained a glacial stare.

'I mean, smoking pot over at the nurses' hostel has been going on for years. It's ridiculous!'

'I thought you knew most of them,' said Slaney, propping himself up against the door frame.

'No, not really… only Jas… he wanted me to warn him if the police were going to raid the place.'

'Good job you didn't, then,' said Slaney.

'How would I know?' she said, leaving the dumb-bells on the floor, leaning forwards with her arms. 'It was his own fault he got caught.'

Imogen rested back on the bench and picked up the dumb-bells to resume her routine.

'How did the investigation go?' she asked, her eyes focused on the ceiling.

'Which one?'

'You know, that poor girl… Annie Buchanan.'

He remained expressionless.

'I hope I don't end up like her,' said Imogen, as she exercised the dumb-bells, left to right.

'I don't think that's likely,' said Slaney.

She leaned forward, arched her back and then stared back at Slaney. She was annoyed he was not paying her the proper attention.

'You can be such a heartless bastard,' she said angrily.

She knew it exuded from every pore, but she also knew whatever she thought meant nothing to him.

Slaney smiled. He would still fuck her, as and when. He was ready to leave now, before it became an even more pointless conversation, and offered Imogen a withering glance.

'Fine…' said Imogen, accepting she would not be seeing him tonight, as he shut and locked the door.

Slaney sat back in his leather chair listening out for Imogen, who had stopped exercising. Good, he thought, she was packing up to go. He opened his drawer and pulled out a plastic jar of pills. He read the label. He had recently changed some of the steroids because his wife had been complaining again about his overly aggressive behaviour towards her. He decided to take three and chewed on them. They tasted disgusting, which he liked.

There was a recognisable knock and Slaney hastily got to the door to unlock it.

'Good evening, Michael,' said Slaney, still chewing his pills.

Fitzpatrick did not reply as he walked to his usual position and perched on the chair angular to Slaney's desk.

'All is well, I hope,' said Slaney, coughing.

Fitzpatrick nodded – almost smiled, which was rare for Fitzpatrick.

There was very little to report, but he began his usual routine of patient numbers, reported incidents, new admissions and discharges. Slaney's phone rang. He picked it up whilst Fitzpatrick was in mid-flow. It was Caldwell.

'Yes, it's Morten here,' said Slaney. 'Just to let you know, the board required your endorsement.'

'They have it,' said Dr Caldwell nonchalantly.

'That's an explicit endorsement,' said Slaney.

'I see…' said Dr Caldwell, who remained silent for a few seconds. 'Has the board so far agreed with the proposals?'

'Yes,' said Slaney.

'Has there been any objections to the preferred bidders for the purchase of the land?'

'No, none,' said Slaney confidently.

There was another pause.

'Have you revealed to the board there is a potential conflict of interest should the tender process for purchase go ahead?'

'If there was a conflict of interest,' said Slaney confidently, 'then the board should certainly be made aware of it. At present there is none.'

'I see…' said Dr Caldwell. 'So, there is no conflict of interest until the tender process has begun?'

'That's the legal advice I have received.'

'So, we can also assume that the internal threat to this enterprise has been effectively neutralised?'

'What trouble there was has been dealt with,' said Slaney, whilst looking keenly in the direction of Fitzpatrick.

'Okay, as I said,' said Dr Caldwell, 'I fully endorse the proposals as they stand.'

'You will need to communicate that to the board,' said Slaney, emphasising the point of their conversation.

'In writing?'

'If that's possible…'

'Okay, I'll ensure the board is made aware of the fact that I fully endorse the proposals.'

'Thank you, Dr Caldwell, and have a good evening.'

'And you, Morten.'

Slaney put the phone down, remaining inscrutable as Fitzpatrick picked up his verbal report from mid-sentence, returning to the exact conjunction which had interrupted his flow. There was a loud crack as the door of the gym slammed shut. Slaney shifted in his chair. Fitzpatrick had been put off his stride. The noise was suspicious. Slaney could tell Fitzpatrick was anxious to poke his nose in. Anyway, there seemed little reason to detain him.

'Okay, Michael, I know everything is under control,' said Slaney, fingering his brow.

Fitzpatrick nodded and shot out of his chair. He was convinced a recalcitrant had been where they were not permitted.

He should have taken early retirement when he had the opportunity, thought Slaney. Still, when you are someone like Fitzpatrick and part of the furniture it will always be a struggle to let go. Not that Slaney had any real sympathy for the man. Fitzpatrick probably knew what was coming: the world was changing, all the old certainties were going, whether that was at Wellington Park or in the new reality outside. The old order had been swept aside and Slaney intended to flourish. Fitzpatrick was just part of the old way of doing things. He would never see selling off Wellington Park as a business opportunity... that was Fitzpatrick's problem.

The door was pushed opened again.

'Oh, I'm sorry... I'm not disturbing you? I'm Sandra Frost, one of the new sisters.'

As she stood halfway in and halfway out, Slaney gave her the usual once-over.

'Are you busy?' she asked, wondering if she was being presumptuous in regards to his open-door policy.

'No, no, no,' he said, waving her in.

'Thanks,' she said, sitting on the hard plastic chair.

'How are you finding it?' asked Slaney.

'Oh yes, it's fine, thanks,' she said, feeling slightly uneasy about Slaney's fixed stare.

'Good,' he said, as he studied the virtues of Sandra Frost.

She smiled uneasily. She was usually quite confident, but this man had a certain aura which was rather unsettling. Then she blushed because of the heightened intensity emanating from Slaney. She flapped her hand in front of her face.

'Ooo… it is hot in here,' she said, pulling her uniform further down towards her knees.

Slaney smiled. Why should he say anything? She was a pretty little thing.

'I must admit,' she said, regaining some of her composure, 'I was a little surprised by the staffing levels on the ward.'

Slaney laughed and leaned across the desk.

'I wouldn't let Mr Fitzpatrick hear you say that,' he said, in a low, sinister whisper.

Her head twitched, unsure how she should interpret Slaney's remark.

'It's a sensitive issue,' said Slaney, as he leaned back in his chair.

'Oh yes, I understand that,' she said, wondering if that was code for not raising the matter any more.

'Do you work out?' asked Slaney.

She blinked hurriedly.

'We have a small gym for staff here,' he said, glancing over at his side door.

'Oh, yes,' she said, 'I think someone had mentioned it before.'

Slaney nodded.

'Do you... work out?' she asked, assuming staffing levels were a no-go area.

'Oh yes,' said Slaney, 'I think it's important... a healthy body is a healthy mind.'

Sandra Frost was frozen, lost for words, feeling out of her depth. *Just say anything*, she told herself.

'Perhaps some of the patients could... learn to exercise?'

Slaney furrowed his brow.

'They would have to get better first... don't you think?'

CHAPTER 41

I AM A MOLE AND I LIVE IN A HOLE

Starr had been operating as a mole deep underground and exploring the undergrowth. One day, as he dug away, drawing mud behind him, he found his hands pushing into a large opening. Intrigued, he removed the mud and clay until he was able to step inside the underground cavern. It was a vaulted hall, lit by fire torches hung on red brick walls. As he explored, he peered down the small annexes which segmented the large, empty space. Then, as he approached the end of the cavern, he detected the faint sound of crying. This was more interesting, he thought, tracking the sound of abandonment down to the last annex. As he peered into the darkness, waiting for his eyes to adjust, he identified the frail figure of Annie Buchanan huddled in the corner.

'I heard you crying,' said Starr, as he moved forwards to get a better view of the sad, crumpled mess.

'I am dead,' she said, lifting her head.

'I am a mole,' said Starr.

Annie paused, shaking, but capable of a half-smile.

'You don't look like one,' she said, scrutinising Starr.

'True, appearances can be deceiving, but how else do you think I got down here?'

'I don't know,' said Annie. 'I can only assume you are dead like me and we are both in hell.'

'Oh,' said Starr, 'is that why you are crying: because you think you are in hell?'

'It feels like hell,' she said, hoping she would be contradicted.

Starr looked around.

'Yes, it is a bit bleak, but I don't think it's hell. It might be hellish on your own down here, but I'm not sure it's hell.'

'How do you know?' asked Annie. 'It feels like a slaughterhouse.'

'That would be hell, but I don't know for sure,' replied Starr.

'Well, if this is hell, then there must be a heaven, which gives me some hope,' she said, lifting herself up from her crouched position. 'Are you the Devil?'

'Afraid not,' said Starr.

No, he did not look like a devil, she thought.

'Well, a proper explanation would be nice,' she said, expecting Starr to have the answers. 'Why have I been left here all on my own?'

'I wish I knew myself,' he said. 'I just dig holes and tunnels.'

'Really?' said Annie, unimpressed.

She walked around Starr and into the main hall.

'I must admit,' she said, 'I have no concept of time.'

'Hmmm… time,' mused Starr.

Annie spun around on her heels.

'I know you,' she said, pointing a finger, which seemed to droop towards Starr's big fat belly. 'All you say is, "Six... one-five... one-five... one-two".'

'Only a fool would say that...'

Starr remained enigmatic, watching as Annie walked through the hall, studiously avoiding stepping into any of the annexes, whilst searching for anything hidden in the mouldy crevices.

'There's not much to this place,' she said, retracing her steps. 'Are you sure you're not dead – like me, I mean?'

'Are you sure you are dead?' replied Starr, continuing to watch her movements.

'I think so,' said Annie, swinging her leg slightly in front of her. 'I killed myself.'

'That's a shame,' said Starr sympathetically.

'I had no choice,' said Annie, her head bowed before she looked up again. 'After that, I can't really remember. It's weird, but time here seems to only last for a few minutes and then it's as if time starts all over again. A minute, and then another minute, but it always feels like the same minute... although, I can remember you, and you've been here for quite a few minutes.'

'It's nice to be remembered,' said Starr.

Annie grimaced. Starr's obliqueness was losing its charm.

'Show me how you got in here,' she said assertively.

Starr waddled forwards and led her back to the other side of the hall. They studied what was in front of them, but there was no hole where he had entered.

'It was here,' he said, pointing at the blank slabs of brickwork.

'Is that a door, then?' wondered Annie, touching the cold surface, feeling for a secret entrance.

But all she could feel was the damp brick wall covered in soft green moss, glistening with a thin, crystalline web. She stepped back, glancing quizzically at Starr.

'So,' said Annie, 'how did you get in here, then?'

Starr pointed at the wall.

'There's no door,' she said.

Starr nodded.

'But you dug your way in…' said Annie, pointing.

Starr nodded again.

'Well, can you not dig your way out,' asked Annie, slightly exasperated, 'so that we can both get out of here?'

Starr shook his head vigorously.

'Are you sure you want to leave?' he said, trying to console her.

'Don't you?' asked Annie.

'I've only just arrived,' said Starr, as he shrugged his shoulders.

'Oh,' said Annie, moving in an agitated semicircle in front of Starr, 'you really think there's a lot to do down here, then?'

'I don't know,' said Starr, 'but I suspect in a place like this, things appear and disappear.'

'Should we wait here then for something to happen?' queried Annie.

'I think we will probably have to wait,' suggested Starr.

'Do you?' said Annie, raising her voice. 'And how would you know anything about that?'

'Waiting? I know a lot about waiting. How time

passes… how things stand still… as if nothing ever happens.'

Annie paused. This man, this person, was something to do with everything else that was going on… she was sure.

'I see,' she said. 'Do you think I am supposed to be waiting, or learning about waiting, or reflecting on how I should have waited before I decided to kill myself? Is this meant to be a lesson for me?'

'I don't know,' said Starr. 'I'd never thought about it like that.'

'So, you are knowing one moment and then ignorant the next.'

'Oh, look!' cried Starr, pointing his stubby finger towards the middle of the hall. 'A table, chairs and some grapes…'

Starr strolled forwards and plonked his bulbous bottom on one of the chairs before casually picking a grape. Annie reluctantly followed, her eyebrows narrowed, ready to declare Starr a fraud, a charlatan, because he was not who he claimed to be (if he had claimed to be anything), and certainly not just a human version of a mole… quite… yes…

'Can dead people eat?' she asked, before she sat down.

'If you are hungry then you should always eat,' said Starr, tucking into the bowl of red and green juicy grapes.

Annie was not hungry. However, to test her dead status theory she plucked a grape and chewed and sucked. *Interesting*, she thought, *perhaps I am not dead?*

'Good, aren't they?' said Starr.

Annie removed the skin from her mouth and placed it in front of him, presenting the evidence for her case.

'Perhaps I am not dead,' she said, 'and I have been forgiven?'

'Why, what have you done wrong?'

'Nothing...' she said, with a deep sigh. 'But not everyone thinks suicide is the right thing to do.'

'You had no choice, surely,' asserted Starr.

Annie sat down and rested her head on her hand.

'If I knew I was going to live once I was dead then I might have changed my mind.'

'Good point,' said Starr, who spat his pip out on the floor.

'Although, I really don't know if I am alive or dead, or in a dream, in another universe, or if any of this is really real...'

'I think,' said Starr coolly, 'a very wise man once said: as I begin to let go, so the world follows me.'

Annie tilted her head upwards whilst keeping it rested on her hand.

'Do you think that's what happened... I haven't really escaped? The ghastly world I couldn't cope with is tracking me down, even though I should be tucked up nice and cosy in some graveyard, all at peace?'

Starr straightened his back.

'All those who I have spoken to, who live in graves, are troubled souls who do not have the wherewithal to do anything. I can assure you, based on my experience, life in a grave is a miserable state.'

'You meet a lot of dead people, do you?' asked Annie, with a sarcastic grin.

'Yes, I do,' said Starr. 'I think, as best as I can understand it, there are powers I have been granted so I can move between more than one type of world… more than just the surface world we live in.'

'Well, you certainly surprised me, as does all of this…' said Annie, spreading her arms to encompass the furniture.

It was then she noticed a new item had mysteriously appeared on the table: a grey Bakelite phone with a dial of characters and numbers. The phone rang. She stared at Starr. He pushed his chair back to indicate he would not be answering.

'For me, then?' asked Annie, raising her voice above the echoing ring.

She picked up the receiver.

'Hi, can I speak to Ms Annie Buchanan?' said a female voice.

'Speaking,' said Annie, pulling a face at Starr.

'Hi, how are you today?'

'I am dead,' said Annie, who was reluctant to participate any further.

'Thank you, Ms Buchanan, I hope you are having a good day today. Is it alright to speak to you now… I hope I am not calling at an inconvenient time for you?'

'Do I have a choice?' asked Annie half-heartedly.

'Of course you have a choice, Ms Buchanan, but I only have a few questions as part of our survey. Would you be willing to take part in this survey?'

'What if I said no?'

'Well, I can always ring back at a time more convenient to you.'

Annie paused. She wondered if she had a choice again, but predicted it was some ritual she needed to go through in order to move on.

'No, no, no… what do you want to ask me?'

'Thank you, Ms Buchanan. I also need to inform you that any information you provide will be treated in the strictest confidence and recording of this conversation will be used for training purposes only. As I say, this won't take too long and if you could just answer a few questions, I would be most grateful.'

'Yes, I have agreed to answer your questions.'

'Thank you, Ms Buchanan. On a scale of one to five, one being where you most strongly disagree and five being where you most strongly agree, what would be your response to the following statement: committing suicide is always a negative, meaningless act?'

'I would say it is wholly inappropriate and insensitive to ask someone who has committed suicide,' said Annie, who continued to stare at Starr, assuming he was now partly responsible for this degrading interrogation.

'I'm sorry to hear that, Ms Buchanan,' said the voice. 'But is it possible to rate your feelings on a scale of one to five, for the purpose of this survey?'

'Do I have to do this?' asked Annie of Starr, the receiver held limply away from her ear.

'Probably,' said Starr.

'So,' said Annie, her hand waving the receiver around, 'you do know more…'

'It takes a while to get up to speed,' said Starr, who felt he had been honest from the time he had crawled into the vaulted space.

'That's clearly not the case, is it, in reality, whatever reality now is?' said Annie, prepared to slam the phone down and demand to know everything from the fatuous fat man.

Starr nodded towards the receiver, as a gentle reminder her obligations needed to be met first.

'What was the question?' asked Annie, back down the phone.

'Would you like me to repeat the question?' asked the telephone surveyor.

'No,' replied Annie. 'What if I don't have a view?'

'I could mark your response down as neutral… which would mean you neither agree nor disagree with the statement.'

'That's me,' said Annie, 'I neither agree nor disagree with the statement.'

'Thank you. In your opinion, is the pain experienced during the act of suicide worth enduring, in order to relieve the pain that motivated these actions? A yes or no answer is required.'

'Can I not have the same opinion as before?' asked Annie, who could now see a strategy to mitigate the supercilious intrusion.

'I only have a response required as a yes or no.'

'Well, that's not a very good survey, is it? I mean, there must be more valid responses other than yes or no?'

Annie smiled at Starr, confident she had triumphed over the inane telephone surveyor.

'I am sorry if this is difficult for you and we always seek to improve our methods. I know I am using up precious moments of your time and appreciate your ongoing participation. However, would you consider you lean more to yes, or more to no?'

'I don't lean towards either,' said Annie.

'Okay, thank you, Ms Buchanan. I will record no, in order to help complete the survey. I only have a few more questions to ask and thank you again for your patience and cooperation. There is an opportunity at the end to make any other comments and I would suggest you provide those comments at the end. Thank you.'

Annie raised her eyebrows.

'Go on,' said Annie incredulously.

'Thank you. Who do you think your suicide has had the greatest impact on? You do not have to mention them by name but only your relationship to them.'

'My mother,' said Annie, without hesitation.

'Thank you. If you were to live your life again, would you still consider suicide a viable option?'

'Yes,' said Annie forcefully.

'Thank you. And lastly, do you believe there is life after death?'

'No,' said Annie. 'I should be dead and that should be the end of it.'

'Thank you. That's the end of the survey and I would just like to thank you for the time you have given. Are there any last comments you would like to make?'

'No.'

'Well, I will note down that you thought there was insufficient scope to respond to question two. Okay, thank you very much and I hope you continue to have a good day. Goodbye…'

The phone went dead. Annie cautiously replaced the receiver.

'I have one thing for you,' said Starr, leaning forward. 'If, on your journey, you come across a Dr Prize-Bomka, please tell him there will be revenge.'

'What journey am I going on?' asked Annie, as she wondered about Starr's obscure statement.

'We must all reach some kind of destiny,' said Starr.

'Destiny... sounds ominous,' said Annie, glancing anxiously around.

Starr moved his chair, gesturing with his hands towards the end of the hall. Annie obliged. Starr let her walk ahead.

'I assume you know what's going to happen next,' said Annie, as she tried to fix exactly where she should stand.

'I don't know,' said Starr. 'I'm as interested as you.'

Childlike, Annie flapped her arms, waiting for something to happen.

'Perhaps it's like waiting for a bus?' said Annie. 'You wait for ages for one to come along and then they all come at once.'

'Get ready,' said Starr, 'and hold your arms out like this.'

Starr demonstrated, holding his arms in front of him and then raising them above his head. Annie held out her arms limply. There was a sudden whoosh of air from one side of the vault which blasted their faces.

'That's it,' said Starr, 'hold out those arms.'

Annie did, stretching up towards the ceiling. The force of air continued to run through the hall, a blast of wind and power which was beginning to destabilise their rooted position. Within this noise the ceiling above began to split and crack, opening a hole, revealing a bright light beaming down upon them. Within the next second Annie caught sight of a golden bird, a phoenix, swooping down through the hall. Before she had time to run, time to scream or cry, it grabbed her, pulled her by her hands and flew effortlessly up into the hole above her head.

CHAPTER 42

JUSTICE IS A WAITING GAME

As the weeks and winter months rolled towards the New Year, Roland uncontrollably collapsed in on himself. He tried to concentrate on things but his split with Sophie kept replaying over and over in his head. There was nothing he could do to soothe the pain; the pain of betrayal which was driving him mad and making his mind run at hundred miles an hour. He wanted to release his anger and scream it in her face: "You used me, you lied to me, you waited until it was convenient for you and then you dumped me!" And he was sure Sophie was avoiding him in case she received both barrels from his wished-for verbal assault. Whenever he knocked on her door she was never in. Then he realised that if she was in, she would not answer because she was always shagging. She was going through them like there was no tomorrow. It just rubbed salt into the wound and made him feel even more stupid and naïve. He was the little boy virgin who had been taken for a ride, the little virgin who pretended not to be a virgin, who needed to be taught a lesson about the grown-up world.

Well, Roland was out for revenge. Sophie's graduation celebrations had been combined with the Christmas and New Year staff and student nurses' party at the Wellington Park Psychiatric Hospital Social Club. Roland had to go, needed to go, to deliver his well-rehearsed speech to Sophie, to puncture her delusions and fantasies, to seek retribution for all the pain she had inflicted. Who did she think she was, causing so much damage... all the hurt and betrayal, without one ounce; one grain of conscience? Roland was going to burst Sophie's bubble, teach her a lesson and demonstrate to all who wanted to hear: this is a heartless bitch, a user and abuser, a liar and deceiver, a betrayer, an unprincipled, self-seeking, callous, cold, calculating arsehole!

This was the invective swirling around in Roland's head as he strode along the tarmac path, out of the hospital grounds and towards the social club. It would be a golden opportunity to humiliate her in front of all her so-called friends, to expose her as an unfettered plague of sexual gratification, where love was a means to an end, a commodity with which to obtain whatever she needed. Me, me, me, self, self, self... that was Sophie's mantra; the mantra of "me before anyone else". So what if he was perceived as a lonely, embittered loser? He knew it would fuck up Sophie if he confronted her with the unadulterated truth.

Roland walked through the door of the social club and into the large hall where small groups of students, graduates and staff sat or stood talking. He recognised the same old music from last year, the same perfunctory decorations, the same drab placement of soulless chairs and tables. He

464

sauntered into the bar where most people were congregated and blushed as he walked through the brightly lit area. He could feel people watching him. *They can fuck off!*

As he stood waiting to be served he scanned for Sophie in the mirror behind the bar. She was not there. Then he had the displeasure of Cranfield moving next to him.

'What are you doing here?' he asked.

'Having a drink,' said Roland, who was certainly not going to be put off.

'She's not here,' said Cranfield, which implied Roland should leave.

Roland shrugged his shoulders. It was none of Cranfield's business. But Cranfield stood his ground, like an expectant bouncer.

'How long you got left?' he asked.

'What, here? Eighteen months, in theory.'

'Where's your next placement?'

'Don't know,' said Roland, who frankly did not care.

'You know you won't survive.'

'What d' yer mean?'

'You know what I mean.'

'No, I don't,' said Roland, determined to get Cranfield to spell it out.

'They'll get you,' said Cranfield, staring straight ahead at his own reflection.

'Who, management, you mean?'

'You must have known it was coming.'

'Why... do you know what's coming?'

'No, but you're the one they want,' said Cranfield shrewdly.

'So, you think I'm fucked, then?'

'Looks like it.'

'So, what would you do, then?' asked Roland, challenging Cranfield to offer something beyond defeat and demoralisation.

'I wouldn't have done what you did.'

'Well, somebody had to do something,' said Roland sullenly.

'Plenty of people have tried and failed,' said Cranfield. 'You should have listened.'

'Yeah, well, the thing is, I don't give a fuck!'

'Really…' said Cranfield, twisting his pint glass on the bar. 'All they need to do now is fuck you over and close this place down. Then it will be buried – history and life will move on as if nothing ever happened.'

Cranfield clasped his hand around his beer glass.

'See yer later,' he said.

'Yeah, see yer later.'

What a fucker, Roland said to himself, *picking over my dead bones like a fucking vulture. What the fuck's happened to him? This place has fucked him up… fucked his mind to end up thinking like that*. Cranfield did not understand… never could and never would.

Self-consciously, Roland sipped from his beer. He decided to stare straight ahead at the mirror above the bar. He might as well admit it to himself: he was a loner, an outsider, an individualist, an introvert. No one gave a fuck about his predicament: betrayed by Bob Jacobs and the useless fucking union, betrayed by Dr Jonas shagging his girlfriend behind his back, betrayed by Sophie shagging anything and everything, betrayed by people who only thought about themselves.

Perhaps Cranfield was right and there really was no point in trying to change anything? What did he and Sophie realistically think they could do when they were just a couple of students trying to change a great big institution? He should have seen it coming; the vengeance for speaking up. What a waste of time in the end. Well, he had certainly learnt one thing: if you are going to change things you can't go along with all the old ways of doing it. You need something new, something different. And there was nothing like that in here, or out there... there was nothing Roland could relate to. There needed to be something more radical, more extreme than all this pussyfooting around. If you play the game they will crush you, eat you up and spit you out. He knew he was going to be taught a lesson. He knew what was going to happen; he could see it all coming. Why wait to be done on some staged incident which led to a disciplinary? What power did he have left except to pre-empt it all, walk out on his so-called career, walk out of Wellington Park and never look back?

'Hello...'

It was Sophie.

'What are you doing here?' she said.

At last, thought Roland, *the bitch is here!*

'That's what Cranfield said, but I think I am entitled to have a drink,' he said, raising his glass, 'if that's alright with you?'

'Why, what's wrong?'

'What's wrong?' said Roland, in a seething, quiet rage. 'You haven't a fucking clue, have you?'

Sophie rolled her eyes.

'I can't believe you're behaving like this,' said Roland, his blood beginning to boil at Sophie's indifference.

'Like what?' she asked, bemused.

'You know exactly what I mean,' said Roland, signalling the intent of his retribution.

Sophie paused. She was going to nip this in the bud.

'If you want to say something to me then say it,' she said, holding a fiver stretched out to buy a drink.

Roland bit his tongue. He looked around and noticed Cranfield ready to pounce and interfere if things got ugly. He couldn't do it here. He couldn't say what he wanted in front of all these people.

'Can we talk?' he asked, in a more conciliatory tone.

'It's over, you know,' said Sophie, who wanted to make sure Roland understood the ground rules.

'Yes, I know it's over, but I think I still have the right to say a few things. You haven't let me say anything to you.'

'It depends… not if you're nasty.'

'I promise I won't be nasty,' said Roland, holding up his hands.

Sophie looked Roland up and down, searching for untruths.

'Let me get a drink first,' she said, attracting the barman. 'A vodka and Coke please.'

That was different, thought Roland – Sophie had always gone for pints of cider.

'What do you want to say, then?' she asked, as she waited.

'Not here,' said Roland, gesturing with his head, indicating Cranfield was keeping a close eye on things.

'Where do you want to go, then?' asked Sophie.

'Outside…'

As Roland waited, he watched her. She was beautiful, even though he hated her, but she was now stunningly beautiful. There was no denying it: ending the relationship had created an even more desirable (and now widely obtainable) Sophie. And in comparison, he probably appeared a complete wreck. Objectively, stood side by side, it was self-evident: Sophie had made the right decision to dump him, to move on. Roland could see that from the outside… it was obvious. But no one knew the excruciating pain it delivered, the tortuous crushing of his self-confidence, the complete loss of meaning to his life.

'Come on, let's go then,' said Sophie, as she collected her drink.

She led Roland through the bar and the hall. He felt a small crumb of comfort that people could see she was still prepared to talk to him; he was not completely *persona non grata*, as most of them seemed to think.

Outside, he could feel the cold pull at his face. They remained only a few yards from the entrance. He nestled his pint in the cradle of his crossed arms, leaning against the pebble-dashed walls of the social club. Sophie was composed, standing in front of him.

'I didn't want it to end like this,' she said, trying her best to address the hurt she may have inflicted. 'I wanted to end it way before it got to this. I just felt one of us had to do it, to finish it, or else it was going to go on forever.'

'I never asked for it to go on forever,' said Roland. 'I just wanted it to last its natural course.'

'Well, it had for me,' said Sophie.

Cranfield appeared in the doorway, balancing on a step.

'You guys okay?' he asked.

What does that creep want? thought Roland. *What the fuck has this got to do with him?*

'Of course,' said Sophie, smiling.

'Just checking,' said Cranfield, as he raised his glass.

'It's okay,' said Sophie, who did not need protection.

'If you need me, just shout,' he said, as he slipped back inside.

'What's all that about?' asked Roland.

'He's only concerned...'

'Really?' said Roland sarcastically. 'Please tell me you're not sleeping with him as well as all the others?'

'No,' said Sophie, shaking her head and laughing.

'He's a fucking arsehole,' said Roland, spitting every word.

'I know,' she said.

Roland paused. Well, he was going to say it...

'I know about you and Dr Jonas... I know what you were up to behind my back.'

Sophie's eyes bulged as she went pink in the light. Roland tilted his head, inspecting his victim, waiting for Sophie to say something.

Sophie bowed her head.

Perhaps she was ashamed? Roland could not tell.

'Why did you do it?'

Sophie looked up. She knew she had to be able to look at Roland, to be able to stand up for herself.

'I don't know,' she said. 'I was just doing what seemed natural.'

It was the answer Roland had been expecting.

'Did you sleep with anyone else?'

Sophie sighed.

'I did love you,' she said, in mitigation.

But that was not good enough, thought Roland; that did not mean anything.

'So, why did you do it then?'

'People do...' she said. 'None of us are perfect.'

Facetiously, Roland was about to say he was.

He leant into the wall, feeling the small stones dig into his back. He was still dissatisfied, frustrated, still struggling to comprehend Sophie's betrayal, her dishonesty and infidelity.

'I never wanted to hurt you,' she said, anxious to fill the void.

But it was too late. He was angry and he'd tell her how it was.

'If you think you're going to be exempt from any pain or feelings then you're wrong,' he said, levering himself off the wall. 'You think you can just walk away from it, and that's it... over. But it doesn't work like that. Things don't just end... there's more to it than that.'

Roland was putting the pressure on. She could feel it. She knew he would do this: have her guilt-trip about the whole thing.

'What do you want me to do?' she said, feeling the watery veins of tears beginning to flow.

Right, she's cracking, thought Roland.

'Do you know how humiliating it is to see you running around shagging anything and everything that

471

moves? Was I so bad in bed that you have to go fuck everything in this place before you leave?'

Sophie laughed, rubbing her cheeks with the back of her hand.

'It's not as bad as you think,' she said, feeling a little relieved. 'But I am leaving, as soon as possible.'

'Well, it's not good for my ego, that's for sure. How do you think that makes me feel?'

'I'm sorry, I know it's a bit heartless of me.'

'You're telling me!' said Roland, whilst at the same time realising (yet again) he was coming to an accommodation with her.

'You're right,' she said, 'I will need to reflect on it. Perhaps it's just a way of avoiding things.'

Then Sophie leaned forward and wrapped her arms around him.

'I will miss you,' she said, resting her head on his shoulder.

Roland was rigid. He had no intention of showing any affection, even though it was good to feel Sophie's body next to his again. She held him tighter as he tried to pull away. Then her tears felt wet on his neck.

'It's okay,' he said forgivingly.

They stayed together a little longer. Roland looked down at his pint dangling in his hand. Sophie let go, then kissed him on his lips.

Did she mean it?

'I won't forget you,' she said. 'You do mean a lot to me. You'll get over it. I know it's not nice being dumped.'

'It's a bit more than being dumped,' said Roland, feeling Sophie was yet again trying to downgrade their relationship.

'You know what I mean… but we couldn't have carried on. Sometimes it takes someone to make the first move. It wasn't easy for me either.'

She did not understand, thought Roland… it was the pain he found unbearable.

She looked at Roland and could tell he was struggling to come to terms with it all. But that was life; it was sometimes cruel and heartless.

'I'll be off soon,' she said. 'I mean, leaving here.'

'Really? What are you going to do?'

'I'm not registering… I'm never going back into nursing. I just want to forget about this place… do something else.'

'When are you leaving?'

'The end of next week.'

Roland sighed, puffed out his cheeks and drank from his pint.

'God, you know,' he said, 'I don't think I'll be able to survive. I can feel they're setting me up. With you and Jas gone, I'm going to be a sitting duck.'

'You don't know that,' soothed Sophie. 'It might not be that bad. You should try and finish your training. You don't have to give it up.'

'We should have seen it coming,' said Roland. 'We should have seen what was going to happen.'

'We didn't do anything wrong,' said Sophie. 'We did our best. Nobody else was going to stand up and say things were wrong. I'm proud of what we did.'

But all Roland could see was defeat.

'I know they're going to get me,' he said.

What more could Sophie say?

'Look, I'll keep in touch,' she said. 'Cheer up, it just feels bad at the moment.'

Roland hated her. She did not understand… and he couldn't make her understand.

'I've got to go back in,' she said. 'You'll be okay.'

Sophie leaned forward and kissed him on the cheek.

'Okay,' she said, 'I hope you feel better about things. Bye.'

Sophie slipped back inside and Roland stood his pint glass on the gravel.

That was it… it was truly over.

CHAPTER 43

DESPAIR

How far did the deceit go? That was the question Roland wrestled with as he lay on his bed, consumed by more despair and misogyny. He had seen (yes, he was sure he had seen; he knew he had seen) Sophie sitting in a car with Bob Jacobs, confirming the rumours, confirming the truth of her final, devastating deceit. How much damage was she capable of? How much more could she do to smash his self-esteem? There was nothing left, nothing left to keep him on a rational keel. He was swirling, drifting out of control, because, so she said, so she told everyone, she had fallen in love.

When did it all start? that's what Roland wanted to know. When did she decide a man twice her age was the one she wanted? Had it been going on again behind his back before she dumped him? Yet again, he had failed to see what was obvious to everyone. He must be the biggest joke that ever walked the earth! Why didn't he see these things? When someone said hello, did they actually mean, "Go fuck yourself!"? Was he so profoundly naïve he lacked the ability to live in this world – the real world, the adult world, with all the secrets, deceits and betrayals permeating everyone's fucked up lives? Was integrity such a bad thing? Was being honest intrinsically wrong? Had he failed as a human being if he was not lying and scheming? Could he really carry on, if he couldn't see what was happening in front of his eyes?

But Sophie was gone, in love with a real man, a proper, grown-up man.

He couldn't help it, but he needed to speak to her again, to say what he wanted to say, having failed when he had the chance outside the social club. She must have been hiding things, hiding the truth, keeping things from him, just so she could protect herself from his anger, his rage.

Roland turned over on his side and curled up into a ball. He could not hold back any longer. He cried and cried and let out childish, baby-like noises. The pain was so great, so acute, so agonising, he could feel it all over his body, in every aching muscle… fatigued, lethargic, unable to move, unable to live any longer. Why, why, why… why had Sophie done it with, of all people, the crusty old fart, the old, useless Labour man, the tired piece of nothingness? He still needed answers as to why she had left him, why did she not love him… what had gone wrong? *Sophie must have the answers*, he thought, *she must know…*

Roland sat up on the bed and wiped his eyes. He needed to pull himself together. He was going to speak to Sophie again. He needed to find out, he needed to let her know, he needed to do something to stop his mind going round and round and round in circles.

He stepped out into the corridor and headed for the phone. The nurses' hostel was quiet for once, with everyone having left for the Christmas break. He looked up and down, as he pulled himself together and dialled the number: 91131 6151512.

'Hello, Bob Jacobs speaking.'

Roland pushed a coin into the slot.

'Oh, hi, can I speak to Sophie Smith please?' said Roland, hoping politeness might get him access to the traitorous bitch.

'Who's calling?'

'It's Roland... Roland Cauldron.'

There was a pause.

'One moment...'

Roland heard the phone being put down and tried to catch the voices in the background. He waited. He heard the receiver being picked up again.

'Hi.'

It was Sophie.

'Hi,' said Roland aggressively.

'Is everything alright?' asked Sophie, her voice sounding anxious.

'No,' said Roland, his anger boiling up inside, 'not really.'

'Oh,' said Sophie.

'Yes, oh,' said Roland, knowing he would have to state the bloody obvious.

'What is it?'

'You,' said Roland, desperate to launch into his tirade.

'Look,' said Sophie, preparing for her defence, 'there's no point in being angry.'

'Really?' said Roland. 'So, you don't think I have a right to be angry then?'

'No.'

'You don't think that what you've done deserves some kind of retribution?'

Sophie sighed.

'If that's what you want, I can't stop you, can I?'

'You don't get it, do you?' said Roland, through gritted teeth.

'What am I supposed to get? I know I've upset you and I'm sorry.'

'Is that it?' said Roland. 'Is that all you can think: you're just sorry?!'

'I don't know what else you expect me to say.'

Roland paused, wanting Sophie to say something, but there was just silence. All he could feel was anger, all he could communicate was an angry silence, hoping the crackling telephone line was translating his rage.

Eventually, Sophie spoke.

'What do you want to say then?' she asked, sounding rather resigned to the inevitable.

Roland found his voice.

'I want to tell you how I feel,' he said.

There was more silence. Then the pips went and Roland shoved another coin into the slot.

'Are you there?' asked Sophie, sounding concerned for once.

'Yes, I am still here… I haven't gone away. Which is part of the problem, isn't it?'

'Okay, I'm listening,' said Sophie. 'You can tell me how you feel.'

'I feel like crap,' said Roland, 'I feel like shit… I feel as if I have been shat upon from a great height… by you…'

'I didn't mean to hurt you.'

'Well, you did!' said Roland emphatically. 'You've really hurt me. In fact, I don't think you know how bad it is for me, how much it hurts. I wish you could feel it… I wish you could feel how much it hurts.'

'I have been there,' said Sophie, rather meekly.

'Have you? Have you really been there? You're not me, you know. I trusted you… I trusted you with everything. I thought you loved me. You said you loved me, but at the same time you were going behind my back. And then this… you've got into bed with Jacobs, who betrayed us!'

'I didn't plan it,' said Sophie. 'It wasn't premeditated.'

'I don't know that, do I?' said Roland. 'How can I believe you after everything you've done?'

'Look,' said Sophie, 'I think you're exaggerating a bit. What happened between us was just normal.'

'Normal… you think what you did is normal?'

'Yes.'

'Fuck me!' said Roland. 'I don't think you have a conscience, do you?'

Sophie sighed even more.

'I don't know what you want me to say.'

But this was what Roland had been waiting for…

'I'll tell you what you can say,' he said, bringing forward his prepared accusation. 'You can tell me that you are a selfish, self-seeking, fucking bitch, who lied and cheated on someone who was desperately in love

479

with you, but for some unknown reason you decided to jump ship, leave me at my most vulnerable, leave me with nothing, nothing to hang on to, as if I was some fucking... one-night fucking stand!'

Sophie whimpered. *Shit, she's doing it again*, thought Roland, *she's fucking crying her way out of it.*

'Look, Sophie,' he said, still animated, 'I'm not having all this tears and crying bullshit any more. I just don't believe it. The point is, you've got what you want, haven't you, but I've got fuck all!'

'If that's the way you want to see it,' said Sophie, now audibly crying.

'Well, pardon me, but isn't that the truth?'

What could Sophie say? She had met someone else... why couldn't Roland see that?

'I didn't mean it to happen,' she said. 'Bob is different, that's all.'

'Is he? So, what's the difference – what's the difference between him and me?'

'It's difficult,' said Sophie, wishing she hadn't said anything.

'Is he better in bed, is that it?'

'No,' said Sophie, 'we're all different. It's just about... confidence, maybe.'

'What do you mean?' asked Roland disconcertedly.

'You'll get your confidence back,' she said. 'I promise you, you'll get over it. I know I haven't handled things properly... I know that...'

The pips went... more money...

'I just needed to be free,' said Sophie, 'so I can be... who I am. And I know you'll always hate me for it.'

He did not hate her... that was wrong... the wrong message.

'I don't hate you,' said Roland. 'I just don't know why you did what you did, and at the end of the day you just won't tell me anything. I need to understand why and you've just left me to figure it out for myself. That's what causes the pain, not knowing, not having a clue... can't you see that?'

'Yes,' she said, 'I can, but...'

'But what?'

'Nothing.'

'Not that fucking nothing again!'

'Look, I really wish I hadn't hurt you. I don't feel good about it, but you've got to try and move on.'

'In this place? You must be joking! I'm humiliated, a fucking joke. Everything is falling apart. Don't you see that? I'm completely on my own.'

'We're all on our own,' she said. 'Look at Jas, we couldn't help him.'

'That's not the same as this.'

'Please,' said Sophie, desperate for her own closure, 'I do love you, but I've got to go...'

'What do you mean, you love me?'

'I'm sorry,' said Sophie, as Bob Jacobs' voice infiltrated the background. 'Good luck.'

Fuck! What did she mean, she still loves me? What the fuck?! What the fuck?!

Sophie put the phone down.

Roland slammed down the receiver. He was no further forward. She'd done it again... blank... blank... blank.

481

He stormed back down the corridor, his feet clumping on the thin carpet covering the concrete floor. He shut the door to his room with a bang and threw himself down on the bed.

Fucking bitch! Fucking bitch! She had done it again. He had let her do it again. She was in control. She was dictating what happened. She had the power and he was powerless.

He stood up. His adrenaline was flowing. He looked in the mirror above his vile institutional sink. He hated what he saw. He hated everything staring back at him. What a stupid, ridiculous fucking face. How could she ever love him? Why did he think someone like Sophie would ever love him? He was not in her league and he was always out of his depth. She was always going to take him for a ride, use him and spit him out. And he had let it happen. Like an idiot he had gone along with it, believing somehow they were compatible. But it was nothing like that... it was an illusion. He had fooled himself into thinking he was at her level, but he wasn't... he wasn't even close.

Well, that was it... he'd never have another girlfriend. Who would ever have him? He was ugly. Now he was back to nothing. Sophie seemed to think it was easy, but it wasn't, not for Roland, because of his circumstances, because of his special circumstances... because he was back to being a naïve little fucking virgin again.

He sat back down on the bed. He was exhausted, drained. There was nothing left in the tank... resigned to his fate, to the horrific endgame. What was the point in carrying on? He was staring at failure. He had got everything wrong. Well, he'd learnt one thing: he'd questioned, searched and discovered yet again that you should never, ever trust people because they can't be trusted. *Sophie was right... we're all on our own. There's no point in having faith in anyone, no point in trying to believe in anything.* He thought he knew; he thought he had convinced himself he should always believe in nothing. There should never be hope because the world was a soulless, heartless hellhole. Life was a meaningless, shallow existence. The only people who flourished were the nasty and greedy... and the psychopaths who were running the show.

He picked up the vodka bottle, unscrewed the top and took a swig. He pulled his face as the spirit burned down his throat. Then the warmth kicked in throughout his body, calming his nerves and pacifying him. He walked to the window with the bottle in his hand. He surveyed the lawns which ran down to the wire fence and the woods. He could do it there, if he wanted to: go to where they all went to do it in the old abbey. Did he want to do it? Was that what he really wanted? It made sense. Everyone else seemed to do it, so why shouldn't he?

No, he was being stupid, really stupid. He shouldn't be thinking like that. He needed to put things in perspective. *Right, let's add things up, let's see the wood from the trees. What's gone wrong?*

So, one: girlfriend dumps me, humiliates me, fucks loads of guys behind my back and makes me a laughing stock in a closed and institutionalised world. Two, we work together to change the place, to improve things for everybody and end up being led up the garden path and teaching everyone that there is no point in trying to change anything. Three: betrayed by some union fuckhead and find out ex-girlfriend has shacked up with the man who betrayed the campaign (fuck!). Four: everyone (apart from Terry, who's a waste of space) has left me... I am on my own, just waiting for my career to be ended by a nasty and vengeful management regime. Anything else? Not really... what a God Almighty fuck up! And perhaps I'm paranoid as well? Yeah, probably got paranoid schizophrenic traits just waiting to come out and bite me in the bum.

Roland took another swig of vodka. He shook his head as the fluid ran down his throat. His body shivered, as the alcohol calmed his nerves and enabled him to see the world for what it was: a vile, pernicious, unthinking world, an absurd world where life was a thankless, painful task. There were just a few who'd get to benefit from this life, just a few who'd sit on top of the pile of shit that was humanity. Well, he'd done his best, he'd tried to change it, he'd tried to do something about it, he hadn't just taken it on the chin and he hadn't buried his head in the sand and pretended nothing was going on. He'd tried to confront it, he'd tried to have a go, to fight back, but it had all gone wrong. He'd lost everything, everything he thought he had achieved; it had all fallen through his hands. And now there was nothing... just a grey, miserable nothingness.

He pushed his head against the windowpane and rubbed his forehead across the glass, backwards and forwards, feeling the harshness, trying to erase the thoughts in his head, the dark, mad thoughts in his mind. *When does it all stop? When does all the pain somehow stop? Should life carry on when things are so bad? That is the real question, the question that matters now. Strip out all the bullshit, strip away all the fluff and stuff and what are you left with?* Roland thought he knew, he thought he had the answers once, back then, when he first met Sophie, when they drank together in the social club, when they sat up all night together, when they first made love (or was that just sex?).

Oh, he missed her so, so desperately…

He lay down on his stomach on the bed. He could smell something on the blankets. It was Sophie… her smell. Somehow it was there. He breathed it in, the smell of Sophie, the last remains, the last bits of Sophie.

More vodka… it made sense, it released the valves. But he was trapped, trapped in this place, trapped in his room; a prisoner. What did it matter where he went? He needed to get out… out of this shithole.

Roland pulled his coat from his wardrobe and fell back on to the bed. He was drunk already, sort of, a bit unsteady. But he did not give a fuck, he did not care… alright, no, he just did not give a fuck. *Do you see? Yes, good, you are listening, good, right, let us get this show on the road, let us hit the road, let us get the fuck out of this place!*

Okay, up we get… whey-hey… phew!

Roland stumbled to the door and fell against it. Perhaps he shouldn't go out?

No… I am fucking going out.

Roland had no distinct aim, place in mind, nowhere to go, but he was getting the fuck out! But not the social club. No way, he couldn't go there.

He had the vodka bottle tucked inside his coat as he walked along the corridor, through the fire exits and down the concrete stairs. At the bottom he laughed to himself at the thick stain of Annie Buchanan's brains and blood. He laughed again. This deserved a drink. In honour of the brave and forgotten Annie Buchanan, whose only crime was to stand up to those bastards.

'To Annie!' Roland took a very large swig, the vodka now moving down easily. He looked at how much he had drunk. Not that much, he thought, considering.

Poor old Annie, he'd let her down as well; hardly his fault, but he'd let her down. She'd done the right thing, though, she'd found a way out; she'd had the courage to go through with it. He admired her for that. *Perhaps I'll join you*, he said to himself; *it must be quite nice there, to be dead, with nothing left, all gone… no more bloody nagging pain, no more bloody meaningless life, all extinguished all in one go. That's the way to do it: get out of this rotten system, no more pretending somehow there's something to live for, no more putting up with all the falseness, no more pretending you can't see when you can. People don't want you to see, or if they do see, they don't want you to go on about it. Best to keep your head down, keep your mouth shut, don't say anything and sweep it under the carpet.*

Bollocks!

Roland pushed open the fire exit door. He felt the cold hit his face.

Fuck it! Let's walk… let's just walk.

He pulled up his hood and headed for the tarmac path. He glanced up at the Clock Tower. *Go on*, he said to himself, *turn me fucking mad if you want! I don't fucking care! I am fucking mad! Mad with this place, mad with all you fucking idiots!*

He stared at the intense light of the high, white-framed windows of the wards as he passed one after the other, moving round and round, viewing the sick madness of it all. *Look at them*, he thought, *shovelling all that piss and shit all day, and then you pretend nothing's happened... you go home to your family, you have a nice cup of tea and watch TV and put your children to bed. And what do you say to them? "I wiped thirty bums today, I shoved food down their fucking gullets, and then I wiped more piss and shit, then I shoved more food down them, then I cleaned up more piss and shit. Kissy-kissy... piss and shit... kissy-kissy... now off to bed with you."*

Fucking bullshit... fucking lies... all shit fucking lies...

Roland could see ahead of him the ark, the boiler house and the potting sheds. He did not want to go near them. To the right of him was the entrance to the old patients' graveyard (creepy, but out of the way). He walked in underneath the arch and felt the soft moss under his feet. He stopped. It was dark, very dark, and he waited for his eyes to adjust. There was a spot where he could sit, behind a headstone, just inside the entrance. He flopped down, felt the cold and wet immediately through his jeans. Fuck it! What a weird place, but a nice place, a strange and peaceful place. How many victims of Dr Prize-Bomka lay here? he wondered.

The drink was getting the better of him. He was so pissed. Wasn't this how they got McEmery? All he had to do now was get up, stroll down the corridors and let Fitzpatrick grab him. Done and dusted. Fitzpatrick would love that… they'd all love that. They must have seen him coming a mile off. *Here comes another one, thinks he can change the fucking system, thinks he can right all the wrongs but hasn't got a fucking clue how to do it.*

Roland peered into the vague, quiet light. He felt warm now; the canopy of trees kept everything at an even temperature. He could just make out the odd shape of bent and broken gravestones, the odd flat surface of a rounded slab. This was where it all ended, buried within the undergrowth, an anonymous signature, returning to our basic form, reducing things to atoms which eventually spun back out into the universe, flying through space, landing on another planet, reforming and reborn. *Out there is where all the metaphysics is. There is nothing to fear, then*, thought Roland, *nothing but the fear of some pain, but only a dying pain, a short-lived bit of pain.*

So he could do it, if he wanted to, if he was ready to join the dead in their resting place. *If they are dead? Are they restless to wake up and seek revenge for what was done to them? Perhaps, like zombies, they can walk again, to mash and smash the skulls of those who did them wrong, to track down their relatives who abandoned them in this stinking hellhole. But who has seen – who has seen the sins? Where are the witnesses? Perhaps it is me? Perhaps I can see?*

Fuck them! He had had enough. He didn't care. He now only needed to care about himself. *Every man, woman and child for themselves… all for one and only for me!*

Roland picked himself up. One more swig of vodka and he was off again.

To his right were the potting sheds where Franks had found the glass he needed to slash his throat. If there was anything Roland had learnt in Wellington Park, it was definitely how to do a good suicide. He kicked around a few bits of broken windowpane, handled a few whilst wobbling on his feet until he found what he needed: a nice, sharp-sided triangle, which fitted neatly into his pocket.

Feel it now, feel the edge of the glass.

He walked back along the tarmac path. He put his hand into his pocket, squeezed tightly around the edges until the glass cut into his hand. He did his best to inspect, in the fading light of day, against the thick lights of the wards which illuminated his walk. He could just make out what he thought were a few shards of glass embedded in the palm of his hand. There was blood, a thin strip of blood oozing out. He smiled with satisfaction before noticing ahead of him a figure, someone else prowling the boring end of the day. They had the gait of a patient… as long as it wasn't some fucking nurse who might want to save him – and he wasn't having any of that, not after he had decided. They stopped and turned back on themselves. *They must know something*, thought Roland.

Just before he reached the nurses' hostel, he veered off across the lawns, squelching through the grass (which really needed to be cut by now), focusing on the wire fence. Who knows, he might even find his dope there in the woods… that would be good: a last smoke.

Fuck it… concentrate.

He put his foot on the wire fence and tried to balance and lever, lifted himself up and then fell head first into the woods. What did it matter? He picked himself up.

The adrenaline was pumping. He did not know why, but he ran... ran as fast as he could. The twigs and vegetation snapped and licked his legs, his eyes shut, his legs like jelly, moving... *am I moving?*

There was light and dark, shadows moving, flowing, light permeating the canopy, fingers of wind catching his ears and eyes, a force propelling, forcing, gorging, pursuing, diving, dying, moving, forever onwards, through shadows, through the mad forces, through the endless paths and tracks, through the never-ending trials of life. *Nothing is the same, nothing is ever black and white, nothing is on the surface, nothing is the same, nothing is ever what it seems, as it changes, fluid, transforming, into dark and light and grey, and lightness, brightness, into grey and dark, exhausted, travelling, running, at a thousand miles an hour... till I stop.*

Roland fell to the floor.

It was almost pitch black. He still needed to get to the place he needed to be, to the place where they all went to do it, but he was tired, drained, exhausted and falling asleep. He could sense he was buried in thick undergrowth, wet, sticky leaves and ferns rising around him; up above, veins outlining the thick branches that consumed him. But it was time. Time to go in, time to rest the anguished pain, time to get rid of a useless, meaningless life, a life that created nothing, a life that was out of pace, out of step and out of time. There were no last regrets, no second thoughts, as he took the glass from his pocket and cut vigorously into his wrist.

It hurt, it hurt like mad, but the warm fluid was running down his hand, the warm, sticky fluid was running down... the warmness was running down... running down... down... and down...

★

Starr stirred, his time in the undergrowth at an end, the cold having sapped all the heat from his body. He was covered in the remains of fermenting foliage, brown leaves, rotting ferns and the twigs and kindle of the trees above him. He sat up and yawned. It had been an excellent sleep (a good snooze), as he looked around the dead quiet of his resting place. He pushed up with his arms and felt the pulse of his muscles flex, shook his head and rubbed his hands through his curly hair.

What more was there to do?

He wanted dinner. He was hungry, which meant he had to navigate his way back through the woods, over the fence, across the lawns, through reception, avoid Fitzpatrick in the corridors, before he could get back on to the ward. That was an effort which kept him sitting there, pondering and anticipating the journey ahead. To deflect from these issues, he pushed out his arms and swept the leaves back around his legs. He touched something soft. It was odd, not part of the woods. He turned to look down at his side and could just make out the crumpled mess of something warm. Yes, it was very warm... like a horse.

He peered at the face. This was, he could tell, another tragedy, but not of the same type, category or person. This one was different. He looked more closely, right into the face, attempting to make out the lines, to

491

establish form and recognition. Instinct told him it was one of them, one of the others, and he did not think it had much to do with him.

'Six… one-five… one-five… one-two,' he said, fondling his lips as they protruded.

He played with the leaves in front of him and across his body. Like a child he threw them up into the air and watched them drop, falling with a suddenness he had not anticipated.

Enough was enough. It was time to get back to where his food was waiting. He stood up and let what wooded debris lay across him fall back down. The body was still there, not moving, not saying anything. They were always quiet when they were dead… they were always at peace. He readied himself for his gallop, ready to launch off back through the woods. He let out a loud braying noise, like a stallion, stamped and curled his foot on the earth. He thrust back his head and strained up into the night sky. It was time, time to leave…

But there was light above… bright, golden light…

He strained to follow the flowing, swooping movement of the light, as it weaved in and out of the fibrous slate of branches. This bird he recognised. It was the phoenix.

Starr waited. Surely it had come to take the body away, just like Annie Buchanan?

The phoenix hovered and swayed, diving to where the body lay. Then, with the same power and force with which it had arrived, it flew up and back out into the night sky.

Perhaps the body needed something? Perhaps there was something he should do? And then he remembered:

he was the one that helped him once, by the sea, looking out across all the land that was the sea. Yes, he would help, if that was what the phoenix wanted.

He took out his star and shone the light, the power and the energy into the face of the body. *Perhaps this will wake him? With the power of the planets and the stars, the power of the universe, the things that matter, the power that has been his gift and cherished and distributed to all the tortured souls, he will wake and stir…*

Starr examined the crumpled body. He knelt down and could still feel some warmth. Just as he had thought, there was always something to give, there was always some humanity. With both hands he lifted up the dead weight. There was a bit of a journey but he had the time and strength. He bent his back. It was not so heavy after all, after some steps. He pushed with his legs. His legs were now like pistons, pumping through the undergrowth, pushing through the tangled wood, driving through the coarse and strangled fibres.

After some distance he could see through the darkness and the lights of Wellington Park. Up against the wire fence he dropped the body over the other side. The body groaned, as Starr forced his way through the gap between two sets of wire. Again, he picked up the body and continued walking, his arms outstretched as if he was carrying a heavy tray. He walked past the nurses' hostel, across the tarmac path and through the severe lights that glowed from the high windows of the wards.

Eventually, he was there, outside reception. He knelt and rolled the body against one of the columns that marked the entrance and slipped inside. He quickened his pace, through the corridors, listening to the hum of the ductwork.

'You!' shouted the voice of Fitzpatrick from behind.

Starr stopped, although he did not look back, but bowed his head.

'Get along to your ward, you're late for your dinner.'

Starr obeyed. After all, it was where he was going.

CHAPTER 44

FULL CIRCLE

'You're a very lucky man,' said Sister Bernice, popping into the post-natal room downstairs, situated at the rear of the Lilywhite Ward day room.

Roland nodded contritely.

'You slept through Christmas Day,' she said, whilst taking his temperature. 'The good news is, the wound is not so bad. You lost some blood, but you just need to recover from the dehydration. There is a small risk of infection, which is why you need to take the antibiotics, but you are not on any other medication. You were all muddy when they found you so you must have been out in those woods. But at least you did the sensible thing by raising the alarm. Do you want me to contact any of your family?'

'No, thanks,' said Roland, as he removed the thermometer and checked the reading himself.

'Well, I just wanted to let you know they have put you on a section, but you needn't worry about anything like that, it's only for a few days, until you feel better. Dr Caldwell's registrar is going to pop in later to review it.'

Roland looked down at his thin crêpe bandage covering the wound. It was just a few blood vessels severed, not the artery. What a mess... what an unadulterated mess he was in.

'Now, things always work out in the end,' she said, recording on his medical chart. 'Sometimes you just need to get to the bottom before you are ready to come back up again.'

Roland acknowledged Sister Bernice's perfunctory wisdom.

'However, it's probably best if you stay in this room for now and away from the other patients,' she said, opening the door to leave. 'The place is almost empty anyway because of Christmas. At least wait until you've spoken to the doctor.'

Roland nodded again. All he could do was appear compliant. If he was on a section, they were bound to want to keep an eye on him.

Roland was feeling cold, so he got out of bed to check the heating, clasping his hands to feel the stone-cold, thickly painted radiator. He looked outside at the bland, nondescript day... neither rain, snow, wind or sunshine, and just more of the woods which he had run into like a drunken idiot. One thing, though: he knew he hadn't made it back himself... someone had carried him... he knew that much.

He felt a presence and looked behind him. Through the glass windowpane in the door, a face, a female nurse, suddenly withdrew.

So, they were keeping an eye on him.

Well, he was up to his neck in it, in the mire, the deep shit. He had unwittingly put himself in exactly the

496

situation they would want him: powerless and captive. But why would Dr Caldwell's registrar review his case? Why should he be involved, because Caldwell's lot never got involved on Lilywhite Ward?

★

Roland sat in the same clinic room where Dr Jonas had completed his now-infamous last assessment. They had also given Roland a shirt and trousers from the linen cupboard and he was dressed in full institutional regalia. Sat opposite was Dr Caldwell's registrar, who had an uncanny resemblance to Dr Jonas: the same smart-casual dress code and thin-rimmed round glasses. Roland felt there was a soft charm about him, a youthfulness which he hoped would help his rationalisation: how a student psychiatric nurse comes to be suicidal in a place like Wellington Park.

As he waited for the registrar to complete his notes, Roland randomly read the didactic health care messages on the noticeboard.

'So, how are you today?' asked the registrar, running his hands through his elongated quiff.

'Okay,' said Roland, 'considering…'

The registrar offered a wry smile.

'Quite a night, I hear…'

'Something like that.'

'Okay,' said the registrar, spinning around the desk on the wheels of his chair so he was side-on to Roland, 'let's just have a little look at that wound of yours.'

Roland offered his left arm and decided immediately he needed to demonstrate a sense of control. He pre-

497

empted the reach of the registrar, unwound the bandage over his wrist and removed the layer of gauze.

'Oh, I see,' said the registrar. 'You've got a few stiches there, but nothing too serious. You'll have a scar of course, but it should heal without a problem.'

Roland nodded, almost proud, a badge of honour, a lasting tattoo of his suffering.

'Eh, Sister Bernice said I was on antibiotics,' queried Roland, 'to prevent infection?'

'Are you?' the registrar replied, slightly surprised, before appearing to correct what he was potentially going to say. 'Well, yes, I would think you are. I don't have your drugs chart with me, but it would be sensible. What did you use to make that cut?'

'Glass,' said Roland.

'Well, in a way it's a good job you didn't have a more efficient cutting tool.'

'I was drunk,' said Roland, submitting his initial mitigation.

The registrar spun himself back round behind the desk.

'You know alcohol acts as a mood depressant?'

'Yes,' said Roland.

'So, probably not the best thing to do when you're feeling a bit blue. It exaggerates those feelings… your emotions.'

'Yes, I know,' said Roland, who was not going to be patronised.

'It's just something you might want to think about if you are ever feeling down again.'

Roland also knew that.

'Well, you're not the first and you certainly won't be the last,' said the registrar, as he made a note on the file in front of him. 'To switch sides, so to speak. When do you finish your training?'

'I've finished,' said Roland. 'After what I've done they're not going to have me back, are they?'

'Why do you think that?'

'Well, they aren't, are they?'

'There is a duty of care… I don't think they would want to wash their hands of you.'

'This is what the school and the management here have been waiting for all along,' said Roland, as he leant forward in his chair. 'For me to mess up, so they can get rid of me.'

'Why would they want to do that?' asked the registrar, intrigued.

'Let's just say…' said Roland, convinced Dr Caldwell's registrar already knew the full story. 'Let's just say that I have been active in trying to change things around here and it's the perfect opportunity for the system to get back at me.'

'I see,' said the registrar, accepting Roland's words at face value. 'But surely, in this instance, you have only done harm to yourself and not the institution?'

'What do you mean?'

'You have only injured yourself, nothing more and nothing less.'

'Look,' said Roland, who felt his best approach was to be explicit, 'you're Dr Caldwell's registrar, aren't you?'

'Yes, for my sins…'

'And you have been sent over here to do an assessment on me… yes?'

'I cover this ward and others.'

Roland paused.

'But I've never seen you before.'

'Well, I can assure you, I do work here,' he said, trying to fathom Roland's train of thought.

Roland prepared himself to raise the registrar's awareness.

'You know,' said Roland, 'there are all sorts of things which go on here that are completely wrong.'

'I don't doubt that for a minute. I've never worked in a hospital where things don't go wrong.'

'Yeah, but it's more than just going wrong.'

The registrar leant back and the wheels of his chair shifted against the wall.

'Did you want to make a complaint?' he asked.

Roland laughed and scoffed.

'A complaint?' he said, moving his head from side to side. 'It's a bit more serious than that…'

And just as Roland was about to reveal the grand conspiracy which underpinned everything, which had ruined his career, his relationship, his friendships and his whole life, he suddenly felt fatalistic, stoical, tired of repeating the same old mantra.

'Take your time,' said the registrar, responding to Roland's demoralised body language.

'Forget it… it doesn't matter any more.'

'Are you sure? You seem to me to be quite passionate about something.'

'I was,' said Roland, who could feel defeatism swarming all over his body.

The registrar moved his chair forward.

'Okay,' he said, as a preface to reverting to the issue in hand, 'maybe we can come back to it later, if you want to, but I think for my purposes I need to determine why you felt the need to harm yourself the other night.'

Harm, thought Roland, *that's an interesting word*. He hadn't thought of it like that... harming himself.

'Is it something you want to go into?' asked the registrar.

'No,' said Roland, recognising the need to find some energy again. 'I mean, I know why I did it: I was drunk, and really upset... things just got on top of me... a whole load of stuff and I was out of control.'

'Have you had suicidal thoughts before?'

'No, not really... I mean, not as much as that. It's just this place... there's a lot of it...'

'Suicide,' said the registrar, smiling.

'Yeah, lots of people killing themselves.'

'Oh, I hope not, or else we wouldn't be doing a very good job, would we?'

'Well, perhaps we aren't doing a very good job?' replied Roland, feeling a little more energetic. 'Perhaps we're just churning the same old crap around and not making a blind bit of difference?'

The registrar nodded sagely.

'It is a strange place to work in at times,' he said, 'but we choose these types of careers in order to help people. What we can't always do is change the environment we have to work in, even if it does need changing.'

'Well,' said Roland, warming to the disclosure, 'I tried to change it and look what's happened to me.'

The registrar paused.

'So,' he said, ensuring what he said next was pertinent, 'would you attribute your self-harming to a failure to change the institution to the way you think it should be?'

'I wouldn't put it like that exactly,' said Roland. 'I wasn't trying to change anything to the way I thought it should be. We were just trying to improve things, stop students being used to cover up shortages, trying to reduce risks by getting more staff on the wards... that's hardly revolutionary, is it?'

'No,' the registrar said, shifting his bottom from side to side. 'But I would imagine it would have upset a few people.'

'So, I'm not mad then?'

'No!' said the registrar, laughing out loud. 'You sound perfectly rational to me. But as you will be only too aware, I do need to establish if you have any potential to further self-harm.'

'Why, so you can section me again?'

'I don't think I'll need to do that,' he said, smiling benignly. 'Trust me.'

Why should he trust him, thought Roland, considering everything he had been through had taught him not to trust anyone, least of all a man who held his captivity and freedom in his hands.

'Tell me,' said the registrar, raising his head to look at the ceiling, 'why did you choose a career like this?'

'Why did I choose a career like this?' said Roland rhetorically. 'I don't know... I must have been mad. All my friends said I was mad. I should have listened to them.'

'You must have had a good reason to want to train to be a psychiatric nurse.'

'Do you want to know the real reason?' said Roland, thinking there was no point in hiding anything. 'It's quite simple, really: I needed to get out of London, find a job with a career and put a roof over my head. I didn't have a penny to my name and for some unknown reason they accepted me here, even though I have a criminal record. I must admit, I was amazed I got accepted, until I realised they'd take anyone to keep this fucked up place going.'

'I would have thought,' said the registrar, 'an intelligent young man like yourself would have had more motivation than that. However, what type of criminal record do you have?'

'My conviction?'

'Yes, is it the only one?'

'Yes: possession of cannabis.'

'And do you still use cannabis?'

'No,' said Roland, without a hint, he hoped, of betraying the truth.

'I see…' the registrar said, clearly unconvinced. 'I assume you also know this can act as a mood alternator, especially if you are a heavy user and were to suddenly stop. It would take time to adjust, don't you think?'

'No…' said Roland, who could see where this was going. 'What I did to myself was down to what someone did to me, nothing more than that.'

'And what did this person do to you?'

'They betrayed me, lied to me, they were deceitful… they treated me like shit and spat me out.'

'That sounds like a powerful experience. Was this through a relationship you had with someone here at the hospital?'

'Yes.'

'A fellow student?'

'Yes.'

'Male or female?'

'Female.'

'I see… so it must have been rather difficult, rather distressing to continue training whilst you were feeling hurt… especially if you are still in the same environment?'

'She's left,' said Roland.

'So, does that give you closure?'

'No, not really…'

The registrar made a note. Roland glanced around the room, partially in an attempt to feign disinterest.

'Can I reflect back to you my thoughts?' asked the registrar.

Roland shrugged. He didn't care.

'I detect two things here: you've indicated to me that you have upset the authorities and you believe this has jeopardised your chances of progression in your training. You have also been hurt by a relationship with someone at the hospital. Perhaps the combination of these two things created an intensity in your own mind and you needed some release – getting drunk, perhaps – and then things spiralled out of control. Would it be fair to say you just needed a bit of time out?'

'Yes,' said Roland, who thought he couldn't have put it better himself.

'Would you mind then if we just explored those two areas a little, simply because I need to be sure there is no further risk to yourself?'

Roland nodded, surprised there might be a way out.

'Do you think there is a conspiracy against you?' asked the registrar, his pen poised over the file in front of him.

'No,' said Roland, watching the registrar start writing, 'not if the point of your question is to suggest I am paranoid.'

'If you are paranoid, you probably wouldn't know you were, so I think we can rule that one out.'

'Well, I know I am not paranoid,' said Roland keenly. 'But this place can't handle dissent of any kind.'

The registrar continued to write.

'Please don't be put off by my writing,' he said.

'I'm not,' said Roland.

'Let me ask you a question, and answer it as best you can… are you fearful of anybody here in this hospital?'

'Look, I'm not paranoid!' said Roland sharply.

'Yes, I have already said you are not paranoid… that's not the point of my question.'

'Well, in what sense do you mean… fear?'

'I think you know what fear is…'

'Yes, I know what fear is… it is not about fear.'

The registrar waited to see if Roland would expand.

'Well,' continued Roland, 'if you challenge something here there is going to be a reaction, consequences. You see that all the time… just look at what's going on.'

Again, the registrar waited for Roland to extrapolate.

'Dissent,' said Roland resentfully. 'Society, the state, the system… it only tolerates a certain level of dissent. Acceptable dissent doesn't change anything and merely plays into the hands of the people who rule. Real dissent, real change, means doing things which upsets people… the hierarchy. Only then will you know if you are making a difference because the bastards at the top are really pissed off with you.'

The registrar put down his pen, genuinely interested to hear what Roland had to say. It was an invitation Roland couldn't resist.

'Look, I'm an anarchist,' said Roland. 'Not the mad type, going around bombing – not that you get that any more… from anarchists, I mean. But being an anarchist puts me out on a limb, outside of the norm. It doesn't mean I'm mad… well, until you come into a place like this, then everything gets exaggerated.'

'But you favour chaos over stability?'

'No… well, only to shake things up… but you can never trust any system. An anarchist must always be a rebel, in a state of permanent revolution.'

'But don't you think,' said the registrar, 'you would never have a system as you would always be trying to change it?'

'No, things have a natural flow and ebb, things move from stability to crisis and back to stability again. And anyway, it's also about questioning, trying to get to some fundamental truths about things. For instance, whether people really are mad, or is it the system that makes them mad?'

The registrar made another note on Roland's file.

'Don't you think that's a difficult way to live, especially when the role of a psychiatric nurse is a rather more practical one? I mean, you could easily see conspiracies where there are none.'

'I am aware of that,' said Roland. 'There are all sorts of risks, but I had to try and do something about it. I just couldn't sit back and pretend there wasn't anything wrong. I did see things, hear things, know things, which by any standard were fundamentally wrong.'

The registrar leant back in his chair, preparing his thoughts, preparing a conclusion.

'Well, Roland, you seem to me to have a lively, enquiring mind. Obviously, your way of thinking, as you've admitted yourself, is bound to lead you into conflict. So, on those terms, your battles, if we can call them that, are a product of your belief system. There is for you no other way to go. Perhaps your only mistake was to take a career to which you are not suited?'

'Well, I'm trapped now,' said Roland.

'Why... ?' asked the registrar, drawing out the question.

Roland shuffled in his chair, annoyed he had to explain the self-evident.

'Because I'm here in front of you!'

'You've lost me,' said the registrar.

'Look,' said Roland, 'it's like this... if the system is mad, absurd, then it probably needs changing. But in trying to change the system, it protects itself by labelling you as mad.'

'I'm sorry, Roland, I'm struggling to fully understand what you mean.'

'Well,' said Roland, who was sure his reasoning made sense, 'the real madness, the real anarchy is in the system... ripping apart people's lives, forcing everyone to live by a new code to be greedy and selfish. We are constantly presented with illusions... look beneath the surface and you will see anarchy is in the system... and not my version of anarchy, but the anarchy of the system.'

The registrar was taken aback by the forcefulness of Roland's reasoning.

'Okay, Roland, I think all I can say is you have a view of the world best contested in politics and philosophy. As interesting as it all is, I am concerned that a few days ago you came close to taking your own life.'

Oh well, thought Roland, *that was a waste of time trying to explain anything…*

'I was drunk,' he said. 'It was a mistake.'

'I accept that… to some degree.'

'And I don't want to be on a section,' asserted Roland.

'You don't need to be… it's probably expired by now.'

'Oh, right…' said Roland, relieved.

'But there is another area I would just like to explore with you, if you don't mind?'

What harm could that do? thought Roland. *I'm free!*

'Would you say you are someone who thinks with their head rather than their heart?'

'I have a heart,' said Roland.

'Yes, a biological organ, but indulge me on this one. I think you've got highly developed reasoning skills and you're very analytical. But do you struggle when you have to deal with deeper emotions, things which are not so tangible?'

'I struggled because I was shat upon,' said Roland.

'I don't doubt that,' said the registrar. 'A lot of the people we have here are victims of cruelty and heartlessness. But it would be naïve if we thought we could go through life without people hurting us. The question is, do you think you have the emotional tools to absorb these kinds of shocks?'

'Well…' said Roland, and he then paused.

'Take your time, please,' said the registrar, leaving his pen in between the pages of Roland's file.

'I don't really know,' said Roland. 'That's a difficult one.'

'What emotions do you feel now, at this moment?'

'At this moment?' said Roland, puffing out his cheeks. 'Anger… at the way I was treated.'

'Is that the only emotion?'

'No,' said Roland, although he was not sure he really felt anything else.

The registrar waited for Roland to fill the space.

'Eh, sad…' said Roland unconvincingly, whilst thinking it reminded him of going to confession and having to make things up. 'Sad it's ended unnecessarily, before its time, even though she, Sophie, was cheating on me.'

'Would you say you are still in love with her?'

'Yes,' said Roland, without hesitation, whilst feeling the emotions the registrar had referred to begin to well up inside.

Then all the tears inside his body came out, uncontrollably, rising up from his gut, flowing through his veins and arteries, pumping from his heart, tears rolling into his eyes and down his cheeks. He had lost the one thing he valued, the one thing that gave purpose to his life: Sophie.

Roland took off his glasses as he tried to control the emotional outpouring. He wiped his eyes, hoping the tears would stop.

'I'm sorry,' he said, letting out a deep breath, 'it's just got on top of me again.'

'Don't apologise,' said the registrar. 'You might feel embarrassed, but there's nothing wrong with crying. You've been hurt and you need to let it out.'

Roland tried to compose himself, putting his glasses back on and then holding his nose.

'I suppose you think there's something wrong with me?' said Roland, feeling he had failed in his task to escape the clutches of Wellington Park.

'Well,' said the registrar, smiling, 'it's what we call in the trade... a broken heart.'

Roland pushed out a belly laugh, relieved at the registrar's common sense.

'I have some empathy with you,' the registrar said. 'My girlfriend left me a few months ago.'

'Did she?' said Roland, taking off his glasses and wiping his eyes again. 'How did you cope with it?'

'I didn't say I had,' he said, with a mischievous grin.

Roland laughed again.

'Okay,' said the registrar, pushing his chair into the table and picking up his pen. 'Here's where I think we're at. There's no need for a further section on you, but I think you should consider taking a bit of time out. How do you feel about staying on the ward?'

'On the ward?!' said Roland, shocked at the proposal.

'I hear from Sister Bernice you've got the post-natal room?'

'Yeah...'

'It would be voluntary. We are in the middle of the Christmas period and the ward is half-empty. You can keep out of the way of the other patients if you like... just take time to reflect and work through some of those emotions.'

'I can't stay on the ward,' said Roland, almost pleading.

'Yes you can,' said the registrar benevolently. 'Although there's nothing wrong with you fundamentally, apart from a reactive depression, I would not be happy with you going back to the nurses' hostel and staying there on your own.'

Roland sighed… but he was fearful of going back.

'Give yourself until the New Year. You can walk out at any time, but while you have the room, why not use it? I can think of nothing more depressing than spending the New Year in a nurses' hostel all on your own. Do you have anyone who can bring a few things over for you?'

'Eh… yeah… Terry, probably…'

'Good. I'll let Sister Bernice know you are going to stay a few more days.'

Was that it? Was the session over?

'Okay?'

'Yes, I think so,' said Roland, getting up from his chair, unsure of what he had really agreed to… unsure if he had been led towards something.

'You'll be fine.'

There was a knock on the clinic door as Sister Bernice invited herself in.

'Oh, sorry, Doctor, I wasn't sure if you were in here.'

Roland turned round.

'How did it go?' she asked.

'Okay, I think…'

'He is good isn't he?' she said, admiring the registrar. 'Just like your father, I suspect.'

Roland looked perplexed.

'Dr Prize-Bomka.'

CHAPTER 45

FLYING TONIGHT!

It was ironic (nothing more) that Roland had been assessed by Dr Prize-Bomka's "youngest", but could he be trusted? Roland kept asking himself. After all, he was Dr Caldwell's registrar. What if they had really concocted something so Roland would end up as a patient voluntarily? Or was he just being paranoid? It was difficult to get a grasp on truth and reality. But think for a minute: they did not control Sophie, they did not tell her to behave like a shit, fuck your boyfriend up so he will feel sorry for himself and try and commit suicide. No, he did not doubt for a second Sophie stood outside all the potential conspiracies he could construct. But there was another thought which kept running around in his head... the seed planted, the question posed: *Do I have the capacity to absorb heartlessness?* Roland had never thought about it like that... that there might be something missing, something not there in his armoury (so to speak). What if he hadn't got the capacity to deal with all the heartless fucking bastards? What then – back to suicide?

The door to the post-natal room was pushed open and Terry walked in, dropping Roland's suitcase loudly on the floor.

'As requested,' Terry said, flopping down on a high-backed armchair.

'Thanks,' said Roland, who was expecting the delivery.

Then he realised he had left some writing open on his bed. He tore a sheet of paper from his A4 pad, folded it into quarters and slipped it into his pocket.

'Cold,' said Terry.

'What's that?'

'It... is... cold outside.'

'Oh, right... it's boiling in here.'

Terry nodded, with some degree of satisfaction.

'Settling in?' asked Terry sarcastically.

'A bit... don't know really.'

Terry acknowledged Roland's ambivalence.

'Anyway, New Year's Eve,' he said, making the announcement.

'Yes, I know... can't stand it,' said Roland.

'Not celebrating then?'

'What, in here, on fucking Lilywhite Ward? You must be joking...'

'Why not? I bet this could be a nice little party room.'

Roland raised an eyebrow. He was not interested... he was not even interested in Terry staying.

'Fancy a cup of tea?' asked Terry.

'A cup of tea... from where?' asked Roland, looking around the room, rather bemused. 'Anyway, I can't stand tea.'

'What, you don't like tea? I love a cuppa,' said Terry, as he removed from inside his jacket a thermos flask. 'You look to me as if you need a cup of tea!'

Terry plonked the flask on the small table in front of him and smiled at Roland.

'I don't have any milk or sugar,' said Roland, as a way of declining Terry's offer.

'Well, you should never put milk in tea,' said Terry, unscrewing the cup on the flask.

'Really, I thought that's what made it palatable?'

'Tea,' said Terry informatively, 'should have sugar, but to retain the flavours you need just hot water and the filtering of the tea leaves.'

'Oh, right,' said Roland, thoroughly disinterested.

Terry undid the flask and poured the steaming tea into the plastic cup.

'Here,' he said, lifting the cup towards Roland, 'I've already sweetened it.'

Roland took the cup and sipped. He winced. It was hot, a strange taste at first, fully saturated in sugar... or maybe it was honey.

'What do you think?' asked Terry.

'Eh... not my cup of tea really,' said Roland, sniggering.

'Try it again, it's an acquired taste, proper tea.'

Roland sipped, feeling under orders to swallow his medication. It definitely had a strange aftertaste, one he recognised but could not quite recall.

'See!' said Terry, feeling he had proved his point. 'Tea's a good drink. It's something you should get into.'

Roland stretched out his hand to return the cup.

'Thanks, but it's not for me.'

Terry scowled.

'Drink the tea!' he instructed.

'Okay,' said Roland, 'I will… drink the tea.'

Bizarre, thought Roland, as he sipped again.

'By the way, I've got some news for you,' said Terry, who was now satisfied his client was following his prescription.

'I've got some news for you,' replied Roland.

But Terry was going to say what he wanted first.

'I'm leaving,' he said.

'I know,' said Roland, recalling his conversation with Terry, before he got drunk and suicidal.

'Well, just to let you know…'

'Yeah, I know,' said Roland again.

'I mean, I'm leaving *now*,' said Terry, emphasising the "now".

'What… you mean you're leaving now… now?' said Roland, slightly puzzled. 'You mean you're leaving now… altogether?'

'Yeah…' said Terry, his face showing a faint sense of guilt at the final abandonment. 'My transfer came through and I'm starting in the New Year.'

'What, Brighton?'

'Yeah, well, near there… and I've bought a boat.'

'A boat?' asked Roland, still trying to assimilate the impact of Terry's imminent departure.

'Well, not a boat that goes on the sea or anything… it just sits there.'

'Sits where?'

'On the water.'

'You bought a boat that sits on the water?' repeated Roland, trying to conjure up an image. 'I don't understand... how the fuck can you afford a boat?'

'I saved up.'

'What, on a student's wage?'

Terry merely shrugged his shoulders.

'Have you been dealing?' asked Roland, suspicious of Terry's access to any form of finance.

'I got a bank loan,' said Terry. 'I know it's a bit crazy, but they gave me the money.'

'So, a bank lent you the money to buy a boat... how much did the boat cost?'

'Not much,' said Terry, 'it's not a sea boat, more like a river boat, but it needs a lot of work done on it.'

'And it floats?'

'Of course it does,' said Terry, laughing. 'You should come down and see it. You know, as I said, it needs a lot of work... but you can sleep in it, live in it.'

'Blimey,' said Roland, who took a large gulp of tea.

'Well,' said Terry, 'that's partly the reason I came to see you.'

'What do you mean?'

'Well, I know you've been through a lot and everything... but do you know what you're going to do yet?'

'I've resigned,' said Roland, as way of delivering his own piece of news, 'from the school.'

Terry was unmoved.

'I thought you would,' he said. 'Makes sense...'

'Does it?' wondered Roland, who was not entirely sure.

'Yeah…' said Terry. 'They wouldn't have let you carry on, not after all the militant stuff and then you trying to do yourself in.'

'No, that's what I thought,' said Roland wistfully.

'You've made the right decision… which is better than letting them doing it for you.'

'I know,' said Roland, who was grateful for the confirmation.

'You need time,' said Terry, 'time to heal…'

'Time's the only thing that cures anything in this place,' said Roland, sipping his tea.

'But you don't want to do it here,' said Terry, shaking his head vigorously.

'Why not?'

Terry paused. He had given it some thought and was now ready to reveal his thinking.

'You're not Annie Buchanan.'

Roland sighed.

'It's easy to think you're just another victim,' said Terry, 'but I think she *was* ill, they just tipped her over the edge. The difference with you is you're not mad… you don't have to be here. There's no section on you… you're free to go.'

'Go where exactly?' said Roland, almost pleading for direction, a destination.

'*Praxis*,' said Terry, with a glint in his eye.

'Is that a spaceship?' asked Roland mockingly.

'It could be,' said Terry, 'but it's actually the name of my boat.'

'Your boat… why would I want to go and live on your boat?'

'Can you think of anything better to do?'

Stay here, thought Roland, who knew Terry would only jump down his throat if he said it.

'So, the invitation's there, if you want it…'

Roland took a gulp of tea.

'I need lodgers to help pay for it,' said Terry, as further inducement, 'but you can live for free, in exchange for working on it. You know, help doing it up.'

'Free accommodation sounds appealing,' said Roland. 'Where is it?'

'It's not too far from Brighton. You need to get to a place called Deanbeigh… Deanbeigh-by-the-Sea. It's moored with a whole bunch of other boats. It's easy to find.'

'Right,' said Roland, discounting the need to remember anything for a journey he thought he would never do.

'But I think you need to decide now,' said Terry.

'Do I?'

'Yes,' said Terry leaning forward in his chair.

'So,' said Roland, 'the options are, stay here and kill myself, or go and stay with you on a boat and do some DIY?'

'Yeah, something like that.'

'I don't know,' said Roland. 'I've got to think about it.'

'Okay,' said Terry, 'I thought you'd say that.'

But he clearly had something else he wanted to say.

'Well…' said Terry, having arrived at the appropriate point in their conversation. 'Well…'

'Well what?'

'Well, you're probably not going to believe me and you're probably going to want to kill me, but I've done something to help you... although you won't see it like that, especially when I tell you, and you will want to freak out... but don't freak out because you'll need to remain calm so you can deal with it... with what I am going to tell you...'

'Is it about Sophie again?'

'No.'

'Jas?'

'No.'

Roland looked quizzically at Terry.

'So, it's something you've done for me to help me, but I'm not going to like it?'

'Well, I don't know, maybe you will like it.'

'Why,' said Roland, laughing, drinking the last dregs of his tea, 'what have you done to help me?'

'You've just drunk magic mushroom tea,' said Terry, straight-faced.

'Bollocks!' said Roland.

Terry remained expressionless.

'You are joking... right?'

Terry shook his head, in a solemn, priestlike manner.

'You wouldn't do that,' said Roland, trying to rationalise for Terry as well as himself, 'because that would be mad, to give someone as fragile as me, in this predicament, a hallucinogenic.'

'They used to do it...' said Terry. 'They used to give patients LSD.'

'Yeah, but that was an experiment and it didn't work.'

'How do you know it didn't work?'

'Because I was in the same class as you when they said it didn't work because it made people who were crazy even more crazy.'

Terry shrugged. He was not going to debate the rights and wrongs of the research because it would be fruitless for someone who was about to go on a "trip".

'You're not joking, are you?' said Roland, beginning to wonder if it was just the power of suggestion making his body tingle.

'It's in your head,' said Terry, pointing to his own head. 'You will only do more damage to yourself if you don't escape, not just from here, but from the prison inside your head. Trust me, this is for your own good. You will thank me for it... eventually.'

Roland stared in horror at Terry, trying to read his mind, trying to get to the truth. Was this another one of his jokes? He couldn't tell. Was Terry mad enough to do it?

'You are kidding, right?' said Roland. 'This is a joke? You are just trying to freak me out... right?'

Terry stood up.

'No joke, mate.'

'Where the fuck are you going?'

'Remember,' said Terry, as he lifted himself out of the chair, 'the option's there if you want it... train to Brighton, go along the coast to Deanbeigh and ask for the boats. I'll be there, on *Praxis*.'

'You're fucking serious... you're fucking crazy!' screamed Roland. 'They'll lock me up! I can't go tripping in this place!'

'Think of it as a test,' said Terry, standing by the door.

'Remember what Dr Jonas said: it's the challenge that counts.'

Roland shut his eyes.

'Oh, my God! Oh, Jesus Christ! You crazy fucking bastard!'

'Don't panic,' said Terry. 'You'll be fine. It's nothing you haven't done before. Remember, you come up faster on tea, it's not like eating them.'

'But not in a place like this... not on my own...' pleaded Roland.

'Brighton... Deanbeigh-by-the-Sea... *Praxis*...'

And with that Terry slipped out through the door.

I don't believe it. Where the fuck is he going? He can't do that: leave me here, tripping on fucking mushrooms... what the fuck?! No. Wait. Terry was joking. He's like that. That's the sort of thing he does: always fucking joking, always trying to freak people out... that's Terry.

Roland stretched out his hand in front of him. It was real. He used his other hand to feel the flesh. No. There was something quite different, something had changed. His hand, his only hand, the one hand he used, was not really part of him, it was going away from him, moving towards the window. He pulled his hand back and it waved and echoed.

Fuck, thought Roland, *I am tripping! Or maybe I'm not. No, actually... I think I am...*

He needed a plan, a contingency, a strategy in order to mitigate the effects of the mushrooms. And perhaps he wasn't tripping? Maybe it was just the power of suggestion, planting the thought, planting the seed of paranoia.

Roland looked again at his hand. It looked and felt normal. It was in his head, then. *I think I'm tripping but I'm not really. That's more like it.* There was no way Terry would have gone that far, to drug him, to trick him. That was just crazy, the worst thing you could do to somebody.

There was a quiet tap on the door. Roland turned around as Sister Bernice entered.

'Oh,' she said, manoeuvring past Roland's suitcase, 'are you leaving us then?'

Roland stared. He was going to say something, something normal, but it did not come out... the words that were meant to come out... they did not come out...

'Are you alright?' she asked, looking quizzically, straight into Roland's eyes.

Roland nodded. That was all he could manage. Sister Bernice hovered.

'You can talk to me,' she said, 'if there's anything on your mind?'

Roland felt his head go up and down.

Sister Bernice stood there, again trying to penetrate Roland's mind, trying to fathom what was wrong, what was not quite right.

Roland had no answers. What could he tell her? Or perhaps he should tell her while he still could? *I've been poisoned. I'm not feeling very well. I need to see a doctor.* No, that was madness. He needed to keep it to himself. He needed to get through this.

'I was just checking,' she said, 'making sure you're okay. It's New Year's Eve. Not much for you to celebrate, I know, but... you know. Well, I'll pop back later, before my shift finishes.'

She looked at Roland's face again. He could see there was another question on her lips, but her mouth did not move. But she still stood there... forever... for ages. Then her face cracked. Like a broken ceramic vase, he could see the detail, fine lines shattering across her face. He blinked and then looked down. *What's happening?* He looked again at her face. It was there again, a type of veined marble, a hard, fixed stone, heartless and immovable. She knew everything now. She could see into his mind. Time was not moving; she was not moving... the fascinating face... the ugly, intransigent face was still in the air.

Then she was gone.

That was close... that was really close. He was on the edge. *Perhaps she might come back? Perhaps she's gone to get somebody? What was Terry thinking? The stupid fucking bastard! What fucking planet is that guy on?!* Yeah, he was in trouble now. It was real... it was definitely real.

So, what's the plan? How to survive? How to survive tripping out of your head on an acute psychiatric ward? There's no fucking survival guide for this.

Think, think, think... what the fuck do I do?

Think...

It's crazy to stay on the ward... madness to stay in this room...

Think...

What's best to do?

Get out!

Yes, get out of here... be out there somewhere... get away from people... stay as far away as possible... find somewhere to go... camp down somewhere, just till it passes... just till it has all gone...

But how bad will the trip be? That doesn't matter now. Just get out!

Roland stood up. He could feel the effects of the mushrooms surge through his body. His muscles twitched uncontrollably. He lurched for his suitcase, pushed it flat on the floor. His fingers touched the locks, but as he pressed down they remained stubbornly locked. He just needed something to wear... something to put on.

Fuck it!

Fucking hell... he was so fucked... so fucked...

Okay... remain calm...

Look again.

He paused. He pressed the locks. He had power. He had powers he did not realise. It was easy. As he rummaged through his clothes he became absorbed in their textures, the different fibres, the rough and the smooth.

Don't get distracted.

No. Okay. He was lucid. He felt normal. It must come in waves. He'd tripped before... he knew how to control it. *Okay... come to terms with it, accept it, don't fight it... let it take you where it goes...*

He put a thick sweatshirt on, a thin denim jacket and his shoes. But things were changing again. The trip was coming back.

He had to go. He had to get out.

He pushed open the door and looked down the corridor to the end of the ward. He could see a few self-absorbed patients but no staff. To his right, a few small steps and then he would be outside. He pushed down on the bar closing the fire exit door. It clanked open. The cold air rushed in...

Fuck, he said to himself, laughing, *I am flying tonight!*

★

Roland wandered around the hospital grounds, passing the odd patient, keeping his head down, keeping himself to himself as the trip came and went. It would grab him suddenly, force his consciousness up to a level where he thought he was going to lose all sense of reality, all certainty and all known parameters by which to understand the world around him. Then he would become lucid again, feel a firmness of mind, the confidence of the usual known qualities, the tangible and the knowable. But increasingly, rapidly, the hallucinogenic was embedding, exponentially setting new thresholds of consciousness. These new perceptions would set a new precedent, deliver the anxiety of a new insight. Each time he was climbing a ladder to a point where he felt he could not step down, where he would be lost to the world of jolting, thudding illusion and hallucination.

He had managed to walk to the boundary of Chaolla House in his desperation to avoid contact with patients and staff, then headed back towards the main hospital, back across the cricket field, then keeping to the tarmac path, passing the school of nursing, marching towards the high windows of Lilywhite Ward, before veering away and sitting on the bench outside the visitor centre.

The prison, thought Roland, what had Terry meant by the prison of his own mind? But as he tried to think, he could feel his heart rate accelerating, a new impetus, a new injection which felt like a dose of adrenaline flooding his arteries and veins. Roland looked to the side and examined the detail of the ironwork of the old bench. It was intense, incredibly detailed. The flakes of metal glowed, and began to move from a fixed position. The whole structure rose up. The ironwork twisted and contorted before arching over his head. The bench was coming to life. Each atom, molecule and particle released from the rigid rules of life. Like a garden pagoda, the fibrous tentacles formed all around him. Like a caged bird, he sat inside. He was transfixed. He knew these things… these things in front of him. There were lights within the tapestry of bending iron, lights which glowed within a thin pinpoint before exploding into colour. There were roses, pink and red roses. The petals appeared at every angle as the iron cage stared down, fusing, firing, burning. They burst into flames, like flickering gas lights.

Fear gripped him. Fear of being inside the prison. It was real. It was there… yes, he could see it was there. But it was the wrong way to be, inside the burning world, inside the box. He shut his eyes. He hoped it would go away, but he was still inside. He had to escape. He needed to be in the real world. He wanted to break back into reality.

I think I need help, he said to himself. Or did he say it out loud?

Turn away.

Run.

Quick… run and hide.

Yes, I must run.

I must escape.

He looked back towards the visitor centre. Did the patients see him? He looked closely. He looked closely at their faces. Then they morphed. Their faces cracked, just like Sister Bernice's, into ceramic lines.

I must run. I must hide. I must escape from the prison.

He wanted to stand, but his body was stuck. Was the prison still there? Yes, it glowed... the ironwork glowed.

I must stand. I must run.

Roland fell forward, landing on the cold stone paving. It seemed to break the spell. He stood up.

Run... run and hide.

But his legs did not move. *What's wrong with my legs? I think I need help.*

I must run.

Run.

Run.

Run.

And... whoosh!

The air took him.

Roland was off like a rocket, his legs thrashing the ground, galloping, riding, pounding... his legs moving faster and faster, thumping the ground, beating the ground... his heart pumping, his blood pulsing, his mind running. But there was no control. He was out of control, heading back towards the woods, towards the boundary...

I will die.

I will die again.

Roland lurched towards his fate, spiralling madly towards what little time and future he had left. Running

527

down the life clock, rapidly moving through time... to finish what he had failed to do.

To where the end is in sight...

Thwack!

Fuck!

'Six... one-five... one-five... one-two...'

Roland stopped.

Starr stood in his way.

Roland swayed as he tried to regain his composure. Starr stared back, sweating profusely as Roland tried to focus.

'Six... one-five... one-five... one-two...'

Six... one-five... one-five... one-two, thought Roland. *Yes... six... one-five... one-five... one-two...*

And Roland laughed, moved forward to touch the bulbous frog man. But his hands were nowhere near where Starr should be. Fumbling forwards, his face went closer to his body, closer still, before laughing again.

'You saved me...' Roland blurted out, like a drunk, his head still reeling from running.

Starr looked down at the cold, wet grass, rummaged in his tracksuit pocket, and held out his hand.

'Star,' said Starr.

Roland looked at Starr's hand. A bright and shining light, a dense and tiny ball shined inexplicably. *So much light*, thought Roland.

Starr's hand remained extended as he offered the light.

'Star,' said Starr again.

Roland reached out and felt Starr's clammy hand and the smooth object in it. He felt Starr's hand close tightly around his, holding him there, keeping him there, passing something to him. Roland held it up in his fingers and watched it glow with organic life. There was something else that needed to happen, thought Roland, something he should give Starr in a fair exchange.

'This is for you,' he said, as he pulled from his pocket the piece of paper he had folded into quarters.

Starr giggled, snatched the paper and then ran, galloping, heading for the woods. Roland was not meant to go there, the worst place to be. But somehow everything felt right, correct, in place, combined and conjoined with Starr, his mutual friend, his ally. They were on the same side, on the same level. It made sense to follow... to follow the galloping Starr.

He thought he would stop at the fence that formed the boundary of the woods, but he seemed to fly over, drift effortlessly through and over the wire.

'How long will I be a part of you?' asked Roland.

And Starr giggled.

And Roland followed.

CHAPTER 46

SMITHY PALACE

Roland was in pursuit, chasing the sound of the pounding Starr, conscious of his breath, the hot breath smoking from his mouth. As he ran, the hot air was the hot air of a horse. Yes, he was galloping like a mysterious horse, following the leader, the thumping, bumping Starr, trekking effortlessly through the frozen woods, who knew all the secret tracks, who was synthesised with the earth, the foliage, the trees and the undergrowth. There was no fear, no trepidation; Starr was his guide to a way out of this madness. Then they stopped and diverted into a patch of ground which Roland felt he already knew. Starr said nothing and just looked. What was he supposed to see? There was nothing. But as he waited, waited for his eyes to focus, so he began to see what Starr wanted him to see. This was it, the place where he had tried to end it all, where probably he would have died if it wasn't for the intervention of Starr. He knew now for sure, the mad, crazy fool, the one person who seemed to have no sense, the lovable child who made everyone crazy with his inane mutterings and phrases, it was Starr who had somehow managed to carry him back to the hospital.

'I know,' said Roland, looking down at the ground remorsefully.

It seemed sufficient recognition as Starr headed off again, this time through the foliage, through the denser parts of the wood. Roland trotted behind, doing his best to keep up whilst Starr brushed aside the obstacles of thick undergrowth. He must not lose him, thought Roland, because he would go crazy left alone in the woods. But suddenly Starr disappeared; the dark shadow vanished. Had he gone through into another world, into another dimension? Roland panicked and rushed forward, kicking aside the dense growth, clawing his way through, his legs struggling in a thick treacle, breathing, wanting to shout out to make Starr stop.

Then Roland stumbled, pushed forward through the wooded barrier, out into an opening, falling, pushing out his hands to stop his fall, collapsing on to something soft. There was light, a bright moonlit night. How bright everything was, how sharp and defined the thin lines of grasses. And there was Starr in front of him, staring up at the night sky too, the pinpricks of real stars illuminating, crowding around the full circle of the moon.

Roland picked himself up. There was calmness about the clearing. He moved towards Starr, who moved backwards, keeping his distance. Then Starr was off again, turning and galloping. There was something there, something solid, but not quite solid. And he could hear

Starr running, baying like a horse. Roland concentrated, forcing his tripping mind to focus. Starr was out there in the dark. Then it became obvious; Roland knew where he was, where he had been before, with Sophie, another type of sanctuary, another type of ending: the old abbey. Feeling with his hands and his legs, fumbling along the sides of the stumps of the wall, there was sufficient outline for Roland to navigate as he listened to Starr running, running he sensed around the circumference of the foundations. He could also hear a strange, rhyming mantra, which Starr repeated, the rhyming getting nearer, the pounding, clodhopping feet, and the mantra, repeating and repeating. Roland stood still as he felt the thunderous rocket brush by him, the fast train rushing through. He remained still, listening intently to Starr's voice:

> *'The mad misfits and mavericks*
> *Who only know the half of it*
> *They clean them up and wash them down,*
> *The mad misfits and mavericks!'*

It made sense, had some sense and logic to it, in all the madness, the psychosis and Roland's induced psychosis. And strangely, although Roland was not entirely sure, but he was fairly sure, so he thought, things were becoming more lucid, less hectic. Yes, a definite calmness, for no tangible reason (and not that there was any reason in anything), he decided it was due to the old abbey, its presence, its ancient bond with healing. In order to avoid being run over by Starr, in order to seek the calm sanctuary of the old abbey, Roland continued to feel his way along the broken walls, the crumbly flint and stone, the grains of old mortar flaking away and sticking to his fingers. There was a route and purpose, an aim, to once more walk through the door, back to the place where he had had the weird dream, back to where he had fucked Sophie under the old oak tree, back to the place where she had been cured.

He stood just inside the interior and looked up at the sparkling night sky. There was complete calm now, a comforting warmth and security. He looked down at the floor and the ground was gently moving in a slow, rippling effect of jagged stone, tufts of grass and weed. Then Roland fell against the thick stump of the old oak tree. He pushed himself up, so his back rested against the brittle bark. *At last*, he thought, *some sanity*. What a crazy, mad, fucked up thing Terry had done to him. *I will never forgive him for this, but I might just survive, I might just get through it if I stay here for the night, out of sight, out of harm's way, with the revolving, bubbling rhyme machine as my guide.*

Roland rested his head between his knees, squeezed his eyes, and colours began to burst out from behind his eyelids. He was still tripping, but how much further did he have to go, how long would these fucking mushrooms last? He had no sense of time. It was just night, just dark. He was lost in time, suspended in the moment, floating through a haze of extended ends. There was no end… no end ever. Time was going on, on and on. *Does it ever stop? It stops for us. It stops us living. It works against us. It gives us life and then stops our life. It says, "You have had enough time, now it is time to stop and to come to an end." It elongates the agony, it fuses life with pleasure and drags out the indeterminate*

nothingness. Starr was right not to look at the Clock Tower…
it has the face of time… the ugly face of time.

Starr revved up his engine. A *brum-brum* sound powered
the gyrating leg motors. *No more a horse then,* thought
Roland, as the motor car screeched around the corner of
the old abbey. Starr got nearer, near to where Roland sat,
so the engine roared again: *brummm… brummm…* and the
pistons pumped. Roland sniffed, coughed. It was odd, but
he could smell the fumes, the exhaust and petrol. And then
a rhyme, as Starr passed by again:

> '*Annie B, Annie B*
> *Swimming in the dead Red Sea,*
> *You had no hope, for you and me,*
> *You had no hope, to try and be.*'

Christ! Fuck! What does that fucking idiot know? Roland tried
to stand. He wanted to get a grip on things, he wanted
to stop this. This was enough! Who the fuck was Starr?
How could he say these things? But as Roland tried to
stand, so his legs gave way. There was no strength. He was
tied to the ground, tied to the tree. It was his place to be,
to listen to the meandering mantras of the omnipresent
Starr. And that was the last thing he needed to hear… to
be reminded about Annie Buchanan. He had done what
he could. He tried to do more than most, he thought.
Or did he? Had he failed her, Annie Buchanan? Had
he feared the consequences? Had he, when it actually
came down to it, done what everybody else did: turn
away, ignore the injustice, the suffering? But what else
could he have done? He was compromised, in a difficult

position, an impossible position. But had he betrayed her? Had he done just the thing he accused everybody else of doing? *Where is the truth in all of this... where is clarity, where are the clear definitions, the boundary, the fence, the protection against all the vile and ugly things of life?*

Stop. Stop right now. He had to stop. His brain was going to explode. He couldn't carry on like this... no one could live their life like this, constantly questioning, constantly doubting. *There must be some certainties? There must be some things that are tangible, something to hold on to as a truth? Or is that the lesson: there is nothing fixed or tangible, all is fleeting, nuanced, pale and bright, grey and coloured? What is fixed is only temporary, briefly knowable, then moves on, transforms and changes.*

Starr continued to whizz around, pumping the ground, pounding the four corners of the walls with his elated chants, his mechanised vehicle and his pounding messages. *Is it better*, wondered Roland, *to be hidden away in a permanent psychosis?* Was that where he belonged, back on the wards, back with the patients? Was there a logic to choosing madness? No, freedom, that was what Terry said, or something like that. Yes, he needed to break free. He needed to learn how to be free. He needed to learn how to fight. It was not enough to have the fight in him. There was more to it... a lot more. Although, it should be simple... injustice is easy to see but doing something about it is not simple... full of pitfalls, full of dangers, full of deep, dark holes to fall into. And he had fallen into one great big gaping hole. Like a blind fucking idiot, he had let people make a fool out of him. Humiliated by everyone: Sophie, Dr Jonas, Douglas, Fitzpatrick, Slaney... they had all had a go, a piece of him. And why… why did they do that? He was innocent. And yet, they all thought they could use him, take him down a peg or two, as if he had no right to breathe, no right to be human.

Perhaps it did come down to one thing? The one thing he hated, the one word he feared, the one thing he had sworn he would never be: naïve. But why was Sophie not honest with him? Or could he not see… could he not see that he was the oppressor? He was part of the truth, the real truth, the inability to be sexually free. He was too rigid. He was too fixed. He was unable to truly see. He was just holding her back, stopping her from becoming, stopping Sophie from expressing… for all of his own selfish reasons, because he was afraid of losing love, of being on his own again and back where he started from.

Then everything stopped. The mad rush of his internal voice, his rambling thinking came to an end. A stillness, a void, a vacuum.

Was it waiting, waiting for him… to take him?

Then Starr's voice came loud and clear, no longer running, no longer pounding:

> *'You cannot see, you cannot see,*
> *You cannot see beneath the tree.'*

'What… what can't I see?' shouted Roland.
Again, Starr repeated the phrase:

> *'You cannot see, you cannot see,*
> *You cannot see beneath the tree.'*

Beneath the tree… what was beneath the tree?

Roland pushed out his hands and touched the ground. He felt the hard, frosty stubble of the roots he sat on. He moved his hands in a semicircular motion, sweeping the ground around him, searching for something. But as he swept with his hands, his arms began to take on a life of their own. He began to feel his arms separating, losing control, divorcing from his body. He pulled them back, but the ground was softer, taking his hands, the power moving up to his arms, taking over his limbs. The ground was taking him. Roland jumped, pushed himself back against the old oak tree. *Fuck! Fuck! I must be tripping again.* He spun round, rolling around the bark of the tree, falling into something, hitting something large and hard, falling on to his back, thumping the ground as he fell. *Please do not take me*, he said to himself, *to the earth, to the musty soil.*

'Please do not take me,' he said again, fearful he was going down, back down into the earth, into the start of it all, back down into the last bits of life, the degeneration and crumbling entropy. He wanted to shout, shout for help, but nothing came out. He fumbled on the ground, looking up at the night sky, the stunning stars, the bright moon, the shining stars, coming through, communicating, letting him know…

Something… about… the body… was there… was… a body…

Hanging there, beneath the tree…

Fuck! Fucking shit! Fuck, fuck, fuck…

Death, stillness of the dead man, hanging beneath the tree.

Then, more silence… a reprieve, a lucidity, a spark of something, a handle to grip… a lifeline. *Let us just see. Let us just look.*

Roland lay on his back and he could feel something press into his thigh… a memory, a reminder of the lump, the gift from Starr. *Of course, it all makes sense, it does make sense to bring me here. Now I understand, to help, to rescue, to revive, to bring back to life where life has no meaning, because I am life, a life-giver, a provider of the breath which must be offered to the dead and dying.*

He sunk to his knees, clasped his hands in prayer and felt the tears run down his cheeks. Starr whimpered, a childlike noise, short, pitying bursts. Above Roland the patient twisted, a half-corkscrew, the rope hanging on to the burden of its weight. Roland pitched forward so now he was on his knees. He felt in his pocket for the power of the star, for the metaphysical things that brought life into being. Like an offering, he held in the palm of his cupped hands the star to help heal and bring relief. With mucus dripping down his nose, a few tears dropping from his face, he tried his best to help. He held his pose in a fragile state, quivering, begging, seeking forgiveness, seeking a way to do something, to cure things, to make things right again. If he looked up, perhaps, to see the face, the chance to see the face, so he could see, so he was looking at the face with no fear, because he had seen death, death looking down on him, which he could now see as he looked into his eyes… so he could see – distorted, but known… now ugly… but it was… *I am sure… I think… who now speaks… which oozes out…*

'I am oak, stretching from the root of the tree to the

538

end of the leaf, stretching from the beginning of life to the end of my seed. The drip-drip, tick-tock of the acorn, the spiral earth feeding drain, putting life into being, into self. The slow strain of transformation, the rapid rise of the sap in my veins, the sudden burst of my new life, the new form, the new transformation, my transmigration, my negation of my negation. You, who are searching for truths where there are no truths, where there is no substance. All that flows through our hands are grains of sand which will refuse to be determinate.

'Let the contradictory ape flare up and flap its arse at the gravedigger. Nonchalant nodding in the vacuum of madness, belly-up and suck the muck and crane the effort into format, form and flowing grown cradle. You resent deceit when you are the creator of that deceit. You have determined they can only move within the framework of their own channel, and you leave them with no choice but to move within the channel of a swollen deceit. The propensity for deceit on the alienated planet, where rocks and meteors thrash and beat the pulse of stars and pending moons.

'The impact of betrayal drives the green fuse and drives the flower through the potting hole into the sand-quick. My friend, it is a contradictory consciousness, the contradictory nature of things, the contradictory burden of unseen truths, of partial sight, of partial knowing, of partially seen glimpses of movement towards the light. When all that is solid seeks melting air and harbours on the shore of some unlikely truth, do not live there, do not believe in safe havens, but desert calls and calling for the trumpet sounding out: I am coming, I am coming.

'Negligent and soiled, unholy and unknown, unworthy and filled with bags of sin, constantly moving truth has no need for wisdom… wise old owl who props up the old oak branch and swoops down on the little creatures… wise old owl who flutters in the moonlit night, craving insight… no wisdom in the corners of the cave, in the crawling vaults and caverns where all wisdom is too late, when all we need is the predator death knell, the revolutionary ark setting sail from the safe dock of cauldron. Zombie ideas, dead ideas that live forever. Barbarity breeds barbarity, the barbarous nub which contorts on the edge of humanity, groping amazement which shows no understanding of the shock.

'From no hope and despair comes the destructive angel, the angel of death, where bombs and guns scream out, where blood and ambulances scream and shout. Move left ultra-seeking and terror stalks the vanguards in their sleeping. Blame runs down the red rivers and spills their monsters into the veins of viewing; obscure psychopathy breeds its entangled nonsense and sets blame against blame, makes cause a defiant, obscure, wanting child who is insatiable and unable to be fed. Make sure you know, make sure you know where the strategy lies and forbid the existence of short answers. Brains are made of thick wire, bulky substance, thought has lived for ages and made the long thought-out cases. Think, live and feed on the essence of existence, transform in the long seas of intelligence and avoid the crowd calling immediacy of short answers, blood red terror and the mangled morality of conscience. Think it through the prism of complexity, delve into the books of library, listen to the wise owl who swoops down from the wooded woods and has grains of wisdom stuffed within its flapping feathers. Wise owl and eagle, mega thought and long, plodding hard work, that is where it lifts its lost head and asks for silence and the parapet to be cured of nonsense. If you can spell it out, spell it out. If you know the answer now then tell me the answer now, or else you are a fool...'

Yes, thought Roland, *I must spell it out:*

X
A
R
M
I
S
M

Then the face stretched out, moving at a rapid rate, towards another shape; a bird-like shape, a beak forming from the end of the nose, coming out, an eagle flying out, flapping his wings, ready to go, ready to fly.

Run.

Run.

Run.

Whoosh!

A roar, a stupendous rush forced Roland suddenly back into the ground. His legs were draining away into the soil. He put his hands out to stop sinking into quicksand. He lifted his head. He needed to breathe. He was suddenly shooting up, rising up, tall and elegant, rising above everything, rising above the trees, the stars and the moon. Roland pushed up with his arms as he still held the star in his fingers. It shone brightly again, sparkling, sending out radiating rays. It was full of life, of substance and meaning. It had come from the distant stars, so Roland realised, it had come from the universe. It had powers beyond anything anyone could know. Yes, Roland could see that now. Starr was right.

Roland steadied himself, adopting a pose that meant he could now walk forwards, watching the star held tightly in front of him, holding the icon open for blessings. He had a mission, it was clear, as clear as day, as clear as night. He must deliver the cure to alleviate the pain.

CHAPTER 47

AS I LAY DOWN

Roland trod his path through the woods, back over the wire fence, around the nurses' hostel and the visitor centre, before veering off towards Lilywhite Ward. This was where the cure must start, he had decided; this was where he must deliver the unadulterated energy, the life force of the universe.

He slid along the side of the walls of the ward, looking in through the high windows at the dirge of life left over on New Year's Eve. The quiet pace of nothingness slumbered in their chairs, mumbling along in drifting thoughts, anxiously fumbling in corners. Roland held up the star and pressed it against the window. It glowed, emanating light and rejuvenating therapy, offering hope against adversity, offering change against stagnation, offering a silver light in the dark ray of cloud, offering goodness, empathy… love.

'Mr Cauldron!'

Roland shuddered.

'Mr Cauldron!'

It was the voice of Fitzpatrick.

Fuck… not now.

He had one chance, one chance if he was to be free before it was too late, before he became the way they wanted him to be. He needed to run, but he felt the breath of Fitzpatrick, the physicality of Fitzpatrick, the gigantic claws of the man coming down to lay his hands on his shoulders, pressing him down into the gravel.

'You, young man, what are you doing?'

Roland collapsed; the shock, the trauma. He was trapped, caught. The life force dissipated in a second. He fell into the cold, stony ground, face down in the wet and the dirt… but he must keep the star (the only hope) and thrust it into his pocket.

'I said,' barked Fitzpatrick, 'what do you think you are doing?'

Roland struggled, wriggled, fumbling to break free from the pressure pushing down on him. He had to get up, he had to break free, manoeuvre and release.

He felt two hands on his shoulder move and then turn him over. He looked up at the face, the cracked and marbled face of Fitzpatrick.

'Get up!' commanded Fitzpatrick, as he hauled the shaking Roland on to his knees. 'Get up and on to your feet.'

Roland shivered for a few seconds, limply managing to stand on his jelly-like pins. Fitzpatrick took a step back, scrutinising Roland in the difficult light.

'What are you doing out here?' quizzed Fitzpatrick. 'You're a patient now and you belong on the ward.'

Roland shuddered. He thought he was shaking his head, but he was not sure. He needed his legs to move, but he was not sure. He needed something to move… so he could run.

Fitzpatrick banged on the window, catching the attention of Sister Bernice.

If he did not do something now, he was fucked… totally fucked.

He held up both his hands and pushed his weight into Fitzpatrick, pushing him away, pushing him further and pushing him back. Fitzpatrick stumbled and fell heavily on the mud and gravel. Roland pounced and pushed down so he was staring into the heart of the man.

'There… is… nothing… wrong… with… me,' said Roland, pronouncing every word, shooting true and accurate bullets into his nemesis.

Time…

He looked strange, thought Roland, in the suspended moment. Not the great, fearful monster. There was something vulnerable about him. For a brief second, the true face of Fitzpatrick (a scared face, a worried face, an unhappy face) revealed itself. This was the moment of truth, he thought, the metaphysical moment he had been waiting for: behind all the mad authoritarianism was just a sad, vulnerable, insecure man, a cog in the wheel, part of the machine, no more in control than the mad Starr he left running around the old abbey.

'We're all the same,' said Roland. 'If I'm a patient, what the fuck do you think you are?'

But the transparency in Fitzpatrick's face dissipated, as a grim anger fused across his heavyset brow. He tried to reach up, to hold on to Roland, the last symbol of everything that was wrong.

'You need to be controlled, to be kept in check, to be kept in order,' spat Fitzpatrick into Roland's face. 'You are a cancer…'

Roland was enraged. He had given him a chance to be human, to be honest, and he had thrown it back in his face.

'Sister Bernice!' shouted Fitzpatrick.

Roland felt more hands grab him and pull him up.

'Hold him there!' roared Fitzpatrick, who was struggling to his feet.

'It's alright, Roland, just calm down,' said Sister Bernice, who stood at Roland's side, holding his hand.

Roland shook his head. He couldn't stay. There was no reason for him to stay. He pulled his hand away and stepped back, back from the approaching Fitzpatrick.

'Please…' said Sister Bernice, begging Roland just to wait, to hold on.

But Roland was moving away, moving on. He was going now. It was all over, finished with. There was nothing more to keep him here.

'I am free,' said Roland quietly.

He took a few steps back. He watched closely for any sudden movements to bring him back. But there was something holding him… another restraint. Roland looked down and could see a thin thread of cotton. He followed the line back to Sister Bernice. Fuck, she was holding his wrist bandage. He thrashed his hands up and down, moving back from every step Fitzpatrick made towards him.

'Please…' said Sister Bernice again. 'Please wait, Roland… let Mr Fitzpatrick help you.'

Roland shook his head. But the bandage kept going on and on, as he frantically flapped his arms up and down. They were both coming for him, walking stealthily, ready to pounce and restrain him. There was only one chance, one way out, one more thing to add:

'Franks is dead,' said Roland, 'you stupid fucking bastards!'

And the thread unravelled, became looser, unravelling, no longer holding or restraining. This was his moment.

Run!

Roland turned, his legs like sludge, treading through quicksand, running like a snail, running away.

Run!

And he ran till he got to the entrance to Wellington Park.

Now... go!

And he burst forwards.

This was it, he was escaping, he was running, he was going to be free.

And on, past the old gate... keep on running... they're probably behind you... keep on running... keep going and you will be free...

He looked to his left, at the bright light from the entrance to the social club. He could hear the music bellowing out, and he looked behind him as he kept running, and there was no one there. He kept going and turned the corner, down the old road, along the side of the street with pavement.

Perhaps he was safe? He felt exhausted. His legs were giving way and he slowed to a walking pace. He looked up and used the lamp post ahead of him as a marker point, his next destination. He focused on the glowing orange neon light. But as he walked he had no sense the lamp post was getting nearer. He looked at the pavement and watched his legs moving. He looked at the lamp post again, but he was not getting closer. He quickened his pace, but the speed he walked made no difference. He was on a conveyor belt, unable to move forwards, stationary whilst running. He concentrated on the lamp post again. Surely, he should be there now? But everything was moving against him, pushing him backwards. He had to get off… off the never-ending treadmill which was holding him back.

He looked to the side of the pavement and threw himself into a field full of tall, wet grasses. He shut his eyes and waited for the constant motion to stop. What should he do now? He was still out of control. The trip was still a powerful motor. He opened his eyes, and by the side of him a tall, incandescent thistle pulsated its purple core.

He weighed up his options. Could he make it any further? Could he walk along the streets without attracting attention? Or should he knock on somebody's door, explain he was unwell, needing help and could they phone for an ambulance? Or was there another option? What had Terry said? Get a train to Brighton… Deanbeigh… *Praxis*… a safe haven.

There was only one way to freedom. Along the suburban streets, follow the path of the bus, don't get on the bus, just walk, keep your head down and try to look normal.

He stepped back on to the pavement. The conveyor belt had stopped. He kept his head down and followed the line of the pavement. He turned a corner and he was heading back, back to town and the train station, back along the route of the 174.

Roland put all his energy, all his concentration into his long march. He knew it was three miles, but he was free... free of everything.

As cars came towards him they thundered and echoed, reverberated in his ears. But he kept going – he was not going to be defeated, he was going to fight this, to get a grip and get a control of things. He began to recognise bits and pieces of reality. He was beginning to make sense of the world. His mind was no longer blasted. The trip was at last easing off. He knew, he was sure, he would make it and be free.

★

Roland was going the wrong way for anybody to be on the train because they were all heading into London for the New Year celebrations. He had no ticket, but there was no way a guard would chuck him off now; his next stop was Brighton. He had no idea if there were going to be repercussions from tonight... but what had he done wrong? Would they come after him, track him down and section him? Perhaps he would have to go into hiding? Who knows? But he felt a keen sense of triumph... he had succeeded against all the odds.

He enjoyed this moment on the train, quietly congratulating himself over and over again. Yes, yes, yes... he had done it: he had escaped from that fucked up institution... he had escaped from the insidious claws of Fitzpatrick, from the pernicious power of Slaney and the perverted legitimacy of Caldwell. He had been on a crazy trip, experienced something close to psychosis, perhaps even listened to the words of a dead man…

But he was tired, exhausted. He was close to sleep and shut his eyes and drifted… drifted with the clatter of the train, the steady motion of the forward movement, taking him away from harm, towards something else…

★

Roland could feel the cold now… cold, exhaustion and shivering. He sunk his body down into the pebbles on the beach, making a small dip in which to hide his body, to keep his flesh cocooned in the knobbly, hard stone. Behind him, higher up on the pebble beach, the sail ropes of the small catamarans were clanking in the wind, ringing out a thrashing bell, lashing a sing-less tune. He could hear the rushing of the sea, the brushing of the waves on the shore. A few voices shouted out into the night, drunken voices that signalled the end of their celebrations. The hotels sat up behind the promenade and shed light down, but they did not cast enough light out into the sea, the flowing, frothing, cold fluid.

Roland pushed his hands into his pockets, hoping this would help retain some warmth. He felt the strange stone, the magic star sitting in his pocket. He had no idea why he had done what he had done. *That's what you do when you go tripping off your head*, he thought. Still, lying in the stones, in the pebbles, it only made sense to lay it down amongst all the others.

Was there anything else left to do, other than wait? No. He would wait, wait until the day woke. For now, he would just lie here, decode, decipher and then start again.

CHAPTER 48

THE RETIREMENT OF MRS FLAMEY

The retirement of Mrs Flamey was a well-kept secret; only Slaney and Fitzpatrick knew the date of her last day at Wellington Park. A new year and a new beginning was the only reason she had given to Slaney for taking early retirement. In truth, she had longed for the day, desperate at times to relieve herself of the drudgery of typing, filing and telephoning on behalf of others. During all her years at the hospital she was someone who had slipped seamlessly in and out of work, barely noticed, hardly commented upon. It was the way she liked it because she had no desire to be visible in such a peculiarly nasty and vindictive workplace. She had also specifically requested there was to be no fuss, no drinks, cards or any such thing which resembled an acknowledgement of her leaving her job as personal secretary to the interim chief executive… that was the way she wanted it.

Fortunately, Slaney had supported her request by attending a chief executives' conference on her last day (all the despised in one place, so Mrs Flamey thought), with the minimum requirement that she type some letters left on his Dictaphone from the night before. One more day of drudgery, servility, and then she would be free. It merely required one passing shot, the icing on the cake, to achieve a sense of fulfilment, purpose and meaning, having her head down all those years whilst all around her lost theirs.

Therefore, she had assiduously accumulated evidence of all the petty scrabbling, all the politics permeating the institution. She knew of hundreds of incidents, accidents, crises, disasters, which she had logged just for safekeeping. She knew all the latest gossip on the troubled young man Roland Cauldron, his suicide attempt, his stay on Lilywhite Ward over Christmas and the fight he had (so they said) with Fitzpatrick and the sister on the ward. She knew Gobi had been called in and castigated by both Slaney and Fitzpatrick for the "appalling behaviour" of this "militant student", which was just another sign the school was going to have to close sooner rather than later.

In fact, she was already typing a letter to Roland's parents, informing them they would be forwarding his belongings as they were unable to locate his whereabouts. She would have liked to have added a few words of her own: how she sympathised with the youthful spirit, the enthusiasm of trying to change things, the lack of jadedness and debilitating calculation. She had also heard all the gossip about the drug-taking going on in the nurses' hostel, the sexual shenanigans which went on with people jumping in and out of bed. She had also heard the young man had been a bit of a victim in that department, taken for a ride by one of the students, who, it was rumoured, had also once had a liaison with Slaney. *Well, that's the only way you learn*, she thought to herself.

There were a few other letters to type: Slaney obviously taking her at her word and treating the day as just another working day. At least there were no scheduled phone calls or appointments to make. She had never got used to using the phone, hated voicemail messages even more and never answered the phone in her own flat.

Given that it was her last day, she felt relaxed enough to sit back and gaze out of her window for a few moments over the small courtyard. Slaney would often stare into the same neglected space and so she would only gaze if she knew he was elsewhere. It was a pale, barren piece of tranquillity, which probably once had more purpose and function, as was the case with all that was left of Wellington Park. It was a great shame such a building was going to come to an end, gutted except for the façades – so she had noted in one of the meetings.

By lunchtime she had all of Slaney's letters typed and ready for signature. She placed each letter within the flap of an appropriately sized envelope and walked along the corridor to his office, so they were ready for signature in the morning. She unlocked the office door (Slaney only left a key with Mrs Flamey when he attended conferences or when he was on annual leave), and placed the letters on his desk in an order that represented the order of dictation. As she was about to return, she heard the door creak slightly, immediately detecting the presence of Fitzpatrick.

'Hello, Michael,' she said, without turning, as she lined up Slaney's letters in a perfect rectangular pile.

'Mrs Flamey,' said Fitzpatrick, as he entered and shut the door behind him.

She remained with her back to him, pretending to perform her office duties.

'I know you're not one for ceremony,' he said, standing a few yards back, 'but I thought I might just catch you, before you go, to wish you all the best.'

She turned around, smiled, then turned her back on him. She had nothing to say and he of all people should know that!

'Well,' said Fitzpatrick, realising his error, 'I wish you well and would like to thank you for all the work you've done… for…'

Then Fitzpatrick faltered.

Mrs Flamey nodded, in recognition of Fitzpatrick's attempts to say goodbye, farewell, or whatever it was meant to be. He huffed under his breath and left.

What an odious man, she said to herself. Men were bad enough, the cause of all the troubles in the world, but there were some men who excelled at being ugly and domineering. They clearly had no conscience in regards to all the damage they did, all their bullying, fear and dread they used in order to command and rule. The sadists, as she liked to call them, the Morten Slaneys and Fitzpatricks of this world, thrived on being heartless, insensitive and cruel. And for what purpose? It was all rather meaningless.

Mrs Flamey slipped back into her office and sat down at her desk for lunch. From her drawer she took out a kitchen roll and unwound two sheets, which she laid on her desk in an exact central position. Also from her drawer, she took out her plastic lunchbox and placed her salt and pepper pots on the right-hand corner of the kitchen roll. From inside the lunchbox she extracted a sealed plastic knife and fork and placed these on the left-hand side. Inside the lunchbox was a smaller container which she removed, peeled back the lid and exposed to the air: her rice, chicken and salad. She had her routines, she knew that, and that was why she liked to be alone, because it had no impact on others.

After lunch, there was little left for her to do. Slaney had said she could put the phone on voicemail if she wanted to go early. There were only a few things she was going to take with her: a few domestic items and a signed photo of Marlene Dietrich.

She unlocked the three-storey metal filing cabinet (she was the only one who had a key), and from the top drawer pulled out a can of polish and a clean yellow duster. She was fastidious about cleanliness and did not want her replacement to feel she worked in a filthy office. She had offered to provide an induction for her successor, but Slaney was keen to leave a gap between "present and future". *So be it*, she had thought, as she envisioned the pressure and oppression that would be coming their way.

She dusted the shelves full of black A4 box folders (with various references in marker pen), and the sides and front of the metal filing cabinet.

Soon, there was no point in waiting any longer. Her time had come… the final day and her last minutes. From the bottom drawer of the filing cabinet she extracted four fairly bulky envelopes. They had already been addressed and postage applied. As she left, she placed the keys to the filing cabinet on her desk, then without looking back, walked outside into the corridor.

She always came and went by the back entrance to the hospital. It was easier to park her car and meant she could slip in and out without people indulging in irrelevant greetings or conversation. She passed a few patients on her way, no more aware of her presence than in the twenty-plus years she had been here. As she pushed through the plastic curtain doors to the cold outside she breathed a sigh of relief, a deep sigh, savouring the moment. She had done it – one way or another, she had done it! All over now, all over apart from one more thing...

As she drove around the hospital she looked keenly at the old building: the Clock Tower above her head, the thick red brickwork and the spidery wards that stuck out. If they could preserve Auschwitz, she thought, why not Wellington Park? Why desecrate a building that had a story to tell? She was going to fix it and put a stop to all the machinations of men like Slaney. They might rise to the top, and most of them might stay there, but if she could bring one or two of them down, it would have been worth it.

The postbox was just outside the hospital grounds, a few yards from the social club. As she posted each envelope, she smiled: one for the editor of the local newspaper, one for the local councillor, one for the MP and one for the minister for the department of health. There was enough evidence, she thought, enough documentation to have Slaney hung, drawn and quartered, to put Dr Caldwell back in his box and to force Fitzpatrick to retire early.

CHAPTER 49

THE FINAL ASSIGNATION

Morten Slaney had been driving around for long enough, considering all he wanted to do was fuck Imogen. He did not want to waste any more time and accelerated with a forcefulness that startled her. She kept quiet as they sped along through the back lanes criss-crossing the green-belt countryside south of Wellington Park. Slaney braked hard and reversed with his usual haste down a muddy track. It was mid-afternoon and the curved cover of hedge and tree seemed to be exactly what he was looking for, with no obvious pathway that might disturb their assignation. Imogen was less impressed and looked through the hedgerow at a soulless steel structure, a leftover from some failed industrial enterprise.

'Are you sure it's alright here?' asked Imogen, sighing.

Slaney stared ahead, keeping an eye on the bottom of the track.

'We're not here to admire the scenery,' he said, looking to his left and right.

Imogen scowled.

'Anyway, that's an old slaughterhouse,' said Slaney,

nodding in Imogen's direction. 'You could hear the pigs squealing in the morning when I was training.'

'That's horrible,' said Imogen, who glanced again through her side of the car window at the hideous structure, its corrugated aluminium sides painted a dark camouflaged green.

'That's life, but don't let it put you off,' said Slaney, who was keen to get down to business.

'Well, we don't have to do anything,' she said, still staring at the desolate entity outside.

That, thought Slaney, was not an option… he was going to fuck her.

'Have you applied for another job yet?' he asked, keen to know when she would be out of his life.

She sighed, which meant she had, but she did not feel like telling Slaney anything.

'When's the interview?'

'I haven't got an interview yet,' she said, examining two wide car tracks in the mud.

'You've got a good chance.'

'Why, because of you?'

Slaney laughed.

'Well, you're a good nurse and you need to grab the opportunities when they come along.'

'What if I apply for something here instead?' she said, feeling increasingly petulant.

'Don't waste your time,' said Slaney, almost as an instruction. 'This place is closing… there's no future here.'

'We all know it's closing,' she said, in the same way that everyone else said they knew it was closing, 'but that won't happen for years.'

'Sooner than you think,' said Slaney. 'Caldwell will keep his little empire, but the rest of it is going.'

Imogen was going to reply, but then thought there was really no point in saying anything.

A car drove past the access point and Slaney watched it continue on down the curving country lane. He breathed deeply, in and out, his muscular chest stretching the taut cotton of his shirt. Another car followed, zipping along the lanes. Slaney watched through the hedgerows until it was also out of sight.

'I've got to get out,' said Imogen. 'I need to pee.'

Slaney frowned.

'I'll keep my eye out,' she said, as she unlocked the car door.

She inspected the ground for an area where her heels could be supported before deciding to tiptoe towards a dense area of hedge and foliage. She whipped her knickers down and crouched. As she urinated into the muddy trough, keeping her eye on the flow, she looked up to see if Slaney was watching. His eyes were still firmly fixed on the track and country lane ahead. With her bladder empty she tiptoed her way back to the car. Slaney was still transfixed, preoccupied…

'Do you think I'm paranoid?' he asked obliquely.

'What, in general, or at this precise moment?'

Slaney ignored her.

'My ex-secretary…' he said, tailing off, as he tried to recall her name.

'You mean Mrs Flamey.'

'Yes.'

'I thought you didn't like her?'

'I don't... didn't,' said Slaney, correcting himself, 'but now I know she's mad.'

Then he paused, reflecting.

'Let's just say... she has revealed herself...'

Slaney remained obscure, much to Imogen's frustration.

'I hope you don't mean in a sexual context,' she said. 'That would be gross.'

Slaney laughed.

'Bizarre as this may sound, I was contacted by the editor of the local rag. He told me he had received a rather strange package, a large envelope full of soiled knickers.'

Imogen burst out laughing.

'Apparently,' continued Slaney, 'with a message, signed by Mrs Flamey... something along the lines of *this is all the evidence required to prove Morten Slaney cannot be trusted to run Auschwitz.*'

'Oh dear,' said Imogen. 'It just shows... you never can tell.'

'Mad old bitch,' he said. 'I mop up this human detritus, the casualties, the ones who can't fit in, moaning and groaning their way through life. Why would she compare me to a concentration camp commander?'

'You can get another job if you want to,' said Imogen.

'Don't be stupid,' he said. 'Why do I need another job?'

'But if they're closing this place down, what are you going to do?'

'I'm the one who's closing it down,' said Slaney, shaking his head.

'You're only closing it because you have to,' she said,

mollifying, 'because that's what the government has told you to do.'

'I could drag it out…'

'Then why don't you?'

Slaney paused, pondering Imogen's mildly pertinent question.

'It's my job to deliver, my job is to understand what needs to be done. There is no point in prevaricating… get it done and on time.'

'Doesn't sound very rewarding…'

'Trust me, it's better to be in the position to make the decisions than the decisions being made for you.'

'But what if you make a wrong decision?'

'I don't.'

That was no surprise, thought Imogen.

'If I admit to a wrong decision,' said Slaney, 'then my job is on the line. So, I never make a mistake.'

'But how can you never,' wondered Imogen, raising her voice so it sounded incredulous, 'make a mistake?'

Slaney smiled, in possession of some secret elixir.

'But what if it's not true?' Imogen continued. 'What about right and wrong?'

'Don't waste your time on morality, you'll end up going mad yourself trying to work that one out. Anyway, I thought you were more grown-up than that?'

'What do you mean?'

Slaney looked to the heavens, mildly exasperated.

'Don't be like that,' said Imogen, shifting her buttocks in her seat, 'we're not all like you…'

'And what are you like?' asked Slaney, looking directly at Imogen, wondering how vacuous the void was.

'I've got a heart,' she said sincerely.

'Oh, that,' said Slaney dismissively.

'Come on, you've got a heart. You're not as hard and cold as you like to make out.'

Slaney failed to answer.

The light outside was beginning to fade. Imogen decided to change the subject.

'You know that music therapist… Annie Buchanan?'

Here we go, thought Slaney, profoundly disinterested.

'What about her?' he asked, looking back down the track.

'Just a rumour,' she said, taking a few deep breaths.

'Oh, that,' said Slaney, acknowledging the rumours.

'So, you know then?'

'I know everything,' he said nonchalantly, 'that's part of my job. I'm not a psychopath, but if people think that, I don't mind. It keeps them on their toes and gives me the distance I need. But in reality, it's doctors who lock people away.'

'Well, I've heard some people say there was nothing wrong with her.'

'If there was nothing wrong with her then she wouldn't have been on section, would she?'

Imogen didn't know. The more fanciful rumours, such as the ones put around about herself, were just as bad.

'So, you didn't sleep with her?'

Slaney shrugged his shoulders. Why did she care who he slept with? It was not something he would admit to.

'Annie Buchanan was on a section,' said Slaney,

knowing this would be communicated by Imogen to the rest of the gossiping community, 'not because I shagged her but because she was a manic depressive.'

Slaney brushed his polyester trousers with both his hands and then smiled unemotionally at Imogen.

'So,' she said, in order to get the facts right, 'there's no such thing as locking people up if they go against the hospital?'

'The conspiracies are fiction,' said Slaney, 'dreamt up by your pot-smoking chums.'

She narrowed her eyebrows in order to let Slaney know she was not going to be compared to them. But what was the point? She couldn't win... not against Slaney. She was there to shag and little else was relevant.

'I think you must have fucked every nurse in this hospital. I bet you even shagged Sophie Smith.'

Slaney grinned and continued to say nothing.

As they waited, waiting for the right moment to start fucking, they looked down the track and could glimpse the top edge of the Clock Tower.

'Well,' said Slaney, 'to be honest with you, no one cares about these places. People want to keep it all out of sight and out of mind. Once we let the lunatics loose they'll be left to fend for themselves... and you'll need a mortgage to get back into Wellington Park.'

'You mean they should keep places like this open?'

'No,' said Slaney, 'there's no going back. We will end up with fragmented institutions of barbarity and a substantial increase in acronyms. So, we will then be able to say we have created lots of FIBs.'

'Oh, that sounds so depressing...'

'Not really,' said Slaney. 'It's not the bricks and mortar that institutionalise.'

'But for some of them, that's their only home.'

'Well, it won't be for long,' said Slaney, who was ready to fuck her. 'Now, shut up and get your knickers off.'

EPILOGUE

He was woken by the distant *clank-clank-clank* of punctuated heavy machinery rolling over the earth, screeching the extension and retraction of their hydraulic arms. It was the sound of the dead, the dead hand removing the skeletal remains of his prison sanctuary, burning in great piles of fire. His heart was crushed, his spirit deflated, demoralised, so far beaten into the ground he struggled to raise himself once more from his wooded haven, in the soft fudge of the autumn leaves covering the moss of the stagnant graveyard. There was no energy, no light, no future, no communication with the stars above, no spirit left to raise the dead, no lust or desire to seek revenge for what was done. He only knew what had gone: the miserable pump which had kept him going for so long had been surgically removed and placed on the burning pyre.

He peered through the jagged bushes, the ivy winding its fibrous tentacles in and out of the knotted twigs of thorns. There was not much left, just the base outline of the old wards, as each excavator ran their tracks in a hurried, flexing crunch, removing the last few walls which remained of the old place. In one area of the devastation, darting in between the protruding arms of the excavator, a gang of three bright yellow and orange fluorescent jackets used improvised poles to poke out the remaining glass windows. The crash of a heavy-sided brown metal truck sped through the old gated entrance, round the old tarmac road to pick up the grades of broken brick and tiling. There was just the methodical hum of activity and the fiery glow of unwanted materials flaming in large piles of unguarded patches.

So, there was not much left to do, then. All had been done, finally pulled down, destroyed by the avenger, the all-powerful One. They had taken it all and spat him out into some other world, an unfeeling, heartless world, where there were so many people it meant nobody existed. Round and round he had gone, a spinning wheel, a spinning cog, a lost, lonely casualty, a remote, useless satellite hurtling uncontrollably to earth and self-destruction.

As he watched another truck crash and crunch its way through the gated entrance, heavy with the debris of his old home, he remembered what Mr Vilnous had said: the white heat, the burning white heat. It was probably the best place to go, somewhere hot and warm and safe, somewhere to feel the heat, the hot, burning heat lapping against his skin, putting fire into his soul, warming the missing heart he had left some time ago.

Time had cast its final shadow. The pale insignificance of life dripped its faint, quiet light across the opaque patches of the old lawns. The liquid fuel, the oil of destruction, the sea creature fluid was raised up to the canopy of trees. With firm, thick hands he wrenched the rusting cap, slowly turning the screw until the rich smell fused his nostrils and nauseated his brain. With one swift movement he held aloft and felt the putrid substance flow uncontrollably down his face and clothes. He struggled to breathe, keeping the foul liquid from stinging his eyes... but he wanted to see... to see everything... all he had come to see...

Because it had come to this...

And it was Time...

As smoke from the burning materials wafted his way, he wobbled, bobbing along in his customary gait. He giggled, snorted like a horse and uttered a few words:

'Six... one-five... one-five... one-two...'

He was heading for one of the fires, and said again:

'Six... one-five... one-five... one-two...'

Then he pulled out of his pocket a thin scrap of paper folded into quarters, with the words and the verses he had come to say...

So he could begin...